KARE

BagHEADs

EMPIRE
PUBLICATIONS

First published in 2012

EMPIRE PUBLICATIONS
1 Newton Street, Manchester M1 1HW
© Karen Woods 2012

ISBN 1901 746 879 – 9781901746877

Printed in Great Britain.

TRY BEFORE YOU BUY

I destroy homes, tear families apart,
Take your children, and that's just the start.
I'm more costly than diamonds, more costly than gold,
The sorrow I bring is a sight to behold,
And if you need me, remember I'm easily found.
I live all around you, in schools and in town.

I live with the rich, I live with the poor,
I live down the street, and maybe next door.
My power is awesome; try me you'll see,
But if you do, you may never break free.
Just try me once and I might let you go,
But try me twice, and ill own your soul.

When I possess you, you'll steal and you'll lie.
You do what you have to just to get high.
The crimes you'll commit, for the narcotic charms,
Will be worth the pleasure you'll feel in your arms.

You'll lie to your mother; you'll steal from your dad
When you see their tears, you should feel sad.
But you'll forget your morals and how you were raised,
I'll be your conscience, I'll teach you my ways.

I take kids from parents, and parents from kids,
I turn people from god, and separate friends.
I'll take everything from you, your looks and your pride;
I'll be with you always, right by your side.

You'll give up everything your family, your home,
Your friends, your money, then you'll be alone.
I'll take and take, till you have nothing more to give.
When I'm finished with you you'll be lucky to live.

If you try me be warned this is no game.
If given the chance, I'll drive you insane.
I'll ravish your body; I'll control your mind.
I'll own you completely; your soul will be mine.

The nightmares I'll give you while lying in bed,
The voices you'll hear from inside your head,
The sweat, the shakes, the visions you'll see;
I want you to know, these are all gifts from me,
But then its too late, and you'll know in your heart,
That you are mine, and we shall not part.

You'll regret that you tried me, they always do,
But you came to me, not I to you.
You knew this would happen. Many times you were told,
But you challenged my power, and you chose to be bold.

You could have said no, and just walked away,
If you could live that day over, now what would you say?
I'll be your master; you will be my slave,
I'll even go with you, when you go to your grave.
Now that you have met me, what will you do?
Will you try me or not? Its all up to you.

I can bring you more misery than words can tell.
Come take my hand, let me lead you to hell.

Foreword

Karen Woods is an author that Manchester should be proud of. Her books play with your emotions and make you feel you are living the life of the characters.

'Bagheads' take you on a journey into the underworld of drugs and crime and depicts the harsh reality of life some people live in our inner-cities. The storyline shows that no matter what happens, no matter what life throws at a mother, her love for her off-spring never dies.

Shaun Cook is the main character. He is mixed-up in the dark world of drugs and crime. I feel he is someone who we can all relate to even though we may not like admitting it! His life shows the misery and desperation that one human being endures and suffers through living such a life.

'Bagheads' also relates to Shaun's family and how living with a drug addict can affect their lives too. It is a story we very rarely get to hear. With every page you turn you learn something new about a world that is a million miles away from many people's lives.

This is a book that stays with you long after you have put it down. The heart-felt emotion pulls on your heart strings.

Karen is truly a talented author who tells it just as it is. She holds nothing back and weaves northern humour through her words in her own inimitable writing style. She is without doubt the best social realist author I have had the pleasure to read in a long, long time.

'Bagheads' is a world that many don't see and hopefully

never will and her story teaches you not to judge people without knowing the full facts about the life they have led.

It is truly an eye-opener and Karen is an inspiration to many. Laugh, cry and be disturbed. Most of all feel the emotion of every single word.

I know I did.

Crissy Rock

Acknowledgements

Thanks to my four children – Ashley Blake Declan and Darcy. I love you all with all my heart and thanks for all your support. Thanks also to my grandchildren – Dolton, Marci and Cruz. A big thanks to James who is always by my side supporting me and my mother Margaret who has spent ages with me going through my books and helping me to become a better writer. Thanks to my dad Alan who is always there behind me supporting me.

I've met some amazing people since I've been writing and my PR Judith Broadbent is one amazing lady, she's always by my side and is always willing to go that extra mile for me. Richard Brecker at Celebrities Worldwide deserves a mention too for all his help and support.

Bagheads has taken me back to my youth living in Harpurhey in Manchester. My brother Darren has always been close to my thoughts whilst I have been writing this book and I know once he reads it, it will bring a smile to his face and pull at his heart strings. "This one's for you Our Kid". You're my brother, my friend and I'll always be your big sis.

Thanks to all my readers because without you all I would have probably given up writing a long time ago. To all my Facebook friends thank you for your support, you have been amazing.

Also to John Ireland and Ashley Shaw at Empire, thanks for your support and believing in me.

Bagheads is dedicated to all those people from Harpurhey, Monsall, Moston, Collyhurst, Miles Platting and Ancoats, who lost their lives to drugs. You will stay in our memories forever and never be forgotten.

Also, a big massive thanks to Crissy Rock for her support and believing in my work she's an inspiration to women worldwide.

"Always chase your dreams and never give up believing in yourself. Anything is possible with self-belief".

My last thanks as always is to my son in heaven Dale. Goodnight God bless son. Love you always.

Karen x

Chapter One

Looking at his reflection in the mirror, Shaun Cook pulled at the baggy skin around his cheekbones. His life had taken him to places you could have only ever seen in your nightmares but even for him this seemed an all-time low. The bathroom mirror was covered in mist as he struggled to see his reflection. Shaun's trembling hand slowly wiped the glass as he stared at a face that he struggled to recognise. As he shook his head, tears started to form in the corner of his eyes.

Shaun's eyes looked like dark grey circles had been drawn around them. They looked bruised and sore. Gritting his teeth together his head drew nearer to the mirror to focus. His hand struggled to find his mouth as he slowly tried to scrape away the brown stains that had formed on his teeth. Shaun placed one hand on the wall trying to steady himself. He struggled to maintain his balance. His gammy finger nails now scratched at his teeth hoping he could hide the fact that he was beyond help. Shaun used to have such a lovely smile and people had always commented on how nice it was. Those days were long gone now. The pearly white teeth he'd once had were now stumps rotted away by the heroin he'd tooted over the years. Struggling to hold himself up from the sink, he swayed. Shaun's frame was like that of an old man's; it hunched over with the years of shame he carried.

Life in Manchester had been hard but then it was like that for lots of other people who lived on council estates. They all lived on the breadline. Shaun was one of three children and he'd always demanded much more love and attention than anyone seemed prepared to give him. Many a night he lay in his bed and wanted to end his life but the call for smack had always deterred him.

Heroin had been the new drug on the streets when Shaun was only thirteen. He lived on a notorious council estate in Harpurhey. Everyone welcomed the new drug with open veins not realising what they were letting themselves in for. They were just kids chasing a buzz but they were soon to find out the consequences of their actions.

Shaun was now thirty-nine and looked haggard. He'd been considered a bit of heartthrob in his youth but those days ended when he'd sold his life to drugs so many years ago. Everyone who'd ever loved him had now deserted him. He was alone. All that was left was the shell of a man addicted to smack.

Shaun left the bathroom and rejoined his mates in the front room. They weren't his mates really, except Ged who he'd known for years. They were just people who also had nothing in life except a demanding drug habit. They clung to each other to feel part of something.

Shaun looked round the room. His eyes were dancing with the drugs he'd just injected into his veins. The place was a total shit tip. Newspapers were scattered all over the floor and empty beer cans filled the small mahogany table on one side. The place smelt damp and the black fungus growing up the walls told you how unhealthy the flat really was. Shaun's pupils looked like pinholes. He looked off his head as he struggled to walk. None of the addicts had a pot to piss in and desperation was written all across their vacant faces.

One junkie marched up and down in the front room. He could be seen wrapping his arms round his shaking body as the call for a fix blasted his brain. They all knew that feeling and sank their heads to their chins knowing there was nothing they could do to help him.

The flat was more like a squat. An old black settee was pushed across the back wall and a bit of an off-cut of carpet sat in the middle of the floor with someone lying across it staring into space. The old battered stereo in the corner played the only CD they owned and "Every Day Is Like Sunday" by Morrissey played at full blast.

Shaun opened the door to the veranda and looked out at the world. You could see children playing in the distance and there was the sound of passing traffic. As he stretched his head over the balcony he could see the estate where he grew up. He smiled as he remembered the days gone by.

The flat was on the fourth floor. They all liked it that way as they knew people couldn't get to them without them knowing. The flat had a security door and no one was allowed in without their say so. As he stretched his head out over the rail on the balcony he wondered if the drop would be enough to kill him. His face looked troubled. The wind howled past him as if it was teasing him to jump. Shaun's body was shaking as the thought of dying filtered through him. His mind was racing and he looked white in the face. The gusts of wind picked up and grabbed at his bones as he stood like a statue waiting to die. His hands trembled as he zipped up his grey parka.

Shaun's head swivelled back as he looked through the rain splattered windows at his baghead friends sat inside. They couldn't care less where he was or what he was doing. His hands shook rapidly as he held the wall to climb onto the balcony. Pulling his hood up, he hid the years of regret that covered his face. With one hand still holding onto the wall he gasped for breath as tears streamed down his face.

Shaun mumbled the words of the song he could hear in the background and nodded his head slowly to the beat as his purple lips trembled. For the last time he turned his head back, looking inside the window for a sign that somebody cared about him. The wind circled his feet as if it was helping him leave the balcony.

Shaun's body lay lifeless after it hit the floor. Nobody in the flat noticed he was missing until they heard people shouting outside. As his friends peered over the balcony they could see people gathering around a body on the floor. "What the fuck's going on?" Ged gasped as he stared down. It wasn't until he saw his friend's familiar grey coat that he realised. Ged began shouting out as his hands dragged at his hair. "It's Shaun. For fuck's sake it's Shaun."

The addicts ran down the staircase as quickly as they could - the lift being out of order as usual. When they reached the frail, motionless body they could see the onlookers scowling at them as if they were lepers. It was obvious the crowd knew who they were.

"That's what taking drugs does to you!" one woman shouted to her teenage son as she held him by the arm. They boy shrugged removing her grip.

"Yeah mam I know. Will you shut the fuck up?" The youth dipped his head and looked embarrassed at his mother's words.

The ambulance had been phoned and the person who'd reported it was sat in shock on a nearby wall. The woman looked about fifty and all you could see was her shaking her head as she gripped the mobile phone in her hands. Someone had placed a blanket around her but she was still shaking like a leaf.

Shaun lay with his hood still pulled over his face. His leg looked deformed and people screamed when they saw it for the first time. Ged quickly knelt by his side and tried to see if he was still alive. Wiping the trickle of blood from Shaun's mouth he spoke in a low voice.

"It's me, Ged. Can you hear me mate? For fuck's sake what have you done this for?" His skinny arms removed Shaun's hood from his face as he tried to find some life in the gaunt face that stared blankly at him. People around him whispered between themselves. You could hear every word they were saying. "Look at his arms the dirty bastard," one man moaned. Ged quickly pulled his sleeves down covering the track marks. His face looked white with shock. The sound of sirens could be heard in the distance and everyone turned their heads to watch it draw nearer.

"Come on mate, hang on in there. The ambulance is here now. Don't fucking give up ya muppet." Ged stayed at Shaun's side until the medics were with him. He managed to stand up and he hung his head in shame as he spoke to the medical team.

"Please help him mate. He's a good lad. He's just been a bit down lately." The man looked at him and quickly assessed the body that lay in front of him. He moved Ged out of the way and told everyone to step back so he could do his job. He now shouted to his colleague to bring him some different equipment from the vehicle. Ged was stood at a grass verge vomiting. The sound of retching could be heard. The spectators watched him spewing his ring up and shook their heads in disgust.

The paramedic took hold of Shaun's cold hand. It looked blue. He felt his pulse while anxiously looking at his watch. He could see something being held in Shaun's grip and slowly unfolded his fingers to reveal a small pebble. He quickly slid it into Shaun's pocket. The other medic joined him now and they made a decision to move his body onto a stretcher. "I don't think he's going to make it," the ambulance man whispered to a colleague. They both sighed as they transferred Shaun onto an orange stretcher. The man was a human being and they didn't want to lose him, no matter who he was. Their faces looked strained as they carried him to the ambulance.

Shaun's friends huddled together as they could hear the comments from the local people in the crowd. A middle aged man spoke in a loud voice and looked directly at the junkies. He wasn't bothered who heard him.

"Well, that's one less smackhead on the streets. They should all fucking jump from there if you ask me. They're nothing but a load of dirty scumbags. Thieving bastards, the lot of 'em." His voice was sarcastic as he focused on Ged and his friends. The comments were getting louder and the residents were making it clear that they didn't care if they heard them or not. As Shaun's lifeless body was put inside the ambulance his friends headed back to the flat like rats returning to a sinking ship.

Ged was asked if he wanted to go with his friend to the hospital but he quickly declined. He told them he would go and tell Shaun's mother what had happened and made excuses why he couldn't go. Some friend he was!

The sirens were turned on and Shaun was taken to North Manchester Hospital. Ged returned to the flat and sat with his head in his hands. As if his tears were locked away he screwed his face up and shook his head. His lips trembled as one of the girls tried to comfort him.

"Why the fuck did he jump? He could have spoken to us about how he was feeling." He held his hands up in the air with a distressed face. "I mean we've all been depressed at one time or another haven't we?" The others agreed, but if they were true to themselves, they knew they didn't care about anything or anyone as long as they had drugs. Ged sighed and walked to the balcony. He stood back from the rail as he peered over it. A few of the others came outside with him. Ged gripped the wall as if he was going to faint. It all seemed too much for him.

"I'm gutted. Why the fuck did he jump?" Nobody could answer his question and one by one they went back inside to the flat.

Ged was the main man in his circle of friends and he ran a tight ship. He organised the grafts every day and drove the girls to Cheetham Hill to sell themselves. Trudging back inside the flat he knew life needed to go on. Clearing his throat he struggled to speak. He was one man down now and had to reorganise his troops. They all needed money fast if they had any chance of surviving another day.

"Right! Let's move our arses. Shaun will be alright, we'll phone the hospital later to make sure." The rest of the addicts nodded. It was obvious they only had one thing on their minds at the moment and Shaun's well-being wasn't it.

Ged carried on as if nothing had happened. Every now and then he would sigh and say what a fucking nobhead Shaun was, but apart from that his emotions seemed numb. Remembering his promise to the medics he told the others to meet him on the market. Watching them leave he headed to Shaun's mother's house with a sprint in his step to break the bad news.

Shaun's mum lived on the Shiredale estate in Harpurhey. The pub it was named after was just a stone's throw away from her house. Lots of wheeling and dealing went on inside the pub and if you ever wanted some cheap knock-off stuff, that was the place to get it. Feeling the cold winds around his neck, Ged zipped up his coat and prepared himself.

Knocking on the door he bounced about on the spot blowing warm breath into his cupped hands. His words were stuck in his throat when she answered the door. Ged coughed to clear his throat before he began. He was fidgeting about and couldn't keep still. Gladys saw his face and eagerly pulled her cardigan tighter round her body. She was a nervous wreck and the trauma of bringing three kids up on her own had taken its toll on her over the years. Her face looked like the colour was slowly draining from it. She looked white.

Shaun had never been far from his mother's thoughts. Every day she worried about him. She would have had him home no problem but it was her eldest son that had banished him from there months before. Shaun's elder brother Paul had promised him the last time he'd seen him that if he ever saw him near the house again he would do him in big time. Rubbing his hands together Ged moved closer the front door. He looked nervous and his mouth looked dry.

"It's your Shaun, Gladys. He's in hospital." Gladys gripped the door frame and her knuckles turned white. Her head sank back as she started to breathe rapidly. "Fucking hell! No!" she mumbled. Gladys shook her head and looked like she was going to have a heart attack.

"He's jumped off the flats." Ged paused and didn't know if she could take anymore. Placing his hand on her shoulder he tried to hold her up. The words were like knives being stabbed into her heart. Paul must have heard the commotion and came to join them. His face was angry.

"What the fuck's going on?" He snarled as he shot a look at Ged. Gladys fell to the floor as if her legs couldn't hold the pain anymore. Ged panicked. He knew Paul of old and stood back from the doorway knowing he could be wasted at any time. His words were shaky.

"It's your Shaun. He's jumped off the flats mate." Ged's voice was low and he was at breaking point. Paul tried to help his mother up from the floor. He shot a look at Ged and gritted his teeth as he spoke to him.

"What the fuck are you telling us about that prick for? Don't you think he's done enough to this family without adding to it. Look at the fucking state of my mam now!"

Paul held Gladys up by the waist. Placing his mother up against the wall he turned to Ged. "Fuck off from the door before I tune you in. Do you hear me? Fuck off!" Ged backed away slowly. He could tell he was treading on eggshells and wanted away as soon as possible. Gladys was screaming as she tried to find out more about her son before Ged left. Paul dragged her back inside by her arms as she yelled through the small gap in the door.

"Is he alive? Where have they taken him?" Her body was yanked from the door as Ged shouted to her what she needed to know. Ged started to walk off with speed, he didn't feel safe. He was watching his back all the time. Paul growled at him one last time as he fled from the doorway.

"Fucking prick" Ged huffed as he watched the front door close from a distance.

Gladys reached for her cigs and lit one with a shaking hand. Her lungs inflated as she inhaled the smoke deeply. She sat at the dining table with her legs crossed and her head dangling onto her knees. Shaun's dad had been off the scene for years now and nobody in the household gave a shit about her son any more.

Shaun's family had their own problems to deal with. His sister Katie had helped Shaun out in the past but she'd given up on him when he nicked her gold cross and chain from her years before. He'd nicked lots of other things but she'd always forgiven him.

Gladys looked at Paul. She held a desperate look on her face. Twisting her fingers she pleaded with him. "Please son, he needs us. We can't just leave him there on his own." Paul bolted from his chair as he paced the living room floor.

"It's always the fucking same mam. All our lives have revolved round that fucking smackhead. He's probably after some attention again." His foot kicked at the bottom of the chair. He was livid. Paul's eyes now turned to Gladys as he shouted into her face. "Well he can fuck right off. He's been dead for years as far as I'm concerned. So don't ask me to be involved in anything to do with that nobhead."

"He's still your fucking brother! No matter what he is!" Gladys screamed back at him. She stood in front of him waving her hands about trying to make him see sense. "How can I just turn my back on him and leave him lying in hospital on his own? Have a fucking heart will you?" Paul made to leave the room. This was his usual way of dealing with situations when he couldn't get through to her.

"Mam, when are you going to accept what he is? He's robbed you blind over the years, and every other fucker that has ever cared for him. Why do you think nobody wants nowt to do with him anymore? He's a fucking drug addict." Paul's hands were held in front of him as he pointed at her. Gladys was shaking from head to toe as he punished her with every word he spoke. "Watch the fucking programmes on the telly. He'll never change. Once a smackhead, always a smackhead. You know that deep down inside. Just get it into your thick head. He's a junkie, a fucking heroin addict." His finger rammed at the side of her head pressing deep into her skull. The emotion in his voice told you how upset he was inside. He left the room cursing under his breath. "You'll never fucking learn will you?" The door slammed and it shook the room.

Gladys lit another cig and paced up and down the front room. Paul was right, Shaun had robbed from her in the past. She didn't have to be told. He'd even hit her on more than one occasion but she'd hid it well and nobody ever knew. He was her flesh and blood and a mother's love for her son would never go away no matter what he'd done. Looking round the room the silence haunted her. She sat back and remembered times when the house had been full of laughter and everything seemed easy. A picture of her children sat on the small cabinet at the side of her. Gripping it tightly she fell to the floor holding the picture frame to her heart. As she sobbed she looked at the photograph and couldn't believe that the boy in front of her was now lying in a hospital bed fighting for his life.

"Where did I go wrong?" she whispered to the picture frame. "I did my best for all of you and look what's happened." She cradled the photograph close to her chest as she rocked. The pain she felt in her heart was like nothing she'd ever felt before. Gladys knew she needed to get to her son and quickly picked up the phone to call her sister for support. Once she'd told her the news Gladys headed for the hospital and prepared herself for the worst.

★

Gladys and her sister sat waiting for the doctor to come. It seemed ages since she'd spoken to the receptionist telling her that she needed to see her son urgently. Looking down the corridor Marie could see a doctor walking towards her with a concerned face. "I think he's coming to see

us," she whispered. Gladys raised her head as she heard the
footsteps coming nearer.

"Are you Shaun Cook's mother?" the doctor asked.
Gladys nodded slowly and hung her head low. She felt like
a failure as a parent and quickly tried to make him aware
of her son's circumstances.

"He's a drug addict, doctor. We've tried everything
to help him, but it's hopeless." The doctor sighed and led
them to a side room and asked them if they needed a drink
before he began. The male doctor now stared at his notes.
Taking a deep breath he looked up and spoke to Gladys.

"It's not good news." Gladys held her breath and you
could see her nostrils flaring. She was on the verge of
screaming out but her sister held her arm and pulled her
back into the chair. He continued.

"Your son is in a coma and has some serious injuries.
His right leg may have to be amputated" Gladys stood up
clenching her fists. The doctor carried on speaking in a
sympathetic tone as he watched her turn to face him. "We
have done everything we can to try and save it, but he
still might lose his leg." His face now looked serious as he
peered over his silver framed spectacles. Gladys sat back
down and now held her knees up to her chest as she jerked
hard to and fro. Her lips quivered as she struggled to speak.
"Is he going to die doctor? Please don't let him die?" she
screamed. The moment was heart wrenching and he took
a few minutes to reply.

"I can't give you an answer Mrs Cook as to whether
your son will ever regain consciousness, but he will be
cared for the best we can whilst he's here."

Gladys was trying her best to keep calm as tears fell
from her eyes and trickled onto her cheek. Her sister
Marie held her hand and cried with her. The doctor now

led them to the room where Shaun lay.

Lots of tubes were attached to Shaun's body. All you could hear was the beeping of his heart monitor at the side of him. Gladys screamed at the sight of her son. Quickly she sat next to Shaun and held his cold hands in her grip. She rubbed at them with her two hands placed together. "He's freezing Marie." Her lips trembled as she spluttered her words.

"Why son? Why?" her words were hard to understand but as her head fell onto his lap, years of frustration were released. Marie sat by her side and patted her head trying to comfort her. She didn't know what else to do. Gladys broke her heart crying as she fired her words.

"It's my fault, I know it is son. I should have done more and helped you." Marie couldn't hold her tongue and hated that her sister was blaming herself for her nephew's addiction. She bent her head down and spoke softly into her ear.

"You did all you could love. The things you have done to help him are countless." Marie looked at Shaun's face and shook her head. He'd always been a handful from being a child and she knew just how badly he'd treated his mother in the past. Even she had told him to never come near her house again. He'd even pinched money from her. Gladys sat up and rocked in the chair as she gazed at the bag of bones that lay on the bed. Regaining her strength she looked at her sister.

"It was me and his dad splitting up that done it you know? He was fine until then. I feel so guilty, that's why I can't ever give up on him." Marie was hanging on her every word and listened as she watched her sister trying to defend her son yet again. "He's been through so much, you don't know the half of it." They both looked at Shaun as Gladys stroked his forehead. She sat looking at his face taking in every line and wrinkle spread across it.

Marie hugged her sister. She knew she hadn't had the best of lives. In fact every member of her family had hit rock bottom at one time or another. Gladys was a tablet away from a breakdown and her own tormented life had been something she found it hard to come to terms with. Gladys's life had left her weak and without any self confidence. She'd stopped caring about herself many years before. All she cared about was her youngest son.

As they watched Shaun sleeping Gladys could see his eyes flickering rapidly. "He looks like he's having a bad dream or something doesn't he?" Gladys whispered as her hand slowly stroked across her son's face trying to calm him down.

"Ssshhh."

Chapter Two

Lying in a coma Shaun went over his life. He was unaware of where he was. He'd drifted off to a place where his life had started to go wrong. Everything seemed real and it was as if he was watching his life over again.

Shaun's thoughts took him back to when he was thirteen years of age. He broke into a smile as he lay in the hospital bed. Shaun was watching himself in his youth. He was a rum fucker and a loveable rogue and everyone loved him. He had dirty blonde hair that felt like a Brillo pad to touch. All his mates had joked about it in the past and it was a long standing joke amongst them. His nickname was "Fanny head" and he'd had many a fight about that down the years. Shaun's mother had bought him every type of hair gel on the market but nothing seemed to control his dry frizzy mop. Shaun was a handy lad amongst his friends. He was known as "The Cock" and nobody ever messed about with him unless they wanted their arses kicking. What he said was gospel and no one ever threatened him. Shaun's skin always had a tanned look about it. His mother had told him that his ancestors were Red Indians and that's where his colouring had come from. What a load of bullshit. His tan was nothing but ground in dirt. Nothing that a bar of soap wouldn't have removed.

Shaun was all skin and bones. A "lean mean fighting machine" he called himself. His mother constantly fed him food supplements in the hope that he would fill out but he never did and he still looked like a bean sprout. Shaun always struggled to finish any meal that was put in front of

him. He was always too busy to eat and he couldn't wait
to get back outside playing with his friends. He was the
champion at the game of British Bulldog and he was as
fast as a whippet. Shaun lived on chocolate and crisps that
he'd stolen from the local shops in Tavistock Square. All the
local kids shoplifted from there and for most of them it was
the only way they stopped the hunger pangs. His mother
didn't know he was eating heaps of the stuff and always said
she couldn't understand why he had so much energy for
someone who didn't eat. Shaun's brother and sister hated
the attention he got and knew the little fucker was having
their mam over.

The family home had been happy back then. Shaun was
living life like most other families living on the breadline.
The kids on the estate all got by any way they could. The
local ice-cream man Marco Rea knew that more than
anyone. He was the victim of theft nearly every day and
hated his ice-cream round in Harpurhey. Many a time the
kids would run off from his van without paying. There was
nothing he could do about it and he took it on the chin
most of the time. The youths would do anything to earn a
few bob and they were all involved in petty crime about
the area.

It all started to go wrong when Shaun was laid in his
bed one night and he heard the screams from downstairs.
He recognised his mother's voice and realised she was
arguing with his father. Of course he'd heard them argue
before but as a young child he never really took much
notice of it. Tonight was different though.

Sitting up in bed he rubbed at his eyes and looked over
at his brother. The moonlight shining through the window
just gave off enough light to see his face. Paul held one
finger firmly to his mouth and stared at Shaun with an

anxious look on his face.

"What's going on?" Shaun whispered.

"Get back to sleep ya nobhead!" Paul replied angrily. Shaun sat listening and could see his elder brother now chewing the edge of his pillow in front of him. He could see his teeth gnawing at the cotton. Paul looked distraught and he could see his hands gripping tightly around the white pillow slip nearly ripping it.

"Why's my mam crying?" he asked again. Shaun pulled his quilt up around his neck as Paul bolted from his bed. He was now gripping his younger brother round the neck and squeezing his throat restricting his breathing. Choking noises could be heard.

"Get to sleep and stop being a little nosey bastard." Shaun knew he'd pushed Paul's temper and once his hands dropped from his neck he turned over and sobbed. He would have had a go back but he knew his brother would have wasted him. He had in the past and he knew to keep his mouth closed even though he wanted to ram his fist into his face.

Suddenly, Shaun's legs felt warm as he lay frozen in his bed. He could feel something trickling down his legs. His face looked frozen. He was pissing himself. This wasn't the first time and it always happened when he was upset. He remained still.

Paul had witnessed the violence between his parents on many occasions and knew there wasn't a thing he could do about it. His father's voice shook the room and all he could do was lie there feeling a failure. Covering his ears with his hands he stared out of the window and prayed for the day to come when he was strong enough to defend his mother. Shouting from the stairs could be heard. Paul lifted his head and listened with one leg hanging from the bed.

"What have I told you about answering me back, you slut! You know how it makes me feel don't you?" Gladys could be heard screaming and she was pleading with her husband not to beat her further. Her voice was low and you could hear in her voice that she'd had enough of his abuse.

"I'm sorry. Please stop it. The kids will hear you."

"Do you think I give a fuck about who hears me?" he screamed. A banging noise could be heard. The sound of her body being dragged up the stairs filled the bedroom. Paul was sat on the side of his bed shaking. His knees were moving up and down towards his chest at speed. Shaun lay in his bed and closed his eyes tightly hoping it would all be over soon. After around twenty minutes the disturbance finally subsided. Silence filled the house.

Paul was now asleep and it was time for Shaun to try and get rid of the evidence that he'd pissed the bed. Creeping out of his covers he peeled his wet pyjama bottoms from his shivering legs. They clung to his skin and he was finding it hard to shake them off. Screwing his face up, Shaun could smell the stench of his piss as he brought them up to his nose. He struggled to breathe and threw the soiled pants into the corner of the room. Looking over at his brother's bed he sneaked over and grabbed the spare blanket from the floor. He wouldn't miss it. Paul was snoring his head off and wasn't likely to wake up. Shaun made his move and grabbed the clean blanket. Placing it on the wet bed he smoothed it out with his fingers. Grabbing a clean pair of shorts from his chest of drawers at the side of him he pulled them over his bony body. His heart was pumping inside his chest and he looked scared as he checked his brother was still asleep. Shaun's eyes were wide open as he stared around the bedroom. All he wanted was some love and affection but it never came. Shaun drifted off to sleep hoping tomorrow would be a better day.

Morning light crept into the Cook household. Paul lay awake for a while as he knew what lay beyond his bedroom door. He couldn't stand the thought of seeing his mother with more bruises on her face. Looking across to Shaun's bed his faced screwed up as he saw the edge of his blanket sticking out underneath his brother's bony arse. "Cheeky twat" he huffed. His body vaulted from his bed and grabbed his dazed brother by the scruff of the neck.

"You little prick. What the fuck have you done to my blanket?" Dragging his body up from the bed he yanked his cover towards him. Shaun rolled against the wall banging his head. You could hear Paul's rapid breathing. His face now changed as he smelt the material. His nostrils were flaring as he realised his brother had pissed the bed again.

"Fucking pissed the bed again, have you?" he scowled. Shaun cowered away from him with his hands held over his face with one leg bent up towards his chest. Paul bent towards him dragging him out of the bed by his hair and threw him onto the floor. Shaun knew what was coming and curled up in a ball like an injured animal. "Pissy arse. You make me sick you little dickhead!" Paul ranted into his face. Shaun lay sobbing with both hands shaking over his head. His legs were drawn up tightly to his chest now trying to protect himself from his brother's fury. Paul drew his leg back and swung it at his sibling with force. Screaming could be heard. "Have that you little shit!" he snarled.

"I'm gonna to tell my mam!" Shaun sobbed hoping the mention of his mother's name might cause him to think twice. His plea fell on deaf ears as Paul dragged his face up from the floor covering his mouth so he couldn't speak.

"Ay sonny boy. Do you think she's gonna listen to you

when she sees what you've done to the bed. You're in deep shit ya wanker." His face smiled down at him with evil eyes as he slowly dripped a mouthful of spit onto his face. Paul went out of the bedroom leaving his brother still crying on the floor.

"Fucking bastard!" Shaun whispered.

The walk down the stairs seemed like the walk of death for Shaun. Each stair seemed to creak no matter how softly he stepped onto it. Reaching the bottom stair he could smell the aroma of burnt toast. Stretching his arms he made his way to face his family. Pulling the door open slightly he could see his father stood at the stove watching the eyelevel grill. He was wearing his navy boxer shorts and a thread bare vest top. He looked fat and out of shape. Hearing his son behind him he told him to get his arse sat at the table for breakfast. Shaun trudged into the front room scratching his head.

Shaun's eyes were still red from crying as he joined his sister and brother at the dining table. Paul smirked at him and mouthed the word "pissy arse" to his sister Kate as he pointed at Shaun. They both giggled and made fun of him without speaking. Shaun asked where his mother was. He needed her protection. Kate kicked him from underneath the table and gritting her teeth at him.

"Shut up ya geek."

"Why what's up?" Shaun moaned. He was now holding the centre of his arm as Paul had reached over and given him a dead arm. His face looked in pain as he tried to hide his torment.

All eyes were on his dad Mike as he brought a large pile of toast into the room. Shaun looked at his siblings across the table. He could see fear in their eyes and tried to work out what was going on. Mike sat on the sofa near them and you could see red scratches around his eyes. Shaun was always outspoken and he chatted to his dad with innocence.

"What's happened to your eye dad?" He could feel Paul's eyes burning into him and wished he hadn't spoken at all now. Mike slowly ran his fingers over the raised skin on his eyes and turned to face his three children. His face snarled as his temper boiled.

"It's your fucking nutter of a mother. I've had just about enough of her and her ways." Paul knew he was lying through his teeth and held his tongue with difficulty. He wanted to plunge his fist deep into his face and you could see his clenched fist near his legs under the table. He'd felt like that for as long as he could remember.

His father was a bully and the sooner he was put in his place the better it would be for everyone. Paul wasn't ready yet and hung his head low. Kate used the opportunity to leave the table and head upstairs to see if her mother was alright. Nobody missed her as her father was in the mirror checking out his injured eye.

Kate crept up the stairs. Facing her was her mother's bedroom. Her hands trembled as she slowly opened the door. The room was dark and the closed curtains didn't help her vision. Kate could just about see a body lay in the bed covered by the blankets.

She tiptoed across the floor and was aware of every creak the floorboards made. The room stunk of stale beer and old perfume. As she reached the bedside she shook her mother's shoulder slowly.

"Mam are you alright?" At first there was no movement, but with another quick shake her mother turned to face her. Kate covered her face with her hands as she saw her for the first time. Her mother's eyes were barely opened and the swelling stopped her from opening them fully. Gladys lifted her hands up and felt her eyes with her fingertips. Seeing Kate's face she tried to calm her down.

"I'm fine. You know what he's like when he's pissed." Her eyes rose to the ceiling as she blew a deep breath from her mouth. "We've just had a bit of an argument that's all." Kate watched the lying face in front of her and held onto her stomach. She felt sick inside and wanted to hold her mother in her arms but an invisible barrier was between them both. It's just the way it was. The family had never showed emotion to each other and they all struggled to show any kind of feelings. The sound of her father's voice sent fear through her body as she heard him shouting her name. "Kate. Kate. Where are you?" His voice seemed near. Kate now looked distressed as she fidgeted about at her mother's bedside. She tiptoed quickly from the bedroom holding a finger up towards her mouth. "Ssshhh," she said to her mother. Coming out of the room she crept into the toilet and replied to her father.

"I'm coming now dad, I'm just on the toilet." The stairs creaking made her look and she could see her father's face looking directly at her. His eyes shot to the open bedroom door and he knew she'd been inside. With a run in his step he raised his large hands up and whacked her round the head. "What's that for?" she yelled.

"Get your arse down those stairs you nosey bitch. Don't think I was born yesterday." He pushed her body to the top of the landing and let her know he meant business. With a forceful shove she was at the top of the stairs. He was still ranting at her. "Get them pots washed. And start cleaning that shit tip downstairs. Tell them two to start helping as well." She never replied. Slowly she headed down the stairs. Her head kept turning behind her to make sure he wasn't following. Kate rubbed the back of her head and made her way back to her brothers.

Paul's face was smiling at her when she entered the front room. "You got slapped. You got slapped," he sung. He'd been stood at the bottom of the stairs and heard the slap she got from their father. He was giggling acting out the slap across the head. As she started to tell them the orders from her father, he playfully pushed her on the sofa doing some of his kung-fu moves on her. It was playtime and they all started toy fighting. They rolled about on the sofa pulling all the cushions from it and even Shaun joined in. Shaun sat on his sister's body while Paul chopped her body with his hand. Laughter filled the room and it seemed to help cover the pain of a broken family. They were just kids having some fun.

Mike walked into the bedroom and spoke nervously to his wife. His voice let Gladys know he was ready to sort things out. This was the usual thing he'd do after a night of drunken violence. He pulled the covers back from the bed and nudged her over with his legs. She kept her back to him and cringed when she felt his hands crawling around on her skin. Mike gripped her closer and kissed the back of her neck. "Sorry love," he whispered. She hated that she had no control of her life and there wasn't a thing she could do to make him go away.

Gladys was in a deep hole of desperation and she couldn't see a way out. Her face told you that she wanted to tell him to take his dirty fucking hands from her body but she knew it would only result in more violence. He rolled her over to face him. As he looked at her face he stroked the bruises with soft touches. He shook his head and realised how bad her injuries were. Mike spoke with sorrow in his voice.

"I'm sorry love. Fucking hell your face is a right mess." Gladys never said a word and just stared at him. No emotion was visible on her face. She was cringing inside. His body now climbed onto hers. Within seconds he'd entered her. She hated every minute of it and hated the man her husband had become. Within minutes the sex was over and he carried on as if nothing had happened. Gladys wanted to die. She felt alone and depressed with the way her life was going. Mike looked proud of himself as usual and he thought everything was fine between them. They'd just had sex so surely it was? Looking at her he spoke with his usual controlling tone.

"Right don't be going out today with that face. Stay in and do something nice for tea. You can do some baking if you want." His face looked surprised as if he was thinking. "In fact you can make a cheese pie for tea." Her eyes closed as she exhaled deeply. Her words were stuck in her mouth and her lips were trembling. She didn't know if she could take this any longer and wanted to end her life there and then. "I might go for a few pints this afternoon if you don't mind?" he chuckled.

"Yeah okay," she mumbled. Any time in the house without him would be appreciated.

Mike jumped from the bed. "Right, bath time I think." Scratching his bollocks he left the room.

"I hate you. I fucking hate you," she sobbed under her breath once he left the room. Her hands gripped the quilt cover and she hid her head away under the blankets crying her heart out.

Shaun helped clean up for a change. Usually he would have just been allowed to go out playing with his mates but today was different because his mother wasn't there to protect him. The three of them cleaned the house. Every now and then Shaun would get a cloth whacked round his face from either Katie or Paul. The three of them played about as they carried out their father's orders. Kate was polishing now and held a cunning look in her eyes. She crept behind Paul and squirted furniture polish into his face .Shaun was laughing his head off as he watched his brother fall to the floor holding his eyes. He secretly wished he would have been blinded forever then he would have been able to pay him back for all the torment he'd given him in the past.

Paul was sixteen and Katie was fifteen. Paul always thought he was the boss of them and tried to demand respect from them all the time. Kate and Shaun had given him the nickname of Sergeant Bilko. He was a complete tosser and always thought they had to obey his every word. Kate and Paul were always fighting and she never gave up without a good fight. Shaun loved his sister and they were very close at times.

The months went by and Mike finally left the family home for some slapper he'd met down the pub. Gladys had taken it badly and tried taking her life a few times. It was always the same; she'd take all her nerve tablets that she'd got from the doctor and neck a bottle of Vodka. She was always saved at the last minute though. She was dependant on Diazapam tablets and her nerves shook every day without them. The small white tablets were the only thing that kept her sane. The family was a mess, there was no doubt about it. Paul and Kate seemed to cope with the break-up better than Shaun and never really missed their father. They were free now to do whatever they wanted and they had no discipline in their lives. Shaun always felt alone and craved attention from anyone who'd give it.

Shaun found a friend that would never let him down. Evo-stick was the glue everyone was sniffing and he loved the way it made him feel. He first tried it for the first time with his mates and loved the buzz it gave him. The glue took him to a place where he felt happy and loved. Nothing seemed to matter when he was sniffing it. School was a distant memory for him now and the wag officer was always knocking at the door regarding his non-attendance. Most kids on the estate were the same and society had just given up on them.

Filling the plastic bag with glue Shaun headed off to a nearby field to rid himself of his family torments. Pouring the yellow sticky looking glue into the bag he sat in some bushes at the top of the hill. Once that was completed he squeezed the air from the bag and blew into it with force His mouth was placed at the top of the bag and he inhaled deeply to get the full effects from it. Shaun looked spaced out within minutes. His eyes were rolling and his head was rocking from side to side. The plastic bag was never far from his mouth as he kept topping up on his buzz. Shaun lay on the fields for hours until his glue was finished. Nobody missed him or even cared where he was. He felt peace within his body as the glue took him to a place he felt safe and secure.

Months went by and the glue was having a serious effect on him. Spots had formed around his mouth and nostrils. Paul knew Shaun was glue sniffing because his mates had told him. He'd wasted him a few times when he'd come in stinking of glue but it didn't deter Shaun from seeking a quick fix. Pickle juice was Shaun's way of disguising his breath after glue sniffing. He must have thought everyone was daft because no matter what he ate the stench of glue was always there.

Gladys was up to her neck in worry about her kids. She'd heard from several people that her children were going wild on the estate but couldn't do a thing about it. She was a single parent now and didn't have the strength to keep them in order. She was always tired and hated the way she felt about herself. If she'd have looked closer at her family she would have seen the truth right before her very eyes. Katie was gas sniffing and Paul soon got into the glue as well. The three of them were a mess and needed a firm hand to sort them out but without a father onboard they were all set for self destruction.

As with everything in life it always came at price. Shaun found that out the hard way. Money was tight and he knew he would have to hatch a plan to fund his habit. As he sat with his friends they all decided they would do bag snatches. They'd seen it on the TV many a time so how hard could it be? The youths planned to watch the banks and watch the people who left with money.

The day was quite cold and everybody was walking around with their heads dipped. Moston Lane was busy as always. The shops were heaving with people. It was around midday and everywhere looked busy. Shaun and his gang hid away in the entry facing the Lloyds bank. Once they'd seen an elderly lady going inside Shaun jumped up from the floor. "Right, wait here. I'm gonna run over the road and see what the old crinkly is taking out of the bank." Steve started to get up to join him. With a flat palm Shaun pushed his head back down. "Nar wait here. It will be on top if we both go over!" Shaun moaned. Steve slid back down onto the floor and shot a look at the others with raised eyebrows. They watched Shaun now pull his hood up and jog across the road.

Shaun was now outside the bank pretending to read the notices on the window. His eyes cunningly gazed at the old lady stood at the cashier point. He could see some notes being slid under the counter and watched her place them neatly into her purse. He chewed on his bottom lip as his eyes danced about with excitement. She was now outside walking slowly up the street. Her bag was hung from her right shoulder and looked an easy target for him to grab. With one hand waving in the air he signalled to his mates across the road. Like a pack of hunting animals they watched the old woman as she walked down the road. They kept out of sight and walked slowly behind her as they huddled together. As soon as the woman turned into a side street, Shaun set off running at speed. As he reached her, he yanked at the brown leather bag hanging from her shoulder. The woman screamed as she tried to hold onto the strap of it. It was too late. Shaun was now running down the side street with her bag concealed inside his tracksuit jacket. The pensioner was screaming and waving her hands about in the air. She looked white in the face and sat on a nearby wall to regain her breath.

Shaun's mates ran to follow him. He'd done well. They knew they'd be in for a cut of whatever was in the purse and ran to catch him up. Shaun ran until he was safely out of the area. He held the bag close to his chest and felt no remorse for what he'd done. Sitting down in some old flats on Fernclough Road he looked around making sure no one was about. His shaking fingers slowly unzipped the bag and cast his eyes over the contents.

The black leather purse was now open. Shaun grabbed a couple of the ten pound notes and shoved them inside his shoe. He was always a bit of a snide where money was concerned. The noise of his friends coming inside the flats made him quickly zip the bag back up. He shoved it back inside his jacket and pretended he hadn't looked inside it yet. Shaun stood up and watched his mates come up the stairs. He stood tall and nodded. All their eyes focused on his tracksuit top as he pulled the bag from it with a smile on his face. He looked like a pirate who'd stolen some treasure. The lads punched their fist into the air. "Result," Steve yelled.

"What's in it?" shouted one of the lads who came to his side. Shaun smiled and with a cocky face swinging the bag about.

"Dunno yet. I haven't opened it," he lied. They all gathered round him like hungry animals. All eyes focused on the handbag. Steve spoke with anger in his voice as he bounced about on the staircase.

"The old cunt flagged a police car down. We saw her didn't we lads?" The lads nodded in agreement.

"Fucking hell, no way did she?" Shaun moaned. Thinking for a minute he shrugged his shoulders and huffed. "I'm not arsed anyway. Let the fucking coffin dodger prove it was me." The lads agreed. Steve tried to put Shaun's mind at rest. "Yeah she's an old cunt and she won't be able to remember you. She was a specky twat!" Steve patted Shaun's shoulder as he spoke. "Fuck me Shaun, you was rapid wasn't you?" Shaun nodded and smiled. He had completed his first mission and now it was time to reap the rewards.

After counting all the money, there was one hundred and eighty pounds in the purse. They also found a broken cross and chain in it too. Shaun claimed it immediately. He held the cross in his hands and knew it could bring him an extra few quid when he was skint. Shoving it in his pockets he went to the large bin and tossed the stolen handbag inside it.

"Right come on, let's fucking get off from here." Steve huffed. Shaun pulled his tracksuit top off and tied it round his waist. He didn't want to take any chances of the police pulling him up because of what he was wearing. His face looked chuffed with his little earner. He swung his hand playfully and punched his mate at the side of him before they all headed down the stairs.

Dipping his head Shaun and his mates headed to the DIY shop on Rochdale Road to get his tin of glue. Only Shaun and Steve went inside the shop. The man in the store knew exactly what they were doing with the glue and didn't seem too bothered selling it them. They were regular customers and he joked with them about the amount they were buying. He always put the glue in a carrier bag and made sure no one was in the shop when he served them.

With everything they needed for the daily buzz they all headed off to Harpurhey fields nearby. Every kid who was there had some kind of home life problem and wanted to block it from their mind. One of them held a tin of gas up his parka coat sleeve, and held it to his mouth as they walked. Sniffing gas was also a big buzz back then and nearly all the youths in Harpurhey felt the need for the cheap buzz. Tip-ex thinner was also another cheap thing the youths abused to get off their heads.

"Fucking hell look at Shaun," Steve shouted. They all watched him from a distance as the bag of glue hung from his mouth. They watched him inhale the fumes as he ran around the fields at speed. His legs were all over the show, Shaun's arms were stretched out and he was imitating a plane. His voice was loud as he ran past them all shouting.

"Come and fly with me you nobheads. I'm off to Australia now." The lads followed his orders and all stretched their arms out running round the field pretending they were flying. In the distance they could see a woman approaching. They came to a standstill as they could see it was Gladys, Shaun's mother.

Gladys was inches away now and they all ran to sit down on the hill. Shaun was still running on the grass with his arms stretched out. Gladys yanked him by the arms. Her hair was stuck up all over and her sandals were full of mud.

"You little fucker what have you been up to? The police have just been round to our house and they're looking for you lot." She now turned to the others and spoke to them. Her finger was pointing at them and her face was red with anger. "You're all in deep shit the fucking lot of you. Steve, your dad's already looking for you, so God help you when he gets his hands on you." Steve's jaw dropped. Gladys now grabbed the bag from Shaun's grip and opened it. Her face looked surprised as she sniffed its contents. The others scattered as she started to scream at the top of her voice.

"You little glue sniffing bastard. No wonder you're not eating. Fucking sniffing glue! Are you right in the head. It can kill you. Do you hear me? It can fucking kill you!" Her eyes were streaming with tears and she looked at the end of her tether as she dragged him towards her. Shaun's eyes were rolling around and he was off his head and not really aware of what was going on. The spots round his mouth looked red and angry. His words were slurred as he answered her.

"We're just having a buzz. I've done nowt wrong so why are the police looking for us?" Gladys dragged him by his arm and started marching him back across the muddy fields. Shaun was trying to shake off his mother's grip but without any success. A few of the neighbours were out on the estate watching her fight with her son. Gladys could see them whispering to each other as she passed them. She leant over to Shaun's face and shouted.

"See what I mean. You've got all the fucking estate talking about us now." Gladys whacked him across the head and Shaun looked at the nosey neighbours. He shoved his two fingers up at them with a smile on his face. "Fuck off back inside, ya beaky bastards!" he chuckled. Gladys whacked him again across his body but he was numb to anything she was doing to him.

As soon as they got through the front door Paul was waiting for him. He dragged Shaun from his mother's arms and pinned him up against the wall with his feet dangling. He was shouting into his face. Shaun was struggling to keep his eyes open.

"Robbing pensioners now are ya? Well wait until the dibble have gone and I'm gonna show you what pain feels like." Shaun looked worried and broke free from his grip. The front door was still open and he took his chance to make a run for it as Paul ran about the house looking for his shoes. There was no way the little bastard was escaping.

"Mam he's done one!" Paul shouted as he slipped his shoes on his feet. Shaun ran like a whippet, he'd lost his brother within seconds. His body was shaking and he had to think quickly as to where he could hide. Remembering his mother had thrown his bag of glue back on the fields he headed back there.

Finding it he took a minute to regain his breath as he flung his body onto the floor. His hand reached for the bag of glue and he brought it to his chest. The glue seemed as fresh as before. Shaun zipped up his tracksuit top and pulled the hood over his head. The glue made him feel loved and as he inhaled he sank back in the grass and went to a place where he had no worries.

He didn't care about anything or anyone.

Chapter Three

Gladys sat at the hospital bed watching her son's eyelids flickering rapidly. She was on the edge of her seat and sat constantly watching the heart monitor. Looking at the door nervously she looked like she was about to shout the doctor in to check him out. He didn't look right. Shaun looked distressed and she wondered if he was dreaming again. Grabbing his hand she stroked it against her face and kissed it softly. His monitor calmed down now and his heartbeat went back to normal. She blew a hard breath and shook her head. It was all getting to much for her.

Shaun's dad had been informed about his son's whereabouts and after a bit of persuasion he was allowed to come to his bed side. The bad blood between them had never subsided and Gladys had been adamant that the bastard was not coming within an inch of her son. Marie had finally convinced her after hours of arguing to let him come to the hospital. After all he was still his father.

Gladys was shocked to see Mike's reaction when he first saw Shaun. She thought he didn't care about his kids. How wrong she was. He looked traumatised. Gladys watched her ex-husband like a hawk as he slithered over to the bedside. Her feelings were mixed for him and she didn't know how to react. This man had abused her for years and she blamed him for everything that had gone wrong in her life.

Mike wiped his eyes as he sat looking at all the tubes placed inside Shaun's body. He was struggling to catch his breath and held one hand around his neck rubbing at it vigorously. The heart monitor showed his son's heart rate at the side of him and he watched it with sadness. His wrinkled hand touched the screen and he wished he could turn back the hands of time. He could feel Gladys's eyes burning into the back of his head. Slowly he turned to face her.

Ruffling the collar on his coat he huffed and dropped his head. Gladys's eyes were still all over him and the look of disgust on her face was obvious. She sat tall in her chair and screwed her face up. He didn't scare her anymore and she was more than ready for him. Gladys's bottom lip was trembling and he could see the heartache in her eyes. Mike licked his dry lips and prepared himself for the fireworks.

Shaun's father was six foot tall and had piled on the pounds over the years. He wasn't always big but the years of alcohol and takeaways had now caught up with him. Mike's unshaven face looked red with the signs of heavy drinking. His nose looked like a ripe tomato. In the past he was always laughing and joking but today he seemed to have lost all his confidence.

Pulling his chair up closer to the bedside, he kept his eyes focused on Shaun's face. He reached for his hands and felt the bony fingers in front of him as his eyes slowly closed. His mouth was moving up and down but no words were coming out. It looked like he was praying. Tears dripped slowly dripped down on his cheek as he remembered holding the same hand when Shaun was only a small boy.

"My boy," he sobbed.

The years of drug abuse were now visible on each of his son's arms. Shaun's veins looked collapsed and they were heavily bruised. Mike sunk his head down and mumbled under his breath. His own tormented life came to the surface now and he needed some kind of forgiveness. Mike had made some bad mistakes in his life but leaving his children was something that played on his mind nearly every day. He told everyone about them but never found the strength to play a part in their lives. Slowly he lifted his head up and turned to Gladys. Pausing for a minute he struggled to speak. He was stuttering.

"It's my fault all this isn't it?" he said as his eyes scanned towards Shaun.

Gladys shot him a look as she sat upright in her chair as if boiling water had been poured down the back of her neck. For years she'd waited for this moment and now it was here she was ready to give the cunt a piece of her mind. She held back as he continued. Gladys looked cold as her hands rubbed up and down against her body. Mike's voice was soft and nothing like she remembered. She looked surprised and wasn't use to seeing this side of him.

"I hold my hands up Gladys." His hands were held out in front of him and a desperate look was across his face. His voice was shaky. "If only I had been a father to him none of this would have happened would it?" His head dropped to his knees and it sounded like he was crying.

Gladys was chomping at the bit and had to restrain herself from diving on him and pummelling her fists into his face. If he thought for one minute he was getting any sympathy from her he had another coming. Lifting his head up slowly Mike stared at her. She could see wetness on his cheeks and realised the bastard did have a heart after all. He continued.

"He would have just been a normal man with a normal life if it wasn't for us." His ex-wife bit down onto her lips as the years of torment hit the surface. Her face was turning red.

"Cheeky bastard," she whispered under her breath. Why was he being so nice to her? She wanted him to be his old self so she could hate him even more than she did already? She looked confused. Gladys wanted to open fire on him but her words stuck in her throat.

The nurse came into the room and checked everything was okay with Shaun. She could see the two distressed parents and it was obvious they didn't get on. Gladys raised her eyes up to the ceiling and shot a look at Mike at the side of her. The atmosphere was there for everyone to see. The nurse looked embarrassed and offered them both a drink. Gladys accepted and seemed to calm down. By the looks of Mike, he could have done with something stronger to calm his nerves.

"Yeah sweetheart, I'll have a coffee if you don't mind." Gladys nearly choked.

"Fucking sweetheart!" she gasped as she looked at him with hate in her eyes. He still wound her up even though the years had passed. He was still a womaniser. The nurse left smiling softly. She couldn't wait to get out of the room as it looked like World War Three was about to start.

"I won't be long," she said.

Mike sat back in his chair. He looked at Gladys and remembered how she looked when she was younger. They should have been so happy together but Mike's own upbringing meant they were set for disaster from the very first moment he placed the wedding ring on her finger.

Mike was one of nine children living on a council estate in Miles Platting. Life had been hard for him and his siblings. Every day had been a struggle for his family. As he sat beside his dying son he thought it was only right that he tried to explain why he was never the father he should have been to his children. The nurse came back into the room and quickly passed them both their drinks. She didn't hang around and quickly left. Taking a drink from his plastic brown cup he stared at Gladys. She looked defensive.

"It was my childhood that fucked me up ya know. It's something I can't ever get over." She could see his eyes filling up and couldn't believe he was opening up to her. He'd always been so hard and never showed any emotions in all the time she'd known him. She held her head back and her nostrils flared as she listened further. "I never deserved a family and I probably never deserved you."

"Too fucking right you didn't!" she mumbled .Gladys wriggled about in the chair and she was preparing herself to have her say. She'd waited years for this moment and she was going to tell him just how much of a twat he really was. As he carried on speaking she saw the pain in his eyes.

"I've never told anyone about my life and the real me, have I?" His eyes looked sad as his thumbs played with his fingertips. "To tell you the truth I find it hard to speak about it and I don't know why I'm talking about it now." He pulled his coat off and stood up as he hung it around the back of the chair. Sitting back down he looked as if he was shivering. He coughed nervously. "My mam tried the best she could for us but once my dad died what chance did she have?" Mike crossed his legs and moved his chair around so he could see her face fully. Gladys was listening and hung onto every word he was saying.

"It was me and our kid that felt it the most. We had fuck all. No food. No money no nothing." His hand reached to Gladys's knee but she moved it away quickly as if it was carrying a disease. "We all missed our dad after he died, but nothing was gonna bring him back. My mam couldn't feed us and we survived the only way we knew how." Sipping more of his coffee he looked at Gladys. Her face was like thunder and he knew she hated him with a passion.

"They took me away from my family you know?"

Gladys shrugged her shoulders and shook her head.

"They should have drowned you at birth if you ask me," she replied sarcastically and her eyes never left his face. Mike shut his eyes for a moment. She was such hard work.

"I went to live with my posh auntie. Fucking hell they had a colour television. I'd never seen a television before, never mind a colour one. They were good to me you know but I missed my family so much, so I kept running away." Gladys blew her nose on the tissue at the side of her and turned her head back to him as he continued. "That's when I fell deeper into crime," he chuckled. "I mean I only done a bit of shoplifting, for fuck's sake there was no need to put me into care. The judge told me I needed discipline in my life and with me having no dad at home the approved school was my only option." Gladys never knew he'd been in care and looked shocked. She'd been married to him for thirteen years and never once had he spoken about his childhood. He'd mentioned basic stuff in the past, but what he was telling her now made her toes curl. Mike pulled at his hair as he ran his fingers through it. He was distressed.

"The fucking care system sucks. You're treated like a machine. They strip any emotions from you and make you feel dead inside." His head hung low as his past gripped him with both hands. He was eager to continue. "Imagine me as an eleven-year-old boy with no mam, no dad. No fuck all. I had nobody to tell me that they loved me. It was a nightmare Gladys I can tell you." She could feel her arms getting ready to hug him but she held back. What was she thinking? He was her enemy.

His look was daunting as he sighed. "The sad thing was though, all the kids in care were like that. It was a dog eat dog world. I learnt that to survive I had to be ruthless, and that's what I did. I bullied, I stole and even got some lads to give me their clothing." Gladys knew he was a bully and scowled as she remembered her own tormented life with him. He laughed out loud and looked chuffed. "I was the best dressed kid in there." He was looking for any signs of forgiveness in her face but she remained solemn. Gladys held her cup of tea and stroked at the rim of it. Her eyes looked over to her son as a single tear ran down her face. She too held years of disappointment and Mike was the biggest part of it. Gritting her teeth she cleared her throat and spoke in a distressed voice. She'd heard enough of his self pitying story.

"So is that why you treated me the way you did?" she screamed. Gladys sat forward in her chair now and looked directly into his eyes. She was struggling not to cry. "You treated me like a low-life and never once did you ever say you were sorry. How do you think that made me feel?" she said jabbing her finger in his face. "Fucking years of beatings, and mental torture you gave me. You destroyed me as a person. Do you know that?" Mike tried to move nearer to her but she held her head high and pulled her arm from his as he tried to comfort her. "Fuck off," she groaned. He tried again to comfort her.

"Take you fucking hands off me Mike. It's too late now for apologies. You ruined my life and our kids." Looking at the floor he slid his feet against the vinyl floor. He could tell by her frozen face that there was no way in this world she would ever forgive him. The years had passed and she'd become bitter against him. The room was silent; all you could hear was the machine bleeping away with Shaun's heartbeat. Gladys wanted to turn the machine off as it was bugging her. Every bleep from it told her that her son was still alive and still suffering. She gripped her body and swayed in the chair. Pulling a strand of hair that had fallen onto her face she turned to face Mike.

"He's better off dead. At least then he won't be in any more pain. What does he have to live for, ay? He's a fucking drug addict. Every day that he continues to breathe will just be more pain for him." Gladys was upset and she shook her head as she looked at Shaun. Blowing her nose she stood up and walked to her son's bedside. With her back to Mike she spoke.

"That's not my son lying there. My son died a long time ago. That's just the shell of someone who used to be my boy." She closed her eyes and hated that she was wishing her son dead. Her voice choked up as she tried to control her heartache but it was no good. Mike bolted up from his seat and placed his arm over her shoulder. She walked back to her chair and her body folded with desperation. Gladys tried to remove Mike's arm but her sorrow was deep and she didn't have the strength anymore for fighting. Standing beside her he leant over and kissed the top of her head.

"I'm sorry love. I know it's years too late, but this is all my fault. Me and my stupid fucked up life." He knelt at the side of her legs. His head sank between his legs as the tears dripped from his face. Mike's large body frame looked like it was melting. Reaching for her hands he pulled them onto his head.

"I've held so much in for years and if I don't get it off my chest I'll go mad. I'm not the big hard man that everyone thinks. In fact I'm a fucking wreck inside." Gladys looked at him and she shook her head. Why was she feeling sorry for him? It was her son who needed her attention not her ex-husband. She pushed him away.

"It's not about you anymore," her eyes turned to Shaun. "It's our son who's lying over there that needs our help. He

needed you, and all you ever done was turn him away."
Her voice was desperate as she stomped about the room.
Her body faced him and she held her hands in the air.
"For crying out loud he was a child when you left. How
do you think that affected him?" Gladys was angry and
her face was turning red as she let out years of frustration.
"You don't know the half of it, Mike. Where the fuck was
you when he cried each night for his dad? Where were
you when he fucking needed you?" Gladys screwed up
her face as she leant in towards him. Her body was shaking
from head to toe. She hadn't finished. "I'll tell you were
you were, shall I?" Mike knew what was coming and sat
up straight. He held his hand up to protect his body as she
shouted into his face.

"You were with your shag-bag. A woman who you
barely knew! Fucking pretending to be a dad to her kids."
She was livid and stood with one hand on her hip as she
continued. "You didn't give a fuck about your own flesh
and blood. What kind of man are you?" she sighed. She'd
done it. Gladys had finally had the chance to tell him exactly
what she thought of him and how he'd let everyone down
not just as a husband but as a father too. She pulled herself
together and fought back the tears. Gladys needed to get
this off her chest for once and for all. This was her chance
and she was holding nothing back.

"Not once did you come and see your own three
kids you cunt. You left me to it all and never gave me a
fucking penny." Gladys spat into his face and her body was
shaking furiously. The nurse entered the room and looked
concerned. She asked if everything was alright and went to
Shaun's side checking his notes. She kept on turning her
head looking at them both. Once she'd finished attending
to the patient she came to where they were seated. She

spoke in a stern voice.

"I don't know what's going on in here, but this man is very poorly and he doesn't need you two arguing at his bedside. Can I suggest that you keep your bickering until you leave." The nurse was a middle aged woman. Her plump figure waddled about the room, her dark hair was scraped back from her face and you could tell she wasn't in the mood for any back chat.

Mike felt embarrassed and told her they were sorry. He promised to keep the noise down. The nurse huffed and left the room. The silence was eerie as Mike wiped the spit from his face, the relationship between them had always been heated from the first day they met.

Mike walked over to the bed and held his son's hand. He rested his head on the bed. Everything in his life had now come back to haunt him. The mistakes he'd made in the past were now staring back at him in the shape of his son. Mike wanted to clear the air. He could hear Gladys sighing behind him but that didn't stop him. He needed her to know the truth.

"Gladys please just let me explain why I was the way I was." Biting her bottom lip she knew she had to curb the anger she felt inside and let him have his say.

"In the home, the care system, whatever you wanna fucking call it, they beat us regularly. I don't mean a slap across your head or a slapped hand, I mean they proper beat us." Mike clenched his fist and shown her what he meant. His knuckles were white as he slammed his fist into his flat palm of his other hand.

"The teachers were bastards. They were all like army sergeants. When I first went into care they seemed okay, but as time went on I knew not to fuck about with them." Gladys nodded slowly. His voice was distressed. "The punishment for anything we did wrong was the cane or the slipper." Gladys looked confused. She didn't understand what he meant. Mike's voice was loud and you could tell he was getting emotional as he stood up and acted out the punishment he received in the care home.

"They made you pull your pants down touch your toes and look the other way whilst they whacked your arse. The first time I had the slipper I screamed. It fuckin' murdered I can tell you." Mike's face was smiling as his body dropped and he touched his toes. Gladys forced a smile as he turned his head acting out as if he was getting the slipper. His body went stiff as if he'd been whacked on the arse and he hopped about the room showing her how the lads all used to run about after the first strike. He made Gladys laugh for the first time. She sat back and cupped her hands together. She looked so different when she smiled. Mike huffed.

"It sorted out the men from the boys I can tell you. We use to take bets on how many whacks you could take without screaming. Fucking hell Gladys by the end of the first few months my arse was like leather. I became immune to the pain." His face looked stern as he showed her the way he looked at the teachers and fear ran through her veins as she remembered the face of her abuser.

"They knew I could take the pain in the end. That's when the real beatings started coming. I should have just screamed like the others and perhaps they would have left me alone, but me being me I couldn't help being a smart arse."

Gladys agreed with him. "Yeah you was always a stubborn sod."

He continued. "The teachers would all gather round me and wait until the final blow had been struck. If there were still no tears they all took their turn in punching me."

Gladys looked at him and wondered why he had never told her this before. The man she saw in front of her was someone she didn't really know, even though she'd been married to him for years. As she watched him she could see the pain in his face as he remembered every little detail as if it was yesterday.

"Mr Woodcock was a right bastard. He knew he couldn't break me and knew it would take something more. That's when it all started." Mike stood up and told her he was going outside for a smoke. He was agitated now and going over his life was stressing him out big time. "Are you coming outside for a cig?" Shaking her head she declined. She was dying for a fag but she didn't want to be too friendly with him. Reaching for his coat pocket on the chair he found his Benson and Hedges cigs. Pulling one from the packet he asked could he borrow her lighter. She bent down and rummaged in her handbag.

"Here, make sure you bring it back!"

"Fucking hell I'm going outside, not to Spain." Mike fired back.

"Once a thief, always a thief!" Gladys replied, shaking her head as he left.

Shaun looked at peace as she stroked his greasy hair. His skin was gaunt and his cheekbones were sticking out from his face. His bone structure looked long and thin. Several spots were round his mouth and his lips looked cracked and sore. Gladys poured a glass of water for herself and dipped her finger inside it. Slowly she placed the water on his lips and softly rubbed it into his skin. Shaun had great shaped lips and some women would have killed for them. As she held his hands she looked at the track marks. As her fingers followed each purple vein up his arm she felt sick inside. She whispered into Shaun ears.

"What's happened to you son? I know I've not always been there for you, but I had things going on myself. You were a handful as a kid you know?" Her head fell onto the bed as Mike walked back into the room. He could see she was upset and came to her side. She inhaled deeply smelling the aroma of smoke from his clothes.

"He's gonna pull through you know. He's strong inside. I know he is." Mike held her hand and this time she didn't pull away. He was all she had at the moment as her sister had left the hospital hours before. If he hadn't been there she would have gladly curled up and died. The sound of the door opening made them both turn round. As they looked Paul was stood there with a look that would kill spread across his face. He'd seen Mike's hands on his mother's body and gritted his teeth together. He looked at his father and snarled.

"Mam, why's he here?" His eyes pierced into his father's head. Gladys removed Mike's hand from her body now aware of how it looked to her son. She walked back to her chair. Paul faced his father and looked him straight into the eyes. It was now his time to set the record straight. He'd waited for this day for years and now it was here he was letting him have it.

"No point giving a shit now is there Dad? It's your fault his head's fucked up in the first place." Mike bit onto his bottom lip and clenched his fist. The anger was written all over his face as he tried to control his temper. Gripping the bedclothes he spoke to his son for the first time in years.

"Listen, Shaun decided to shove drugs into his body not me. He is the one to blame for his life. We've all had shit to deal with haven't we?" Paul sat on the chair next to his mother. He stared at the floor for a few minutes and couldn't hold his tongue any longer. The man he saw in front of him now was old and he knew he could floor him with one punch. He felt no remorse as he continued.

"What shit did you have to deal with? You fucked off and left three kids and led a single life. So don't tell me about dealing with shit. I did your fucking job for you." Paul was livid as he spoke with hatred to his father. "If you would have only showed one bit of interest in any of your kids' lives we might not be here today." Paul's words cut Mike in half. His shoulders melted and he knew his son was speaking the truth. Mike sighed and started to speak but Paul stopped him dead in his tracks as he held a flat palm in front of his face.

"Save it for someone who gives a fuck, ay dad. Don't try and explain anything to me because I don't want to hear it. If you want to cleanse your soul, tell my mam because she's listened to your bullshit for years. It doesn't wash with me, so don't waste your breath." Gladys shook her head and tried to calm him down. Mike sprung to Paul's side with his temper pumping.

"Who the fuck do you think you're talking to? Where's your respect gone?" Paul held his head back and laughed before he stood up to meet his dad's eyes. They were nose to nose. Gladys jumped between them pushing them apart.

"For fuck's sake this isn't the time or the place for this. Will you both leave it out?" Paul never lost eye contact. Mike looked from side to side and knew she was right. Grabbing his coat from the chair he told them he was going outside for another cig. Paul watched him leave and let his mother have a piece of his mind.

"Tell you what mam, you must be fucking desperate." Gladys looked puzzled.

"What are you going on about?"

"Fucking holding hands all nicey, nicey. Have you forgotten what he's done to you in the past? Your son's lying there half dead and you're all over him like a rash. Get a grip woman and sort it out otherwise I'm off." Gladys jumped up and defended herself.

"It's not what you think," she was by his side trying to stop him moving away. "Just listen for a minute will you, before you get on your high horse." Paul couldn't look her in the face. "I was upset and he was just trying to comfort me, that's all."

Paul shouted at her as he paced the room with speed in his step. "Shame he didn't comfort you when he used to knock ten bags of shit out of you isn't it? Have you forgotten what he did to you?" He raised his arms above his head and pulled at his hair. He focused on the bed and with tears in his eyes he sat next to his brother. His mother sat shaking her head but left him alone as she could see he was angry. She grabbed her coat and headed outside carrying her cigs.

"Oh I don't know!" she mumbled.

Paul had always hated that his brother was a heroin addict. He could never come to terms with what had happened to Shaun over the years. It was much easier to blame everyone else for his life so that's what he did. The room felt cold and Paul just stared at Shaun, shaking his head as tears ran down his face.

"Fucking hell our kid, how has it come to this? I know I've disowned you but I still fucking love you, ya muppet." Gripping the lifeless hand he placed it on his head and sobbed. Shaun's body twitched and Paul raised his head in shock. He stood from his chair and shook his brother softly.

"Wake up, wake up," he ranted but Shaun remained

comatose. His words were wasted as Shaun was in another world and by the look on his face he was in some kind of pain.

"Please God don't let him die!" Paul whispered.

Chapter Four

At the age of fifteen Shaun Cook could see himself stood in the juvenile courtroom in Manchester. He looked confident and as if he didn't give a shit about anything that was going on around him. He'd been to court loads of times in the past and all he ever got was a slap on the wrist, so he thought today was going to be no different. How wrong he was! As the charges were read out they consisted of shoplifting robbery and burglaries. To look at the angelic boy that stood in the dock you would have thought butter wouldn't have melted in his mouth. Shaun's dirty blonde hair just covered his eyes and his golden skin made his blue eyes stand out. He was fidgeting.

Shaun was dressed in a white thick knitted jumper and faded jeans. As you watched him you could tell the jumper was aggravating him round the neck as he yanked at it. His mother sat at his side whispering for him to keep still. Anton, Shaun's solicitor, read out his personal circumstances as Gladys held her head in shame at the side of him. Shaun never showed any emotion as the sentence was passed. He was trying to look strong. To tell you the truth he didn't realise how serious it all was. His eyes were all over the courtroom as his hands gripped the wooden frame in front of him. The words of the magistrate were like swords being stabbed into his mother's heart. He looked at her face as he told the young boy he was going into the care system. She looked white in the face. Shaun swung his body around and chewed on the sleeve of his jumper.

The social worker came to his side and led him

through a side door closely followed by his sobbing mother. Gladys's heartache was visible as she passed the people in the courtroom. "Heartless bastards," she whispered. The prosecution were whispering to each other and she knew they all felt she was a failure as a parent. Pulling her coat together with a shaking hand she passed through the door at the back of the courtroom.

Shaun was sat on a chair swinging his legs about as his mother entered. He wore a vacant look as she sat beside him. Gladys watched all the people pass her and stared at her son before she spoke.

"You've done it this time lad. I can't save you now." Shaun screwed his face up and folded his arms across his chest. His face was cocky and he spoke with an attitude.

"Mam, I'm not even arsed. It gets me away from round here doesn't it?" Grabbing his arm she pulled him towards her and cradled him in her arms. Gladys inhaled the smell from his head and slowly kissed his head. Shaun sat and looked around the room. He didn't look bothered about what had just happened. The social worker now came to his side and knelt down in front of them both, looking into Shaun's eyes. She could see his mother was struggling to cope and gave her a moment more before she spoke.

"How are you Shaun? My name is Joan and I'm going to be dealing with you whilst you're in care. You are going to Beachvale care home in Blackpool. It's a lovely place."

"Fucking Blackpool!" Gladys screamed. "How on earth am I supposed to get up there. I haven't got a pot to piss in!" she gasped. Joan didn't know how to answer her question and continued speaking as Gladys huffed at the side of her.

"There are around fifty boys there. The care workers are great." Shaun held no expression on his face as he read the notices on the board in front of him.

Joan was a middle-aged woman with frizzy brown hair. Shaun looked at her large brown spectacles and covered his mouth as he whispered to his mam. "She looks like Deirdre Barlow from Coronation Street doesn't she?" Gladys tried to force a smile but her heart was broken in two. Her hands looked old and wrinkled as she rubbed her son's hand in hers. Joan told them that once all the paperwork was ready she would be the one taking Shaun to his new home. Gladys burst into tears and spoke. Her voice was desperate and at one stage she was nearly on her knees begging Joan to help her.

"When can I visit him? Say he doesn't like it, can he come home?" The social worker stood to her feet. Joan had seen this heartbreaking moment so many times in the past and felt the woman's pain. Looking around the room she began to speak.

"You can visit once a week, but he can write to you every day if he wants." Shaun shrugged his shoulder.

"Fuck that!" he mumbled. He could barely read or write and knew deep down inside he wouldn't be writing endless letters. Joan now asked them to follow her. The time was nearing for him to say goodbye to his mother and the life he knew in Harpurhey.

Walking outside, Shaun squeezed his eyes together. The sun was bright and he struggled to see. Lifting his hands up, he covered his eyes. Shaun and Gladys both followed Joan to her red Corsa and watched as she opened the door. Shaun kicked the floor as Gladys spoke eagerly to Joan. A few other people stood close to them who looked like security. Shaun looked bored. Once they'd finished talking, his mother came to his side. Searching her coat pocket she pulled out an old tissue and placed it into her mouth to wet it. She quickly wiped his face with the edge of it. Shaun started to moan as she wiped the tissue around his face.

"Mam stop it. It's got your breath all over it. It stinks of arse." Gladys scrubbed his face and grabbed him towards her. Her grip was tight as she spoke her last words to him. She looked weak and ready for the knacker's yard.

"Orr son I love you so much. How have you ended up like this?" Her head fell onto his shoulders. "I'll come and see you every week son. I promise, just be good and you'll be home before you know it." Shaun shoved her away from him with a gentle push. He was a big lad now and didn't need his mother's love anymore or so he thought. Dragging the car door open he plonked his body inside.

Gladys stared through the window at her son. Watching her face sent a wave of fear through his body. For the first time he felt scared. Joan started the engine and he nodded his head at his mother as they started to drive off. As he looked through the back misted window he could see her shaking from head to toe. "Silly cow," he whispered. Turning his head back to the front he bit onto his bottom lip to stop his tears flowing.

The time passed quickly on the way to Blackpool. The traffic was heavy and cars were speeding past them as they joined the motorway. Joan looked stressed. Her fingers gripped the steering wheel and as she picked up speed to join the traffic she was mumbling under her breath. Shaun thought about Blackpool and smiled as he remembered family holidays there. Those happy days were long gone now. The rain banged on the car windows as if it was trying to get a grip of Shaun's body. He looked uncomfortable.

The windscreen wipers started to swish from side to side. Shaun followed them with his eyes and seemed hypnotised by them. The motorway wasn't that busy but the weather was slowing the traffic down. Shaun sat staring with a cunning look on his face. His fingers were tapping rapidly on his knees. He was up to something.

Joan glanced over to where he was and asked if he was okay. A quick nod of his head was enough for her and she carried on driving. Shaun asked where they were and once she told him he knew he would have to act quickly. The traffic was coming to a standstill as the road works approached. Shaun quickly jumped into the front seat and yanked at the door handle with trembling hands. Joan started screaming.

"What are you doing, you lunatic? Close the bloody door!" She tried to grab him but her seatbelt restricted her movement. Shaun ignored her and flung himself from the moving car onto the road. The traffic was starting to move again and she knew she would have to get to the hard shoulder. "Fucking hell! fucking hell!" she panicked.

Pulling over to the hard shoulder, she ran to the fence which she had seen Shaun jump. He was almost halfway across it by the time she got there. Joan knew there would be no chance of her catching him. She lifted her hands to her head and sighed.

"The little bastard!"

Shaun ran and ran and didn't turn back once to see if she was chasing him. The field was full of cow shit and he dodged it as if he was avoiding landmines. Once he reached the other side he looked behind him. He couldn't see anyone. "Result!" he shouted as he punched his fist into the air. He was gasping for air until slowly his breathing returned to normal. Digging deep into his socks he pulled out the packet of cigs he'd stashed earlier and lit one. His mam had also shoved twenty pounds into his hand before she left him so he knew he could get back home safely if he wanted.

As he inhaled his cig he pulled his hood up over his face. Sat with his knees up to his chest he planned his next move as he took cover in some nearby bushes. Shaun didn't really know where he was but the money he had in his pocket was enough for now. The rain now became heavier as the heavens opened. It was pissing down. Flicking his cig into the grass verge he sat thinking for a minute. He looked sad. Looking round the area his eyes focused on the houses he could see in the distance. Jerking his body up from the ground he kept his head low as he trudged towards the gap in the fence.

Shaun seemed to walk for ages before he saw another person. As a middle-aged man approached him he prepared his words. Licking his lips he spoke in a confident manner.

"Excuse me, can you tell me where the train station is to get to Manchester please?" The man looked at him and couldn't really be bothered standing about in the rain. He was still walking as he gave Shaun the information he needed. Shaun jogged at the side of him.

"You need to get to the town centre son. Just get the bus there." The man pointed down the road as he continued. "Ask the driver if it takes you into town. Then you should be fine from there." The passer-by walked away with his hands in his pocket and his long trench coat buttoned up tightly. Shaun stood looking at the bus stop and read the times the buses were due. Glancing over the road he noticed a DIY shop and wondered if they sold glue.

Shaun crossed the road with a spring in his step. He entered the shop. It was quite old fashioned and an old man stood behind the counter wearing a light brown overall. The man's grey hair was combed over his bald spot and Shaun was amused how the hair fell out of place every time he bent down. Slowly he walked round the shop as the eyes of the man focused on him.

"Can I help you son?" the shop keeper asked. Shaun now played the part he'd played so many times before. He deserved an Oscar for this performance.

"My dad has sent me for some strong glue. I can't really remember the name of it." Shaun started to sound out some words as the man stood watching him. "Epo, edo, glue?" The man knew exactly what he meant and laughed as he grabbed his shoulder.

"You mean Evo-stick glue sonny." The man now reached up onto the shelf and grabbed the tin. The red container made Shaun smile because he knew in a few minutes he would be off his head and he could get the rush he desired. As he stood at the till he casually asked for a plastic bag to put his purchase in. After all without the bag he couldn't sniff could he? The man obliged and handed him the adhesive. Shaun stood swinging his body as he waited for his change. Leaving the shop Shaun shouted goodbye to the man and headed back to the deserted bus stop.

Looking both ways he sat on the small red plastic seat inside the bus shelter. Once he'd unscrewed the lid from the glue he poured the thick yellow liquid into the bag. His hands were shaking as he gripped the bag by the neck and pushed all the glue to the bottom of it. As he opened his tracksuit top he placed the glue-bag down deep inside it. Shaun left the top of the bag hanging out so he could get his mouth into it.

The first sniff was always the best and today was no different. He inhaled deeply and you could see his body melting. The bag inflated and deflated in his hands as if it was a lung. Mellow moments followed. Standing from his seat Shaun tried to read the timetable on the plastic notice board screwed on the bus shelter. His eyesight looked disturbed as he tried to focus on the words. He looked pissed.

Once the bus arrived Shaun quickly asked the driver if it went to the town centre. Once he'd confirmed where it was going he paid his fare and headed to the upper level on the bus. As he reached the top of the stairs he clocked all the people and where they were sat. He needed a quiet place to sniff his glue and headed to the back of the bus where he would be alone. Shaun placed his skinny legs along the back seat. His face disappeared as his head went inside the top of his coat.

Later, when he got on the train, the chugging noise brought a smile to Shaun's face as he tapped his fingers on the window. The noise of it seemed like the beating of a drum. He held his hands out over his legs and pretended he had a set of drums in front of him. People in the carriage looked at him and shook their heads. He looked drunk to them and they whispered to each other as he sat in a world of his own.

Shaun picked at the spots round his mouth as his eyes struggled to keep open. Some of the spots were red and inflamed but that didn't deter him scratching at them. His mouth was open as he gawped at his surroundings. He was on his way home.

As the train came to a standstill in Manchester, he knew he was back on familiar ground. The sound of a man's voice shouting "Get your Evening News" brought a smile to his face. Everybody was rushing around as he slowly made his way to the exit. His steps were clumsy and he nearly lost his balance a few times. Shaun remembered he was a wanted man. He pulled his hood up further around his face only leaving his eyes on show. Shaun began to quicken his steps and once he was outside the train station he jogged a little until he reached a nearby side street.

The glue was nearly gone now. His face was deep inside the plastic bag as he inhaled the last bit of it. He tossed the bag to the floor. Seeing a red phone box in the distance he searched his pocket for some change. Once he was inside it he dialled the number of his family home. The voice he heard was that of his brother and he paused for few second before he finally spoke.

"Tell me mam I want her. Tell her to be quick before my money runs out." Shaun held the phone away from his ear as his brother screamed down the line.

"Get your arse home ya little prick! The police have been here all day looking for you!" Shaun spoke again but this time his voice was low.

"Just get my mam will ya." The phone was silent and he pressed his ear against the phone as he heard the voice of Paul shouting his mother in the background.

"Mam, that nobhead's on the phone. You better tell him when I see him I'm gonna do him in. The little twat."

"Fucking dickhead," Shaun growled. Gladys's voice was shaky and low as she replied to her son. Shaun sounded frantic.

"Mam it's me." His mother's sobs could be heard as he continued. "I'm not going back there. I want to stay with you."

His mother tried to reason with him and as he held the phone by the wire he could hear her piercing voice telling him to hand himself in at the police station. Shaun placed the receiver down and mumbled under his breath.

"Fucking sell out. No way I'm going back into care." He flung the door open from the phone box and kicked the side of the glass panel. His hood was still covering his head. Standing for a minute he thought about where to go. With a little jog in his step he made his way to the bus stop that would take him back to Harpurhey.

There were a few people waiting for the same bus as Shaun. His hands gripped the rusty pole at the bus stop. Leaning against it, he held his arms out and swung around it into the road. The cars honked their horns as they just missed him, but his face remained calm as he rammed two fingers up at the traffic. One woman grabbed her child's hand and shook her head at him with a look of disgust on her face. "Fucking nutter," she huffed.

Shaun stepped on the bus and dug his hands into his jeans for the fare. His trousers hung from his arse and the top of his boxer shorts could be seen. His eyes looked glazed over and he stank of glue. The driver took the fare and nodded slowly at him. He watched him through his rear view mirror take his seat. The woman behind him couldn't wait to fill the driver in about Shaun's antics as he took her fare. Her head turned away from Shaun and once she knew he couldn't hear her she began.

"He's a couple of butties short of a picnic him. You should have seen him before. He swung right out into the road without a care in the world, he could have been killed you know." The driver shook his head but didn't speak as he gave her the bus ticket. He watched her as she walked past and carried on taking the fares.

Shaun pressed his face against the window and blew his warm breath onto it. Once the window had misted over, he wet the end of his finger and wrote his name in it. "Shaun of Harpurhey" he scrawled. The man next to him smiled. He couldn't see any harm in the kid's artwork and carried on reading his newspaper.

Shaun suddenly stood up at the window and started banging on the glass as he spotted one of his mates. His voice was loud as he shouted through the glass. The bus was at a standstill waiting for the traffic lights to change.

"Dillon! Where ya off to?" he shouted as his face scrunched up at the window. You could see the other lad nearing the bus as he shouted back.

"Just on my way up to Mark's. Are ya coming?" Shaun waved his hands at him and shouted at the driver to wait while he got off the bus. The driver was reluctant at first but felt intimidated by him so he pressed the button to open the door. The other passengers could be heard sighing, but they were glad to see the back of the youth. Shaun jumped off the bus as it was still in motion and bounced toward his mate.

Dillon nodded as he approached him and passed him half the cig he'd been smoking. "What ya up to then?" Dillon sniggered. Shaun hunched his shoulders and smiled with a cocky face.

"I'm on my toes aren't I?"

His mate giggled. Shaun was now aware he had to be more careful in the area. He pulled his hood back up and took a deep drag of the cig. Dillon wanted to know more and delved deeper into his business.

"What ya on the run for? What ya been up to now ya nobhead?" Shaun bit onto his bottom lip as he spoke. This was the first time he'd realised exactly how deep in shit he really was.

"I'm supposed to be in care. They tried taking me today, but I got off." Dillon smiled and punched him on the arm playfully.

"Ya muppet. What did ya do?" Shaun had to think and tilted his head to the side.

"Nar nothing much, just a few snatches and that. They think I'm out of control because my dad has fucked off."

Dillon watched his friend's face. He could see sadness in his eyes. He was a lot older than Shaun and always looked at him as the brother he never had. Dillon was a good kid and never got involved with the street life in Harpurhey. He'd much rather concentrate on his schoolwork unlike most kids in the area. Dillon was considered an outsider by lots of the youth in the area. Shaun's other mates use to take the piss out him for associating with him but he always told them to lay off him and fought his corner well telling them he was an alright lad.

They carried on walking. They crossed the road that led to some nearby fields. Shaun felt the money in his pocket and told Dillon he would meet him later at Mark's. He made his way to the hardware shop and quickly hid his glue in his coat once he'd bought some more. Mark was a glue sniffer as well and now he had some, they could have a buzz together. Secretly he was hoping Mark would let him get his head down at his gaff, well at least for tonight anyway. His mate's parents were pissed all the time and didn't give a fuck who stayed in the house as long as they didn't bother them.

The thought of the solvent inside his coat made him quicken his pace. He held it like it was a bar of gold. This was his remedy to take all the pain away he felt inside. Nothing mattered when he was as high as a kite on glue. If he'd have had his way he would of stayed that way forever.

Shaun rapped at Mark's door. The letter box was full of dirt and grease. After he knocked it he wiped his hands on his jacket. "Scruffy twats," he whispered. Music could

be heard playing at full blast inside. Lifting the letter box
up he scanned through it to see if he could see anyone.
Scrunching his mouth inside it he shouted Mark's name.
Within minutes a man came to the door looking pissed
out of his head. He took a while to focus on Shaun and
walked away leaving the door wide open.

Shaun walked inside and stood for a minute. When he
saw Mark's drunken dad shut the living room door he made
his way upstairs. The music was blasting downstairs and he
found it hard to hear as he shouted Mark. Once he heard
his voice he jogged up the rest of the stairs and entered the
bedroom. The bedroom was poorly lit. It looked like a shit
tip. The curtains being fully closed didn't help. A bare bulb
hung from the discoloured ceiling and the two double beds
in the room were covered in clothes and coats. A few other
lads were lying on the beds.

Dillon stood up ready to leave. He had only called
to swap a game with Mark and now he saw the glue in
Shaun's hands he knew it was time to do one. Shaun felt a
little embarrassed when he saw his eyes focus on his guilty
pleasure and tried to raise a smile, but Dillon left straight
away.

Mark ran downstairs and got some plastic bags as the
others waited eagerly for him to return. When he came
back he threw them all a bag each and watched as Shaun
shared it out. Before the sniffing began Shaun made sure
he could have a bed for the night. Once he explained to
Mark what was happening he began to relax knowing he
had somewhere to stay for now.

All four lads inhaled the glue and slowly they all went
into a world of their own. The music being played by Pink
Floyd set the scene. They mumbled the words to "Another
Brick in the wall" as the solvent took effect. The noise of

someone coming in the room made them hide their glue bags. As they looked up it was Mark's mother stood at the door. She had a cig hanging from her mouth and her words were slurred as she spoke. She looked a disgrace.

"Get this shit hole cleaned up. Look at the fucking state of it in here!" The lads hung their heads low as Mark spoke.

"Chill out will ya . I'll do it later, what's the big rush." His mother could barely stand up and gripped the door fame to steady herself.

"No wonder I'm always pissed, the state of this fucking house," she slurred before slamming the bedroom door. Mark screwed up his face as she left.

"She's a fucking nobhead isn't she? Every time I have my mates in she always says the same thing. She thinks she will shame me into cleaning up." He looked embarrassed as he ranted. "She wants to look at herself instead of my fucking bedroom. She's a walking wreck."

No one replied as their heads were now sunk into their plastic bags. Eyes rolled and jaws dropped as they inhaled the fumes from the thick yellow liquid. Each kid had their own personal problems but to look at them you couldn't tell. They all had smiles on their face and didn't seem to give a shit about anything in life.

Later that night, just Mark and Shaun were left in the bedroom. They'd been downstairs and grabbed a butty. The fridge was bare except for two curled up pieces of ham inside it. They buttered some bread and made the most of what was there.

Mark's parents were flat out on the sofa. Empty cans of lager were scattered around them. The ashtray was full to the top with cig ends. The smell from the room was putrid. Mark sighed and felt embarrassed. He just shook his head and closed the door as they trudged back upstairs. Once back in the bedroom they flung their bodies onto the soiled bed sheets. The duvet cover should have been a cream colour but to look at it, it was covered in all different colours of food and drinks.

Shaun dragged the blanket over his body. He snuggled inside it leaving only his face showing. The moon shone in through the net curtains and made everything look magical. Shaun placed his hand into his pocket and pulled out the pebble he'd found earlier when he was waiting at the bus stop. The pebble felt cold as he stroked it. Twisting it around in his fingers he slowly closed his eyes. The pebble felt like a magic stone to him and he promised himself to keep it by his side always. His head rose one last time to look at Mark, and once he knew he was out for the count he closed his eyes to and tried to find sleep too.

Police sirens could be heard outside and some locals were stood outside their houses talking loudly. Today had been one big failure for Shaun and he just hoped that the morning light would bring some changes in his life.

Chapter Five

Shaun could hear the birds tweeting outside the window. He stretched his body and scratched his nuts as his hands disappeared down his boxer shorts. The room was still dark. Looking round the room he stretched his legs across to Mark's bed and kicked him softly. Mark didn't move at first but when he kicked him again he started to moan.

"Fuck off and leave me alone ya dickhead."

Shaun was wide awake now and sat up on his bed. He yanked the curtains open and let the bright sunlight in the bedroom. Mark screwed his face and hid his eyes under the covers "Close the curtains. Fucking hell Shaun, I'm trying to get some shut eye here." Shaun looked for his shoes and pushed Mark's with his hands.

"Come on, let's get some cash earned. I'm on my arse and need some money." Mark liked the sound of that and suddenly sprang into life.

"Just hang on for fuck's sake my eyes are still closed." Shaun moved towards the window. He scratched his head as he hatched a plan. Turning his head around to Mark he looked excited.

"Let's nick some lead. There's loads on the roofs near the market. We should earn some decent cash from it." Mark's eyes popped open. He was skint and the chances of getting fed by his parents were zero. He needed money to survive. Nicking lead was a good little earner for the kids in Harpurhey and today was no different. They finished getting ready and quickly grabbed their coats as they left the house. Breakfast wasn't going to happen at Mark's and

they didn't even try looking for something to eat before
they left as the fridge was always bare.

A few youngsters were out on the estate playing in
front of their houses in their pyjamas. As they walked past
them Shaun slapped the sides of their heads pushing them
to the ground. The kids were now up in arms and tried
grabbing Shaun and Mark's legs as they carried on walking.
Mark laughed as he tried to free the kid from his calves as
Shaun pissed himself laughing. Mark nearly lost his balance
and fell to the floor at one point as the youngsters dragged
at him. It was only Shaun's arm that saved him. The joke
was over now and they let the kids know the game had
ended. They told them that on the way back they would
have a re-match with them. That seemed enough for the
kids to let them go without giving them any more shit.

Conran Street market was a well known landmark In
Harpurhey. The locals called it the bargain market. You
could get cheap cigs, hooky CDs of all the latest pop bands
– it was counterfeit heaven. The market was also a local
haunt for a lot of drug addicts trying to make a few quid.
They could be seen lingering near the entrance of the
market sweating and getting ready to make some cash.

Shaun knew a few of the druggies and nodded as he
passed them. Each of them looked a lot older than they
really were. Their faces looked sallow and they seemed to
have grey skin. Shaun had always been fascinated by the
junkies and the lives they lived. Everybody had told him
to keep away from them but for some reason he felt like he
was drawn to them.

As they passed through the market they could hear the
banter between the market traders. Shaun kept his head
low and let on to the odd person who he knew. Shaun's
sister worked on the market and he made sure he kept

right out of her way as he walked through. Shaun loved his sister and they got on well. She hated him sniffing glue and would have gone sick at him if she had seen him with any. Their bond was strong and they looked out for each other, but at the moment he couldn't be arsed with the earache she'd give him about running away. He turned his head to the stall where she worked and he could see the side of her. Half of him wanted to run to her and the other part of him wanted to go and earn some cash. With that in mind his pace quickened and left the market.

As the lads stood back looking at the old terraced houses in front of them they could see the lead on the roofs. The large wall at the side of the houses was their only route to the metal. They checked the area to make sure no one was looking and grabbed a dust bin from the nearby alleyway. Shaun dragged it to the side of the houses and knew once they threw the lead down to the ground they could gather it together and use the bin to transport it to the scrap yard.

Shaun climbed up first. His legs held the drain-pipe for dear life. Mark watched as he saw him pull his body onto the roof and followed his lead to reach the top. Once Mark was by his side, he pulled out a screwdriver and the Stanley knife that he'd brought along with him. Shaun pressed the blade deep into the lead and dragged it along to the end of the roof. Once that was done they used the screwdriver to lodge underneath it to help lift it up from the roof. Rolling it together they crossed the slated roof and threw it down onto the floor near the bin.

Shaun's face was black and all his clothes were too. Mark was laughing as he looked at his face and found it hard to keep his balance. The sound of the boys laughing filled the air and they never heard the old woman from the street shouting up to them to get down. Shaun and Mark carried on doing what they were doing and were oblivious to the sound of police sirens in the distance.

A crowd now gathered beneath them. They watched the lads larking about throwing stones at each other from across the roof as they gathered more lead. A police car drew up and took a look at the two boys up to mischief. He pulled his radio from his pocket and spoke to someone on the other end of it. Once his radio was back in his jacket he made the lads aware of his presence. His voice was loud as he shouted. Mark nearly slid from the roof when he realised they'd been caught bang to rights. Shaun climbed further up the roof and got a proper view of the crowd. Mark's face looked white with fear as he turned to Shaun for guidance.

"Fucking hell Shaun. It's well on top. How are we gonna get out of this one? My dad's gonna leather me now." Shaun knew there was no making a run for it this time and just remained still. The police down below shouted for them to stay seated. They told them the fire brigade were on their way to get them down safely. A few young kids were shouting down below and they made Shaun and Mark smile as their voices got louder.

"Soldier it lads. Don't let them take you alive." The copper chased the kids away much to the amusement of the two thieves. Shaun thought about his words and a plan was hatching in his mind. After all he had nothing to lose anyway. He was already on the run and what was the worst that could happen? He gritted his teeth and spoke to Mark.

"No way am I getting down from here. I can stay here for hours. I saw it on the telly. If we are up here for so many hours they have to feed us. Some Human rights act or summat." Mark looked shocked. Shaun hesitated before he continued. "I remember my mam watching it on the telly and laughing as they took food to some thugs who were stuck in the trees." Mark forced a smile but Shaun could see he was shitting himself. He looked at his face and gave him the words to make things easier.

"When the fire brigade comes, you're better off getting down. I'll take the shit and say you weren't doing owt. No point in us both getting done for it, is there?" Mark smiled and tried to say "No" but after a few minutes he agreed with him. Mark moved his arse about on the roof with the palms of his hands flat to the roof. His words were shaky as he spoke to his mate.

"Yeah I'll get down when they come. My mam's gonna go sick at me for being in trouble again. Are you gonna be alright coz I'll stay up here with you if ya want?" Shaun looked at him and shook his head.

"Nah, you get off. I'm gonna have some fun with these fuckers before they fling me back in care." The police officer who'd attended the incident recognised Shaun straight away and sent an officer round to inform his mother where her son was. Within minutes the fireman was up at the side of the house. They were helping Mark down. Shaun watched as the crowd cheered as his mate was the first to leave the roof.

Once Mark was gone Shaun began to rule the roof. His voice was loud as he shouted. He started to throw lumps of lead at the fireman who tried to help him down. The stocky fireman stayed near the roof for a minute, but when a lump of metal nearly caught his face he gave the orders to be lowered back to the ground.

Shaun walked across the roof and people could be heard crying as he stood at the edge of it threatening to jump if anyone came near him. One woman covered her eyes and sobbed as she grabbed the officer's arm telling him to leave the kid alone.

Shaun saw a police car pull up. He could now see his mother for the first time. "What the fuck is she doing here?" he snarled. Gladys looked sad as his eyes caught hers. She pulled her cardigan tightly round her body as she saw the crowd focus on her. The policeman filled her in on what had happened so far and she shook her head as her eyes focused on her son. Before he'd finished talking she stepped back so she could see her son fully and let rip.

"Get yourself down from there, you're making a show of yourself. What do you hope to achieve by sitting up there?" Shaun looked angry and let out a big scream as he continued.

"What the fuck are you here for. You don't give a shit about me. Why don't you tell everyone that you've had me put in care? Go on!" He stood waving his hands in the air. He continued as he spat at her from the roof top. He was on a roll now and wanted everyone to hear his story.

"Orr I thought you would be quiet now mother." Shaun looked happy with his words and watched the onlookers whispering to each other. Gladys looked around and felt the shame of everyone knowing her business. If she could have climbed the ladder she would have got up there and smacked his arse until it was red raw the way she felt. She knew Shaun would play the scene out and prepared herself for a long wait. The voice of her son made her look up again.

"I want summat to eat. I've been up here for ages. I've had nowt for ages and I'm starving. Mam tell em about that programme we watched on telly. I have human rights don't I mam?" Gladys knew it was true and looked at the officer for help. Her face looked anxious as she spoke to the officer.

"Can he have something to eat? He's been on the run and probably hasn't eaten today." The policeman got back on his radio and walked away from the crowd while he spoke. He was gone a few minutes then returned.

"What does he want to eat? I've checked with my seniors and we can get him some food." Gladys shouted up straight away and waited for him to answer. Shaun was starving and knew he had them where he wanted them. His face was cocky as he sat with his legs up to his chest dangling from the edge of the roof top.

"I want chips, peas and gravy from the chippy and a can of Coke." His eyes lit up as he said the words. He watched them from above as one officer drove away to collect his food.

Digging in his pockets Shaun pulled out his pebble. His fingertips stoked across it as he held it up to the sunlight to see all the other colours in it. The stone looked like it had fragments of diamonds in it as it sparkled in the sunlight. Under his breath he whispered to it but his words were too low to hear. Placing the stone firmly back in his pocket he stood up and looked at the area in full view. Everything looked so small and even his mother's face was difficult to see.

Shaun balanced across the roof with his arms stretched out at either side of him. He looked bored now and decided he would have a little fun. Pulling a loose tile up from the roof he glided it into the air. The crowd muttered in disgust. This only encouraged him to continue. His mother shouted in a piercing voice for him to stop but he just put his two fingers up in the air to her and carried on launching the slates.

The policeman now made it clear he was committing an offence and told him he would be charged with criminal damage if he continued. Shaun knew he was right and slowly made his way to the chimney at the top of the roof. The chimney looked old and the red bricks were loose. As he gripped his arms round it he knew it wasn't safe and slid back to his original position. He now sat tapping his feet humming a song.

The fireman climbed back onto the ladder and left the food in the place where Shaun had requested. He told them once he'd eaten his food he would admit defeat and come down from the rooftop. Sliding his fingers into the paper he could feel the heat from the chips. Nothing seemed to bother him as he scanned the food in front of him. Shaun ate the food quickly and finished it off with a cold can of Coke. He burped loudly and launched the paper from his food down below.

Looking down into the crowd he now nodded for them to come and get him. The rescue was done in minutes and Shaun was soon sat in the back of the police car with his mother at the side of him. The officers showed some compassion for the situation and left his mother talking to him for a while as they stood at the side of the car. Half of Gladys wanted to pummel his head in but the other half of her felt the love of a mother for her distressed son. She placed her arm round his neck and watched as he moved away from her sitting more towards the window. Her face was sad as she started to speak.

"Shaun, why are you being like this with me? It's not my fault son. You have brought this all on yourself. There is nothing I can do, you know?" her face was distraught as she moved closer to him. "Don't you think I would if I could?" Shaun remained looking out of the window and pressed his face against it as he spoke.

"It is your fault. Yours and my Dad's. That's why I've ended up in trouble because you two didn't care." His words crucified her and she slowly closed her eyes as the words hit her like knives being plunged into her heart. She took a few seconds to regain her strength and tried again to make him see sense.

"You have to go back into care you know. It won't be for long. You'll be home before you know it. I'll come and see you all the time. I'll bring our Katie?" He didn't respond. He banged his fist on the window to the officers.

"I'm ready now. Can you get her out of the car, she's doing my head in?" Gladys tried to comfort him one last time but his look was enough for her to know that he meant business. He'd always been a smacked arse even from being a small child. She knew if she didn't leave now he would probably start screaming and making a scene. With one last breath Gladys told him she loved him and he would be home soon. Shaun acted as if she wasn't there. He continued tapping on the window with his fingernails.

He watched his mother talk to the police for a few minutes and saw the officers shaking their heads as they looked towards him. He knew they thought he was a nobhead but he didn't care anymore. All he wanted to do now was to get to the care home and see what it was all about.

The police took him to Collyhurst police station and he waited there until the social worker came to attend to him. It was decided that the police would escort him to the care home as they didn't want him escaping again.

Shaun was lucky that he wasn't charged with criminal damage. He sunk his head low as the officer gave him a lecture about his previous behaviour. The policeman had seen hundreds of kids like Shaun and knew his words were wasted as he watched him stare into space. They all walked to the car. Shaun and his new social worker Jenny sat in the back of the car. Joan had told them she didn't feel safe with Shaun anymore and requested he was moved into someone else's care as she couldn't cope with him. She was still traumatised.

Jenny was a middle-aged woman and her voice was always animated when she spoke to him. She read through Shaun's personal file and felt sorry for the youth at the side of her. The car was over halfway there now and Shaun kept asking how long they had left as he needed a piss. Jenny looked at the signpost and told him just a little bit longer.

The care home was set in woodland. It seemed to take forever to reach the home once you'd come through the main gates. Shaun's head swivelled around in the car as he tried to take in everything in. Jenny stroked his hand to comfort him but he pulled it away from her straight away not needing any comfort. The house looked Victorian. Shaun had seen something similar on the TV. He felt a little scared as the car door opened.

"Come on lad," the officer prompted. "This is your new home. It looks alright doesn't it?" Shaun placed his hand in his pocket and felt his pebble. The stone was his only friend now and he gained comfort from rubbing it in his pocket. His words were few as they entered the house. Within minutes a scruffy looking man appeared. He looked like a hippy gone wrong. His hair was long and wild and his clothing looked old and worn. The man spoke to Jenny at the side of the reception and nodded as he looked over to where Shaun stood. The officers were offered a cup of tea and a sandwich before they set off back to Manchester. They both declined as it was getting late and they wanted to get home early before their shift finished. Once Jenny had walked them to the door and said goodbye she came to sit with Shaun. The man now came to join them and introduced himself as Bernard. As he spoke to him Shaun tried to refrain himself from looking at the spots on his skin. The blemishes looked red and some of them had yellow puss trapped inside them. The man spoke with a deep voice.

"Right Shaun it's late now, so in the morning I'll show you around and introduce you to all the staff. I'll just show you your room for now. So just get your head down for tonight and we can go through the induction in the morning. Is that alright?" Shaun was knackered and couldn't wait to get into bed, so he just nodded his head and agreed with him. Before they went any further he took him into the large kitchen and looked inside the fridge with one hand on his hip.

"I've got ham or cheese, if you are hungry? I can make you a sandwich or a toastie, which do you prefer?" Shaun loved toasties and jumped at the chance of one.

"Can I have cheese and ham on it?"

Bernard agreed and grabbed the stuff he needed. Shaun watched as he cut the cheese and licked his lips as he saw him put it under the grill to melt. Jenny had just left the room and just the two of them sat around the pine table waiting for the food to be done. At first they both sat in silence and it was Bernard who spoke first.

"It's not bad here you know. At first it will seem strange because you're away from home but after a few weeks it will get better." Bernard held his head up to the ceiling as he stretched his arms out. He looked tired. "There's loads for you to do here and the lads are alright. You should get some good mates here." Shaun's words seemed glued to his tongue and he struggled to speak. His mouth was dry as he stood to get a drink of water. He watched Bernard from the corner of his eye taking the food from the grill. His stomach was making noises as he watched him cut the toastie in half.

Bernard placed the small white plate on the table as he waited for him to return. Drinking the water Shaun made his way back with the glass still held to his mouth. As he dragged the chair from under the table he spoke.

"Thanks for that, I'm starving." Bernard nodded and started to tell him about the activities they had at the home. Shaun felt a lot calmer now. He sat chatting with Bernard. Shaun knew he had to get his head down and try and get home as soon as he could so he told Bernard he thought he was going to do well there.

The bedroom was dark as they entered. Shaun focused on the beds placed on each side of the room. All in all there were eight. He could see people were asleep in them but he couldn't see any faces. Bernard led him to his bed and told him he would see him in the morning. He ruffled Shaun's hair and left the bedroom.

Shaun sat on his bed and slowly pulled his trainers off. He could hear snoring nearby and giggled as the sound of a pig grunting filled the room. Once he was undressed he jumped into bed and snuggled down. The bedding smelt fresh. He inhaled deeply as he held the blanket up to his nose. It smelt of roses.

Shaun could hear his heart thumping in his ears and tried to calm himself down by blowing his breath slowly through his mouth. As he lay still he looked through the large window and looked at the moonlight shining through. The moon always made him feel safe and he knew his family would be looking at the same moonlight as they went to sleep too. Shaun reached down into his pants and searched for his friend the pebble. As he found it he held it in his grip and stoked across it with his fingertips. Holding the cold shape to his face his eyes began to close and he felt sleepy.

Chapter Six

As the morning light shone through the care home's windows and the birds outside sang like they were celebrating something, Shaun hid his head under the blanket and wanted to shut out the world. He could hear movement in the bedroom and slowly peeled the sheets from his face.

A mixed race boy stood near his bed and met his eyes for the first time. Shaun nodded at him as he focused on his massive afro hairdo. The lad was wearing shorts and a t-shirt that didn't cover his stomach. He scratched his bollocks as he spoke to Shaun for the first time.

"When did you get here then?" Shaun sat up from his bed and folded his pillow under his head. He slowly turned and faced the lad who had now plonked himself on the end of his bed.

"It was late last night. I just got straight into bed and got my head down." The boy now introduced himself as Colby. He seemed friendly enough and shouted out to the others in the room.

"Ay lads we've got a newcomer. He sneaked in last night," he chuckled. Some of the others came over but some stayed in bed where it was nice and warm. The lads all dressed the same in boxer shorts and t-shirts. He could feel their eyes on him and felt daft as he fidgeted about in his bed. The tallest lad now walked over and moved Colby from the bed so he could sit down. The lad pulled the blankets from the bottom of the bed and snuggled in at the bottom much to Shaun's embarrassment. Once he was comfy he raised his head and began to speak.

"I'm Shaky. Well that's my nickname," he said with a grin across his face. "But my real name is Joseph. I hate Joseph so just call me Shaky." Shaun smiled and told them he'd never had a nickname and the lads laughed as Colby shouted out so the room could hear him.

"You will have soon Shaun. We all have nicknames in this place including the staff." Shaun felt at ease and started to ask some questions.

"What's it like in here then? It looks boring as fuck." Shaky sat up and a few of the others joined in.

"Boring! You must be fucking joking. You should see what we get up to. The staff are mint. We get money and clothes from them and everything," a lad at the side of Shaun spoke with excitement in his voice.

"I had nowt until I came here and now I've got loads of shit!" Shaun's eyes lit up as the day just seemed to be getting better and better. One of the lads shouted that breakfast was ready and they all jumped from their beds like they'd shit themselves. Shaun remained in bed until Shaky told him to come and join them. Pulling his legs from the bed he picked up his trackie bottoms and went to join them all for breakfast.

All the lads sat round two tables and a woman in her mid thirties was at the stove cooking. Shaun sat next to Joseph and grabbed his brew in front of him. The first slurp of it made his face screw up, but as soon as he put his normal three sugars in it, it tasted better. Piles of toast were placed in the middle of the table now. Hands from every direction grabbed at it rapidly. Shaun was starving and made his claim to a piece too. The smell of bacon filtered through the room and each lad inhaled as the smell from the pan filled their nostrils. Big steel pans on the stove were cooking something else but Shaun couldn't see what it was. More members of staff came to join them. Bernard came straight over to Shaun placing his hands at the back of his chair. He dipped his head towards Shaun.

"Did you sleep well son?" Shaun nodded and carried on munching on his toast. Bernard coughed and asked them to be for quiet for a moment while he introduced Shaun to the group. As he started speaking Shaky stopped him dead in his tracks and shouted out.

"We all know who he is and we're sorted. We'll show him the ropes don't worry about it." Bernard smiled and shook his head.

"Shaky, I bet you will show him the ropes, but I'm on about the rules we don't break, not the ones we do." Shaky laughed out loud as the others joined him. Shaky was a bit of a handful and had been in care for just over a year. He was nearly sixteen but still had a baby face. His ginger hair looked like wire and his pale complexion looked spotty. Bernard told Shaun after breakfast he would give him a tour of the place and tell him all about the rules in the home. The sound of munching filled the kitchen. The lads ate like it was going to be their last meal as sparks flew from their cutlery.

Rubbing his belly and feeling full Shaun swigged the last mouthful of his cup of tea. Everyone's plate was empty. The cook now started to clear the table with a disgusted look on her face. "Messy fuckers," she mumbled under her breath.

Shaky stood first and the lads seemed to follow his lead. Shaun followed them back to the bedroom. As they reached the room the noise level started to rise as they started toy fighting. Shaky jumped on Colby's back and pulled at his big afro. That was it, within seconds a big pile on started and all you could hear was Colby's voice from the bottom of the pile telling them he couldn't breathe. Shaun loved it and bounced about near the top of the bodies. The next thing he could feel were his boxers being pulled tightly into the cheeks of his arse.

"Wedgie" shouted another lad. They all attacked each other now yanking their boxers in the cracks of their arses. Colby was still laid on the floor doubled over in pain ranting that they'd broken his ribs. The laughter could be heard throughout the hallway and it wasn't long until Bernard and Marion were stood at the doorway screaming at the top of their voices.

"Lads, lads, come on. Keep the noise level down ay." The boys all fell about laughing and Shaun tiptoed about the room trying to pull his underwear from his arsehole. Marion started to pick pillows up from the floor and told them to get the room cleaned otherwise they wouldn't be allowed to watch the film tonight. A few of them started to clean up, but Shaky just lay on his bed with his arms folded underneath his head. Marion looked straight at him and he knew she meant business. She was one of the tougher care-workers and he knew she took no shit. Marion had had run-ins with him in the past and he knew how far to push her. Slowly he slid off the bed and picked a few clothes up at the side of him. He could feel her eyes burning into him and found it hard not to laugh. He was giggling.

Shaun helped clean the room. Just before they left, Bernard turned around and told Shaun that when he was dressed he was to come down to the office to see him. Once they'd disappeared a few more pillows were flung about, but most of them started to get ready and obey the rules. Colby was now up and about but still moaning that his ribs were cracked. No one was listening to him and they carried on getting ready. Sundays were good days in the home and most of the day was spent chilling and doing whatever they wanted to do. One lad called Mike had a visit today from his parents and told the others he couldn't go wherever they'd planned. Shaky checked his money and had over a tenner in his pocket. The lads in care all got pocket money on Saturdays and Shaun complained that he'd missed it. Shaky was right by his side and told him when he went to see Bernard to make sure he told him that his trainers had holes in them and that he didn't have any money. Shaun laughed and asked him why, but as soon as Shaky told him a smile spread across his face.

"No way do they get you new trainers and that?" Shaky was waving his hands around in the air. He was telling him of all the things you could get while you was in the home and Shaun couldn't believe his ears.

"Well I'm deffo gonna ask for some new trainers then", Shaun snarled. "These ones are knackered. I thought this place was gonna be hard, but by the sounds of things I'm gonna like it here." He told Shaky to wait for him until he returned. His mate agreed and wished him luck in getting some cash.

The hallway smelt old and musty. The walls were painted in a grey pastel colour. The carpet had seen better days and traces of dirt and mud could be seen all over it. The ceilings in the home were high. As he walked to the office he tilted his head back and looked at them in more detail. The care home reminded him of a museum.

Bernard's office was just in front of where Shaun stood. He knocked softly on the wooden door before he entered. Bernard shouted for him to come in. As he went inside the office he could see him sat round a small table with Marion. Shaun's eyes cast over all the paperwork scattered all over the table. Moving the papers over to one side Bernard told him to come and take a seat at the table. When he sat down he could see his name on a large yellow folder next to Marion.

Marion was in her fifties and her large round figure just fitted under the table. Her legs looked the same width all the way down. He watched her closely as she sank another chocolate biscuit into her mouth. "Fat bitch," he thought as she wiped the chocolate from the side of her lips. Bernard finished whatever he was doing and turned to him with his arms folded. His tone was friendly.

"Right son, this isn't going take long. Here are some rules about the home. You can have a read of them when you have a spare minute." Taking the piece of paper from him, Shaun roughly folded it and shoved it into his back pocket. Marion now started to speak.

"I'm Marion and I'm going to be your case worker while you're here," Shaun didn't understand her and chewed on his lips. Marion widened her eyes and continued. "That means I'm going to get the best out of you." She tilted her head back and laughed revealing the inside of her mouth. His face screwed up as he saw all her black fillings inside. She quickly glanced through his notes and spoke to him as she carried on reading with her head held down.

"You've been in a bit of a mess lately haven't you?" Her head lifted up slightly as she gazed at him. "I'm not here to dictate. I'm here to help. If you have any worries or something that is bothering you, I want you to know you can always come to me for a chat. Every problem has an answer and together we can get through most things." Marion looked pleased with her speech and turned around to face Shaun. His eyes looked all round the room and he felt uneasy. She's a proper dick-head he thought but tried to listen to her without laughing. Remembering what Shaky had told him he changed his face to a look of sadness and spoke with his head dipped.

"Marion I do have a problem, my trainers are wrecked. I feel scruffy in them. Look they have holes in the bottom." Pulling at his trainers Marion watched sympathetically dipping her head over the table. He could see her concern and knew he was on a winner.

Looking at Bernard Marion asked for some cash and the receipt book. Once he'd given it her she filled it out and passed Shaun £80 for some new trainers. His face glowed with happiness and now he was on a roll he asked was it too late for him to have his pocket money too. Passing him another ten pound note to him he thanked them both. He was buzzing. Bernard nodded at him and told him they expected him to look after the new trainers as he wouldn't be getting anymore in the near future. Bernard now had a look of concern on his face and remembered the call he'd received from Shaun's mother.

"Your mam phoned last night son. Just to see if you got here safely and all that. She seemed upset. Do you want to give her a ring to tell her you're okay?" Standing to his feet Shaun refused but told him he would phone her later. Marion could see the hate in his eyes as he spoke her name and knew he had some real issues with his mother. Part of Marion's job was to get him to open up to her and speak about problems he faced in his life. As she looked the lad up and down she knew sooner or later she would find out what was eating him away inside.

Returning back to the bedroom Shaun fanned his cash out for all to see. Shaky was by his side within seconds and inhaled the smell from the cash with a smile on his face.

"Told you didn't I? I knew you would get some money

from them. Where we off to then? It's your treat." Looking round the room he saw a few faces smiling at him and felt under pressure to share the money he'd got for his new trainers. Shaun picked up his cash, and looked at the lads.

"Come on then, where we going? I'm new round here don't forgot. And I don't know my way around." Shaky smiled cunningly and told him not to worry he would show him the area. Colby came to join them, but the look from Shaky told him he wasn't welcome. Colby backed away and called Shaky under his breath.

"Prick," he mumbled.

The two lads left together. You could hear the others left in the room cursing Shaky calling him an arse licker. One of the lads spoke up as he paced the bedroom floor.

"Ginger tosser. Who does he think he his? He bugs me the way he thinks he can speak to us like little nobheads." The young lad clenched his fist and his face was going red. "One of these days I'm gonna waste the ginger ferret trust me." His words fell on empty ears as the others shook their heads. They were all used to Shaky and the way he thought he was the boss of them all. Gary hated him with a vengeance.

Gary was just a little younger than Shaky and he'd had a few dealings with him in the past. He swore before his time was up in the care home he would get his own back on the bully. As he sat there sulking on his bed with his fist clenched. "One day, one day soon," he whispered.

Shaun and his new mate walked out of the home. It took around ten minutes before they reached the main gates. They both were dressed similarly in tracksuit bottoms and trainers. Shaun held his hand down the front of his pants and squeezed at his nob as he walked. Shaky led them to the bus stop and they both sat talking as they waited for the bus to arrive. Shaun felt his cash in his pocket with a pleased look on his face. All that was on his mind was getting high. He didn't know if Shaky was a sniffer and approached him with caution.

"So what do you do to have fun round here?"

Shaky looked at him and told him they got pissed at weekends. The look on Shaun's face showed he wasn't impressed. He continued talking as he stood up and swung his arms from the bus shelter dangling from it like a monkey.

"Don't you sniff?"

Shaky looked puzzled. You could tell he didn't have a clue what he was on about. Shaun sat back down and began to fill him in on the new craze doing the actions with his hands.

"Gas, glue, Tip-ex thinner? Fucking hell everyone's doing it around our way. Don't tell me you've never tried it?" Shaky shook his head and felt stupid. Shaun saw his embarrassment and told him they would get some in the town centre and he'd show him what it was all about.

Shaky was from Yorkshire and Shaun laughed loudly calling him a sheep shagger. He joked about with him telling him that he bet that all his mates sniffed sheep's arses for a high in Yorkshire. Shaky was up in arms now. He stood tall as he reeled off his past experiences. None of them was anything to be proud of and Shaun let him know how much of a geek he thought he was. Shaky saw the bus approaching. He stuck his arm out for it to stop. Once they'd paid the fare they both sat at the back. Shaun got straight back on the subject of sniffing and knew he'd found another glue sniffing partner.

"Right when we get into town we'll get some Evo. We can sniff it when we get back to the home." Shaky agreed and led him to the shops that sold the trainers he wanted. He looked apprehensive but didn't let his mate know he was shitting himself inside.

The town centre wasn't that busy and they both walked around it as if they owned the place. As they walked towards the shops they barged past people without a care in the world. To look at them you would have thought they had stones in their shoes that made them walk with a limp.

Entering the sports shop they headed straight for the footwear section. The music was pumping and Shaun nodded his head to the beat. Picking up nearly every pair of trainers Shaun examined them fully. Finally he got the assistant to get him the pair he wanted to try in a size seven. Once the assistant returned he left the trainers with Shaun and went to deal with another customer. The shop was mad busy.

Shaun walked up and down the store in his new sneakers. He looked in the mirror turning his feet this way and that. Shaky gave a nod of approval and his choice was made. Bending down to take the shoes off Shaun froze. Looking round he saw everyone was busy. He stood straight away and nudged Shaky in the waist.

"Come on let's get off." Shaky looked around the store and followed him pulling his hood up as they left the shop. They both set off running and never looked back. Shaun was in front and kept dodging people to get into the side streets. Once they were out of sight Shaky placed his hands on his knees and tried to regain his breath .Shaun was panting for breath too but the rush he was feeling inside made him feel strong.

"Fucking hell, that was mad wasn't it?" Shaky smiled and called him a dickhead, as he carried on blowing through his mouth. Shaun walked up to the end of the alley way and peeped out just to make sure they weren't being followed. Once he knew they were safe he called Shaky to join him.

"Come on let's go and get high. Where's the DIY shops around here?" Shaky sunk his hands into his coat pocket and led him.

Shaun poured the glue into two bags as they got back into the care home. They headed into the gardens and found a quiet place where they wouldn't be disturbed. Shaky was nervous and you could tell by his actions he was shitting himself. He watched the plastic bag inflate as Shaun placed his mouth around it. His eyes focused as Shaun took a deep breath from it. Shaky copied him as he passed the bag to him.

Shaky loved the glue. His body fell back onto the grass as his head exploded with the buzz from it. Shaun smiled and felt like he'd introduced him to some great fun. The bags of glue were held in their hands like trophies and both of them were off their heads on it.

Hours passed before they both headed back into the home. Bernard was looking at them with suspicion as they walked passed him. He was talking to another boy as they passed him and he got a whiff of something strong. He stopped them and asked them if they had magic markers on them. They both looked at him and shook their heads but Bernard was on to them and followed them as they walked into the kitchen. Shaun went straight to the fridge and grabbed a jar of pickles. He quickly drank the juice from it and passed it to Shaky. He sniggered as he spoke.

"Hurry up and get a drink of that. It takes the smell of glue from your breath." Grabbing it with both hands Shaky lifted it up to his mouth and took a gob full. As he turned his head he could see Bernard stood at the door. Bernard wasn't happy as he raised his eyes at them.

"I don't know what you two are up to but believe me I'm watching you. Where have you been all day?" Shaky remained quiet as Shaun took over. He pulled the bottom of his pants up and revealed his new trainers.

"We went into town for my trainers didn't we? I told you where we were going before. Did you forget?" Bernard looked to the ceiling and he had a blank look on his face. He came to where they stood and looked down at the trainers more closely.

"Smart them aren't they?" He bragged. Bernard held his hand out to him. "Did you bring a receipt back for me?" Shaun dipped his hands into his pocket and pretended to search for a receipt that he knew wasn't there. After a few minutes he came up with the answer.

"It's in the box that I threw away. I put my old trainers in it and launched it. Sorry did you need it?"

Bernard studied Shaun's face and could tell he was lying. He knew he was up to something and promised them both he would be on their case if he ever caught them trying to have him over. As he left he turned and watched them whispering to each other. He knew they were up to no good and set his mind to keep a close eye on them both in the future.

"Fucking tosser isn't he?" Shaun laughed. "Good job I'm a quick thinker otherwise he would have been onto us?" Shaky nudged him with his arm and nodded his head. He looked quite white in the face and looked like he was going to be sick. Shaun looked closer at him as he pulled him nearer.

"You okay?" Shaun asked. He now watched as he Shaky ran to the kitchen sink. He was spewing his ring up. The noise of retching made Shaun screw his face screw up.

He came to his side and patted his mate on the back.

"It's the glue that mate. First time I had it I was the same." Shaky lifted his head and wiped his mouth on his sleeve. His eyes were glassy and his words hesitant.

"Orr I feel ruff as a bear's arse. I need to get into bed. Don't think that glue agrees with me." Shaun's face dropped and he quickly assured him that it was normal to be sick after his first sniff. Panic took over Shaun now and he ran to get him a cold drink of water. Shaky was his new sniffing mate and he didn't want to lose him.

Once Shaky drank the cold water they both headed for the bedroom. Shaky fell onto his bed and pulled the covers over his head. Colby was in the room and saw something was wrong and went to Shaun's bed to see what was going on. Shaun sprawled on his bed and kicked his shoes off. When he saw Colby at his side he nodded his head slowly. He could see he was after something and sat watching him like a hawk.

"What's up with him?" Colby whispered as his eyes shot over to Shaky's bed. Shaun remained still and told him his new mate didn't feel well. Colby smiled and you could see he was enjoying every minute of his pain. He sat on the empty bed next to him and laughed.

"Hope he's up all night shitting and spewing. It what he deserves the prick. It bugs me how he thinks he can speak to us all like pieces of shit." Shaun giggled and turned to face him.

"Nar he's alright you know. Why don't you like him?" Colby gritted his teeth as he looked at Shaky lay asleep on the nearby bed.

"I have my reasons. He's a turd. One of these days he'll get my fist in his face the prick."

Shaun liked Colby, he made him laugh. He couldn't

understand the hate he showed in his eyes when he looked at Shaky. Colby turned his head back to him and kicked his feet on the floor. He seemed like he wanted to tell him something but he couldn't get the words out. Shaun looked at him and waited. Colby fidgeted about with his clothing and you could see he was nervous. His words were angry as he whispered.

"Don't trust him Shaun. He's a snidey twat." Shaun sat up from his bed as Colby continued.

"I'm not saying anymore, but watch ya arse. And I mean that in more ways than one," he snarled. Colby's eyes were wide open now and he watched as Shaun pulled his knees to his chest.

"What do you mean? Watch my arse?" Colby tipped his head back and laughed. He quickly changed the subject and left Shaun with a puzzled look on his face. The conversation carried on but no more was mentioned about Shaky's antics.

Darkness fell and Shaun lay in his bed tossing and turning. He struggled to sleep as Colby's words played on his mind. As he fidgeted in his bed he looked over to his new found friend's bed and stared at the body in front of him. He decided that the following day he would find out more about his history. Closing his eyes he pulled the quilt tightly around his body. In his grip he held his pebble and twisted it in his fingertips until he drifted off to sleep.

Morning came quickly and the noise of two boys woke Shaun from his sleep. As he opened his eyes his vision was blurred. He twisted his knuckles in his eyes. Colby was pinned up against the wall and Shaky was in his face shouting insults at him calling him a "black fucker." Shaun watched for a moment and could see it was getting out of hand. As he watched Colby's face he knew he needed to help him. Kicking the sheets back from the bed he came to their side.

"What's going on?" Shaun growled. Shaky's face was screwed up as he touched noses with Colby.

"It's this nobhead thinking he can chat shit to me." Colby tried to free Shaky's hands from his body but he was struggling. Clenching his fist he connected with Shaky's chin. Shaky punched him back but a lot harder and was livid that the cheeky bastard had even thought he could take his title. Colby now screamed out and went for him with rage in his eyes. The other lads in the room all sat up from their bed and couldn't believe someone was challenging Shaky. They huddled together and watched with amazement. Colby was now bouncing about with his hands up in the air shouting at the top of his voice.

"Think you can chat shit to me do ya? Well come on then let's have it." His body jumped up into the air as he flung himself at Shaky with his arms spinning like a windmill. Shaun stood back and chewed on his bottom lip unsure of what to do. Colby was standing his ground and within minutes he was sat on top punching him from left, right and centre. Shaky's head seemed lifeless as each punch sent his head to the other side. Shaun knew he had to stop the fight and pulled Colby up by his arms but he just stared him down with an evil look and shouted "Fuck off and don't get involved."

He grabbed Shaky by the hair. The silence in the room was eerie and you could have heard a pin drop at that moment. Colby sprung up from the floor and gave him one last kick into his stomach. The others cringed as they felt the force of it. One lad bit into his pillow as he closed his eyes with all the trauma. Colby stood tall as he walked away. For months Shaky had made his life a misery and now he didn't have to be scared anymore. He had defeated him. The boys nodded at Colby as he went to his bed. Flinging his body onto it he let out an enormous scream.

"I knew he was a fucking shit-bag. He thought I was just another nobhead who he could terrorize. Well he knows different now, doesn't he?" Shaun leant down to Shaky and pulled him up from the floor. His face was covered in blood and his eye was swollen. Shaun shook his head, but didn't want to take sides. He liked both of the lads and found it hard not to get in the middle of it.

Shaky was like a wounded animal. His pride was hurt and the image he'd set for himself in the home was shattered. He could hear the comments from the others in the room and knew his life was going to be a nightmare from this day forward. He struggled to get to his bed. Pulling the blankets over his head he hid his shame from the others. Shaun held his hands up in desperation waiting for one of the others to give him some support. One lad who wasn't a fan of Shaky's spoke out. His reign of terror was over now and he wasn't afraid to voice his opinion anymore.

"Leave him there the shit stabber." He ranted as he looked at Shaky's bed. Colby snarled. He was exploding with temper.

"It's about time he got a taste of his own medicine." Shaun could see the anger in the lad's faces and looked at Colby lying on his bed looking like he'd conquered the world. Watching him sit up he trudged over to him. Finally Shaun turned to Colby.

"What was all that about then?"

Colby threw his eyes to a smaller lad at the end of the bedroom and gritted his teeth. Looking over to the lad Shaun could see the young lad shaking in his bed. He looked like he'd cried a thousand tears. As he focused on his face closer he seemed to have black circles around his eyes. The youngster's face looked gaunt and lifeless. Shaun could tell the youth was scared and looked away from him quickly. As he turned his head back Colby stood up from the bed and told him to follow him to the bathroom.

The bathroom was cold as he walked inside it. Shaun rubbed his arms. You could see goose bumps starting to appear on his skin. Six sinks sat on the wall at the side of room. Colby walked to them and started throwing cold water all over his face. Jumping on the ledge at the end of the bathroom, Shaun kicked his legs as he watched him clean his face up. Colby dried his face with his t-shirt and stood looking in the mirror. He felt the cut on his face and growled. At first he just looked over at Shaun but remained silent. Walking to the bathroom door he closed it firmly and walked back. He looked distressed and you could see tears forming in the corner of his eye. Taking a deep breath he began.

"Shaky's a liberty taker. He's been doing it for ages and everyone just lets him get away with it."

"Why what's he done?"

Colby's face looked tormented. "I heard the pervert at it last night. I just couldn't take it anymore." Shaun jumped from the side and stood next to him. His face looked as if he didn't understand what he was saying. He asked him again what he meant. Colby turned his face away from him and couldn't stand the shame he was feeling inside. Tears trickled down his cheeks as his body fell to the floor.

"He's only done it to me once. But as soon as a new lad comes in the home he's on them like a rash. The young lad in our room has been here for about two months and I know he's been in his bed more than once. He's a wrong 'un ya know?" Shaun sat beside him. He knew what he was saying about Shaky now but just couldn't get a grip of what it exactly meant. Feeling stupid he asked for more details.

"What does he get in bed with em for? Is he scared at night or summit like that?"

Colby raised his head from his knees and screwed up his face. "He gets a wank from 'em ya nobhead."

Shaun's face froze. His eyes nearly popped out of their sockets. He felt sick inside and blew his breath out through his mouth. Colby sat shaking his head.

"It's a wonder he wasn't in your bed the first night you came. He must have thought he would befriend you first."

Shaun stood up and ran to the sink and vomited. The sound of his retching brought more shame onto Colby. He'd been a victim too. Shaun was the first person he'd ever told. As he stood up he made his way over to Shaun. Placing his hand on his back he rubbed it slowly.

"I feel like shit ya know. I feel dirty inside. Every time I look at him I want to end my life. He's fucked my head up big time." Shaun turned to face him. His face looked white and he gritted his teeth as he shook his head.

"He seemed an alright lad. Why didn't you tell me he was a queer fucker? If I would have known what he was like, do you think for one minute I would have been chilling with him?"

Colby was lost for words. His own secret was out now and he was waiting for Shaun to comment about what Shaky had done to him. Colby felt like a cloak of despair had been lifted from his shoulders as he walked to the door to leave. Shaun watched him like a hawk as he left.

"Wait a minute. Where you going? I mean erm…" Shaun followed him to the door and ranted. "He needs to be fucked off now doesn't he? Surely he can't stay here with us lot. He's a dirty scum-bag. I want fuck all to do with him. How can I look at him the same now I know what he's been up to? Ewww he makes my skin crawl."

Colby agreed and they both left the bathroom. They were united now and a friendship was formed that no one would ever break. As they walked back into the room everyone stared at them. They were the new leaders and the lads sat like soldiers awaiting their instructions. Shaun looked over to Shaky's bed and noticed he was missing. He quickly ran to his bed and pulled the covers from it throwing them onto the floor.

"Where's nobhead gone?" he shouted out at the top of his voice. One of the lads walked over to him and told him that as soon as they went into the bathroom Shaky got off. Shaun kicked at the bed-frame. Grabbing the bedding from the floor he wrapped the sheets up into a ball. His face looked angry and he wiped his hands on his clothes as if the sheets were carrying some kind of disease.

Colby picked up the bundle of bedding and opened the bedroom window. At first he struggled to get it through but as Shaun helped him they launched the lot outside. Shaun wanted to smash Shaky's bed up but Colby made him see sense, and calmed him down.

The others lads were all gathered round his bed and Shaun needed to tell them just how much of a tosser Shaky really was. As he started to tell them what he'd been doing to some of the lads, a few of them sank their heads onto their chests. As he looked at them closer it was obvious Shaky had messed about with them too. Shaun continued speaking to the group.

"Listen up yeah. We all know what the ginger faggot has been up to don't we? Well it's all over now. If any of you are thinking of doing the same, think again coz I'll personally chop ya fucking dick off. We're all in the same boat and need to stick together don't we?" The lads agreed and one by one they left his bedside.

Bernard's voice could be heard in the hallway and everyone pretended to be busy. He stuck his head into the room.

"Colby, Shaun, office now!" Shaun looked at Colby and had a worried look on his face. As they started walking from the bedroom Shaun was mumbling under his breath.

"Bet he's grassed you up hasn't he? What ya gonna say?"

Colby was quiet and remained silent. As they reached the office they entered it with worried looks on their faces. Bernard and Marion were sat at the table. Marion was tapping her pen on her teeth as she spoke.

"Right you two get in here and take a seat." Shaun shrugged his shoulders and shoved his hands down the front of his pants. He stood at the table and didn't sit down until Colby was seated first. Marion looked at them both in disgust as Bernard began.

"Right you two. As you may be aware Shaky has been removed from the building. He came to us in a right state." Bernard shook his head in disgust. "It's bullying at its worst what you two have done to him. He wouldn't even wait for his clothes to be packed. He was in a right state." Bernard starting writing a report as Marion asked them further questions. Her glasses hung over her nose as she looked Colby straight in the face.

"So have you anything to say young man?" Looking at Shaun for guidance he shrugged his shoulders.

"Nar," he mumbled. Bernard started to read the allegations aloud and they both looked at him in disbelief. They knew they weren't going to tell them the truth and

sat staring around the room with nothing to say. Bernard
wrote as Marion told them to leave the room. She told
them this situation was far from over and to be expected
to be called back to the office at any time. As they left the
room they looked scared. The thought of the police being
involved sent shivers down their spines. Shaun suggested
they run away but Colby wasn't having any of it. Walking
back to the room Colby had a brainwave.

"Right we need the lads to go and see Bernard and
tell him Shaky was the one who started it all. We'll tell
them to say he jumped on me and you came to pull him
off and he set about you as well." Shaun looked anxious
but agreed. They ran to the bedroom and spoke to the lads.
Once Colby told them what he wanted them to do he was
a bit calmer knowing that they would get away with the
allegations.

They all sat on the bed and went though the scene
they were acting. Some of the lads were acting it out in
front of them. Colby knew they could pull it off and sent
two of the lads down to Bernard's office.

Around fifteen minutes passed and the youths returned
with smiles across their faces. They nodded their heads and
high-fived each other on their acting skills. Shaun went
straight over to them and made them go through every
word they had spoken. Colby remained on his own bed
and looped his arms behind his pillow looking satisfied.
Shaun looked happy and celebrated by jumping on Colby's
bed.

"It's sorted mate. No need to worry now. I hope the
prick is put somewhere where they bum him every fucking
night. That will show the dinner masher." All the others
laughed and even Colby had a smile to his face. Shaky
was now a bad memory to the lads and they could all get

on with their time spent in care knowing their arses were safe at night. Shaun and a few of the other lads planned a celebration and decided the next night they would all sneak into Blackpool town centre for a night of fun.

Chapter Seven

Three weeks passed and Shaun was still in a coma. Gladys looked at her son's face. His facial expression seemed to have changed. She stroked his head and looked at all the machines for any signs of distress. The doctor had now confirmed he wouldn't have to have his leg amputated but it would never be the same again. He told her that it was deformed and he would not be walking fully for a long time. Her face was sad as he told her the news but she was just glad he was still alive and didn't think about the days that lay ahead.

The hospital door opened and in walked Ged. He looked ill and his hands shook rapidly. His face was covered in spots and Gladys looked at him with hate in her eyes.

"What the fucking hell do you want?" her face was leant towards his. "It's been three weeks and you haven't been near the hospital. I thought you were his friend?" Ged dipped his head. It looked like tears were forming in his eyes. He walked to the side of the bed and sighed.

"Gladys I wanted to come but I've been skint. I didn't even have the bus fare. I was scared as well. I've not slept since he's been in here ya know." His lips were trembling and as he sat down he dropped his head into his hands. "Gladys all I can see in my head is his body lying at the bottom of the flats, twisted up." She looked at him in disgust. She blamed him for her son's downfall and wasn't afraid to let him know.

"Yeah whatever Ged. It's always the same old story with you lot." He screwed his face up and looked at her. "What do ya mean by that?" She pulled at her cardigan and walked to the chair at the side of the bed.

"You know what I mean. Fucking smackheads. You're all the same. No respect or morals." Ged seemed to be calm when he answered her but his shaking hands told her she was right.

"Gladys, he jumped from the flats. We didn't push him. I know what I am and I feel ashamed the way my life has turned out but don't blame us for the way Shaun has ended up. He's a heroin addict."

He watched her turn her eyes away from him, and he knew he'd hit a nerve. Gladys had always been the same about her blue-eyed boy over the years. He knew she would never blame Shaun for anything he'd ever done. It was always someone else's fault. He sat at the side of the bed and Gladys grabbed her cigs. She left the room with an angry look on her face. "I'm going for a fag. Hurry up and piss off because I want you gone when I get back." She left the room.

Ged was roasting and needed a fix. He looked round the room and looked for anything with any value. He was talking to himself as he searched the drawers near the far wall. Once he'd pocketed a few bandages and syringes he walked back to Shaun. His mind was already doing overtime thinking who he could sell the bandages to and his words were shaky as he spoke to the lifeless body.

"Fucking hell mate. It's been hard without you .We're not even earning anymore." His hands were placed on the bed now and he looked at all the machines hooked up to his friend.

"I should just turn the machine off on you, shouldn't I?" His hands now stoked the wires at the side of him. "What's the point of living ay? At least you're not shaking for smack all the time like I am." Ged stood wiping the sweat from his brow. He chewed on his lip as he held the tears back. "It's fucking hard mate. I wish it was me lying there and not you." He dropped his head on the bed as his hand played with the bandages in his pocket. Gladys walked back into the room and he knew it was time for him to leave. He placed his hand on Shaun's head but never spoke. His face was filled with sadness as he left. The sweat dripped from his head into his eyes. He quickly wiped it with the sleeve from his coat. As Ged left Gladys mumbled "Scumbag" under her breath. She was glad to see the back of him.

Ged sat in the flat once he was home. He sat staring at the walls. His body couldn't rest as Shaun played on his mind more than ever. Gladys was right, he hadn't been near the hospital since he'd been admitted and it felt like his right arm was missing without his side-kick. Ged and Shaun had met years before and they were like brothers in arms. They grafted together and shared everything they had. Life for them both had been at rock bottom lately and he too had thought about ending his own sad life.

Looking at his bruised veins his head sunk low. His arms were just skin and bones. If a gust of wind came along he would be blown away. His family had given up any hope of him sorting himself out years ago. He still saw them every now and then but that was only when he needed a fix and was desperate for money. The last time he'd seen his mother was a few weeks before. He promised himself he wouldn't put her through any more pain after that day. Ged had been desperate for cash and waited for his mother outside the Post Office in Harpurhey where she cashed her pension. He knew she couldn't bear to see him roasting and joined her in the queue with his rattling bones. Everyone watched him as he begged her for cash.

"Mam, please. I'm ill. Come on it's only a tenner. Just until I get myself back on my feet." He grabbed at her arm and sunk his head onto her sleeve as the onlookers turned away in disgust. His body looked cold as he shivered. Spit hung from the side of his mouth as his eyes rolled. Ged's legs looked as if they were going to give way as he pleaded further. After a while his mother broke down and cried. Searching in her tattered purse she pulled the money out and threw it at him.

"Go on take it. If all you care about is drugs then you're welcome to it. Get out of my sight and don't ever come near me again." Ged picked the money from the floor and stood to face her but her eyes were filled with tears and he couldn't bear what he'd done to her. As he held the money in his hands he wanted to return it back to her but the drugs were calling him and he needed a fix. He left his mother's side that day with sorrow in his heart and would never forget the way she looked at him with disgust.

Heroin had been his life for many years. His life was ruled by it. Ged had no real friends and the only person who understood him was now lying in a hospital bed fighting for his life. Ged stood up and walked about the flat. All the other druggies were out trying to earn some cash. He looked lonely and depressed. Tears poured from his eyes as he wrapped his arms around his rattling body. He so desperately wanted to change his life around and he'd spoken about it so many times with Shaun in the past but that day never came. All he wanted was to feel normal again, perhaps even have a family. Ged had had girlfriends in the past but all they wanted him for was for him to supply them with smack. His last girlfriend had overdosed on heroin and burying her nearly finished him off. He still thought about her every now and then, but the drugs seemed to help numb any emotions he felt about her.

Drying his eyes he looked for his coat. The flat was a shit tip and everything was a mess. Clothes were all over the place. The CD that Shaun always played was still in the CD player. The Smiths CD was Shaun's pride and joy and no matter what, he never sold it. Probably due to the fact it was worth only a few quid. Slowly Ged turned the CD on and sat with his arms wrapped around his body. His head nodded as each word seemed to relate to him. Shaun had told him the history about what the CD meant to him and how much he cherished it. Ged sat listening to the music.

The sound of the door opening made him lift his head and he could see Donna and Steve walking in holding a briefcase. As he watched he could see the excitement in their eyes as they flung it onto the floor in the living room. They were desperate to open it.

"Get a knife out of the kitchen Steve. We can open it with that." The woman's voice shouted. Donna had long blonde hair. It looked like it hadn't been brushed for months. The dark circles round her eyes showed that she too was another heroin addict. Donna had been staying at the flat for a couple of months now and she was known to sell herself down Cheetham Hill when times were hard.

Steve hurried to the kitchen. You could hear him searching the drawers. The kitchen was filthy and brown grease was all over the few tiles around the sink. Once he'd pulled one from the sink he wiped it on his pants and headed back to them. Steve was thirty six but looked like death warmed up. His hair was long and the beard that grew around his mouth hid the unsightly spots.

"Give it here then," he moaned. Steve grabbed the briefcase from her hands and sat on the floor with his legs spread. Ged was now sat upright watching. Donna urged him to open it as fast as he could. Minutes passed and finally the case flung opened. They were like flies round shit and Steve told them to fuck off out of his way while he rooted about in it.

Papers were being slung across the room. They were all looking for something of value. A mobile phone was uncovered and they sighed with relief knowing they could at least sell it for drugs. Donna examined the phone and knew they could get at least fifty quid for it. It was one of the latest models. She eagerly watched the rest of the case being emptied and when she knew there was nothing of any value she told them she was off to sell the phone. Steve told her to hurry up and carried on reading the letters in the case. As he read them Ged picked up the briefcase and walked around the front room with it held at his side.

"Does it suit me? Do I look like a businessman or what?"

Steve chuckled, "Do you fuck, ya nob. You just don't have that look." Ged looked disappointed and threw it to the floor. He would have loved to have been a man who carried that kind of briefcase about. He sat back down disheartened. He watched Steve as he read one of the letters from the case.

"Listen to this Ged. Fucking hell this cunt must be loaded. Check this out.'Dear Sir. having looked through your account I can now tell you that your account is in credit of five thousand and sixty two pounds'."

Ged shook his head enviously, "More money than sense some people haven't they. I mean I can't get a borrow of a tenner never mind five fucking grand." Steve agreed.

"Tell me about it Ged. Tell ya what, this week has been so hard. There is nowt about to have off. We got lucky with this case. Donna saw a guy through the window in

Costa Coffee putting his case at the side of him. We got straight on it. She just walked straight in, no fucking about and picked it up as if belonged to her and walked out." Steve slid all the paperwork to the side of the room and lay on the floor. You could tell he needed a fix as he looked agitated.

Ged sat thinking about the life of others and how successful they were. He started to look back at his own life and tried to see where it had all gone wrong for him. As he lay back he could still see the demons he tried to rid his mind of every night. He knew he would never lead a normal drug free life because of his past.

When Ged was sixteen he was abused by his uncle. To this day he'd never told anyone. It all started when his uncle came to stay with them. His mother was always working and she saw it as a chance to get some help with her four kids. Ged's dad was working away from home. Ged was the youngest of the four children and his three sisters had always called him a puff because he was always whinging. His uncle always protected him and let it be known to his sisters that they didn't stand a chance of hurting him while he was around.

At first Ged loved it and was never far from his uncle's side. His uncle Mike even slept in his bed sometimes and told him stories about things from his past. He looked up to him as his second dad. One night when his sisters were asleep in the next room Ged's nightmare started. He'd fallen asleep with Mike at the side of him. At first he thought he was dreaming but as he opened his eyes he could see his uncle knelt above him masturbating. Once Mike saw his nephew was awake he rammed his penis in his mouth and nearly choked him to death. Ged was wriggling about but he yanked his hair and made sure he didn't move. Once he'd finished he lay next to him and touched Ged between his legs, before long he was doing things to him that the child knew was wrong. Ged cried and dug his head into his pillow. He sobbed all the way through the ordeal. Once it was finished he lay staring into space as his uncle's breath warmed his ear at the side of him. Mike grabbed his face in his hands and whispered.

"If you ever breathe a word of this ya little prick. I'll kill you. Do you understand?" Ged nodded and watched as his uncle left the bedroom.

Ged became a nervous wreck over the next few months and his mother kept asking him if everything was okay. Ged just nodded to her as Mike was always sat there watching him like a hawk. As he left the room he could hear Mike telling his mam that his sisters were still giving him a hard time and he would deal with them. "Lying bastard," Ged whispered. His skin crawled when he heard him telling his mother that he would move his bed into his bedroom so he didn't feel lonely anymore. As his words filtered through the wall his body crumbled and he knew he couldn't go on. His head was spinning as he left the house and he wanted to die.

Ged walked over a bridge towards school. He looked over it and watched the traffic underneath. His legs started to shake as the thought of throwing himself over hit his mind. Tears fell onto his cheeks and he screamed out. His knuckles were white as he held the iron railing. He swallowed hard and took a deep breath. Dressed in a black hooded top he pulled it tighter round his head and fell to the floor. His knees were up at his chest as his head sank between them. He didn't have the courage to jump.

Ged walked away from the bridge that day and came up with a plan that would stop the torment he felt inside.

Later that night he searched the kitchen drawer for his mam's sharpest bread knife. Once he'd found it he placed it under his bed out of sight. As night-time fell he waited in his bed with fear running through his body.

"Move over then," Mike whispered as he climbed in his bed beside him. Ged could feel him at the side of him and shook with fear. The smell of his breath was all over him and he knew he was pissed yet again. Ged waited until he placed his hand down his boxers and knew it was now or never. His breathing was rapid. He had to get the knife from its hideout without Mike noticing. He dropped his hand down onto the floor and Mike didn't seem to notice. He could feel the cold blade in his grip and slowly he raised it up onto the bed. As he watched Mike's face he lifted the knife up and quickly dug it into him as fast as he could. Mike screamed in pain as he jumped out of the bed with a menacing look on his face.

Ged thought about running out of the room as Mike stood up, but as he looked at him he realised he was the one in control now. Mike was shouting aloud and Ged could hear his mam shouting from the other side of the wall.

"What's going on in there? Will you keep the fucking noise down? I'm trying to fucking sleep." Ged remained silent and waved the blade near Mike's face. As he saw him fall to the ground he kicked him with all his might. Ged's words were low and fierce.

"You dirty fucking perv. I should kill ya for what you've put me through. I'm a kid, you're my fucking uncle. I thought you loved me?" Mike realised that he was in danger of getting caught and lifted his body up off the floor. Ged paced the room with the knife firmly in his grip. Mike was bleeding from his leg and holding his arm as blood pumped from his wounds.

"Get out of our house," Ged spoke with a chilling voice. "If ya don't, I'm going right in there to my mam and telling her everything you have done to me. Do ya hear me?" He was pointing his finger to his mother's bedroom. Mike stood and grabbed his clothes. He remained silent for a few seconds. Mike looked at his nephew with a menacing look in his eyes.

"No one would believe ya anyway. You're a little puff who needs to grow some balls," Ged ran at him and tried to hurt him further, but Mike just threw him to the floor as he collected his shoes. His words were whispered as he left the bedroom.

"Tell ya what son, you give a great wank. Shame it's over ya little gay twat," Ged quivered and stood shaking from head to toe. The light was poor but you could see tears streaming down his face. As the light from outside the bedroom door shone in all he could see was the shadow of his uncle leaving. Ged flung himself onto his bed and watched the door like a lion waiting for its prey.

The sound of his uncle opening and closing cupboards could be heard and each time he heard a bang in the next room his body shook. Finally the front door slammed and he dived to the window to see the back of Mike leaving carrying a few bags to his car. His heart pumped inside his chest and he cried with relief. Still holding the knife in his grip he felt strong and in control for once in his life. His head sunk to the pillow and for hours he sat looking at the door, but his uncle never came back. Ged never slept a wink all night.

"Mike, come on I've brewed up and I want ya to go and get the papers so I can check my bingo numbers," Sheila banged on the bedroom door and slowly opened it. Mike's bed was empty and she could now see it hadn't been slept in. Ged was wide awake and looked directly at his mother's face as she spoke.

"Orr fucking hell Mike where the fuck are you?" her body moved around the bedroom seeing if he was lay on the floor. She sighed. "Bet ya with that dirty little tramp down the road again.." His mother raised her eyes at Ged and asked him would he run to the newsagents instead. As he agreed she walked over to him and she could see blood on his hands. She grabbed his hands.

"Where's all the blood from?" her eyes glanced round the bedroom and she could see more evidence of blood all over the carpet.

"Orr for fuck's sake. What have you done now? I hope you haven't been hurting yourself." Sheila quickly gripped his hands and rolled his sleeves up. Her actions were frantic as she checked all across his body. Once she was sure he wasn't hurt she looked at him with a screwed up face. "If you're not hurt, where's the blood from?"

Ged thought quickly and told her Mike had had a nose bleed during the night. He told her he was drunk and he remembered him falling all about the bedroom. Sheila sighed and that seemed to be enough to set her mind at rest. She urged him to hurry up and get ready to go to the shop. Once she had left the room he got ready quickly and slid the knife down his sock. This was his new friend now and no one would ever hurt him again.

His uncle Mike never returned to their house again. His mother still couldn't understand how he could leave the family without saying goodbye. Ged was a changed person now and everyone had noticed how different he was. Even his sisters stopped bullying him as they saw a look in his eyes that scared them. Ged had previously got hold of his oldest sister and pulled a knife on her telling her if she ever messed with him again he would stab her up. The message he sent to her seemed to work because from that day forward she never picked on him again. In fact they became quite close. Ged was now part of the family and his dark days of being a loner were over.

The kids on the estate feared Ged and his street cred was high. He was known as 'the rusty blade' but no one ever told him this because they knew he would slice them up at the drop of a hat. Ged met some older boys and he was now in their circle of trust. They give him a mobile phone and set him up selling drugs on the estate. The other lads all had smart cars and the best clothes. Ged wanted to be part of it. As he sat in the cars with them collecting the drugs he knew one day that it would be him sat behind the steering wheel looking the way they did.

At first, he only sold weed. Ged sometimes smoked it himself but generally he couldn't be arsed with getting stoned all the time. His personal look had got a lot better. Within a few months his old image had changed. He now wore smart clothes and even had a few lads selling drugs for him. The phone never stopped ringing and he was always on his mountain bike delivering somewhere or other.

Ged's mother never seemed bothered that he was dealing drugs and sometimes she would even ask him for a spliff to calm her nerves. His pockets were never empty. He secretly loved the power he felt over his customers. Some of them even brought gold necklaces and stereos, to exchange for drugs. Ged would always knock them down in price as he knew they were desperate for drugs and ended up with some great bargains. One of his prize bargains was the thick gold chain he wore round his neck. It was his pride and joy. He always wore it hanging out over his clothing for everyone to see.

Reece was the main supplier of drugs in Harpurhey and he took a shine to Ged. He let him ride round in his sport car and often took him out for something to eat. The way Ged felt as he sat in the car was unreal. He felt important and looked at all his friends as he drove past them nodding his head. Reece had told him he could start earning some proper cash if he wanted to, but it would mean he would be selling brown. Ged had questioned him when he'd mentioned the word brown and wasn't sure what he meant. Reece lit a spliff and leant back in the car as he started to tell him.

"Brown is smack, you nob. HIt's where the big cash is these days. You can earn some big bucks if ya fancy it?" Ged didn't really understand what it was, but the thought of earning more cash and getting a smart car made his eyes light up. "Yeah, fucking dead right I will. I want to get some proper cash earned now and fuck off from around here." Reece told him he would sort out a phone and told him about the kind of customers he should expect. He chuckled as he spoke.

"The smackheads will do owt for gear. They would steal your eyes and come back for the sockets, the dirty bastards." Ged watched Reece skinning up. Reece was twenty-five years old and mixed race. His hair was cut short. Ged loved the patterns he'd had shaved in the side of his head. They looked like waves. Reece started telling him the perks of selling drugs.

"When I was selling heroin I even got offered sex from the girls." Reece's head rested on the car seat as he flicked the ash from the spliff. "Fuck that mate. I wouldn't touch 'em with a bargepole," he sniggered. Reece's nudged him in the waist and winked at him. "Mind you, I have to admit.

I did get my cock sucked a few times off em when I first started out selling."

Ged laughed with him. He was still a virgin and the thought of someone sucking him off interested him. They now spoke of where he was going to sell the smack and Reece told him he wanted to set up a new phone in Blackpool. Ged looked shocked that he wanted him to go so far from home, but Reece grabbed his leg and explained further.

"Don't worry. We'll look after ya. There's already a few kids up there selling for us. You'll have somewhere to stay and a few runners to deliver it for you. When can you go up?" Ged was a bit scared, but he wanted to impress Reece and tilted his head to the side.

"Erm, anytime. I'll just tell my mam I've got a bit of a job up there that's all. She won't be arsed anyway. I think she will be glad to see the back of me." Reece nodded and took him to buy a new pair of trainers. He had him in his grasp now and wanted to keep him sweet. Selling smack carried a big jail sentence, but never once did he tell Ged how much it would affect his life if he was ever caught.

The following day Ged packed a small sports bag with some clothes inside it. He sat nervously waiting for Reece to come. As he heard him honking his horn outside his house he stood up and looked through the window.

"Right mam I'm off. I should be back at weekend." His mother never batted an eyelid and just sat in the armchair watching some chat show that was on. He repeated himself. "Mother! I said I'm off. See you at weekend," she now turned to him as she stubbed her cig out in the ash tray.

"Yeah I heard you. Make sure you behave ay." Ged smiled as he picked his bag up from the floor and threw it over his shoulder.

"You know me mam, I always behave." They both smiled and Ged left the house and headed to the car. He could hear the music pumping and loved that his neighbours could see him getting into the big flash car. As he stepped out of the gate he saw a girl he'd fancied for years. Lauren had gone to the same school as him and was quite popular among the lads. She had a great figure and her raven black hair always shone brightly. Ged wished he could tell her how he felt about her, but for now all he could manage was a quick hello. He watched as she walked past and laughed at the things he'd done to her in his fantasies. He always masturbated about her. He could see her turn her head as he got into the car and smiled knowing he would have her one day.

As the car pulled away they drove past her and their eyes met again. Getting Reece to slow down, he asked where she was going and did she want a lift. He could see she was interested, but she pointed to her friend who was waiting for her just a bit further up the street. Driving away he blew her a kiss. He felt confident and on top of the world.

The drive to Blackpool took an hour. The traffic wasn't that bad and he couldn't wait to see the landmark that was Blackpool tower. He remembered going on school trips there and how all the kids were sat up in their seats shouting saying they could see the tower. He had to remain calm when he first noticed the tower in the distance and quickly mentioned it to Reece in conversation.

"Oh there's the tower, Not been up here for ages." Ged turned his head to the signpost. "Not long now then is it." Reece agreed and told him they should be there in fifteen minutes. The music was turned up full now and the windows were wound down. They both sat singing the tunes on the radio and Ged was miming the words.

The area was nothing like Ged expected. The times he'd been to Blackpool before, he'd only ever stayed on a caravan park. The houses he saw in front of him looked old. The estate itself looked rundown. He could see a few lads sat about on a wall. As they drove past them their eyes met for a few seconds. Reece pulled his mobile phone from his pocket and dialled the number.

"Yo it's Reece. I'll be there in five so open the door." He threw his phone on his lap and continued driving. When they pulled up outside their destination he parked up and gave Ged the nod to follow him. Ged grabbed his bag and slammed the car door shut. There were a few kids playing on the street. They looked dirty and neglected.

A woman opened the door and let them in. As soon as they walked through the front door Ged could smell wet dog. He screwed his face up and hoped things would get better. As they entered the front room three men were sat there and a young girl who only looked around seventeen years of age. She looked pretty but as he looked closer he could see she looked stoned or something. Her blonde hair was clipped from her face and her big blue eyes stared vacantly at him. They sat down and Reece introduced the newcomer to the group.

"This is Ged. He's looking after things for a while." Ged stood tall and nodded his head as Reece continued. "I want you to show him the ropes and look after him." The young girl smiled and chuckled.

"I'll look after him don't you worry." Reece shook his head as she spoke.

"Ay dirty knickers. Just leave him alone. He's only been here five minutes and you're trying to get into him." The girl smiled and introduced herself as Emma. Ged grinned

at her. Reece stayed for around half an hour and the phone
the other man had in the room never stopped ringing. Ged
couldn't make out what he was saying. The man sitting
opposite him would just answer the phone and ask a few
questions. He listened more carefully to the call.

"So you want one brown, two white and a stone?
Right be outside the phone box in ten." Ged looked at
Reece for answers as it was obvious he didn't have a clue
what different drugs the slang was used for. Reece held his
shoulder and spoke to him like a teacher to his student.

"Right. Brown's fucking heroin. A stone is crack and
white is cocaine. Do you get it now?" Ged nodded as they
all laughed. Reece now stood and gave Ged the eye to
follow him. Ged walked him to the front door as Reece
whispered under his breath.

"Right, watch them fuckers like hawks." His eyes
focused on Emma as his head turned back to the front
room. "Especially that little slapper over there. She would
do anything for drugs, trust me mate." Grabbing his arm
before he left he joked with him. "Ay get a suck off her,
she's not bad." Reece winked and ruffled his hair leaving
him to go back into the front room. The others told him
where his room was and Emma was all over him like a rash.
She started grabbing his stuff from the floor.

"Come on I'll help with that." Ged picked up his bag
and followed her as she led him upstairs. The hallway carpet
was tattered and torn and stunk of cat piss. It looked like it
hadn't been hoovered for years. The wallpaper was hanging
from the walls and the whole staircase looked dirty. Emma
opened the bedroom door and kicked it open with her
foot. She let Ged pass her and followed him inside.

The room had a double-bed in the middle of it and
a wardrobe with no doors on it. Ged walked over to the

window and looked outside. All he could see were houses and a few gardens. Emma lay on the bed. As Ged turned round from the window she patted the bed for him to sit down. His heart pumped inside his chest as he remembered what Reece had told him. Emma fluttered her eyelids as she spoke to him.

"Bet you're hungry aren't you? Have you had anything to eat?" Ged shook his head. "Tell ya what give us some money and I'll run to the chippy for you. It's only around the corner it shouldn't take me five minutes." Ged searched his tracksuit bottoms and pulled out a twenty pound note. Emma's eyes lit up. She stood up from the bed and fidgeted.

"What do you want then?" He sat thinking as he watched her swaying at the side of him. She looked agitated.

"What's the curry like up here?" Emma told him it was nice and quite spicy. He quickly made up his mind.

"Get me meat pie, chips and gravy. Oh get me a buttered muffin as well and a can of coke." Emma couldn't wait to get the money off him. As soon as it was in her grasp she was off out of the room. She shouted to him as she left.

"Meat pie, chips and gravy, yeah?" Ged shouted

"Yeah," Emma mumbled over her shoulder as she ran down the stairs and out the front door.

Ged lay on the bed. He quickly shoved his hands down his boxers and felt his nob. As his hand came out of his boxer shorts he brought it up to his nose and sniffed his fingers. He mumbled to himself with a big grin spread across his face.

"Smells okay that. Fucking hell, I'm gonna get a suck. I just know I am." As he giggled, he lifted the blankets to his nose. His face changed as the smell of sweaty feet filtered his nose. He quickly stripped the bed and ran downstairs to the others. He held the dirty bedding in his grip before he passed it over to Johnny.

"Have you got anymore bedding? This lot stinks of cheesy feet." Johnny sat scratching his head and told him to tell Emma to check the box room, as that's where all the bedding was kept. As Ged told them Emma had gone to the chippy for him they both started laughing. Johnny sighed.

"No fucking way did you give her money?" Ged looked gutted and nodded his head.

"Yeah I've give her twenty quid. She said she would go for me. It was her idea." Johnny stood up and started to go upstairs. He stood with his hand on the door frame and smiled.

"Listen mate she's had you over. Emma will do owt for a quick fix. She's not gone to any fucking chippy for you .She's probably tooting as we speak." Ged was angry and ran up the stairs behind Johnny.

"Where the fuck does she go? I'll fucking twist the dirty little slag up, thinking she can have me over." Johnny opened the door to the box room and started searching for some clean bedding. He tried to calm him.

"She will come back later mate. She always does. There is no point searching for her. She will give you some excuse but once bitten twice shy, ay. At least you know for the future." His head lifted from the floor and he winked at Ged. "I'm sure she will pay you back in some way or another." Johnny laughed out loud and Ged knew exactly what he meant. He grabbed the bedding and headed back in the bedroom ranting under his breath.

Using his hands he cleared the mattress of any debris.

He placed his nose to the mattress and inhaled. Checking his bag he pulled out some deodorant and sprayed it all over it. The clean sheets weren't much better than the old ones but at least they didn't stink. As he held the sheets up he could see stains all over them. He tutted and shook his head. Once his bed was made, he unpacked his clothes. His trainers were his pride and joy and he lined them all up against the wall admiring them.

The walls were decorated in woodchip wallpaper. It was painted in a horrible yellow colour. The top of the paper had black fungus on it and Ged cringed as he looked at it. The bed was made and Ged headed down stairs to join the others. As he walked into the front room he could see them with a lighter in their hands burning some tinfoil. As he looked at them closer they seemed in a world of their own. He seated and watched them further. Johnny now spoke. His words were slow.

"Do ya want a toot?" Ged shook his head. The mobile phone started to ring and he watched as Johnny picked it up from the table. Once the call had ended he gave the other guy a few plastic packets that he pulled from the side of the chair and told him where to go. The other man found it hard to stand up and struggled to put his coat on. Ged watched with interest and told him he would go with him just to see how it all worked.

Johnny agreed and he told Paul to take the new recruit with him. Ged followed Paul to the front door. As they walked Paul was nearly running and Ged had to tell him to slow down. He looked like he was a speed walker.

Paul was about thirty five and his arms were covered in tattoos. His hair looked like you could fry an egg on it. Ged wondered how long it had been since he washed it. His jeans hung from his waist and nothing but an old

tattered leather belt kept them from falling down. As they
approached the phone box, Ged could see a man and a
woman stood there shivering. Paul walked up to them
and gave them the eye to follow him round the corner.
Once out of sight he checked the money was right and
passed them the drugs. Ged was stood back from them and
watched how the couple looked desperate for the powder.
Once the drugs were in their hands, they walked away at
speed. Ged noticed how the man and woman both looked
sallow. He hadn't come to terms yet with what heroin
could do to a person. Ged didn't think in a million years
that drugs could affect people so badly.

Walking back to the house Ged bought some food from
the chippy. His eyes were all over the place still looking for
Emma but he couldn't see her. Holding the tray in his
hands he started to eat his food. He offered Paul a chip but
he refused. Ged wanted to know more about this man and
started to ask him questions.

"What do you do then mate?" Ged enquired. Paul
laughed out loud.

"What do ya mean, what do I do?" Ged laughed and
felt a little embarrassed.

"I mean do ya work or owt."

Paul zipped his coat up further and carried on walking.
He chuckled. "Me work? Are you having a laugh? I've never
worked in my life. I've done eight years in prison so if ya
wanna call that work ya can." Ged didn't know if he'd heard
him correctly and was on him for more information.

"Did ya say you done eight years in the nick?" Paul
nodded. "Fucking hell what was that for?"

Paul looked shameful and hung his head low. Ged
could see he'd hit a nerve and spoke in a low voice. "Go
on tell me I won't say owt." Paul looked at Ged and shook

his head.

"Some other time ay. My head's up my arse at the moment and I don't want to be going over it." His smile was soft as he glanced to him. Ged knew he wasn't in the mood and backed off. Ged reached the front door of his new 'home'. Paul shouted through the letter box to Johnny to let them in.

The rest of the night went on more or less the same. Ged was eager to start taking the calls. He felt like a business man and loved selling drugs. When it was time for bed he placed the phone on the table. He was about to turn it off when Johnny shouted at him.

"What the fuck are ya doing? Don't switch it off." Ged stood up with an angry face.

"I'm fucking knackered. I'm not serving anyone. I'm off to bed." Johnny grabbed the phone and turned it back on.

"Ya nobhead. You don't turn it off. That's when we get most of our customers. It's a twenty- four hour service this phone. Me and Paul are up most of the night so we do it between us." Ged sulked and grabbed his jacket and headed to bed.

"Oh right," he mumbled.

The bed felt cold as he jumped into it. He left his t-shirt on and his boxer shorts. His body wriggled about in the bed as he tried to get warm. He could hear the phone ringing all the time downstairs and placed the pillow over his head to drown out its tones. He went to sleep eventually. Ged was in a deep sleep when he felt someone climb into bed next to him. Emma knew she was in trouble and tried to make amends the only way she knew how. She slowly slipped her hands into the young boy's boxers and started to stroke his manhood. Ged felt her and in his half conscious state was reminded of his uncle's late night antics. He quickly grabbed her hand and punched his fist into thin air. One of the punches connected with her cheek and it wasn't until she screamed out he realised it was her. Emma screamed.

"For fuck's sake Ged. I know what I've done is wrong but I'll pay you back. There is no need for that." Ged's eyes opened fully and he realised where he was. He sat up and looked at Emma rubbing her face.

"What the fuck are doing ya little slag. I was asleep." Emma was crying and trying to get him to feel sorry for her. She looked off her head.

"I was just gonna give you a suck or something, to make up for the money I took. I'll get it back for you. I was desperate, Ged." He was awake now and knew he was in control of the situation. The light that shone through the window just gave off enough light so he could see her face. Emma looked quite angelic. Placing his hands behind his head he lay back down. Emma lay at his side and before long she was paying her debt back in full. Ged wanted to laugh when she first started sucking his nob but as he got into it he held her head and forced his cock all the way down her throat. He loved it and would have paid double the amount she'd stolen from him for the suck she was giving him but he never told her that.

As the night went on Ged lost his virginity. He didn't tell her he hadn't had sex before and just let her take control. As she sat on top of him his hands felt breasts for the first time in his life. Emma's tits weren't big but they were enough for Ged to place his mouth around them and suckle on. He felt like a man. He loved sex and shot his load for the second time. He lay with a smile on his face and regained his breath for a moment. Reaching over the bed he grabbed a cig from his pocket. He didn't smoke a lot but he'd seen it on films that after sex they'd always lit a cig and he didn't want to seem childish. Emma was laid next to him. She was high as a kite on drugs. Her words were few as she pulled the blanket over her body.

Ged was now getting a better picture of what a smackhead was really about. He knew they all had a story to tell and more than anything what they would do to get their hands on the drugs their bodies craved.

Looking at the back of Emma's head he knew sex would be on tap from now on. He could also learn some sex tips from her before he went back home. Finishing his cig he decided that the next night he would go to the fun-fair. After all he was in Blackpool and he wanted to go on the latest ride there. So far he was having the time of his life. Little did he know these would be the best days of his life.

Chapter Eight

Shaun and Colby and a few of the lads from the care home stood at the bus stop. They were all heading to the town centre for a night of fun. The boys were all giddy and fooling around. Colby and Shaun had bought a bottle of brandy from the off-licence earlier. They had blagged a man to buy it for them as they were all under-age. The bottle was hidden in Shaun's jacket. They all took turns swigging at it. Night time was just falling and they couldn't wait to get to the funfair to cause some havoc.

Colby had been smoking weed with Shaun earlier and their eyes looked glazed over. Their plan was to get into town and find some hot girls. None of them had had sex yet and they all spoke about what they would do as soon as they got a girl. Colby was the one to speak first.

"Tell ya what my bollocks are massive and need to be emptied soon!" The others giggled. Colby continued. "Fucking hell I need a wheel barrow to carry them around." The boys agreed as he flashed his ball bag to them as they laughed their heads off. They were now speaking about masturbating and how they had nearly been caught. Shaun felt a tingle in his groin. He wanted some female company desperately.

The bus stopped and they all ran off it like animals escaping from the zoo. The noise from them was loud and the few passengers that sat on the bus looked at them shaking their heads in disgust. Colby was leading them. They all made their way to the funfair laughing and joking. The smell of food hit the back of their throats. Everyone they looked at was eating some kind of food. Shaun grabbed a hot dog as he walked along the golden mile. He couldn't wait to sink his teeth in it. The ketchup reminded him of home and he felt a slight pain in his heart as he missed his family. The Pleasure Beach was minutes away and they could hear all the sounds of the rides.

"Fucking hell, let's get on that one it looks mint!" shouted Colby. As they looked ahead they could see the rides over their heads twisting and turning about. They could hear screams from the people on it and decided they would make "The Big One" the first ride they went on. Standing in the queue they were all giddy. Colby was at the front of the queue where he'd pushed in and shouted for Shaun to come and join him. As he passed the other people in the line he could hear them moaning but he didn't seem to care. Once he was next to Colby his heart pounded. Rides weren't really his thing but he didn't want to seem like a shitbag in front of his mates. A lad stood in front of him and he smiled at him in a friendly way. The time came to get on the ride and every ride had three seats in each compartment. Colby was on the far side from Shaun and the lad who'd stood in front of them in the queue was now sat beside him. The lad smirked and he spoke in a shaky voice.

"Fucking shitting myself ya know. I don't even know why I'm on here." Shaun agreed and told him he felt the same way. As the ride started, the three of them tried not to scream but as soon as the ride started to twist they were screaming at full pelt. After it had stopped the three of them got off and were laughing their heads off.

"What a fucking buzz that was. Are you coming on some other rides with us or what?"

Shaun watched as the new lad agreed. He introduced himself as Ged and told them he came from Manchester.

Shaun told them that's where they were from and when they started speaking they realised they didn't live that far from each other. The other lads went their own way and left the three of them to do their own thing. They shared some of the brandy with him and before long he was as pissed as them.

A group of girls sat near the wall where they were heading and Shaun was straight over to them trying to work his charm. Before long he knew they weren't his kind of girls and told them they were stuck up their own arses. The girls frowned and jumped off the wall. As they left one of the girls turned and called them a bunch of dickheads. Colby wanted to run after her and punch her lights out but Shaun held him back. As he laughed in Colby's face he said, "For fuck's sake. You can't go belting her. She's a girl." Colby removed Shaun's grip and spat on the floor as Shaun tried to make light of the matter. "Anyway that's our dream of getting a shag out the window now isn't it." Colby raised a smiled and agreed. Ged bounced about at the side of them and joined in the conversation.

"Nar no way is it. It's only ten o'clock. We've got plenty of time yet haven't we?" Ged hatched a plan in his head. He couldn't wait to tell it to his new found friends. He held a cunning look on his face as he spoke.

"How much money have you got?" They both looked at him and asked why. "If you've got cash I can make sure you get a shag tonight," Ged whispered. They both dug deep in their pockets and placed some crumpled notes on the wall. Shaun was counting the change in his hands and after they'd counted it all, it came to round about £30. Ged looked at it and started jumping about where he stood with excitement.

"That's well enough money. You can get a suck as well

for that much." Shaun wanted to know more details and once he'd told them his own story they were well up for it. Both Colby and Shaun were holding their groins. They wanted to go straight away to meet Emma.

As they walked back to Ged's house, Shaun was quiet. He had lots of questions to ask Ged. He wasted no time and started to quiz him about his life.

"If you're from Manchester why are you in Blackpool?" Shaun stopped walking and waited for his answer. Ged made no secret about what he was doing in Blackpool and told them both he was a dealer. Both Shaun and Colby loved it and wanted to know exactly how much he earned. They both wanted a part of whatever he was doing to earn money.

"Can't you get us in on it? We could be good grafters." Shaun nudged him in the ribs and ruffled his hair. "Come on Ged we are after all fellow Mancs and all that." Ged smiled. He felt important. He joked with them both.

"I don't know about that lads. I can ask Reece for you both." Ged changed the conversation quickly. "Anyway why are you two in Blackpool?"

Shaun felt ashamed, but Colby didn't give a shit and told him straight they were both in a care-home. Ged felt sorry for them both and tried to work out how he could help them as they neared the house.

The front door opened and Paul let the three of them inside. He looked at the two new housemates and walked back into the front room. Ged followed him and asked where Emma was. Paul was rocking as he spoke.

"She should be in soon. She's just nipped out." Ged rubbed his hands together and took them both upstairs to his room. Shaun and Colby swigged the brandy and passed Ged the bottle. Colby searched his pocket for the last bit of weed he had and started to skin up. Once the spliff was made they all smoked it and lay flat out on the bed. Ged felt in control and reminded the boys why they were there.

"Hope your cocks haven't shrunk. Emma will be here in a minute." Ged quickly checked his watch. He lay kicking his legs on the bed as he continued. "I swear to God lads she sucks it right down to ya spuds." Laughter filled the room and they all played around kicking each other. Colby needed the toilet and asked where it was. Once he'd left the room Ged tried to get more background on Shaun.

"So what's he in care for?" Shaun was just about to tell him when Emma opened the door. She stood there wearing a short black skirt and a small red belly top. Her hair looked ruffled and she had a smile across her face.

"Paul said you were looking for me. What's wrong?" Ged smiled and told her he needed a quick word with her on the landing. He jerked himself up from the bed and followed her outside. Shaun could hear her laughing outside the room and covered his eyes with his hands. Minutes passed and Emma walked back into the room. Her eyes looked strange as Shaun looked at her. He felt scared. Emma kicked her high heels from her feet and lay on the bed. She puckered her lips together and touched the side of his face.

"Ged tells me you're wanting some loving?" Shaun felt like a right dickhead and he searched his pocket for the money they'd got together earlier. He remained silent and placed the money on the bed. Emma counted every penny and shoved it into her pocket. As she stood up she slipped her skirt off and Shaun could see her black lacy knickers for the first time.

Shaun lay back on the bed and waited for his experience

to start. He'd always imagined sex to be with someone he loved. He could feel her hand on his nob and his feet curled up as she stroked it. He was hard within minutes. Emma placed his manhood in her mouth and he could feel her warm wet mouth sliding up and down it. Once she knew he was ready she climbed on top of him and pulled her knickers to the side. She smiled as she looked down at his face and knew he was a virgin. She slurred her words as she gave him instructions.

"I'll do the work, so you just keep still for now." Shaun felt like he was going to explode and he could feel himself inside her. Her hips were gyrating and he could feel something strange happening inside his body. He'd wanked loads of times in the past, but this was the dog's bollocks, he thought. His arse moved up and down beneath her and he could feel he was going to come. As he looked at her he saw she had her eyes closed and she looked to be enjoying it. His arse movements became rapid and within seconds he exploded. Emma remained still as he held her hips. As he opened his eyes she smiled at him and jumped off.

Shaun lay lifeless for a minute. He felt like a man. He was staring at the ceiling with a smile right across his face. Ged must have been listening from outside the door because he seemed to know when to enter. As he opened the door Colby was at his side peeping behind him inside the bedroom. Shaun found his pants and slipped them back on. His face was cocky as he walked to the door and whispered to Colby.

"Get in there lad. Fucking mint mate. I can tell ya. Ay I got a suck as well." Colby looked at Emma laid on the bed with the cover over her. He was nervous but couldn't back down because Shaun and Ged were pushing him through the door. As he closed the door behind him he headed over to the bed. Once Emma saw him she sat up. Her eyes were nearly closed and Colby hoped she wasn't going to collapse on him. Emma told him to take his pants off. Once he did she pulled him back onto the bed. She was just about to mount him when he asked her to suck him off first. Emma pulled her face and wanted to just get it over with, she wasn't really in the mood to suck him off as well.

"Fucking cheeky aren't you", she moaned. "The money you've gave me was a shag each not a suck as well." Colby felt daft but told her straight.

"You've just sucked Shaun off, and the money was mostly mine not his." Emma sighed and climbed to the floor and got between his legs. "Well I'll do it this time, but in future you will have to pay the full price alright?" Colby nodded as she started to lick his shaft. He felt like laughing when he saw his cock disappearing inside her mouth. He had to control the laughter in case she stopped. She only sucked him off for a few minutes and told him to lie on the bed. His legs were shaking as he lay down. Colby closed his eyes and could feel her inserting his cock inside her. Emma only moved her body a few times on his manhood and he shot his load. She smiled at him and told him sex would get better in time to come. Emma jumped off him and put her skirt back on. No words were spoken between them.

When she left the room Shaun and Ged came straight back inside after her. Ged playfully pushed Shaun and they could tell by Colby's face he was happy. Shaun jumped beside him and lay on the bed. He dug him in the ribs as he laughed.

"Mint innit?" Colby smiled and looked for his pants. Once he dragged them on his body he started to discuss the sex with Shaun.

"I shot my load straight away. I was gutted." Ged laughed as he watched him dig his hand down the front of his pants. He watched his face screw up as he spoke.

"Ewwww my dick stinks of tuna." The three of them fell about the bed laughing. Shaun now smelt his cock too and laughed as he shoved his fingers in Ged's face. Shaun shook his hands in the air.

"She's a dirty fucking minger. She better wash her fanny next time." Ged pushed him away and laughed.

"Beggars can't be choosers. It's a start innit? So stop moaning. At least you're not a virgin anymore." They agreed and Colby looked at his watch.

"We better get off mate. Look at the fucking time." Shaun agreed and they got the rest of their clothes and followed Ged downstairs. Once they got in the living room Colby could smell weed. He quickly popped his head round the door and found the man who was smoking it. He nudged Shaun and asked him to get a spliff off him to walk home with. Ged heard the conversation and took control.

"Paul do us a quick reefer for my mates." Colby was impressed how they asked no questions and just followed his instructions. They all watched him as he sprinkled the skunk into the Rizla paper. Once it was done he twisted the end of it and passed it over to Ged.

Ged looked at the spliff and casually passed it to his mates. He walked them to the door. Colby lit the spliff and inhaled deeply. Ged loved his new partners in crime and wanted to make sure he didn't lose them.

"Right lads, are ya coming back tomorrow? I'll see if I can get you any work and that." Shaun and Colby looked at each other and nodded. They were impressed at what this lad could offer them. They told him they would definitely be in touch. Ged scribbled his mobile phone number down and passed it to them as they parted.

Shaun and Colby were quiet as they walked to the bus stop. Colby could be seen still smelling his fingers and smiling. Shaun took the rest of the spliff from him and finished it off. Once they sat at the bus shelter Shaun spoke as he pulled his hood tighter round his face.

"He's mint him isn't he?"

Colby nodded and couldn't be arsed speaking as he was stoned. The journey back to the home was spent more or less in silence. They both sat at the back of the bus and stared out of the window.

The next day Colby and Shaun spoke about their antics. They decided that from that day they would make the most of their time in care. They phoned Ged and told him they would work for him. They hoped to make a lot of money and just prayed he would get them onboard with him.

Chapter Nine

The day Shaun finished his long term care order was a sad time. All the lads were stood there hugging him. Gladys had come to pick him. She looked a nervous wreck. Her clothes hung from her body and she looked anorexic. In the time Shaun had spent in care you could count on one hand how many times his mother had visited him. He always told her to stay at home and save her money from the train fare for herself. Colby had left months before and they still spoke to each other every day.

Colby and Shaun had hatched a plan to sell heroin when they got home. Ged was in on it as well and they had everything sorted out. They'd even got a few lads from Harpurhey involved as runners. Reece wasn't happy when he'd heard what Ged had planned and tried to make him stay with him but Ged was older and wiser now and wanted to go it alone. Ged had got a name for himself and some people on the street were calling him ruthless. He didn't give a fuck who he hurt as long as he got the result he wanted.

The flat was already set up by Ged. As soon as Shaun got in the car with his mother he told her he wasn't staying at the family home. She was upset and cried but his words were strong and she knew he wouldn't change his mind.

Once they got home Shaun ran to his old bedroom and started to gather some clothes. His mam had rigged his wardrobe with a few new clothes. As he looked at his old room he noticed it had been decorated. His heart melted for a moment but he was in too much of a rush to thank his mother for all the effort she'd made. As he piled the clothes into a bag his mother stood at the bedroom door. A cig hung from her mouth as she rested her arm on the door frame.

"Where are you going then? I mean you have only just got home. Why don't you stay for a few days then go?" Shaun's head was dipped and he couldn't look at her face.

"Mam, will you fuck off pecking my head. I'll still come and see you every day but I've got a job and I don't want to fuck it up." Gladys heard the word job and looked happy. She felt proud he'd found work.

"Oh what job is it son? Have the care home sorted it out for you?" Shaun just huffed and picked up his bags. Paul could be heard shouting his mother from outside the room. Shaun met his brother for the first time in ages. Paul immediately hugged him. It was obvious he'd missed him.

"Alright our kid. Bet ya glad to be home aren't ya?" Shaun smiled at him and nodded as he ruffled his hair. Paul noticed his bags in his hands and looked at him with a puzzled face.

"Where ya off to? Don't tell me you and my mam have been arguing already. For fuck's sake you haven't been home two minutes." Shaun answered as they both headed downstairs.

"Nar, I've got a job so I'm moving in with my mate. I should be earning some good money." Paul looked angry and was just about to give him a lecture but Shaun ran out and shouted his goodbyes. Paul joined his mam in Shaun's bedroom. Gladys had lifted the net curtain from the window and was watching him carry his bag on his shoulder. The kids on the estate were shouting at him as he passed them and you could see his smiling face joking around with them.

Paul gripped his mother's shoulder. He could see she was upset. He placed his chin on her shoulder and watched his brother leave.

"Come on mam. You've wasted enough tears over him. He'll be fine, he always is." Gladys dropped the net curtain and went downstairs. Even though he'd been home for just one day her nerves were on edge. Gladys always knew from Shaun being a baby that he would bring her nothing but trouble and she'd always told her sister the same thing when he was a toddler.

Shaun was always the child who was up to mischief. Whenever she heard a child crying in the distance she always knew her son would have had something to do with it. Reaching for her cigs she turned the TV on and sat watching a daytime chat show. The programme was about everyday people and their lives. Gladys sat shaking her head as she listened to them.

Shaun reached the flats in Harpurhey and pressed the button for the number of the door. He waited until he heard a voice on the intercom. He heard a buzzing noise and the door opened. Dragging his bag he made his way to the lift. There were two sets of lifts: one for even numbers and one for odd numbers. He entered the lift for even numbers and pressed the button for the second floor. He could smell piss and you could see his nostrils flaring as he breathed deeply. As he looked on the floor he could see green spit all over the show. He mumbled under his breath, "dirty bastards".

The doors opened and he could see three doors looking at him. Quickly checking the numbers on the door he tapped the letter box with his hand. After waiting a few seconds he could see a shadow approaching the door. As it opened he saw Colby's face.

"Alright lad. How's it going?" Colby hugged Shaun and they shared a moment. Grabbing him by the shoulder he escorted him to the living room. The flat looked quite clean. The few things they had in the gaff were all top of the range. The large TV stood on a silver stand, and the music centre stood next to it. The flat had crisp white net curtains up at the window and the carpet on the floor looked new. Shaun was impressed.

Ged could be heard coming from the bedroom and a young woman followed behind him. Shaun couldn't see her face at first but when she turned around he noticed it was Lauren. Shaun knew Lauren from years before and he'd always had a soft spot for her. He watched her place her hair back into a ponytail and it was obvious her and Ged had just had sex. Feeling an ache in his stomach Shaun tried to raise a smile. He nodded his head at Lauren as he sat down. Looking round he could see loads of small plastic bags on the table and a small set of scales. Colby came back in the room and smiled.

"Well come on then. Get stuck in we need to get this bagged up before six o'clock". Shaun leaned forward and weighed the heroin onto the scales. He could see Ged now mixing some other powder with it. He looked at him and asked the question that was playing on his mind.

"What's that ya putting in it?"

Ged winked at him as Shaun watched him empty some tablets onto the table and started to crush them. He scooped a spoonful of some other powder and mixed them all together.

"Just some paracetamol and caffeine mate. It helps it go further. Reece showed me how to do it. Clever innit".

Shaun shook his head and moaned. "Fucking hell ya could kill em".

Ged shrugged his shoulders and held his head back as he laughed. "Does this face look as if it gives a fuck? I'm in it for the money mate". Ged could see Shaun was annoyed and explained himself further. "If they want to shoot smack into their veins, then that's up to them".

Shaun chewed on his fingernails for a minute. Ged was right he thought and backed down. He sat at the table and started crushing some of the tablets with him.

Lauren sat smoking her cig. She looked different to Shaun. Her face looked thin and her eyes seemed vacant and her once long hair now looked thin and brittle. He wanted to speak to her but still felt shy.

Once all the drugs were bagged up they sat back and just looked at it scattered all over the table. Ged moved Lauren from the chair where she was sat. He told her to go and brew up in the kitchen. As she stood Shaun could see her jeans hanging from her arse. Watching her leave the room Ged grabbed at his penis.

"Just got a suck off her, it wasn't that bad either." Ged nudged Shaun as his eyes focused on the door. "You'd better shift all that brown out of her way, otherwise the little skank will try and have it away. The dirty smackhead." Shaun sat forward in his chair, he looked shocked.

"What, is she a baghead now?" Ged raised his eyebrows as he watched the door making sure she wasn't coming back in the room.

"Yeah, fucking hell she's been on it for years. She was one of the first people round Harpurhey who I sold it to." Shaun shook his head and couldn't believe Lauren had got herself mixed up in the drug world. She was always a top class girl. He wanted to know more and asked further questions.

"Well that's surprised me. How does someone like her end up on shit?"

Laughter filled the room as Ged chuckled. "I think that was down to me mate. When we set up round here we had to get everyone interested in heroin, so we gave them freebies first just to try it. Lauren tried it a few times and she couldn't get enough of it. Mind you so did a lot of the others." Ged reeled off loads of names of kids that Shaun knew and watched his face sink as he told him they were all junkies now. Ged explained how he'd also fancied Lauren years before and they both laughed knowing they fancied the same girl.

Lauren carried the brews back into the front room. She was struggling and Shaun could see her fingers were burning as the others grabbed them from her. Placing the other drinks down on the table she stood up fidgeting about. Ged knew what she wanted and quickly reached over and grabbed a bag of heroin from the table. Throwing it to her, she grasped onto it for dear life. Shaun felt sick inside and wanted to help her. For some strange reason he felt warmth towards her and he knew in time he would help to sort her out. She was too nice to end up like this. The sound of the door slamming could be heard as she left.

The mobile phone was ringing non-stop. Shaun shook the sadness from him. He reminded himself he was a drug dealer and asked Colby if he fancied a walk. This was his first day home and he wanted to see all his old mates to find out what they'd been up to. Colby agreed and grabbed his coat. Ged decided to stay at the house and told them he would man the phone until they got back.

Shaun felt strange. His words were stuck in his throat.

He loved the money that drug dealing would bring him but hated what it did to people. As they walked from the flats they hit the main road. Rochdale Road ran right through the estate where he'd been brought up. They both walked for a few minutes and went to a local hangout looking for all his old mates.

Tavistock Square was where all the wheeling and dealing went on. If you ever wanted to find someone or get some hooky stuff, someone in the square would always be able to help you. The square had five lots of shops on it. And a pub situated in the middle of it called the Ark Royal. A few lads could be seen stood near the pub's entrance. As Shaun recognised a few of his old mates he started shouting.

"Yo lads how's it rolling?" The youths looked twice at him. They didn't recognise him at first but when they did they came to his side and playfully pushed him about.

"How's it going Shaun? Fucking hell you've been gone for time. You look well though." With a grin splattered over his face Shaun tensed his muscles and encouraged them to feel them.

One of the lads who he used to glue sniff with reminded him of the times they spent together tripping. The lad was loud as he broadcasted his story.

"Got any Evo ay Shaun?" Shaun pissed himself laughing and told Colby some of the stories about what happened when they were high on glue. Colby wasn't saying much and looked each of the lads up and down. Shaun finally introduced him to his old mates and it seemed to clear the air. They all spoke for a while and Shaun looked at a lad walking not far from them. He had to look twice at him as he thought he knew him. The others started shouting at the lad and Shaun looked shocked.

"Ay ya fucking baghead. What ya selling today. Have you got out?" The lad turned to them and started to walk over carrying a white plastic bag. As he reached them he started to pull out lots of different items from the bag.

"I've got Mach three blades. Electric toothbrushes, and a few packets of bacon. Do any of yas want any?" Shaun watched the lad's shaking hand as he held the goods out in front of him. The smackhead looked familiar to Shaun. And then it clicked who he was. It was his old mate Mark. Shaun was in his face.

"Fucking hell Mark how's it going?" Mark looked at him and he seemed to look right through him. Shaun explained who he was and Mark smiled as he chatted to him.

"Fucking hell you look well. Don't ya want any blades or owt to shave that bum fluff from round ya mouth?" Shaun punched him playfully.

"Do I fuck, I'm growing a beard." Mark laughed and started to put all his stuff back in the bag. He stood for a few minutes and you could see he was eager to get away from them. He told Shaun to call to his house when he had time and left them watching him leave. Shaun stood in disbelief.

"Tell ya what, he looks rough. He used to be a right fat cunt in his day." The lad at the side of him screwed his face.

"Rough isn't the word? He's a fucking raving smackhead. What do ya expect?" Shaun shook his head. He seemed to be walking back into an area that even he didn't recognise anymore. All the people he once knew looked like zombies and they'd sold their souls to heroin. Colby looked fed up. He was skinning up in the doorway. Once he'd finished he urged Shaun to hurry up. They said their goodbyes to his old pals.

"See ya later lads. Ay don't forget, if ya need any drugs we're the suppliers around here now not Reece's crew anymore." They walked away and Shaun ran into the chippy to grab something to eat, he was starving.

"Can I have chips, pudding and gravy please, and a buttered muffin?" The lady behind the counter waddled to get his order. She looked fed up and you could tell her heart wasn't in the job. He watched her wrap up his food and she placed the plastic fork on top of it. Once he'd paid her he said goodbye, she never replied.

As they walked up towards the local park Shaun scranned his food. He hadn't eaten anything all day. Once he'd finished he tossed the tray onto the floor as he walked. In the distance he could see a few kids sat messing about. His idea was to tell as many people in the area that they were the drug suppliers now. When they got nearer Colby pointed out that Lauren who was at the flat earlier was stood in the distance.

Something inside Shaun wanted to help her. He knew what she was but he wanted to save her. His pebble was in his tracksuit bottoms. As he reached inside he felt the coldness from it. At first Lauren didn't notice him but as she did she smiled. Her teeth were rotted away and looked minging but that didn't deter him. Colby informed the crowd of the service they were providing and Shaun sat on the wall next to Lauren. As she spoke she held her hand over her mouth so he couldn't see her broken teeth.

Shaun gazed into her eyes. He could still see the girl who he'd a had a crush on all those years before. He didn't feel nervous and spoke to her casually.

"So what have you been up to then?" Lauren dipped her head and felt ashamed of what she'd become. She mumbled a reply and he could see tears appearing in the corner of her eyes.

"Erm. Nowt much. Just trying to get off the shit and that, but it never seems to happen."

Shaun bit on his lip and his words came from nowhere. "I'll help you get clean ya know. You can go to the doctors and get some methadone that weans ya off it." Lauren smiled and grabbed his hands. Her hands looked ancient. They looked wrinkled and full of bruises where she'd injected into her veins.

"I know what I should do, but I just never seem to get there" she mumbled. Shaun was in her face now. He seemed angry.

"What about ya mam and dad won't they help you?"

Lauren wiped the tears from her eyes and shook her head as her chin fell onto her chest. "No. I've done too much to them." She hid her face in shame as she continued. "I mean I've robbed off them and caused them nothing but shit. They want fuck all to do with me since they found out I was on the game."

Shaun felt sick at her words. He wanted to speak more to her but Colby was at his side pecking his head. He told her to come to the flat later and she agreed. As they left he looked over his shoulder at her and knew she was in deep shit. They both headed back to the flat.

Ged was sat smoking weed when they entered. The living room stunk of it. Colby didn't mind because he smoked it but Shaun pulled his jumper up to his nose and tried to avoid breathing in the fumes. He'd smoked it in the past but it didn't agree with him. He always felt himself going under when he smoked weed. The last time he'd smoked it he'd had a panic attack and promised himself he wouldn't touch the stuff again. Colby started to shout out over the music.

"Ay Ged, Shaun's got the hots for smackhead Lauren." Ged chuckled and took a drag from his spliff.

"Arrhhh no way, she's a dirty slag. Fucking hell Shaun, keep well away from her. She's alright for a suck every now and then but don't go fucking falling in love with her." Shaun went red in the face and twisted his body in the chair.

"Fuck off you two. I just feel sorry for her that's all. I've known her for years." The sound of the banter between them all filled the room. The mobile phone that sat on the table started ringing and Colby jumped to answer it. He took the order and asked Shaun to deliver it.

The night went on much the same and the phone never stopped ringing. Shaun didn't realise how many people In Harpurhey were on drugs. All the people he delivered to differed in age. Some of them lived in nice houses and you wouldn't have suspected they were using drugs in a million years. One of his customers was a solicitor and he had to be sworn to secrecy that he supplied him.

Lauren came to the flat later that night. It was past midnight because Shaun looked at his watch as he heard her knocking and shouting at the door. Shaun jumped up from the bed and let her inside. As she got near him she smelt stale. He could smell booze and cigs on her. Lauren's eyes were dancing all over the place. She was wearing a short red mini skirt and a black netted top. Her bra was see-through. Lauren's legs looked cold as he led her to the front room.

Ged was in the bedroom with some girl he'd picked up and Colby was out making a delivery. As Lauren sat down he passed her a can of lager from the side. She opened it and swigged at it. She now pulled several notes from her coat and counted them. Looking at Shaun she passed him a twenty pound note and asked him for a bag of brown. He felt like a hypocrite. Leaving the room he returned with the drugs. She quickly took the wrap from him and shoved it into her coat. Lauren tried to make light of the matter.

"At least I won't be rattling tomorrow morning now will I?" He didn't answer her and turned the television over. As he watched her, her eyes were half closed and she was struggling to stay awake. Her mouth was open and he could see spit hanging from the corner of her mouth. His head was telling him to fuck her off out of the house, but his heart was telling him to help her. Walking over to the chair he softly kicked at her leg.

"Go and get in my bed if ya want." She struggled to open her eyes and mumbled under her breath. He kicked at her again. "Go and get ya head down. You're wrecked." Lauren stood and wobbled.

She placed her hand on her hip. She was cocky.

"What do ya want a shag or summat." Shaking his head he led her to his bedroom. The room was in darkness. Lots of clothes were scattered over the floor. He moved a large sports bag from the bed and watched as she fell onto it. She sat up and squeezed her eyes together. She could see him starting to leave and shouted him back.

"Don't go, please come and lie with me. I don't want to sleep on my own. I'm scared of the dark." Shaun stopped dead in his tracks. His heart raced in his chest. He turned his head slowly and he could see her eyes shining in the moonlight. She looked so sad. Slowly he headed back to the bed. Sinking his arse on the bottom of it he watched her lie down. She patted the space next to her as she spoke.

"I don't bite ya know. Come and lie here and get me warm. I'm fucking freezing my tits off." He kicked his slippers off and his socks hung from his feet. Crawling up the bed he lay on his front and started to speak.

"Ya off your head you. Why are you scared of sleeping on ya own?" Lauren pulled the blankets up round her neck and lay on her side. The moonlight shining through the window let them see each other's faces.

"I'm scared of everything me. I'm scared of tomorrow and everyday that follows. Look at what I've become. I'm a fucking junkie." Shaun listened as he made himself comfortable. Lauren was talking. "The last three years of my life have been shite. I had everything and I've blown it. My family hate me, and to tell you the truth I hate myself." Shaun watched as she pinched her skin and dragged at it. His heart melted for her. He tried to make her see sense.

"Why are you talking like that Lauren? You can get help and do summat about it. It's not too late ya know". Lying down he could hear her sobs. He pulled at her arm to try and see her face but she pushed him away.

"I've done some bad things ya know. Selling my body is only the half of it. I'm a thief and a low life fucker. My dad was right when he kicked me out. He told me I'm the scum of the earth and to never darken his door again, suppose he was right wasn't he?"

Shaun moved to the top of the bed and cradled her face in his hands. She felt so fragile. As he grabbed her hands he felt every finger and stroked them. He could see tears falling from her eyes and slowly wiped them away. Watching her cuddle into his chest she felt so helpless. He wanted to fix her. His voice was low as he spoke to the top of her head.

"I'll come with you to the doctor's tomorrow. If you want to change and get off the gear I'll help you." He could feel her head nodding and squeezed her tightly as they both drifted off to sleep.

Chapter Ten

Lauren had been free from heroin for six months now and she and Shaun were in love. As she felt the baby growing inside her she knew she had a shot at life again. The methadone was down to almost nothing and the doctor predicted before she gave birth she would be drug free. It had been a long hard battle and one she was still fighting every day.

Shaun was her rock and he cared for her in every way despite the shit he took from his mates. Most days she was fine but sometimes when she was stressed she just wanted to ram a needle deep into her veins to take the pain away. She never told Shaun that she still felt the urge to have a fix and she always felt like a fake when she listened to him telling people how well she'd done getting clean. Her family were slowly but surely welcoming her back into the family but they were always watching every move she made in the house.

Her drug worker had helped her to find a home and furnish it. Shaun was still dealing but he kept her well away from any drugs. Ged and Colby had called him a nob-head for taking her on and told him that once a smackhead always a smackhead. He defended her to the max and always sung her praises telling them she was clean now. Ged missed Shaun and the fun they had together. He hated Lauren with a vengeance and decided to call round to see her to see if she really was all Shaun made her out to be.

Lauren now lived in Miles Platting in a two bedroom house. The area was quiet and sometimes she missed the wheeling and dealing that went on in Harpurhey. All her drug- addict friends had long since disappeared and she felt lonely. The knocking at the door made her jump. She never got any visitors and looked happy as she ran to the front door. Opening the door fully she saw Ged. Lauren smiled and invited him in straight away. She loved having someone to talk to.

"Do ya want a drink or owt Ged?"

"Yeah I'll have a coffee," he replied as he watched her going into the kitchen. Making his way into the front room he checked out the house and commented on how clean it was. He shouted into her.

"You've got it nice in here haven't ya?" The sound of tap water could be heard and he could hear her shouting back from the kitchen.

"It will be. That's all I do every fucking day. Cook and clean. I'm a proper little housewife now ya know." Carrying the brews into the front room she sat down on the sofa. She now looked at him with a curious look on her face.

"What's wrong? Is Shaun alright?"

Ged picked up his brew and laughed. "Yeah he's sweet. I was just passing and thought I would call in and see how you are. I've brought a birthday card for Shaun as well." He slid the card onto the table. His eyes cast over her. "You look really well ya know." Lauren felt embarrassed and flicked her hair from her face.

"I know, I can't stop eating. Since I've been pregnant I never feel full. I think I'm addicted to food now."

Ged chuckled and spoke about everyday events. He wanted to make sure she wasn't fooling anyone and secretly pulled a bag of heroin from his pocket. He casually planted it at the side of him on the chair. Ged quickly drank his brew and glanced at his watch. As he stood up he made sure the heroin was in sight. He thanked Lauren for the brew. A smirk formed across his face. As he left she followed him to the door.

"Thanks for calling, Ged. It's nice to have visitors every now and then." He waved as she watched him get into his smart black car. Once he pulled off she headed back into the house to wrap Shaun's birthday present.

The Smiths CD lay on the table and she searched for the wrapping paper she'd bought earlier. Once it was wrapped she sat playing with it on the table. Writing his birthday card she sat with the pen hanging from her mouth thinking of the right words to say. As her hand started writing she felt a lump in her throat as the words poured from her heart.

"To Shaun. My life . My rock. My everything. You have saved me in more ways than you'll ever know, and I'll always be true to you. My love forever Lauren xx" As she walked to the table she placed the card alongside his present and stood looking proudly at it. For years she'd never bought a card or a gift for anyone and as a matter of fact she'd never wished anyone a happy birthday in a long time.

Looking round the front room she saw a small package on the chair. As she moved closer to it her heart missed a beat. She knew straight away what it was and ran into the kitchen. She covered her eyes and pulled at her hair. As if the drug was calling her she stood at the door staring at the little plastic bag. Time stood still and every bone in her body shook. She cried as she fell to the floor. Her knees were up at her chest as she pulled her grey sweatshirt over them. The drug was calling her. She covered her ears to try and help drown out its call. She was sweating and water trickled from her forehead. She looked in a daze as her body floated towards the drugs. Slowly she picked up the small plastic bag and held it like a dead mouse as she licked her dry lips.

Searching for some tin foil, she couldn't fight the urge any longer. She was whispering under her breath as she prepared to toot the drugs.

"Just one last time that's all. I promise I promise." Her body hurried about the front room as she rushed to the front door to lock it. Pulling the curtains together she sat in the darkness. The green lighter in her hand shook as she began to burn the silver tin foil with the drugs on it.

The sound from the television was low as her body melted into the carpet. Her eyes slowly drifted to a place where she felt safe. Her fingers could be seen falling from a tight grip. Lauren's body suddenly started shaking. It shook for a few seconds and Lauren remained still. Her chest wasn't moving anymore and she remained in the same position.

★

That night Shaun couldn't wait to get home. He knew Lauren would have got him a present and he couldn't wait to see what she'd got him. Checking his face in the car mirror he wiped the food he'd just eaten away from his lips. The key slid into the door and he walked straight in. He was shouting in an excited voice.

"Where are you my princess? I hope you have got gifts for your prince?" Pushing the living room door open he could see her lying on the floor. He quickly turned the light on and bent down towards her.

"Ay sleepy head, come on I need some TLC." He shook her slowly but started to panic when she remained still. His eyes were drawn to the table and that's when he saw the burnt foil. He shook her frantically and screamed at the top of his voice.

"No! No! Lauren ya fucking muppet. What have you done?" His hands shook rapidly as he tried to pull his mobile phone from his pocket. He quickly called an ambulance and sat by her side with her head on his lap. His words were desperate.

"Lauren wake up, wake up please." His eyes were wide open and he remembered his unborn baby. As he lifted her top up he looked for any movement. When he saw there wasn't any sign of life he screamed out as she shouted up at the ceiling.

"Not my fucking baby as well. Fucking hell Lauren what have you done to me?" He cradled them both in his arms and prayed that they would survive. Her face looked at peace and he cursed her for killing his child.

The sound of knocking at the front door made him place her cold body back onto the carpet. As the medics came into the room they could tell by his face that she was already dead. They tried reviving her but gave up after a few attempts. Shaun stood by the door and knew she was gone before they told him. He gripped the man's hand and spoke with desperation in his voice.

"What about the baby. Is it dead as well?" he sobbed. The medic nodded his head and started to prepare to take her to the hospital. Shaun was stood with his hand in his pocket and twisted his pebble at speed. He wanted to run at them and rip their heads off but his body was weak and he couldn't find the strength to talk anymore. His legs melted as he fell to the floor. The ambulance man ran to his side to give him some medical help. Shaun was shouting out now as he rolled about on the floor as if he'd been stabbed in the heart.

"You dirty no good smackhead. You lied to me and me,

like a prick, believed you. I'll never forgive you Lauren."
Tears fell from his eyes as he watched them take her from
the room. He slowly followed them to the hospital and
listened as the doctor confirmed they were both dead.

Later, as he knocked on the flat door, Ged answered.
Shaun fell inside and Ged thought he'd been shot or
something.

"What's up Shaun? Are you okay? Fucking hell mate,
speak to me what's wrong?" Shaun punched the floor and
sounded like he couldn't breathe. Ged looked worried and
turned him over. "Tell me what's wrong ya prick and then
I can help." Shaun sat up and shouted at full pelt.

"You can't do Jack shit mate. She's dead and never
coming back. She even took my baby with her." Ged's face
dropped and he needed to know more. Once he'd told
him Lauren had overdosed his body shivered. Ged could
be seen rubbing his arms as his face went white. He slowly
let Shaun fall from his grip onto the floor. Shaun sobbed as
he looked at Ged.

"Fucking hell mate I'm done in. How do I cope with
this shit?" Ged led him to the front room and sat watching
him from the armchair as Shaun's head dropped into the
palm of his hands.

"I just can't understand it. I thought she was off the
shit." Ged sat hiding his guilty secret. He knew he was the
cause of her death and felt like his throat was closing up
as he struggled to breathe. Grasping his t-shirt he pulled it
down from his neck and walked to the balcony for some
fresh air. Shaun could be heard sobbing from inside the flat.
Slowly Ged turned his head and could see the pain on his
mate's face through the window. He lit a cig and his hands
were shaking uncontrollably.

"Fuck fuck fuck!" he mumbled.

Shaun stood and told him he'd just told Lauren's parents the heart-breaking news. He put his tracksuit top on and told him he was going back to Lauren's house. Ged quickly grabbed his coat and told him he was coming with him. Ged was frantic as he followed him.

"Wait up, ay. No way am I letting you go on ya own. You need your mates at times like this don't you?" Ged placed his arm round his shoulder and escorted him to the front door. Colby had heard the news from the bedroom and shouted to Shaun.

"I'll get some beers in mate. You need a drink at times like this." Shaun made no reply. They both left the flat and headed to Miles Platting.

The front door of the house seemed daunting to Shaun. The overgrown garden looked worse than ever. He cringed at the jobs that he'd never done in the house. Slipping the key into the front door felt strange because he knew the woman he loved wasn't there anymore. The room looked empty and he could smell death. Shaun paced the front room and noticed his birthday card and present on the side of the table. His mind was all over the show. He quickly sat down before he collapsed. Taking a deep breath he asked Ged to pass him the card.

Slowly he opened the blue envelope. Pulling the card out from the envelope his eyes focused on the words on the front. "To the one I love" it read. Shaun felt like his fingers were stuck. He couldn't find the strength to open the card. Ged noticed the plastic bag on the floor and wanted to get rid of it before Shaun saw it. This was the evidence of his sins and the only thing that connected him to Lauren's death. Casually walking over to it he placed his foot firmly over it. He could see Shaun's eyes welling up as he read the card and took his chance. He quickly bent his body and he slid the drugs bag from under his foot and casually placed it in his pocket. Then, seeing the birthday card on the fireplace that he'd brought earlier he paced over to it and quickly shoved it inside his jacket. Shaun was too heartbroken to see his friend's evil ways.

Every word Shaun read from the card was like a knife being plunged into his heart. Once he'd read the words he held the card to his chest and shook his head. Ged was at his side now and passed him the wrapped present. As he opened it his tears fell onto the paper. Reading the songs on the track he lifted his head up and spoke to Ged.

"This is all I have left of her and my baby. One fucking lousy CD. She knew I loved The Smiths."

Ged needed to get out of the house as he felt like Lauren's spirit was present in the room with them. He kept getting a cold chill throughout his body and was seen rubbing his arms. Shaun stood up and shoved the disc into his back pocket. He too felt strange in the house and questioned his own mind about the reasons she'd given into drugs again.

Two weeks later Lauren was laid to rest in Moston Cemetery. The service was small and only a few people turned up to pay their last respects. Lauren's mother sank to her knees as they lowered her coffin into the ground. Shaun bit onto his bottom lip as he listened to the heartbreaking sound from the mourners. Ged pressed the play button on the music player that they'd brought along and a song called "All I Want Is You" by U2 played as everyone threw some soil down the hole on top of the coffin. The coffin was a light brown colour and the gold plaque displayed her name and the date her life ended.

Lauren's dad held his wife's hand and kept her strong as they left the graveside. Shaun wanted to drag Lauren from her coffin and shake her. She'd ruined his life. She'd taken his child and all that he had left was a daft fucking CD. He wanted to smash the music centre to pieces and the CD with it but Ged held him back and told him he'd only be sorry later.

The black suit he'd worn looked too big on him. All the bottom of the pants was now covered in thick brown mud. Shaun's mother had come to the funeral with his sister and they both watched as they saw him fall apart.

Gladys kissed Shaun as she left, as did his sister. He just nodded at them and didn't say a word. Katie told Shaun to call at her house when he had time and he just nodded in agreement. He missed his sister and knew when the chips were down she would always bring a smile to his face. His hands played about in his pocket and the cold feeling from his pebble brought him calm. He twisted it frantically in his pocket. Shaun stood shaking as he spoke to his mate.

"Get me out of here Ged. Please. I can't do this anymore I need to get wrecked." Ged was like his lieutenant and held his arm firmly as they left the cemetery. The car was nearby and once they were in it he drove off at speed. There was no wake and everybody went their separate ways.

The next few weeks broke Shaun in two. He spent most of his time laid in the flat in his bedroom. His face was unshaven and his eyes were dark underneath through lack of sleep. Colby had stayed up most nights with him chatting until the early hours.

One morning Shaun walked into the front room. Colby and Ged sat bagging the drugs. He hated the sight of all the powders spread across the table and remembered the last time he'd seen his girlfriend's face. Wearing nothing but his boxers his sparrow like legs looked as if they were going to snap. He sat down.

"That shit ruined my life, but ya both still sit there like witches round a pot bagging it. Have a bit of respect ay." Ged raised his eyebrows to Colby and shook his head. They both knew he was having a bad time and ignored him. Shaun's face was white with temper as he stood up. Using the side of his arm he swept the drugs from the table and screamed. He'd lost the plot.

"Fucking heroin fucks people up. I've lost everything because of it ya wankers." He screamed round the room. "Do you hear me?" he was in their faces. Ged was fuming and ran at him.

"Listen ya prick. She was a smackhead. A dirty no good baghead. Did ya think she was gonna change?"

Shaun clenched his fist and ran at him while Colby tried to break them up. Shaun was raging and couldn't be controlled. Making his way back to Ged he headbutted him and pummelled his fist into his face. He screamed out loud.

"She was my smackhead, carrying my baby. She did want to change. She was trying ya know." Ged broke free and started shouting.

"I knew she was a lying twat, that's why I left the drugs there for her. I wanted to show you that it was only a matter of time before she went back to them, and I was right. Wasn't I?" Shaun played with the words in his mind. He wasn't sure if he'd heard him right. He screwed his face up as he growled.

"What ya saying dickhead? Are you saying that you gave her the smack?"

Ged realised what he'd said as Colby now zoomed in on him too. Shaun was in his face now and they were nose to nose.

"Did you give her heroin? Go on tell me, or are you not man enough to admit you killed her?"

Ged pulled his face away from Shaun's and walked away, but Shaun ran and jumped onto his back.

"Did ya give it her ya wanker." The two of them rolled about the floor and Colby was doing his best to split them up. Ged shouted out as he took control of the fight.

"I gave her the drugs, yeah. Lauren decided to take them not me. It's her own fault she's dead, not mine." He looked cocky as he replied. "She would never have made a good mother anyway. You're lucky you found out sooner rather than later." Shaun rolled about underneath him, but was unable to break free. Colby looked at Ged in shame and shook his head. Quickly jumping up from Shaun, Ged made a run for the door. You could hear Shaun screaming behind him.

"Fucking murdering bastard. What was it ay? Couldn't you stand seeing anyone else happy? This isn't over Ged. Mark my words ya wanker. One way or another I'll make you pay." The sound of the door slamming could be heard. Colby left his half smoked spliff in the ash tray. He looked at Shaun and sighed.

"Fuck me man. That's some heavy shit. How could he have kept that in? It's proper shady what he's done. I wouldn't blame ya if ya stabbed the cunt up. He's well out of order."

Shaun was in his bedroom. He grabbed some clothes from the old wardrobe. If he'd have had a gun he would have shot the bastard right there and then. He needed to cope with this in his head and knew his sister could help him think straight. He shouted to Colby where he was going and could hear him shouting behind him as he left.

"If you need back up with Ged, I'm with you all the way mate. Don't forget that will ya?" Shaun ran down the stairs and didn't stop running until he reached the bottom.

The warm summer air hit his face and he felt strange. Loosening his jacket tighter round his body he looked round the area to see if he could see Ged. As he started to walk he felt the anger bubbling inside him. Mumbling under his breath he crossed Rochdale Road. Shaun felt the adrenalin pumping around his body and decided to run. His sister Katie didn't live very far and he set off towards her house with speed.

Katie and Shaun were close. Through their youth they'd stuck together. Shaun's sister was pretty but the tosser of a boyfriend she'd ended up with always tried to drag her down. Shaun hated him with a vengeance and some of the stories he had heard of what he had done to her, made his blood boil. Shaun had only been a kid at the time, but now he would stand up to him and make sure he treated his sister well.

Katie opened the door to Shaun and knew something was wrong. As if someone had pressed a button on him, all Shaun's emotions fell out of him.

"Shaun what's wrong, come on get in." She pulled at his coat and helped him inside. As he fell onto the sofa she watched as a river of tears left his eyes. His body shook and she felt every inch of his pain. She shook him by the arm.

"Tell me what's wrong our kid. Please tell me." Shaun bit his lips and lit a cig. Katie was watching him like a hawk as he began to tell her exactly what Ged had confessed to. She lit a cig and sat next to Shaun as she started to speak.

"I always knew he was a wrong un ya know. Tell ya what, I'll never speak to him again."

"What are ya gonna do?" Katie asked as she reached for the ashtray. "You should go to the dibble and get the twat locked up." Shaun took a deep drag of his cig and shook his head slowly.

"Nar Katie, that's not my style. He'll get what's coming to him, don't you worry. I've told him that as well. My head's fucked at the moment I just need time to think it through." Katie sat by him and placed her hands round his neck. Her eyes filled with tears as she held her brother closer.

"Fucking hell you've had a bad time lately haven't you? Things will get better in time. It's just raw at the moment." As he pulled her hands from round her neck, he could see bruises. He looked at them closer and looked into her eyes.

"Where's the bruises from? Don't even try covering up for him because I can tell by your face it's him that's done them" Katie stood up and made her way to the window. As her body bent over she pulled the net curtain back and looked outside to make sure her boyfriend wasn't in view.

"We had murders the other night. You know what he's like when he's pissed. Don't think I just sit and take it because I don't." Shaun knew he'd upset her and stood up and opened the back door. Katie smiled and turned to him.

"Should we get a few beers? The weather's mint, we can sit in the garden." Katie told him she was skint but he found some cash and told her not to worry. Shaun left to go to the shops and Katie started to clean the garden up and get rid of some of the rubbish.

Katie's house was always clean. She made the most of what she had. She lived on the same estate as her mother and knew her life was set in stone if she didn't try to change it. Brian, her boyfriend, was a big mouth and not a lot of people liked him. He was well known on the estate as a bit of hard man but he was a bully that preyed on vulnerable people. Brian was a grafter and himself and a few others on the estate earned quite a bit of money from the thieving they did.

When Katie first met Brian he seemed nice and she fell head over heels in love with him. He treated her like a princess at first. As time went by Katie was kicked to the kerb by him and his mates took first place in his life. His plastic mates were always there when he'd earned a few bob but as soon as the cash went he was left on his own. His fists didn't start to hit Katie till he started on drugs. Whizz and weed was his life. As soon as he had any cash he was right at the drug dealers' doors. Ged had served him a few times in the past. He was a well know whizz head in the area.

Katie's life was boring. She used to have so many friends but once Brian got his claws into her he made sure one by one they disappeared. She felt alone and her world revolved around him. If she was true to herself, the only reason she stayed with him was because she had nowhere else to go. Sometimes she'd dream of leaving him and finding her Prince Charming. But the grey days she faced every day never seemed to leave her side.

Shaun returned with several cans of beer. He placed them on the table and told her to get one. The neighbour next door leant over the fence. When he saw the beer he invited himself in with his girlfriend. The hours passed and the tunes were pumping from the house. Loads more people had come to join them and the garden party was in full swing. Each visitor brought beer and Katie was pissed as a fart as she danced about in the garden. No one heard Brian come in. He stood at the door with a face like thunder watching every movement she made.

Brian was around six foot tall. He was a large framed man with dark brown hair. He looked angry as he held one hand on the door. Looking at all the other people in the garden he nodded his head and knew one of them would be getting a belt before the night was over. As he turned the music off he could hear the moans from outside. Katie shouted inside the house.

"Get the music back on ya muppet. We're listening to that." Brian appeared at the back door and Katie looked shocked. She could be seen mumbling under her breath as she dropped her head. Katie looked white but the beer she'd drunk gave her courage and she stood tall.

"Brian! Turn it back on will ya. Just because you've come in we're not all gonna sit here in silence." Brian gave her a look to kill and her friends knew it was time to go home. One by one they filtered out of the back gate as he sat at the garden table smoking his weed. Shaun hated the way he could ruin a great night and he sat staring at him. Looking at his sister he knew if he gave her any shit he would be on him like a ton of bricks. Clenching his fist under the table you could see his knuckles turning white. Katie was still in the party mood. She danced her way over to Brian. Her short skirt showed off her long slender legs and she knew she looked good. She shook her arse in a sexual manner at him.

Katie reached over Brian to get her drink from the table. As she did he pulled her hair dragging it to his face.

"You little tart. What the fuck do ya think you're doing strutting ya stuff all around the place? Get in the fucking house ya little slag." As he released his grip on her hair she jumped into his face.

"Fuck off back out, ya fat cunt. Every time you see me having a bit of fun you're always the same. What is it? Can't you stand to see me happy?"

Brian jumped from his chair as it fell to the ground and ran at her. Shaun got up too and this time he was in Brian's face as he tried to capture her. Shaun spoke low at first.

"Leave it out ay. She was only having a bit of fun." Brian's face raged. You could see his nostrils flaring with temper. Shaun knew he'd have to fight him now and prepared for him by pulling his small penknife from his pocket. Brian grabbed him and tried head butting him, but Shaun's blade connected. Shaun was quick and continued slashing him. Brian felt the blood on his face and lifted his hand up to wipe the blood that was trickling down. As his hand came back down he looked at his hand covered in blood and became like a caged animal. The penknife was now out in full view and Shaun waved it into his face.

"Come on prick. I'll fucking kill ya. You think you can take the piss out my sister do ya?" Their eyes locked and Brian sprung on him like a lion attacking his prey. Within minutes Shaun was on the floor and Brian was knocking ten tons of shit out of him. Katie was screaming as she tried to free her brother but she was weak and couldn't move him. Shaun's head could be seen being knocked from side to side and blood hung from his mouth. Brian wanted to hurt him bad but knew he'd had enough. As Brian stood up he gave Shaun one last kick to his body. Katie was at the side of him ragging his arm begging him to stop. Brian gripped her face and shouted into it.

"See what happens when ya think you can take the piss out of me. I'll destroy anything that gets in my way including you. Do ya hear me?" Her body shook with fear as she stood on her tiptoes at the side of him. He spat in her face and went inside. Running straight to Shaun's side, Katie tried to help him up. His eyes were swollen and blood ran from his nose. She sobbed.

"I'm sorry, he's a prick. Just fuck off from here otherwise he'll come back out for you. You know what he's like. Go to me mam's. As soon as he's asleep I'll be round and see ya." His body struggled to get up and the neighbour next door came in to give him a hand. The man checked Brian was gone and spoke to her in a distraught tone.

"Katie why the fuck you stay with someone like that is beyond me. He's a fucking nutter. Look what he's done to ya brother." Katie was ashamed and felt guilty. She hung her head low and watched Shaun being led out of the back gate. Standing for a minute she looked deep in thought. Entering the house she could see Brian sat watching the television as if nothing had happened. Her blood was boiling and she knew her next move.

On the table lay a big marble ashtray. Slowly she turned and made sure the back door was still open. She positioned herself at the side of him and slowly reached for the ashtray. Bringing her arm back behind her, she swung it right into the side of his face. Her legs nearly gave way as she ran out the door. She could hear his screams behind her but she never turned back and kept running.

Shaun could be seen in the distance and Katie's legs just about carried her towards him. "Run, fucking run!" she shouted. As she reached Shaun she told him what she'd done. The neighbour now left them both and crossed the road back to his house. He looked scared and didn't want to be a part of it any longer.

They both headed to their mother's house. Once inside they locked all the doors because they knew within minutes Brian would be there. Gladys was sat watching TV and when she saw the state of them both her heart was pounding.

"What the bloody hell has gone on?" She jumped from her chair and grabbed Shaun. "Oh fucking hell Shaun. Look at your face." Cupping his face she ran into the kitchen to get her first-aid kit. She could be heard shouting and she always made things ten times worse than they were. When she returned with the first aid kit, she opened it on the chair and started to pull out all the bandages. Shaun was angry and told her straight.

"Mam will ya fuck off with all ya shit. I don't need any fucking bandages. It looks worst than what it is. It's only a black eye." She didn't listen and tried to get a further look at him.

"I don't care. It still needs medical attention. Do you need an ambulance?" Katie stood at the back window like a soldier on guard. Gladys was running about the room now and she came to Katie's side. Katie told Gladys what had happened. Her mother's face was angry, "Oh I hope the fat cunt comes here," Gladys ranted, "He will get a piece of my mind."

Katie shook her head. "Mam you're full of shit. When he comes, you will be up his arse like you always are. It's always the same. He kicks fuck out of me and you always send me back to him." Gladys huffed, and stood tall shaking her head.

"I send you back because it's always your fault. You and your big mouth!" Katie looked upset.

"Mam I'm your daughter. How can you send me back to him, when ya know exactly what he does to me? Any normal mother would phone the police on him, but not you." Katie mimicked her mother's action from the past. "Oh Brian it doesn't matter what the fuck you do to her as long as she's not bothering me." Katie was being sarcastic and Gladys tried to ignore her but Shaun stepped in.

"She's right mam. Ya need to fuck him off if he comes here for her. Do ya hear me?" Walking for her cigs Gladys huffed.

"Oh I might have known I would be to blame for this. What about your father? He's got a quiet life, no fucking mither. I'm expected to do everything, right? Well I'm sick of it." She sat at the table with her head held in her hands as she cried. "Why can't I have fucking normal kids who don't bring any trouble to my door?" Katie looked at Shaun and they both knew she was on one. If Brian wasn't walking up road, Katie would have reeled off her years of frustration.

"Shaun! He's here. Fucking hell what we gonna do." Shaun ran about the house looking for some kind of weapon. He came back in the front room with an old stick from under the stairs. Gladys was shaking and telling them she didn't need all the stress but it was too late as Shaun opened the door and stood waiting for him to enter the garden. Katie grabbed an old hockey stick and together they knew they could take him. Gladys locked the door behind them and phoned the police as quickly as she could. Once the call was made she ran back to the door and opened it. She could see Brian just coming in the gate. Shaun and Katie had their tools ready. Brian clocked them and laughed.

"What the fuck do ya think ya gonna do with them. I'll shove em up ya arses if ya don't put them down." Shaun looked edgy.

"Ya won't do shit mate," Shaun replied shakily. Gladys was now out in the garden and she was in Brian's face.

"Look at my son's face, ya big fat cunt. I've phoned the

police so fuck off before they come for you." Brian was confident. He looked over to Katie as he spoke to Gladys.

"I'm not going anywhere until she comes with me. Trust me Gladys, if she doesn't come I'll make ya life a misery." Turning her head Gladys gave Katie the eyes as if it was all her fault again. Katie stood closer to Shaun and shook her head saying.

"Nah, not this time Brian. You can fuck off. You think you can treat me like shit. I'm not putting up with it anymore." Brian hunched his shoulders. He looked ready to make a move.

"Don't be smart Katie. Just because you think you have some backup with you. I'll still waste you ya know." The four of them stood waiting for someone to make the first move, but they all remained frozen.

The police finally arrived and moved Brian on. They wanted Shaun and Katie to press charges against him for assault but they both said no. Grassing was the lowest of the low in Harpurhey and no matter what happened no one wanted to be called a snitch.

Brian screamed out as the police took him. He shouted to Katie that he would be back for her. His words sent shivers down her spine but she tried not to look bothered. All the neighbours were out in full force. They stood gossiping amongst themselves. Gladys looked at Katie and raised her eyebrows.

"You happy now? All the estate are talking about us again." Katie wanted to open fire on her but she was used to her moaning ways and just left her to go back into the house. Shaun and Katie stood with a few people from the estate and filled them in on all the finer details. They all knew Brian of old and told Katie to watch her back in future.

Shaun felt sick and went back into the house with Katie following behind him. The front room looked dirty and clothes were scattered about. Half drunken cups of tea were on the table and the ash tray was filled with cig ends. Shaun went into the kitchen and started washing his face. Gladys just sat watching television and completely ignored Katie.

Once Shaun returned Gladys examined his face as he tried to push her away. She managed to get some Savlon cream on his cuts. He sat moaning as his face started stinging with the antiseptic. Katie watched her mother with Shaun and wondered why she wasn't treated the same. All her life she'd had to fight for any affection from her. Her heart sunk as she tried to straighten the front room up. As she reached for the cups from the table her mother ignored her again and acted like she wasn't there. Shaun could see it too and gripped Katie's shoulder.

"You're gonna be alright ya know. I'll make sure of it. You can't go back to him Katie, you'll end up dead." Katie's eyes filled up and she knew he was right. They both discussed the options and it was decided they would both move back into their mother's house. When they told Gladys the news, she couldn't hide her disappointment. She paced round front room huffing and puffing and made several remarks.

"Well if you're staying here I'll need some keep. Money doesn't grow on trees you know!" Shaun searched his pocket and pulled out two twenty pound notes. Once he'd passed her the money her face changed but she still carried on moaning.

"What's gonna happen if he comes again? I can't be doing with this every night, so you better sort it out Katie. Do you hear me?" Shaun stepped in before Kate blew her temper as he could see her face going red.

"Mam, what the fuck can she do about him? We'll just have to keep phoning the police if he turns up again, won't we?" Gladys rocked in her chair and somehow Katie knew she wouldn't be staying long with her. They were like chalk and cheese and they both just about tolerated each other.

That night all the family were back together. When Paul came home from work and saw them there he was distraught knowing what had gone on. Gladys was still playing the victim and walked round the front room telling her side of the story.

Over the next few nights Brian rang the house phone several times throughout the late hours. There were even bricks thrown at the windows but still Katie remained safe and away from his grip.

Shaun spent some time thinking over the last few weeks and he'd decided he was going back to Blackpool to start drug dealing from there again. It would be a chance to make a fresh start after Lauren but first he had to get in touch with Colby as he didn't want to do it alone

Chapter Eleven

Colby and Shaun were on the train heading back to Blackpool. They'd already found somewhere to stay up there. The new phone was already set up and ready to take calls. The lads they knew from years before had helped them sort it out and everything was set when they arrived.

Colby had stolen Ged's drugs from the flat. Once Ged found out he knew he would be a dead man. The sound of the train moving along was peaceful and Shaun closed his eyes as he touched the pebble in his pocket. His friend beside him looked a lot older. His once big afro hairdo was now shaven to the bone. Colby had lost a fair amount of weight and Shaun had asked on several occasions if he'd been dabbling in smack. Colby was angry and sat at the side of him waving his arms in his face defending himself.

"You cheeky cunt. What ya saying? That I look like a bag-head?" Shaun smiled and knew he'd hurt his feelings.

"Nar, I just thought I'd ask that's all. Come on let's face it. You've lost pure weight though." Colby pulled his sleeves up and looked at his arms. They did look thin and he admitted that he'd not been eating properly for a while. His face looked distressed as he spoke.

"It's all the shit that's gone on with you and Ged. I've lost my appetite ya know. Fucking hell I still can't get a grip of what he did to Lauren." Mention of her name plunged Shaun into sorrow. He patted Colby's leg.

"Ged's a twat and as I've told him, he'll be paid back for what he did to her. I don't know how and I don't know when but believe me, the twat will pay." Colby listened to his words and nodded. He was now paranoid over his weight and pulled his jeans up looking at his scrawny legs.

Once they arrived in Blackpool, the lads ordered a taxi to take them to the house where they were staying. The sun was shining and lots of holiday-makers were out and about. As they passed the funfair they could hear the screams of people enjoying themselves. Shaun remembered the few family holidays he'd had as a child and smiled as he remembered his mam running up the beach away from the sea water. Colby didn't have good memories of Blackpool and as soon as he got off the train the vision of Shaky and the things he'd done to him in the past came flooding back. He never spoke about how he felt inside and sometimes he'd even thought about ending his life because he still felt dirty inside.

Pulling up outside the house Shaun paid the taxi fare. They both picked up their bags containing their clothes and stood rapping at the door. A blonde girl opened it and looked at them with a smile.

"Oh you must be Shaun and Colby. The guys are expecting you. Come in." They both walked into the house and headed into the front room. A few familiar faces were present and Shaun nodded his head at them. Within minutes the drugs Colby had brought with him were on the table and the lads were bagging it up. The mobile phone was ringing constantly and the dealers were taking orders before they were bagged.

The night went on and the blonde woman from earlier had taken a shine to Shaun. He'd checked her history out with the lads and she seemed a nice girl. She wasn't a junkie and she didn't do drugs they told him. He found it hard to believe because she was staying at the house. Shaun sat by her side and started to find out for himself.

"What's ya name then?" As she looked at him she smiled and said.

"Becky. What do ya want to know for?" He started to tickle her side and loved her dry sense of humour.

"I want to know because I think you're sexy and I wouldn't mind ragging ya fanny about, that's why." She giggled and fluttered her eyelashes at him.

"Well think again. I'm not dirty. I'm a good girl." Shaun could see she was a bit hurt by his words and tried to make amends.

"I'm only joking, mard arse. I just wanted to start a conversation with you that's all." Becky smiled and introduced herself. She was twenty and had long blonde hair. Her figure was fantastic. Her big tits made Shaun's eyes nearly pop out of their sockets. Shaun carried on talking to her and asked her about her background. Becky told him she was a lap dancer in a club in the city centre. She also told him a little about her past and how she'd run away from home at the age of fifteen. His eyes were hypnotised by her and he watched her mouth moving as she spoke.

"It's been hard you know. I've lived everywhere. The job I'm doing is alright, but there are too many perverts out there now. When I was sixteen I used to get the odd punter having a feel of me every now and then but these days they're all over you like flies round shit."

Shaun laughed and carried on finding out more about her. She asked him to come into the nightclub where she was dancing tonight and he agreed. He was buzzing with her and told Colby about the arrangement for the night. He asked him to come along with him but Colby was unsure of what he wanted to do.

As the day went on Shaun took care of business. He got in touch with his suppliers and sorted out the arrangement for getting more drugs on the streets. The main supplier was called Bobby and he knew him from years before. Bobby was just a runner to start with but now he looked like he was doing well for himself. He drove a silver BMW and wore all the smart clobber. He'd even opened a few sunbed shops in the area. Shaun looked at him and knew one day he wanted the life Bobby lived. The deal was done and Shaun headed back home to get ready to go and watch Becky dance at the club.

Shaun had so many ideas in his head. He was thinking of other ways to make some money. As he entered the house Colby greeted him. His face looked wrecked and he could tell he'd been smoking weed again. Shaun shook his head and sat on the arm of the chair.

"What the fuck are ya smoking weed for again. I thought you'd given it up." Colby shook his head.

"Nar mate. I need it to get through the day. It chills me out." Looking around the front room Shaun noticed a young lad around fourteen years of age sat in the corner. His eyes looked dark underneath and his skin looked grey. His knees were pulled up to his chest and his jumper was pulled over his knees as if he was cold. Shaun looked at him more closely and asked Colby in a whispering voice who the lad was. Colby told him and didn't care his voice was pretty loud.

"He's a fucking rent boy man. Jerry's just told me. I couldn't believe it either." Jerry was nearby and heard the conversation. As Shaun looked over to him he nodded and made a funny gay gesture with his hand. Shaun huffed.

"Fuck me he's only a baby. What's he doing here anyway?" Colby passed the lad a bag of heroin and took the money from his hand. Shaun felt sick inside. The lad walked past him and nodded. Once they heard the door slam behind him Jerry couldn't wait to dish the dirt on him.

"Yeah he's a fucking rent boy. He's been on gear since he was twelve. Tell ya what though he earns pure cash because he's always here for brown at least three or four times a day. You should hear some of the stories he has to tell you. He's had a fucking hard life."

Colby was sat up in the chair as he puffed on his spliff. He looked at Shaun and screwed his face up at Jerry.

"Go on then, don't tell us half a story. What do ya know about him?" Jerry kept on mixing the drugs on the table and began to tell them what he knew about Lenny.

"I believe his mam was a baghead and when he was ten or summat like that she started to let her punters have a feel of him for extra cash." Shaun's mouth dropped as he listened further. "She was a prostitute herself and didn't give a fuck about him most of the time. Anyway, " he paused as he sat back in his seat, "she started to sell his arse to get the money she needed for gear"

"Fuck off!" Shaun shouted. "No way am I having that. I mean what kind of mother would sell their son's body for money." Jerry looked at him and rolled his eyes.

"Mate, we're talking about addicts now. They will do owt for a fix. Fucking hell, when ya gonna wake up and smell the coffee." Colby was pissing himself laughing at the side of him and Shaun felt daft. He defended himself.

"Fucking hell what ya laughing at? How the fuck am I supposed to know every fucker's background?"

Colby lay back in his chair and his face changed. He looked sad as the words came from his mouth.

"There are some sick bastards out there Shaun. Everyone has a story to tell. You don't have to be a baghead to have shit happen to you" Shaun knew exactly what he meant and took the conversation back to Jerry.

"So what happened to Lenny's mam, surely she got
arrested or summat?" Jerry chewed on his lips and hunched
his shoulders.

"She's still on brown mate. We serve her up sometimes.
I know she got time for whatever happened to Lenny, but
she denies it all if you ask her." Shaun wanted to know
more.

"So did he get put in care and all that or what?" Jerry
stood up and stretched his arms over his head.

"Yeah mate course, but he just got lost in the system
and ended up running away. He's told us bits about himself,
but only when he's off his head." Jerry lit a cig and plonked
his arse back down on the chair. Blowing the smoke from
his mouth he sighed. "I remember one night in here when
he broke down crying and poured his heart out. Fucking
pulled right on my heartstrings he did."

Shaun felt Lenny's pain and wished he could help him.
As he closed his eyes he could still see his sad face looking
at him. He promised himself that the next time he was
at the house he would have a talk with him and see if he
could help him in any way.

Running upstairs Shaun started to run himself a bath.
The bath was disgusting and he poured some bleach around
the side to try and clean it. The whole house was dirty and
he'd already decided the following day he would clean it
up and try and make it look half decent.

Sitting in the bath he looked in the cracked mirror.
His face looked older than he could last remember. He
was twenty-two now and his boyish face had now turned
into a man's. As he shaved he couldn't stop thinking about
Becky. He liked her and knew there had been some kind
of connection between them both. Lauren was still in his

heart but he only felt anger towards her now.

As he dried his body he flexed his muscles and looked into the mirror. Walking into his bedroom he turned on his CD player and played the only CD he owned. The Smiths started to play and he thought about Lauren again. He wanted to turn it off but the words of the song soothed him in some strange way.

Heading downstairs he popped his head round the door. The lads made comments about the way he was dressed and caused him to check himself over again. He was wearing his black jeans and a tight white t-shirt. He giggled to the lads.

"You two have no dress sense that's all. I'm a fanny magnet and you both know it!"

Laughter filled the room as Shaun strutted his stuff. As he started doing some sexual movements against the door they all pissed themselves laughing. His arse was swaying to and fro and he pretended to smack his own arse as they watched him in fits of laughter.

"Go on fuck off ya gay twat," shouted Colby. Shaun smiled and jumped on him and started kissing his head. He laughed loudly as he tickled him.

"I'll show you who's a gay twat. Come on get ya mouth round this." Shaun stood in front of him and tried to push his head down towards his crutch. Colby's laughter stopped all of a sudden, his mood changed and he broke free. His looked angry. Colby mumbled under his breath as he straightened his clothes.

"I said fucking do one. Ya prick." Shaun still teased him but could see the distress in his eyes so he left him alone. Shaun looked one last time in the mirror and said goodbye. Colby was still sulking and Shaun blew him a kiss just to see if he would laugh. Colby smirked and shook his head.

"Nobhead," he muttered.

Shaun felt on top of the world and was singing The Smiths song he'd just listened to. The sun was still out as he headed to the bar where he'd arranged to meet Becky. As he walked in the music was pumping. He headed straight to the bar and ordered a bottle of Budweiser. The place was packed and he found it difficult to find Becky. Once he'd got his drink he walked towards the dancefloor and from the corner of his eye he saw her. Waving his hand up in the air he finally got her attention.

Becky looked stunning. Her long blonde hair had been curled and her skin looked fresh. She was wearing a small pair of white shorts that just about covered her crotch. Her heels made her tower over him and he felt quite small stood next to her. He was slavering at the mouth as he gawped at her.

"You look mint," he whispered into her ear. Becky smiled and took him over to a table at the back end of the pub. As they reached it she started to introduce him to some of the other girls. All the girls were stunners and Shaun thought he'd died and gone to heaven. They had a certain look about them that you knew they were dancers of some kind. Shaun gulped from his bottle and asked Becky if she wanted another beer. She declined.

"No thanks we're heading over to 'Bare It' now." Becky told him 'Bare It' was the club where she worked. As he walked down the busy promenade he felt special. All the men were looking at the girls and you could hear the girls telling gangs of men where they were going. Some of the wives of the gawping men could be seen punching their men in the side and Shaun laughed to himself.

The Blackpool nightlife was buzzing. Lots of hen and stag parties were out in full force. All the parties had themes.

The girls who'd just walked past them were all dressed as nurses. Becky saw Shaun looking at them and dragged his arm towards her. She joked.

"Ay dirty balls. Don't be looking at other girls when you're with me." He smiled and pulled her closer for a kiss. Her lips felt warm. As he kissed her he could taste her cherry lipstick. Her eyes focused on him and she carried on walking. She held his arm tight as she pulled him closer.

"I have to tell you now Shaun that the men will be all over me tonight. It's only a job ya know. Just remember that and don't be getting the green-eyed monster." His head fell back and he chuckled.

"Get a grip will ya. For fuck's sake I know what you do. I'm not the jealous type anyway." Becky held her head back and laughed.

"Yeah that's what they all say Shaun. Just let's see ay." He held her hand as they walked in the club and the bouncers all let on to her. She introduced Shaun to them and he was made to feel part of the family. Becky showed him where the bar was and told him she was up dancing first so she shouldn't be long. He kissed her on the cheek and watched her leave. Rubbing his hands together he got a drink and headed to the front of the stage. Lots of men were already there and he watched them as he sat down. He was buzzing.

One man caught his eye. He looked twice at him because he thought he knew him. As he looked closer the ginger hair made him realise it was Shaky from the care home. "Fuck me!" he whispered. Shaky looked fatter and his ginger wig was in need of a haircut. He was dressed in some grey pants and a white shirt. As he watched him closer he reminded him of a paedophile. Shaun turned his chair the opposite way and hoped he didn't have to talk to him. He looked uneasy.

The music stopped and the song "Temptation" by Heaven 17 started to play. Shaun's eyes focused on the stage and there she was in all her glory. Becky was dressed in a red bikini. Her silver shoes caught his eyes and as he watched her take the stage as if she owned it, he looked proud. Shaun watched every move she made as he touched his crotch.

Becky's hips gyrated to and fro and at one stage she was sat in front of him with her legs spread apart nearly showing all her fur burger. His cock felt hard in his pants and he wanted to part her tash there and then. The men at the side of where he stood were placing money in Becky's bra. She was like a goddess to them and each of them looked at her with wanting eyes.

As she moved along the platform he could see Shaky searching his pockets. He watched him pull out a note and whistle for her to come over to him. As she walked near him she bent over and looked at him through her legs. She could feel the money being shoved up her arse cheeks and slowly kicked him away with a look of disgust on her face. Shaun wanted to run over and punch his face in but before he knew it Becky was on the other side of the stage still collecting money.

The song seemed to last forever. She finished her last move over near him. Every muscle in her body looked toned and he couldn't wait to be inside her later. As the song finished she winked at him and left the stage. Shaun turned his head to the right and saw Shaky on his phone. He was curious as what he was up to and followed him outside when he saw him leaving.

Shaun lit a cig and stayed in the doorway out of sight. He watched Shaky pacing up and down the street. He looked like he was waiting for someone as he kept checking his watch. A few minutes later he watched him talking to a younger lad. As he watched more closely he could see Shaky grab the lad's arm and drag him closer.

"It's Lenny!" Shaun mumbled.

Taking a deep drag of his cig he followed Shaky round the corner into a dark alleyway. He could hear bits of moaning and didn't want to go any further. Frozen for a second he knew he had to make sure Lenny was alright.

The alleyway was eerie and as he walked further into it, he could see a shadow. Creeping slowly behind him he could see Shaky's pants were halfway down his arse. It wasn't until he got nearer that he could see Lenny bent over the bin with his pants down too. Shaun felt sick and stood on a can that made some noise. He could hear noises in front of him and decided to fuck off back to the club. As he left he was gritting his teeth and clenching his fists. His words were angry as he mumbled under his breath.

"Still the same old Shaky I see. Well you're another one who will get what's coming to them. You dirty bent bastard." Shaun stood in front of the club and lit another cig. His hands were shaking and he was struggling to breathe. "Dirty twat," he snarled. Becky now came to join him.

"I've been looking for you everywhere. I thought you'd fucked off." Shaun tried to laugh but felt sick in the pit of his stomach. One hundred and one things were going round in his mind and he was already planning Shaky's downfall inside his head. He put a smile on his face and tried to act normal.

"I just needed to get some fresh air. Your dancing made me all hot and sweaty." Becky smiled at him and hurried him back inside the club. She was pulling at his arm.

"Come on I've got another three dances to do before

we can leave." He followed her back inside but he kept turning his head watching the exit. Becky guided him to a small office at the back of the club. Once they were inside she locked the door and pulled a small bag of white powder from her bra.

"What's that?" he asked with a soft voice.

"Just a bit of sniff that's all. Do ya want a line or what?"

Shaun felt uneasy. He'd had stuff in the past but nothing as hard as cocaine. He watched everything she did and followed her lead. Within minutes he felt the rush of the white powder. He was on fire and full of life. Becky pulled him closer and kissed him passionately. He could feel her wanting him as she ground her crotch against him. Within a short space of time he was inside her and riding her like the wind. His cock felt like it had a mind of its own. It felt massive as he slid in and out of her. Becky must have had lots of sex in the past because the things she was doing to him set him on fire. He was screaming with pleasure and never wanted it to end. Becky reached orgasm first and he watched her face as she came. Never in a million years had he thought sex could be this good.

They lay entwined on the floor for a while. Shaun smiled over to her and held her hand. Becky started to get ready and told him she was back on stage again soon. He pulled his pants up and held her by the waist.

"That was great. You're one top woman." She tossed her hair back from her face and giggled.

"Ay and that was for free. Imagine if you was paying what you would get." Shaun was shocked and shot her a look.

"What do you mean? Are ya a prostitute as well?" She screwed her face up and waved a finger in his face.

"Am I fuck. I've done some escorting in the past, but not for years now." He looked relieved as he straightened his t-shirt. Before she opened the door she turned back and kissed him.

"I can see me and you are gonna go far together you know." Shaun agreed and headed back into the club. As she left his side he could see Shaky sitting back at the table. He wanted so much to run over to him and punch his face in but he knew he would have to wait. The time would come for him and when it did he wanted Colby to be at his side.

The night went on more or less the same and Shaun snorted more and more lines of cocaine. His jaw was swinging by the end of the night and his eyes looked fucked. Becky was at his side and they decided to go back to the house.

As they walked down the streets the midnight air cooled them down. They were both swaying about and looked as pissed as farts. Becky wanted to know more about Shaun and asked him a bit about his background. He told her about Lauren and his baby and she could see the pain in his eyes as he spoke about her. She gripped his hand as they walked and she told him more about her life.

Becky had some big dreams. She told Shaun she was saving her money to go and live abroad. He looked shocked. She could see his face change and laughed.

"What do you think I dance each night for, the fucking fun of it? I've worked it out, if I dance for another few months I'll have enough to go and find somewhere to live and some money to keep me going until I find work" Shaun's head wobbled as he looked at her. "And what about me? Where do I come into this dream?"

"You can come if you want Shaun. Fucking hell I've

only just met you and you want to be included in my dreams," she huffed. His face was blank as he hunched his shoulders.

As they reached the house he searched his pocket for his key. Once he'd found it he struggled to put it in the door.

"Fucking give it here!" Becky giggled. "You're bobbins." Sliding the key into the lock she could see Shaun flopped against the wall looking like he was going to be sick. "Come on ya piss head," she chuckled. The house was silent as they headed straight upstairs to bed.

Both of them fell onto the bed. They remained fully clothed as they lay in each other's arms. Colby could hear them from the next room and relaxed knowing his friend was back in the house.

★

The following morning Becky rushed to get ready. She had to meet her friend at twelve o'clock. She quickly checked her watch and kissed Shaun on the cheek telling him she would be back later. He tried grabbing her back into bed for a bit more loving but she wriggled free telling him she had to leave. As he listened to the front door closing, the night before came flooding back to him and he remembered seeing Shaky. He tossed and turned and no matter how hard he tried he couldn't get back to sleep.

Lying wide awake he could see the door opening slowly. Colby dipped his head around the door. Once he knew he was alone he ran and jumped onto the bed.

"Where's Becky then? Has she gone home or what?" Shaun nodded his head. He looked rough. Looking at Colby's face he couldn't decide whether to tell him or not. After a few minutes Colby sprawled on the bed at the side of him.

"So what did ya do last night? Was it a good night or what?" Shaun looked in a world of his own and Colby punched him in the arm to wake him up.

"Are you listening to me or what ya muppet?" Shaun realised he was talking to him and answered.

"Yeah fucking top night mate. You should have come out instead of being a boring twat." Colby placed his arms behind his head and fell back onto the bed.

"I got stoned and had a good night with Jerry." Colby made himself comfortable. "So come on what did I miss?" Shaun reached for his pants and grabbed two cigs. He passed one to Colby. Shaun's face looked serious.

"You missed quite a lot mate." Colby was intrigued and watched his face change as he carried on. "I was in the club with Becky. Just watching her dance, and all that," he inhaled deeply on his cig, "as I looked over my shoulder I thought I recognised this bloke who was sat near me." Colby was sat up now, hanging onto his every word. Shaun licked his dry cracked lips and slowly shook his head. "It took me a while but his hair was a dead giveaway. He looks a lot older than I remembered him but I still knew it was him." Colby was frustrated.

"Fucking who? Come on who did you see?" Shaun gulped.

"Shaky."

Colby's face changed. He stood from the bed and marched around the room with the cig hanging out of his mouth. As he looked out of the window, Shaun continued telling him what he'd witnessed with Lenny. Colby was livid.

"The dirty, dirty fucker. Why did you walk away? You should have done him in right there and then." The room was silent as Shaun sat thinking. Colby was now at his side and he wanted to know every last detail about him. Once he knew it all he grabbed Shaun's arm.

"We need to go and see him. We can get hold of Lenny and find out all we can about him. Lenny will help us. I know he will."

Shaun agreed, but Colby was scaring him. He told him he wanted to abduct him and slice the fucker up. Shaun wanted revenge but nothing like Colby was saying. He was happy just to beat him up and all that, he never wanted to kill him. Colby was like a man possessed. He reminded Shaun of all the times he'd stood by him in the past and wanted to be sure he would help him seek Shaky out. Shaun gave him his word but dreaded to think what would happen to Shaky when Colby got his hands on him.

A few days passed and there was still no sign of Lenny. Every phone call that was taken went through Colby. He was feeling at an all time low. He looked depressed all day long.

A few days later there was a knock at the door and Shaun answered. Once he'd looked through the spyhole he could see it was Lenny. Half of him wanted to turn him away but the other half remembered the promise he'd made to his best friend. He looked a mess. He had a black eye and was struggling to walk. Shaun let him inside and brought him straight into the front room. As soon as Colby saw him he was all over him like a rash. Shaun had to tell him to leave him alone for a minute while he sorted the kid out.

"Fucking hell man!" Colby moaned as he sat back down on the chair chewing at his finger nails.

Lenny looked tired. As they examined his face they asked him what had happened. His voice was low and he seemed too weak to speak. Shaun spoke to him as he knelt by his side. Grabbing his hand he spoke with a soft caring voice.

"When was the last time you've had summat to eat?" Lenny shook his head and shrugged his shoulders. Jerry made his way into the kitchen and started to make a ham butty and a glass of milk. Shaun sat by his side and asked again what had happened to his face. They both listen eagerly as he started to tell them.

"It was a punter. I was with him last night. He wouldn't pay me, the slimey cunt. So I pulled a blade on him. I sliced his fucking hand, but it never stopped him from beating me." Colby was sat on the edge of his seat with his body rocking.

Shaun's heart was beating like an express train in his chest and he felt guilty in case it was Shaky who'd done it to him. He urged him to tell him more details.

"Where did it happen? Can you remember round about what time it was?"

Lenny looked worried and became cagey. Colby had to assure him he wasn't in any trouble and told him they just wanted to help him. "It was behind that club 'Bare It' or summat like that." Shaun looked over at Colby and nodded his head. Colby bolted from his chair and dragged his hands in his hair.

"It's him isn't it?" he shook his head and dropped his chin onto his chest as he closed his eyes. Shaun asked Lenny a lot more questions as Colby paced the front room. He eventually found out a lot more about their old friend Shaky. Apparently he was well-known by all the rent boys. He was known as "The Rammer." The lads had given him that nickname because whenever they were having anal sex with him he always rammed his cock in. Colby felt sick inside but needed to know more. He was onto it now and began firing questions.

"Where does he drink? Do you see him all the time?"

Lenny was now eating his sandwich and struggled to speak with a full mouth. He nodded his head at them both. "Let him have summat to eat first, then he can speak to us," Shaun pleaded. Colby sat back down. Kicking his shoes off he brought his feet up beside him.

Lenny eventually told them everything they needed to know about Shaky and within minutes Colby was thinking about setting up a meet with him. He spoke calmly to Lenny. He held a cunning look in his eyes.

"Lenny. I need you to let me know the next time he wants to see you. As soon as he does, give me a ring and I'll take it from there." Lenny looked scared. Colby grabbed his hand and reassured him that he wasn't in any kind of trouble. "We just need you to get him to a certain place for us that's all. Then you can fuck off." Lenny wanted to know more and tried to ask questions but Colby shut him up by throwing him a bag of smack.

Shaun sat thinking and knew it was too late to turn back. He would have to see it through. He listened to Colby and agreed with all his plans.

Chapter Twelve

Lenny stood in his usual spot waiting for punters. The night was warm as he wore his white shorts and pink shirt. His body looked weak and tired. Lenny held his arms round his shoulders as he looked around the area. This spot was a local haunt for the rent boys in the area. The crowds of tourists who walked past him were unaware of his trade.

Blackpool was alive and kicking. The noise of people having fun filled the air. Lenny had just scored and his eyes looked pinned. His words were slurred as he spoke to another rent-boy stood not far from him.

"Yo, Mark. What time you working until? There is a party at Jonas' later if ya fancy it?" The other lad shook his head as he come closer.

"I'm not arsed tonight mate. Just want to get home as quick as I can." Lenny smiled at him and watched as he saw a familiar face approaching. He shouted over to his mate before the punter got any closer.

"Fucking hell. That's all I need to start my night. It's the Rammer." The lad smiled and watched him getting closer. Shaky looked like a fat, scruffy pervert. He just had that look across his face that made him look like a wrong 'un. Lenny's face changed and he remembered what Colby had told him. He knew if he was to set the fat cunt up he would definitely get some brown off the lads as a reward. He quickly dipped into his pocket for his phone and searched for the number. Once he found it he turned his face away from Shaky who was nearly at his side and spoke with speed.

"Ay mate, he's here. I'm outside 'Bare It'." I'll take him to the entry behind it. You better hurry up though. I don't know how long I can keep him there." Lenny shoved the phone back in his pocket. Colby could be heard speaking but Lenny cut him off. Shaky placed his hand on Lenny's shoulder. As he turned to face him his heart was pumping.

"Hello. What you after?" Lenny asked. Shaky looked at him with an evil look in his eyes and tried to pull him away. Lenny struggled and spoke.

"No way am I moving till you pay me. Remember last time?" Shaky looked blank as Lenny pointed to his eye. It still had some traces of bruises around it. Searching in his pockets, the punter pulled out a roll of crumpled notes. As he counted it out in the dark doorway he wafted £20 in front of his nose.

"That's how much you charge isn't it?" He threw the crumpled notes at Lenny. "Well come on then you better fucking earn it." Shaky watched as Lenny picked the money up from the floor. Screwing his face up he looked around the area hoping the lads would be here soon. He hated Shaky with a vengeance and prayed he would get a chance to kick the fucker while he was down. Shaky's breath was stale and Lenny screwed his face up as he spoke to him.

"Okay, okay. What's the rush? Have you never heard of romance?" Lenny cheekily smiled as his lips trembled. Giving one last glance over his shoulder he slowly headed to their destination. "Hurry up lads, please!" he whispered as he trudged away from the street.

Once in the dark deserted alley he could see Shaky undoing his large black leather belt. He had one arm on a nearby bin balancing as he slid his pants down over his arse cheeks. Lenny watched him like a hawk as he summoned him closer. His voice was chilling.

"Here, get this in your mouth for a minute. I need warming up." Lenny could see his cock nesting in his pubic hair and fell to his knees at his side. His mind was far from together. He looked desperate as his hands found the man's penis.

The taste of the man's cock made him heave. He could smell sweat and shit as he grabbed hold of the penis to suck him off. Shaky held his body up against the wall. His hands gripped tightly round Lenny's head. The rent boy looked distressed. A noise from the distance made Shaky freeze. As he held Lenny's head still in his hands he lifted his head up and looked into the darkness. The lighting was poor and all he could see were shadows at the end of the alley.

Shaky's eyes searched further into the darkness. Once he was sure he wasn't being watched he urged the rent boy to continue. His eyes were closed firmly and he was enjoying the gobble. Lenny carried on sucking him off but as his head turned to the side he could see the feet of two men. The trainers he saw told him help had arrived. Colby spoke.

"You dirty cunt!"

Colby now stood in front of him as Shaky opened his eyes in shock. Shaky threw Lenny to the floor and tried to pull his pants up with one hand. Shaun stood still and watched as Lenny ran off.

"You don't remember me do you?"

Shaky shook from head to toe and tried to focus on the face in front of him. Shaun came into view now and held his head low. Colby had a menacing look in his eyes and his teeth were grinding together.

"I see you're still abusing young boys then. Some things never change do they?" Colby chuckled. Shaky looked at his face in more detail and it clicked who he was.

"Colby, bloody hell it's been years hasn't it?" he now looked to Shaun and recognised him too.

"Fucking hell Shaun. You haven't changed one bit either. How are you two doing anyway?"

Colby neared him and gripped his shirt with his hand pressing him up against the brick wall. Their noses were touching as he ranted into his face.

"How the fuck are we doing? Ya dirty bastard. I'll show you how we're doing."

Shaky fell to the ground with a knockout punch as Colby kicked ten tons of shit out of him. Shaun paced the floor and knew if he didn't stop his friend soon he would surely kill him. Shaky's screams could be heard and Colby placed his hand over his mouth as he leant over him.

"I should fucking kill you, shouldn't I? And leave you here to rot. You dirty bastard!"

Shaun stepped in and slowly pulled the back of his jacket. Colby loosened his grip and stood up. He quickly gave Shaun instructions.

"Right, make sure no one comes down here. You fuck off, I've just got a few things that need saying before I'm finished with him." Shaky was rolling around in pain. He was gripping his stomach screaming that he couldn't breathe.

Shaun jogged down the alley and kept turning back as he heard the sounds of more punches being thrown. Once Colby knew he was out of sight he dragged Shaky up by the scruff off his neck.

"You have ruined my life ya know? Every night when I go to sleep all I see is your fat ugly face." Shaky's face was swelling already. You could barely see his eyes. Colby turned him on his side and ragged his pants down.

"Let's see how you like being bummed ay." Shaky

made no attempt to fight back. His body was still as Colby shoved his cock up his arse. With each stroke into him he pummelled his head and before long Shaky was lifeless. When he'd finished he pulled his track suit bottoms up and stood over the body. He was sobbing.

"I should cut ya nob off shouldn't I? That way you'll never abuse anyone again would ya?" His foot swung back and with one almighty kick he sunk it into his head. Colby walked away and started to jog as he came to the end of the road. Once he arrived on the street he searched for Shaun. Every inch of his body was shaking and he couldn't think straight.

Shaun saw him coming out of the entry and quickly ran to his side gripping his arm.

"Fucking hell mate. You nearly killed the fucker. Are you alright, you look weird?" Colby was sweating and his fists were still clenched. Shaun could see blood all over his hands and looked at him with a concerned face.

"You didn't kill him did ya?" Colby was walking away and remained silent as Shaun asked him again. This time Colby stopped dead in his tracks and looked him in the face.

"I fucking hope so. He deserves to be dead."

Colby searched his pockets with shaking hands and couldn't find a cig and asked Shaun for one. Once he passed him one they sat on a nearby wall. The traffic seemed quiet on the roads. Every passer-by seemed to know their sins as they looked at their faces. Holding his head with one hand he took a deep drag of his cig. He spoke to Shaun.

"I think he's dead ya know. We'll have to fuck off back to Manchester until things have quietened down."

Shaun stood up from the wall and pushed Colby's shoulder with one arm.

"What the fuck do you mean go back to Manchester. He can't be dead .You just gave him a few digs that's all. Didn't you?" Shaun was bouncing about kicking the floor. Colby shook his head and spoke in a low voice.

"I've give him what he deserved. Are you forgetting what he did to me? If he's dead, so fucking what. I don't give a flying fuck." Colby spat on the floor as his temper exploded. Shaun looked at him in disbelief and left his side. He motored back to the alleyway and he ran back to where the attack took place.

He crept back to the body. Once he was stood above Shaky his right foot tried to move him. His breathing was rapid as he bent down and pulled Shaky's body over so he could see his face. The body rolled over and Shaun covered his mouth with both his hands. Slowly he bent down and shook the lifeless man in front of him. He lifted his eyelids and tried blowing in his eyes to see if there was any sign of life. His head quickly swivelled as he heard a voice shouting from a nearby window that overlooked the alleyway. It was a woman's voice.

"I've seen it all don't worry. I've phoned the police. You dirty no good bastard." Shaun panicked and ran as his head turned he could see a woman hanging from the window watching him flee from the dead body. His pace quickened and he ran back to Colby who was still sat on the wall. Running past him he shouted.

"Quick, fucking do one. Someone's phoned the dibble." Colby seemed in a trance and it took a moment for him to stand to his feet. Shaun jogged on the spot and ranted.

"For fuck's sake, move ya arse." Shaun ran back and grabbed him. They both ran off with speed down the back streets pulling their hoods up in the process. Sirens could be heard in the distance. When they were out of sight Shaun pinned Colby up against the wall.

"You daft twat. I thought you said you were only gonna give him a few digs. He's fucking dead ya prick!" Colby broke free and jumped about in front of him.

"So fucking what. He deserves to be dead. Are you forgetting what he did to me?" Shaun ran at him and flung him to the floor.

"I don't give a fuck. I'm not going to jail for murder. Arrrggghh." Colby was screaming at him, his voice was loud.

"Ay nobhead! Who was there when you needed him, ay? When everyone else fucked you off. Yeah me. No fucker else. If you want to get off, go on fuck off. I can deal with this on my own." Shaun stood and was looking from left to right scanning the area. He spoke in a distressed voice.

"Just let's get back to the house ay. We need to get away from here as soon as possible. Fucking hell I don't believe this mess."

They both hurried back to the house. As soon as they got through the front door Shaun told Colby to get his stuff together. He quickly searched the kitchen drawers and shoved a screwdriver in his pocket.

Entering his bedroom Shaun grabbed his bag and opened the wardrobe. He grabbed all his clothes and threw them into the open bag. His face was sweating and he was mumbling under his breath. Colby now stood at the doorway and watched his every movement. Shaun knew he had his reasons for what he'd done but still wanted to waste him. He grabbed his last remaining trainers from the floor and headed downstairs.

As they entered the front room he told the lads to manage the phone for the drugs and he would be back soon. He didn't give them chance to ask any questions.

He quickly left the house slamming the door behind him. Shaun looked at all the parked cars. He handed Colby his bag as he approached a black car not far from them. Colby could now see him shoving the screwdriver into the door and within seconds he was inside it.

The car screeched at the side of him. Colby picked the bags up from the floor before he jumped inside. Shaun checked his rear view mirror and quickly headed towards the motorway. As they drove down the side streets Colby slouched into his seat. The car radio played music. As he listened more carefully he could hear one of his favourite tunes playing. The Smiths were singing "There is a light that never goes out." Turning the volume up to full blast he sang along to the words. The song had so many memories for him. He felt a wave of sadness ride through his body. Tears were running down his cheek. Colby knew his mate was still angry with him and tried to make amends. He turned to face him as he watched him drive.

"We should be alright ya know. It's our secret. No one else has to ever know do they?" Shaun kept his eyes on the road and carried on singing. When the song had finished he turned the volume down and answered him.

"I just hope that woman didn't get a good glimpse of me otherwise I'm fucked." Colby placed has hand on his shoulder and squeezed it. His face was looking straight at him.

"I owe you big time ya know. If there's anything you need. Anything you want I'll always be there for you." Shaun nodded and moved lanes on the motorway. Colby sighed and mumbled.

"Fucking hell. I forgot about Ged. He will be out for my blood when he knows I'm back. I nicked his shit didn't I?" The sound of Ged's name made Shaun sit up straight.

He looked as if he was thinking and finally spoke after a few minutes.

"Fuck the tosser. Let him come. I'm sure we can sort him out, he's a prick." Colby banged the dashboard and agreed. Lighting a spliff he pushed his seat back and lay back getting stoned.

Manchester was minutes away and Shaun phoned his mam to ask if they could get their heads down at her house for tonight. Gladys was asking lots of questions but agreed for them both to stay there. Driving through Harpurhey brought a smile to Shaun's face. He felt a warmth ride through his bones as he looked at the familiar landmarks. He was home.

The back door was open when they got to his house. Gladys was sat in the chair with a worried look on her face. The old familiar cardigan she always wore was draped from her shoulders like a blanket of despair. Her eyes focused on them both as they entered. As she saw her son's face she knew she couldn't interrogate him as he looked tired and ready for bed. Shaun smiled at her.

"Mam do me and Colby a butty will ya. We've not had chance to grab owt to eat." Gladys pulled her frail body from the chair and headed into the kitchen. Once he heard her making the sandwich he whispered to Colby.

"Right let's have a quick look at the news and see if there's anything on about it. I'm sure the news is on at this time." Colby moved to his side and watched as he searched through the channels. Gladys returned into the room carrying two plates. She passed them to the lads and sat at the dining table situated at the back of the room watching them. Lighting her cig she made conversation.

"Told you Katie would go back with him didn't I? A few days after you fucked off she went back." Her face looked anxious. "I've not heard from her for weeks." Shaun wasn't listening properly as his eyes were focused on the TV screen. He slowly turned from the television and asked Gladys what she had just said. She huffed and repeated herself.

"Fucking deaf lugs, I said your sister didn't last long. She's back with that bastard again. I think he had a big graft and you know how he promises her the world when he's got money." Shaun shook his head and asked where Paul was. Once she'd told him he'd moved in with his girlfriend he started to relax. They all sat discussing the latest gossip. Shaun nearly collapsed when she told him Ged was in jail for supplying drugs.

Colby smiled from cheek to cheek when he heard the news. He asked her lots more questions to ease his mind. When she told him he'd got three years shoved up his arse he winked at Shaun and listened as Gladys rambled on.

"Apparently they caught him bang to rights. They busted the flat and got loads of drugs and money. They even got firearms so it said in the newspaper." Her head was in the air as she preached to them both. "Well I think he deserves everything he gets, fucking killing people with his drugs." Shaun knew what she was on about. She was just about to start another lecture but he stopped her dead in her tracks.

"Right mam. For fuck's sake. Why do you always go over the top? The guy just got caught selling drugs that's all." His mother stood up and placed her hand on her hip as she emptied the ashtray.

"Drugs are the lowest of the low. They fuck so many people lives up. Look at your friend Mark. He was such a lovely lad ya know. His mother's at her wits end with him these days. He's robbed anything she had of value. So don't you try and defend that Ged. He's a fucking scumbag."

Colby dipped his head as Shaun smiled at him. He felt daft the way his mam was going on and told her to shut up and go to bed. Gladys screwed up her face and spoke as she left the room.

"I'm entitled to my opinion. I still think he's a drug dealing bastard. I hope he rots in jail." Shaun told her to fuck off to bed again and this time he glared at her to let her know he was getting angry. She said goodnight to the boys. They listened as they heard her plod up the stairs to bed.

Shaun munched his butty and lifted the bread up to look at its contents. His mam could always make a good sandwich. He loved the way she threw loads of dressings all over the salad.

Both lads looked tired and after a few minutes Shaun turned the lights off and headed to bed with his partner in crime following closely behind him. The lighting was poor as they walked up the stairs. Shaun held the banister and guided himself to the top. As he opened his old bedroom door he smiled. Everything was the same as he'd left it. Kicking his shoes off he told Colby he would have to get his head down on the floor. Shaun passed him a blanket and a pillow.

Shaun snuggled into his bed and smelt the bedding. They smelt so clean and fresh and a million miles away from the ones he had got used to. Reaching down into his jeans he gripped his small pebble and stroked it slowly. His body turned to face the wall. He could still hear Colby fidgeting about on the floor at the side of him. Shaun's head was on fire with thoughts and he knew the police would find them sooner or later. He prayed they would get away with the crime they'd committed but he knew deep down inside they were on borrowed time. The pebble felt cold in his hands and he slowly rubbed it up and down on his cheek.

Chapter Thirteen

Lenny sat in the police cell and his body was rattling from head to toe. After all the investigations the police had arrested him knowing he was the last person to have been seen with the dead man. Lenny was the prime-suspect for the murder. He was shitting himself.

Lenny had been held in police custody for over forty-eight hours now. The drugs he needed were making his body feel weird. His forehead was covered in rivulets of sweat when the investigating officer came into the interview room to join him. The murder detective knew it wouldn't be long before he got the smackhead to squeal like a pig.

DCI Jordan sat down with his colleague at the side of the young lad. He told Lenny about the procedure and switched the tape recorder on. The officer was used to dealing with roasting heroin addicts and knew the rent boy was nearly at breaking point. He watched as Lenny nervously fidgeted about with his fingers. The interview began.

"So Lenny, do you want to tell me again what happened on the night this man was murdered." He showed Lenny a picture of the victim. DCI Jordan placed the photo back on the table and continued as he saw the distress in the suspect's face.

"Because," he paused as his eyes focused on Lenny, "at the moment it looks like you're going to prison for a long, long time." Lenny sunk his head onto the table and rocked about. He looked like he was in pain as he gripped his stomach. His eyes looked like they were rolling about. He couldn't focus for long. Lenny closed his eyes and chewed on his bottom lip. The officer prompted him again.

"Lenny, if you tell us everything you know you could be out of here within a couple of hours. I know you're roasting mate, so do yourself a favour."

Lenny lifted his head up and gripped his hair. His fingers ran through his greasy hair. He was desperate as he spoke. "I've told you before. Fucking hell what more can I do. He was a punter that's all. We did the business and I fucked off and left him." DCI Jordan knew he was covering something up and asked him again. This time he meant business.

"Lenny you know what happened, so just tell us. Why are you denying you don't know anything?" The other officer tapped his pen on the table and looked at Lenny with a concerned look. The lad he saw in front of him was still a child and part of him felt sorry for him. The two officers were ready to turn the tape off when Lenny broke. He was at his wits' end.

"Wait. Don't go. Just give me a few minutes." They both looked at each other and knew they'd struck gold. Patiently they sat there and waited for the grass to start talking again. Lenny asked for a drink and a cig before he started and they were only too happy to oblige.

The water cooled Lenny down. He gulped it back in one mouthful. They watched him carefully as he pulled at his sweat drenched t-shirt in front of them. He was roasting his nuts off. Lighting the cig he shook his head slowly and blew a laboured breath. Lenny's hand was trembling as he tried to take a drag of his cig. The officers were eager for him to start talking and switched the tape back on and repeated the legal procedure.

"When you're ready, Lenny," DCI Jordan coaxed. All eyes were on him now.

Lenny folded his arms under his chin and rested on the table as his feet kicked into the floor. He took a deep breath and gasped. "I just phoned them when he was there. That's all they wanted me to do. As soon as he come, I fucked off." The officer looked shocked and prompted him to continue. He was on the ball now and wanted more information.

"Who fucked off?" You could see Lenny biting down on his lip as he continued.

"The two guys from Manchester. I'm not sure what their names are. I just get my drugs from them that's all. Can I go now or what?" Lenny stood up from his chair and paced the floor. He didn't look well.

The two investigating officers leant back in their chairs. PC Jordan explained to him he would need more details about the suspects. At first Lenny wasn't giving anything away, but once he heard he could be out on bail before the night was through he gave them all they needed to know. He was singing like a Canary. Once the interview was over Lenny knew he'd betrayed the lads. His body was shaking rapidly and the officers agreed for him to see the on-call doctor before they continued. Lenny looked like death warmed up.

Within a few hours the house in Blackpool was raided and everyone was arrested. The police found a substantial amount of money and drugs. Lenny finally told the police everything they needed to know and once the other lads from the house were in the police station too it was confirmed who the suspects were. The police had the names of the murderers.

The Preston police worked together with the

Manchester force and in the early hours of the morning a
warrant was issued for Colby and Shaun's arrest.

★

The following night Shaun hadn't been asleep long when
he heard someone banging at the front door. He quickly
jumped from his bed and nearly fell over. He flapped about
the bedroom as he peeped through the window. Moving
the net curtain slightly he could see it was the dibble at
the door. Gladys was now at his bedroom door rubbing
her eyes.

"Who is it? Is it our Katie?" Shaun told her to go back
into her room. He was running around like a headless
chicken. As he kicked Colby on the floor they both started
to get ready. Colby didn't fully understand at first what was
going on but once he heard the hammering on the door
he grabbed his clothes and started to get dressed.

Both lads crept down the stairs. Shaun quickly glanced
into the living room. He could see the shadow of the
police officers outside the door. He whispered to Colby
at his side.

"Fucking hell it's swarming with dibble. Let's have a
look around the back." Colby followed him and kept his
body low. Shaun peered through the little side window and
couldn't see anyone. Within minutes he had the key in the
back door and opened. Looking both ways he made his bid
for freedom, but it was too late the police saw him from
over the fence and gave chase.

Shaun could hear Colby screaming in the distance. He
could be seen trying to fight the officers off. There were
more than four of the fuckers on top of him. They twisted
him up straight away and placed the handcuffs on him.
Colby was still trying to break free but it wasn't long before

they had him in the back of the police van. His distressed voice could be heard screaming from inside. You could hear him kicking at the back doors. "Let me out ya daft bastards." He was yelling at the top of his voice.

Shaun's legs felt like jelly. He could hear the police shouting from behind him to stop but it didn't deter him from trying to escape. He was on his toes. Shaun made his way to the old market on Conran Street and jumped the wall leading to the market stalls. It was pitch black and he couldn't see a thing. His body froze for a minute trying to think of his next move. Shaun rolled his body under a stall and lay quivering. You could hear dogs barking in the distance. "Fuck, fuck, fuck," Shaun muttered. He was debating moving his hiding place but decided to stay where he was as it was too late.

As he lay like a scared animal he could see the beams of a torch searching near where he lay. His hand covered his mouth as he tried to control his breathing. The noise of dogs barking seemed to be getting closer. He panicked. Rolling out in full view Shaun made a run for it but a dog saw him and chased after him at speed.

Climbing the wall Shaun felt a yanking at his leg. As he looked down the police dog had the bottom of his jeans in its mouth. Shaun watched as its head shook his pants from side to side. He tried kicking it but it was no good, the mutt wasn't letting go. Losing his balance Shaun fell to the ground with a crash. The hound was now all over him and shaking his body as it got a better grip. "Fucking mutt," Shaun growled as he wriggled about.

Shaun kicked and punched at the animal but the Alsatian dog wasn't giving up. He raised his fist and plunged it into the dog's face. Loud growling could be heard. His fist pummelled its face several times but it just made the dog more determined to restrain him.

Voices in the distance could be heard and the sound of footsteps getting closer let him know his number was up. The streetlamp gave off enough light to let the officer know where the dog was. Within minutes crowds of officers were all over him. They were shouting at him to remain still but he was still wriggling about. Once he was cuffed they led him to the police van. One of the officers recognised Shaun and made a comment.

"I've not seen you for years Cook. I thought you were going straight now?" Shaun didn't reply as he was thrown onto the cold floor of the white van. As he pulled his body from the floor he could hear the police talking outside. He pressed his ear closer to the doors but couldn't make out a word they were saying.

The journey didn't take long. Once the engine stopped he prepared himself to meet the arresting officers again. The van doors swung opened and a voice told him to come outside. He thought about trying to make a getaway again but the officers had all the escape routes covered. As he stepped out of the van he realised he was in Collyhurst police station. He'd been there so many times in the past and it didn't look any different than he'd remembered it.

As Shaun came through the doors a large desk stood in front of him. He remembered it was the charge desk. They led him past it and down a small corridor to the holding cells. He could hear Colby shouting in a nearby cell and shouted back at him as the custody officers pushed him past.

"Colby it's me Shaun. Say fuck all mate until the solicitor gets here." He didn't hear his reply because he was pushed into a cell and the door was slammed behind him. At first he stood behind it and kicked at the iron door a few times but he knew there was no point and headed towards the back wall.

The cell was bare. A small ledge was situated on the back wall and a wafer thin mattress covered it. Walking over to it Shaun cupped his head in his arms. "I don't fucking believe this," he ranted. Looking down at his shoes he hated that they'd taken away his laces, otherwise he would have strung himself up there and then to escape the days that lay ahead.

Lying with his hands looped behind his head he stared at the ceiling. It just seemed that whenever he was doing alright in life something always happened to knock him for six. Shaun knew how much trouble he was in and prayed Colby could hold his tongue. He racked his brains and thought about what evidence the police could have that would put them at the scene of the crime. With a grin on his face he thought he was safe and started to relax thinking he would be let out pretty soon.

Hours passed and his solicitor finally came. He introduced himself as Anton. He shook his head as he read the evidence from the police. Anton was a middle-aged man with thick black hair. He looked like he worked out because when he hung his jacket round the back of the chair his muscles bulged through his crisp white shirt. The room where they sat was quite warm and four chairs were situated around the table. Pulling his briefcase to the table Anton searched for a pen. Shaun was sat on the chair facing him and watched his every movement.

Shaun listened to the allegations and shook his head as Anton repeated them over and over again. Rocking on his chair he asked what they had on him. His solicitor read further papers and shook his head as he told him about the witness's statements.

"Witnesses!" Shaun screamed. "What fucking witnesses?" Anton leant on the table and rolled his pen in his fingers as he continued.

"They have a witness saying you had a rent boy set up a meeting with the dead man." Shaun's face changed and he looked white. His mind was doing overtime and he couldn't believe Lenny had stitched them up. Shaun struggled for breath as he held a tight grip around his neck. Shaun now folded his arms behind his head.

"It's a load of shit. Get me fucking out of here. They've got Jack shit on me." Anton started writing and asked lots more questions. His face looked stern when he listened to the answers the suspect was giving him. It wasn't adding up. Shaun knew this wasn't going to be easy. He denied any knowledge of knowing the murdered man and told Anton that he'd been with his girlfriend all night long.

After a long interview with his solicitor the police came and locked Shaun back up. On his way back to his cell he could see Colby stood at the charge desk with his arms behind his back still cuffed.

It wasn't long before Shaun was stood there too. The officer read the charges out and told him he would be in court the following day. His face looked cocky as he spoke.

"I've done fuck all wrong. Why the fuck are you keeping me?" The charge officer made no comment and carried on reading the allegations. The other police officers in the room looked at the young man and shook their heads. They'd seen it so many times before and knew by the evidence they had in front of them that Shaun wouldn't be seeing the light of day for many years.

Leading him back to his cell they locked the door behind him. The sound of the door slamming sent a chill down his spine. Goosebumps appeared on his skin. Making his way to the bed he fell front first onto the plastic mattress. Punching the side of the bed he screamed out.

"It's a load of shit. Colby if you can hear me you prick. You better sort this fucking lot out." He sat up straight. He remained still to see if he could hear his co-accused answering him. Nothing. All he could hear was a drunken man next door singing "Collyhurst Road" at the top of his voice. The words of the song made him smile as he remembered him and his brother Paul singing it with their dad when they were kids.

Reality set in within minutes. Shaun lay down on the stinking thin mattress and pulled the blanket over his body. He looked cold. All night long he could hear doors slamming and his eyes stared into the darkness as he listened outside his door.

★

Morning came and the police officer arrived at his cell offering him some breakfast. Shaun was sarcastic and spoke to him with his head tilted to the side.

"Do I look like I want any fucking breakfast?" The man smiled at him and left his cell. Shaun stretched his body out and pulled his trainers on. He could hear noises outside the door. He was sure he could hear Colby's voice. As he ran to the door he placed his ear next to it, but couldn't really hear anything. His body felt like a ton weight as he sank to the floor. Shaun sat thinking and hoped Becky would defend him if the police questioned her, but he wasn't holding his breath. The door opened and a police officer was stood watching him.

"Come on lad, let's get you to court." Another officer joined him now and watched his every move as he stood to his feet. Shaun couldn't be arsed arguing with them. He trudged to the corridor as one stood in front of him and one stood behind. "Fucking hell," Shaun mumbled.

Shaun was in the sweat box and he could hear other criminals being escorted to their places to sit for the journey to court. The white van had small compartments in it. Behind every door was a small seat and a window. Shaun watched the door close behind him and stared out at the view. As the engine started he held his head back and fidgeted about in his seat. Passing familiar landmarks he knew it wouldn't be long before he arrived at Preston magistrates courts.

The journey took just under an hour. It was a ballache that they couldn't be heard in Manchester but his solicitor had told him because the crime was committed in Blackpool, they would have to be dealt with in Preston. As they pulled up he was glad to stretch his legs as he was getting cramp. The door opened and he cupped his hands over his eyes to avoid the sunlight. The Group Four security men didn't take long to get him inside and he didn't see any other criminals.

Anton came to his cell before court and asked him what he wanted to do regarding his case. He told him that if he pleaded guilty he would be remanded. Shaun looked confused and knew he had to be straight with him. His solicitor was an alright guy.

Colby had already confessed to the murder of Shaky much to Shaun's surprise. He'd said in his interview that Shaun had nothing to do with it, but the witness statements had said something different. Looking at Anton for guidance Shaun shook his head.

"Fucking hell mate. I don't know what the fuck to do. I mean like I told you, I was there but I didn't do fuck all."

Anton read from his notes and chewed on his lip.

"Basically you're fucked Shaun. They have two strong statements putting you at the scene of the crime. No matter what, you're involved in it one way or another."

Shaun itched at his skin. It looked and felt like it was on fire. Taking a deep breath he told his solicitor that he would go into court and plead not guilty for now. He wanted to wait to see all the evidence they had against him first. His solicitor agreed but in the back of his mind he knew the young man in front of him would be getting a few years shoved up his arse no matter what.

After meeting his solicitor he was led into the courtroom. For the first time he saw Colby as he sat next to him in the dock. He looked broken and he refrained from any eye contact with Shaun. Before the judge started to speak Colby whispered under his breath.

"Don't worry, it's my mess and I'll sort it out. I've said you had fuck all to do with it." The usher looked at him with a frown on his face and ordered that they both sat in silence. The judge sat in his black leather chair at the front of the courtroom. He peered over his glasses every now and then looking at the accused men. The prosecution began to read the evidence out and told the courtroom why he wanted both men to remain in custody. Shaun had put a bail application in and he kept his fingers crossed that the court would see he was an innocent man.

Once both parties had spoken the judge took a minute. He asked them to stand up. Shaun fidgeted around while Colby looked like an empty shell. Bail was refused and both the accused were now taken down to the holding cell. Few words were spoken and once they were out of the court Shaun shouted to his co-accused. "Colby you better put this right! I'm not getting slammed for something I haven't done!" The security guards pulled at his hands as he waited for a reply but Colby just walked off in a world of his own. He looked like his head was gone.

The cell looked as depressing as ever as he lay on the stale mattress. Looping his arms behind his head he stared at the flaking gloss paint above. The noise from outside made him sit up and lean on his side. As he fell back down he knew it was just another lad being brought back from court declaring he was unfairly treated.

At around half-past three his cell door opened. The security guard stood with a clip board in front of him. He read from the white piece of paper, scrolling his pen up and down it.

"Cook, Shaun?" He looked at Shaun's face and waited for him to reply.

"Yep that's me. Where am I off to, boss?" The man smiled and told him he was off to Preston jail.

Shaun nodded and knew the journey would be short. The Group Four man looked quite friendly and Shaun started to joke with him.

"Fucking hell. Preston is a shite nick, I've heard. They're all tractor drivers and sheep shaggers." The man laughed and led him from the cell. Shaun quickly asked him to check the list for his mate Colby and asked if he was going to Preston too.

With another quick glance the officer confirmed his mate was going to Strangeways in Manchester. Shaun's face screwed up and he tried to argue with him.

"For fuck's sake can't you get me there as well? What chances have I got of a visit all the way up here?" his hands were waving about in front of him, he looked distressed. "All my family's in Manchester. Can't you work it so I can go there as well?" Another member of staff came to his side now and he wasn't as friendly as the other. He gripped Shaun's arm and spoke in a firm voice.

"It's not a fucking travel agency. I suppose you want an apartment facing the pool as well don't you?" Shaun knew not to answer back and trudged to the sweatbox.

"Prick!" he whispered under his breath. He'd wanted to open fire on the cocky cunt but he bit his tongue.

The doors closed behind him and he punched his fist into it as they closed. You could see he was bursting with temper. The sounds from the others convicts in the van sent a cold shiver down his back. He held his arms around his body as his nose pressed up against the window.

Chapter Fourteen

Colby and Shaun were both found guilty of murder. Colby got life for premeditated murder and Shaun got five years for his part in it. The courtroom moaned as sentence was passed, neither prisoner made a noise. Gladys sat in court and rocked about as they spoke about her son as if he was a piece of meat. At one point she had to grip the edge of her seat so she didn't stand up and defend her own flesh and blood. Tears dripped down her face as they led her son out of the courtroom. Katie could see her mother getting ready to blow and yanked her back down in her seat before she tried to make a show of herself. "Leave it mam, leave it!" she whispered.

Not one member of Colby's family came to court as his sentence was passed. Colby gritted his teeth and scowled at the jury. As they led him out of court he wriggled from the grip of the security guard and shouted out in a loud voice. "It's what he fucking deserved. He was a fucking sex case." He was gone.

Shaun stared over towards his mother and sister before he left the courtroom. Katie could be seen crying and holding her mother in a cradled grip. The mascara dripped down his sister's cheeks as she mouthed the words "I love you" over to her brother. The dead man's family were inside the courtroom and shouted abuse at Shaun's family as he was led down. Shaky's brother was up in arms as he shouted out.

"Scum that's all you are. Life isn't long enough for what he's done to my family. I hope you burn in hell the pair of you!" The people in the courtroom all stared at Gladys and Katie now. Katie stood up and held her mother's arm as she started to lead her from the courtroom. The look on her face told Shaky's family how she felt. Katie screwed her face up at them and raised her two fingers in the air. She could hear them muttering under their breath as she made her way to the large wooden exit door.

Gladys held onto her as she left the courtroom. She looked as if she might pass out. Katie led her to some nearby chairs. She quickly ran to get her a drink of water from the cafe on the ground floor. Shaun's mother looked ill. Her face looked like a blanket of white snow had fallen onto it. She held her body back on the chair and struggled to catch her breath. Gladys could be seen exhaling slowly.

★

Shaun nodded his head in a cocky fashion as they told him he was now going to Strangeways. He was buzzing that he had now been convicted and was no longer on remand. Shaun was relieved that he wasn't going back to Preston as he didn't think he could stand another day there with all the carrot-crunching fuckers. He didn't know where Colby was being shipped out to but he made a guess that it wouldn't be the 'Ways. The last time he saw Colby was when they led him past him ready to be transferred. Colby shook his head at Shaun and just said sorry to him as he passed him. Shaun's heart went out to him. Even though he'd ruined his life, he still couldn't help but feel sorry for him.

Strangeways was the local prison in Manchester. Shaun had walked past it so many times in the past. He never thought in a million years he'd be inside it one day. Walking out of the sweatbox into the daylight he looked at all the other convicts for the first time. They all looked the same, hair stuck up and clothes hanging from their bodies. Shaun pulled at his jacket and tried to remain calm. Inside he wanted to scream out and run away forever but he knew this was his reality and he had to face whatever was in front of him.

The convicts lined up at the reception and were issued some prison clothing. There were no designer names any more for the convicts. Prison issue clothes were all they would have. The screw laughed as he passed an inmate a shirt.

"Get hold of this lad. It's Ralph Lauren that one. I'll just get you some Armani strides to go with it." The lad didn't have a sense of humour and grabbed the clothes as the screw chuckled to himself. Next in line was Shaun and he smiled as he took his clothes from the hatch.

"Have you got these pants in any other colours our kid?" Shaun giggled. The officer loved it and was joined by his mates as they all got in on the joke as well. The screws chuckled.

"I've got pink and pastel blue chuck if that's what tickles your fancy." The others started talking in a gay tone now and more of the other prisoners joined in. For a moment Shaun forgot where he was and smiled from ear to ear.

Once all the lads had all their stuff they made their way to their pads. The prison smelt stale as Shaun walked through it. He gripped his stuff and sunk his chin into the top of it as he walked the landings. One by one the lads were disappearing into their cells and it wasn't long before Shaun was inside his.

The cell door opened with a bang and he could see two beds. A large man was lying on one of them. Shaun casually nodded at him as they made eye contact for the first time.

The door closed behind him and he walked a few paces to the end of the bed. Once he dropped his clothing onto the side of it, he made his way to the small window between the two beds. He could feel eyes burning into his back and slowly turned around to introduce himself.

"You alright mate? I'm Shaun." The other man wobbled as he sat up and held his hand out for him to shake his hand. As he gripped his fingers Shaun turned to check the rest of the room out. The other man introduced himself as Bert. The convict tried to get as much information out of Shaun straight away.

"How long ya in for mate?"

Shaun threw himself onto the bed and pressed his back deep into the mattress trying to get comfy.

"A five stretch mate. How long you in for?" Bert sat on the side of his bed as his stomach hung between his legs like a sack of spuds.

"I've got three long 'uns left lad. I got seven years shoved up my arse for armed robbery. What you in for?" His eyes narrowed as he waited for a reply. Bert looked relieved when Shaun told him he wasn't a nonce or anything like that. Shaun told him the story of how he'd landed in jail and watched as his pad mate rolled a wafer-thin cig.

Examining the cell Shaun pulled his face. He touched the brick walls with his fingertips and commented on the battleship grey colour the walls were painted in. Bert showed him the storage for his clothes and watched as he placed his belongings inside them.

The small toilet in the cell was at the side of the room. A white wash basin stood at the side of it. When it was quiet all you could hear the droplets of water falling from the silver taps. Bert laughed as he told him he would get used to the noise in time and told him how it helped him get to sleep some night.

Strangeways was a notorious Manchester prison. A lot of hard criminals had spent time there. The door to the cell opened and Bert told him it was time to stretch his legs. Waiting for his lead, Shaun followed closely behind him like a lost sheep.

Lots of cell doors faced him as he walked onto the landing. He could see lots of inmates making their way down the steel staircase in the middle of the prison. The prisoners all seemed to have a similar look about them. They all had stubble around their faces and their hair all seemed like it needed a good cut. A few lads nodded at him as he walked behind Bert. Shaun looked apprehensive as he took in his new surroundings.

Holding the cold handrail he made his way to the ground floor. Shaun stood against the wall and watched a few lads running for the pool table. Other games were available but the playing cards seemed favourite. The noise of everyone speaking soon filled the room. Shaun felt like a spare part at first but some of the lads welcomed him with open arms into prison life. A man nearby shouted at him.

"Ay, mate. Grab a chair and get your bony arse sat over here next to me." Shaun smiled and welcomed the friendship. The man looked thin and his high cheek bones made his eyes look like piss holes in the snow. His hair looked that thick with grease that you could have fried an egg on it. The inmates watched Shaun as he sat down. They quickly dealt him in a hand of cards. Some of them were guarding their cards as if their lives depended on it. Rolled up cigs were pushed in the middle of the table as stakes. Shaun looked embarrassed as they searched his face for his contribution to the kitty. He placed his cards faced down on the table and leant back into his seat. Shaun told them he hadn't got his canteen yet so he couldn't play. A voice from behind him piped up and he could see three rolled up cigs being thrown onto the middle of the table.

"I'll stand him until he gets sorted."

Shaun turned his head towards the voice and shit himself. He recognised Ged straight away. Standing from his chair Shaun prepared to fight him. Ged looked gaunt and half the size he remembered him in the past. His old friend stood at the side of him and refrained from any eye contact for now. Shaun felt his body shaking. He was surprised when Ged told him to sit back down and play the cards he'd been dealt. Cautiously Shaun sat back down but he kept one eye on Ged at the side of him. His heart was thumping inside his chest.

Half of Shaun wanted to get it over with there and then, but as the card game went on he realised he had nothing to fear from his former best friend. Once the game was over Shaun stood from his seat and headed for the toilet. He could feel the warm breath of someone following him and quickened his pace. Shaun unzipped his pants and stood at the urinal. As he turned his head he could see Ged stood at the door watching his every movement. Shaun shook his nob and slowly zipped up his pants. Ged chuckled.

"Fucking hell. Long time no see. I heard you'd be getting time but I didn't expect to see you in the Ways. Where's that black cunt Colby? He still owes me money ya know?" Shaun walked to his side and shrugged his shoulders.

"They shipped him out somewhere. I don't know where he is yet but he'll be in at another Cat A jail won't he?"

Ged screwed his face up and rubbed his mate's hair as he tried to get past him. "Well I hope they don't send him here because I'll rip his fucking head off, thinking he can have me over." Shaun couldn't be arsed with him and walked from the toilet area but Ged followed him mumbling at the back of him. Shaun sat near a few other prisoners and Ged joined him. He was all over him like a rash. When Ged spoke Shaun looked at his face and slowly shook his head in disbelief.

"Why don't you get moved into my pad ay?"

Shaun gasped and spoke in a low voice into the side of Ged's ear.

"Are you forgetting something ya daft cunt?" his eyes burned into Ged's face. It was obvious that he knew what he was talking about but he tried to make light of the matter. He placed his hand on Shaun's shoulder.

"Mate, that wasn't my fault. She was a smackhead no matter what she told you?"

Shaun's anger spilled over and he threw his arm from his body.

"She was my smackhead who was carrying my fucking baby you twat. You killed her and like I said I'll never forgive you. So do ya self a favour and fuck off out of my face."

Ged hung his head and sighed. The other inmates heard the shouting and watched them eagerly. Ged lifted his head and stared into space thinking. He chewed on his lip as if the words were stuck in his mouth. A few minutes passed and Shaun lit a cig. His body was trembling inside and every drag he took seemed to calm him down. His eyes focused on Ged and he could tell he was struggling.

Association time was nearly over and Shaun let his guard down. As he spoke about his life since they parted his face looked sad. Ged was now his only back-up in the jail and he knew he had to keep him on his side. He told him of the crime he'd committed and spoke about Colby.

"He's off his head now ya know? Couple of butties short of a picnic he is." Ged was hanging on his every word as Shaun told him the details of the murder. Once Ged was up to date on it all he coughed loudly.

"Fucking hell. His head must be well fucked. I mean, to meet the cunt who abused you years later and know he was still doing it." Ged shook his head and sighed. "Fuck me man that's some heavy shit to deal with." Shaun agreed.

The screw came over to them both and told them it was time to head back to their cells. Ged stood up as if he'd shit his pants. The screw looked at Ged and laughed.

"What's up with you lad?" Ged kicked his foot into the floor as he spoke. He had a smirk across his face.

"Can ya get my mate padded up with me or what? The pad-mate I've got at the moment is a scruffy twat. He doesn't have a wash for days." Ged scowled. "Come on mate, sort us out will ya?" The screw was a middle aged man. He was well-built and going slightly grey. He was an alright guy and all the inmates got on with him well. He softly pushed Ged towards his cell.

"I'll see what I can do, but I'm not promising anything. Fucking hell you lot think its Butlin's in here." Ged smiled and looked at Shaun.

"He's alright him Shaun. I know he'll do his best for us." Ged winked at the screw as they left each other's side.

As the inmates walked up the big steel staircase you could hear banter going on between them. Life in the Ways was hard but all prisoners could do was make the most of their time behind bars.

Some of them looked hard as fuck. Shaun wondered what they were all in for. An old man now barged past him on the way up the staircase. Shaun was ready to knock the old cunt out until a guy at the side of him told him to leave it. He explained as Shaun stood with an anguished look spread across his face.

"Mate, just leave him to it. He's always like that. The prick's got some serious issues. He done his wife and kids in ya know?" Shaun froze on the staircase as he held onto the cold iron banister. The lad at the side of him smiled and continued walking as he filled him in on the other inmate's crimes.

"Come on lad he won't hurt you. His bark isn't as bad as his bite." Shaun's legs felt like bricks had been tied around them and he was finding it hard to move. The reality of prison life started to hit him hard. He held his shirt open as he climbed to the top of the stairs. Shaun felt like he was in a bubble and he was walking on fresh air. The screw urged him to hurry up but his legs weren't functioning properly. His cell door was already open. As he went inside it the door was slammed behind him. Shaun collapsed onto the bed and kicked his shoes from his feet. They felt like they were on fire. Looking round the pad his mind was working overtime and he had cabin fever. A wave of emotion passed through his body and he ran to the toilet away from Bert's eyes.

The toilet stank of shit. Bert must have just dropped a load before he entered. The walls felt like they were closing in on him. Shaun held both his hands over his mouth to try and cover his emotions but he was sobbing loudly. His body fell to the floor as he gripped the toilet basin. Bert could be heard outside and he was now kicking the bottom of the door. He shouted in a concerned voice.

"You alright in there son?" Shaun blew his breath through his hands and spoke in a distressed voice.

"Yeah mate. My guts are off that's all." Bert walked from the door and the sound of the radio playing could be heard. It was ironic really because Shaun's favourite band The Smiths were playing. "This Charming Man" filled the toilet walls. Shaun sat with his back against the toilet door and held his head on the top of his knees. His body was shaking from top to bottom. As he looked at the walls he spoke in a low voice.

"For fuck's sake. Please get me through this." Each painted brick looked at him as if they felt his pain. Wiping his eyes on his sleeve he stood up and had a piss. The sound of the toilet flushing made Bert watch the door. As Shaun appeared he knew he'd been upset by the state of his eyes. He'd seen bigger men than him cry in the past and gave him some words of comfort.

"Listen pal. It's early days yet. Everyone has their down days you know. It will get better in time trust me." Shaun stretched his arms over his head and headed for the small window. The wind on his face made him close his eyes as he spoke.

"Yeah, I know Bert. I'm just having a bit of a shite day that's all. It's fucking hard innit? One minute you're outside with ya mates and the next you're in this fucking shit hole locked up all fucking day." Bert sat on his bed and felt like he needed to help him.

"Shaun, I was the same you know. Even now I still have days when I just wanna do myself in and end it all. You have to keep your chin up son and get through it the best you can." Shaun listened to his wise words. His hands gripped the bars inside the window. You could see his knuckles turning white as he pulled at them. Finally he turned and flung himself onto his bed. Pulling the thin blankets over his head he hid from the world and secretly wished he would die in his sleep. Bert shook his head as he watched him. Picking up his newspaper he continued reading.

Chapter Fifteen

Ged lay on his bed and smiled at Shaun as he returned from his exercise. Quickly jumping up to the door, Ged placed his hands down his boxers and stuck his fingers into his arse hole. Shaun was watching and wondered what the fuck he was doing.

A small package was now in his hand. Ged held it from his body as he ran to the sink. He quickly returned and showed Shaun the smack he'd just got in from a visit. Ged had been on heroin now for over a year. At first he just took it to help him get through the days in Strangeways but now he took the drug because his body rattled for it. Shaun had watched him a few times toot the drug but he never wanted to try it. Ged started to tell him about the visit he'd had earlier and how he got the drugs inside the prison.

"Angela was a walking wreck mate. She was shaking from head to toe." Ged had Shaun's full attention and carried on talking. "Good job that fucking dog wasn't on duty today because it would have smelt the shit in Angela's knickers." They both sat laughing. Ged continued. "She said they searched her from top to bottom as well, but she stuck it into her bra the cunning twat." Shaun was watching Ged as he was setting up to get his fix. He watched as he found the silver foil that he'd saved from his Kit-Kat earlier in the day. Ged guarded it with his life. He kept a low voice as he spoke.

"Yeah the visit was sound. Only a few screws were on duty today. Took me ages though to get the drugs from her tits and get it plugged up my arse." Shaun's eyes never left Ged's face as he watched him toot from the foil. He could see the pleasure he was feeling as he fell back onto the bed.

Ged looked in a trance as his eyes rolled to the back of his head. Shaun felt something inside him and held onto his stomach. His head was in bits and although he knew it was heroin Ged was messing about with, he also wanted to take the pain away he felt inside too.

Not long after, he succumbed and before long he was tooting the smack. Shaun looked white and his body managed to sink back onto his bed as he melted into the mattress. Now his body looked relaxed. Finally he spoke to Ged who was now lying on his own bed chilling.

"Fucking hell mate, I feel so relaxed." Ged gave no reply and lay staring into space. Both inmates were now junkies. Shaun never knew that this day would haunt him for the rest of his life. There was no going back.

Morning came and Ged looked rough. As his eyes focused on Shaun, he smiled. Being a smackhead was a lonely life and now that his friend was on the gear too he knew there would be more chance of getting a fix. They spoke about his first experience of heroin and Shaun felt ashamed that he'd given into it. He couldn't hide the fact that he enjoyed it though. It took him to a place that was peaceful and free of misery.

Finally Ged spoke about getting more, "I know some girls who will bring it in, but you need to get some cash to them before they will do shit. Can you get hold of some cash on the out or what?" Shaun screwed his eyes up. The only person he had on the out was his mother Gladys. He knew she was skint but it had never stopped him before to play on her emotions. He told Ged it wouldn't be a problem and winked at him. Shaun had a visit from his mother and his sister later that day. He knew if he turned on the tears he would surely get them to hand over some cash.

★

The visiting room was filled with inmates waiting to see their loved ones. They all wore red bibs over their clothing and sat at the small tables watching the door to see their visitors. The door opened and one by one the visitors walked in. Shaun watched as a man near him gripped his wife in his arms. He could see the torment in the convict's eyes and felt a lump in the back of his throat. Behind the line of people walking in Shaun could see the smile of his sister Katie walking in. She looked thinner than he remembered. Gladys was now in sight. Shaun waved his hands in the air so they could see him. His mother looked twice her age. Her once golden locks now looked like grey wire. Deep wrinkles filled her face. He knew somewhere deep inside he was the one to blame for them.

His family sat down at his table and he leant forward and kissed them both on the cheek. His mother smelt of tobacco and her yellow teeth suggested she was still a heavy smoker. A queue was now forming at the back of them for the canteen. Katie asked him if he wanted something to eat. Shaun squirmed. He looked at the other inmates at the side of him and told her to get him a sandwich and a drink. She asked if he wanted any chocolate but he refused for now. Once Katie left them he knew he only had a few minutes to get into his mother's ribs for some cash. Pulling her hand over the table he looked directly into her eyes.

"Mam. I need you to sort me some money out. I'm seriously fucked if you don't." Gladys wriggled away and pulled at her cardigan.

"Where the fuck do you think I'm gonna get money from? I don't have enough to live on never mind give it to you!" His head sunk and he secretly watched her through his hands that covered his face. Gladys could be heard sighing.

"What do you need money for anyway?" Shaun knew he had her attention and checked where Katie was.

"Mam, you don't know what it's like in here. Some guy's giving me shit. If I don't pay him what he wants he's gonna do me in big time." His mother looked horrified. She was already looking around the room to report her son's problem to an officer. Shaun screwed his face up. Gladys spoke with a huff in her voice.

"Well what have you done? You must have done something for him to be demanding money from you." Shaun forced a tear from his eyes and shook his head.

"It's a guy who I owe money to from when I was outside. I never paid him and got off with his stuff. For fuck's sake mam are you gonna sort it or what." His voice was loud now and she tried to calm him down. She could see people looking over to their table.

"How bloody much? I'm just as skint as you. I don't fucking believe this! You better pay me back!"

Shaun's eyes opened fully now and he placed his arms around her neck across the table. "I will Mam, don't worry. I need fifty quid. I'll get someone to call to your house for it." Gladys looked puzzled. He told her to have the money ready by the following day. Katie now joined them and she could see Gladys looked annoyed.

"What's up Mam?" Shaun stared at Gladys and she tried to shake the anger off.

"Oh nothing. It's just this place. It's so depressing."

Katie studied the other convicts. She was amazed at some of the characters and asked her brother what some of them were in for. The screws paced the room and let everyone know they were present. In the middle of the room four wardens sat higher up than everyone else. They scanned the room for anything untoward. Katie looked at Shaun and started to fill him in on all the local gossip. She made him laugh and for a moment he forgot where he was. Shaun's eyes focused on the visiting room and planned his next visit to get the drugs in.

The noise in the room was filled with kids crying and talking. As his eyes focused he could see a couple on the next table. The inmate was raising his voice at her and it was obvious the woman was upset. She looked scared to death of him and he could see him dragging her jumper closer to him.

Katie looked at her mother and they all pretended not to watch them. Shaun felt uneasy and told them to stop being nosey as he didn't want the prisoner on his case. Katie now told Shaun that one of his old mates was now selling drugs on the estate. He looked shocked as he never expected it from his clean-cut mate Dillon.

Gladys remained silent. Her face looked stern as she sat back in her chair. Every now and then she would speak. Looking around the room she spoke in a harsh tone.

"They're all in here for a reason, Katie. No good feeling sorry for them." Shaun shook his head and knew she was on one. He sighed.

"Mam why are you always Chief Black Cloud? We know they have all done something wrong, that's why they are in fucking jail ya muppet."

Holding her head up and shaking it from side to side she made her point anyway. "Fucking three meals a day.

No bills, no worries. Tell ya what I could do with a few years in here. It's a holiday camp not a prison." Katie smiled at Shaun and they both knew Gladys wasn't happy. Once she'd finished moaning the visit was nearly over.

Shaun watched as all the visitors stood to leave. He could see them kissing and hugging each other. The inmate who sat near him sunk his head on the table as his wife left and you could see him pulling at his knuckles making them crack loudly.

Katie stood first and hugged Shaun. As she started to walk off Shaun gripped his mother. "Mam, don't forget that money. I'll tell em to call tomorrow for it. Alright?" Gladys nodded but her face was full of sadness. She wanted to take her son home with her. In her eyes he was just a mixed-up kid. She never classed him as a murderer. He would always be her blue-eyed boy no matter what.

The visits were now over and each inmate walked back to their cells with their heads hung low. They were searched first. Shaun made a mental note of every part of his body they searched. He felt heavy and he seemed to be in a world of his own as he entered his pad. As he flung himself onto his bed he noticed Ged ruffling about under his bed sheets. He smiled to himself and knew he'd been masturbating. It was an unwritten law in jail that when your pad mate was out on a visit you could bash your bishop until your heart's content. Looking at Ged's face, it seemed he certainly had taken advantage of this rule.

Shaun took the pen in his hand and rolled it about in his fingers. He had no one really special to write to. As he sat staring at the piece of paper in front of him, his mind was blank. Standing at the window he could see a pigeon on the far wall. The bird looked at him as if it was smiling. There it was: free to go wherever it wanted and there he was locked away behind bars. Shaun smiled and spoke to Ged.

"Tell ya what mate. Even the pigeons in Manchester walk around with a fucking attitude. Come and check this cocky fucker out over here." Ged pushed his head to the bars and they both laughed as they watched the bird balancing along the ledge. Shaun was right, the bird's chest was stuck out in front of it and it walked about as if it didn't have a care in the world. Ged shoved his arm through the bars and held a small mirror out so he could see the pad next door. He shouted out of the window and within minutes he could see a man's reflection in it.

Shaun was learning all about prison life every day. He learnt how to get a light when he didn't have one. Ged had shown him how to shove two pieces of foil into the plug socket to get a spark. At first when he watched the whole episode he thought Ged would end up killing himself but as he watched further he was amazed. Prison life was funny and if he didn't laugh about it all he would have cried his eyes out all day long.

Months went by and Shaun was soon a full blown addict. Each day that passed was all about where he and Ged could get drugs. Shaun had been devastated when he heard the news about his friend Colby and not even the smack could take away the hurt he felt in his heart. Colby had committed suicide. Apparently he'd strung himself up. Shaun had received a letter from him weeks before and he knew even then that his mate wasn't coping well. He'd tried to get to the funeral, but because he wasn't direct family his application had been refused.

Shaun now had a girlfriend. He'd met her through Ged. She was the one bringing the drugs into the prison. Over time they'd become close and started to write to each other. Julie was an addict too and her life hadn't been easy either. Just like most addicts she had a story to tell. Her kids were in care and all that she had left in the world was drugs. Julie had strawberry blonde hair. The perm she'd had many years before was still growing out. Her body was thin and her complexion was spotty. Julie tried to make herself look respectable but no matter how much make-up she caked on she could never cover up the damage years of injecting heroin into her veins had caused.

Shaun and Julie got on well. She was all he had to keep him going. To kiss a woman made a big difference to any man serving a sentence. The first time he kissed her he cringed. Her stump like teeth were brown and her breath stank of horse manure. The kiss wasn't that bad he thought and he told her to get some mints when she came on the visit to freshen her breath. Julie had no inhibitions. She would touch his cock and squeeze it all the time on the visit. At one time she nearly made him come she rubbed his nob that much. They were both making plans for when he was released from jail. After time passed Shaun thought he really loved her.

The years passed and Shaun was due to be released. Ged had been gone a long time ago and life inside the jail had been hard. Drugs were still a big part of Shaun's life and he couldn't get enough of the stuff. He'd fleeced his mother of any money she had. Lying in his bed the night before he would be a free man was hard. His eyes were heavy but he couldn't sleep. He lay there thinking of life on the outsdide and planned to turn his life around once he was a free man.

Chapter Sixteen

The light hit Shaun's face as he stepped from the prison gates. He was a free man. Ged and Julie were waiting for him outside. He smiled at them as he dragged his belongings towards them. The sunlight hurt his eyes. Holding his hand up he walked towards his friends. Ged stood out from the car with one arm resting on the roof. He looked more or less the same as he did before. His visits had been few to Shaun during the remainder of his sentence but he always promised him he would be there to meet him on his release date. He'd kept his promise.

"You alright mate?" Ged shouted. Shaun grinned and ducked his head to get inside the car. Julie smiled at him as he turned his head over to kiss her. Sitting in the back of the car he dragged his belongings to the side of him. Ged quickly got in and turned the engine on. The music was low as Ged spoke.

"Right I've still got that flat in Harpurhey. Are you getting ya head down there or what?" The thought of going to his mother's house depressed him. He quickly accepted the offer. Julie looked wrecked as she sat in the passenger side. Her hair was roughly held in a ragged bobble. Her clothes stunk and looked like they needed a good wash. Shaun looked at her and spoke.

"Fuck me Julie; you look as rough as a bear's arse. Are you okay?" She smiled and turned to face him.

"Yeah I'm just knackered that's all. Why I don't look that bad do I?" She pulled down the car mirror and shoved her face towards it. Licking her finger she wiped under her eyes. Shaun could see her eyes in the mirror and watched her. She saw him looking and quickly folded the mirror back. She giggled and spoke in a sarcastic tone.

"I think I look alright. Fucking hell you've only been out a few minutes and you're going on." Her face turned sour as she retaliated. "Shut it anyway, and take a look at yourself. You're no oil painting ya know." Shaun could see he'd upset her and laughed at Ged in the rear-view mirror. Shaun gazed through the window as the journey to Harpurhey began. Everything looked so different around him. Even the people walking in the street seemed to be walking quicker. The world had changed and he knew it . He felt strange inside and a worried look appeared on his face.

Ged's flat was a dump. Car radios were scattered all over the floor. Bits of burnt foil were tossed all over the place. Every ashtray and old cans of drinks were full of dimps. It was a proper shit tip. Shaun opened the window and looked from the high-rise flat. His breath was laboured as the wind hit his face. Ged could be heard shouting him. He trudged back inside.

Ged prepared the drugs; after all this was a celebration of his mate's freedom. Julie held herself and rocked as she sat patiently waiting for her hit. Ged was now injecting heroin into his veins. He tied a shoe lace tightly around his arm and was shooting up. Julie was also preparing herself and told Shaun to do the same. At first he refused and said he would just have a toot but Julie moaned. She told him he would get a better buzz if he injected it. Copying her he tied a shoelace around his arm and clenched his fist in and out repeatedly. Within a few minutes his veins were prominent. He watched the others inject.

Julie pulled the needle from her arm and passed it to

Shaun. Ged was at his side and nursed the sharp needle into his vein. As the needle dug deeper Shaun could feel the rush of the smack entering his body. His body folded as he collapsed onto the draylon chair. Three bodies lay staring into space. Each of them looked in a world of their own. Julie kicked off her tattered shoes and held her head back. Her eyes were flickering slowly and spit hung from the corner of her mouth.

The flat wasn't even decorated. Old wallpaper hung from the walls. The black fungus at the top of the discoloured ceiling looked like it had years before. Ged had told him earlier the local council had given him a wallpaper and paint grant to do the place up but he sold it all for next to nothing to earn a quick few quid.

Shaun's mind was awake but his body was motionless. His arms hung from the chair as if they had died. He tried to speak but it took a few seconds for him to get himself together.

"Have you got a bedroom for me or what? I don't wanna be kipping on the floor." Ged didn't answer straightaway and took a few seconds to register what Shaun had said.

"Nar mate. You don't need to sleep on the floor. I rescued a double bed from the skip last week for ya . It just needs a wipe down." Julie wriggled about on the floor and finally managed to pull herself up. She stood near Shaun swaying and bent down to grab his hand. Once she managed to get a grip on it she led him to the bedroom. "Fun time," she whispered.

The bedroom looked like a bomb had hit it. The bed stank of cat piss. Shaun looked disgusted as he pulled the mattress onto the bed. Looking around the room he realised there were no sheets to cover it. Julie didn't mind and threw her stinking body onto it. Falling beside her

Shaun complained about the smell.

"Is that the mattress I can smell, or your sweaty fanny?"

She smiled and dug him in his stomach. "You cheeky cunt. I've had a wash today."

Shaun smiled but as he looked at her he knew she was lying. She'd stunk all the time in the past and he couldn't see today being any different. Julie struggled to focus as she un-zipped her jeans. Her legs looked white as milk. They hadn't seen daylight in a long time. Shaun clocked her knickers and wondered how long she'd been wearing them. He looked disgusted. The knickers were a faded grey colour. The once sexy white lace at the front of them had seen better days. Shaun lay beside her. He wasn't ready for sex but she was touching his cock and getting him aroused.

Julie leant in to kiss her beloved. She had never been in love before but she told herself things would be different with Shaun. Julie had been selling herself for years now and every punter that came along she thought they could be the one that saved her. That day never came. Shaun was her world now and nothing else seemed to matter. She hid this secret from Shaun and hoped in time he would understand. Pulling his pants down Julie swallowed his cock. She watched his face fill with pleasure as she saw his eyes close. Shaun was a million miles away. His thoughts were not on the job in hand. Within minutes his penis shrunk. It looked like a walnut whip and he sat up looking at it in disbelief. Julie was annoyed.

"What's up? Don't I turn you on or summat?" Julie scowled. His voice was defensive and he slapped at his manhood trying to bring it back to life.

"Must be all the shit of coming out of jail. Fucking

hell this has never happened to me before. It might be the drugs ay?"

Julie flung herself back on the bed and felt deflated. "Well it must be the drugs because this kind of shit doesn't happen to me. I suck a mean cock so it must be you," she moaned.

Shaun lay flat next to her and hugged her closely. She was still moaning and he knew he would have to kiss her. He braced himself as the smell of shit from her mouth hit his face. Taking a deep breath he connected with her lips. Julie kissed him passionately and he was forgiven. She still stroked his cock but it didn't respond. Ged could be heard shouting from outside the bedroom.

"Ay lazy fuckers. We need to get some graft done. We need some cash don't we?" Julie looked at Shaun and knew he was right. She told him she had to get off anyway. She never told him that she was off to Cheetham Hill to sell herself.

Shaun reached into his belongings. Digging deep he searched the large transparent bag. All the years of his prison life were stored inside it. His hands trembled as his pebble fell into his grip. Touching the stone gave him instant calm. He dragged himself up from the side of the bed he stroked the pebble across his face. Julie left the room shouting "goodbye" but he couldn't be arsed replying to her. Ged entered and dragged at his feet.

"Come on then. We can get down town for the last hour. Loads of mountain bikes are left unattended round about this time. Me and one of the lads got one each last week. Top bikes as well," he poked Shaun in his arm. "Come on pull your sweaty arse out of bed."

Shaun felt glued to the mattress. The heroin was still flowing through his veins and all he wanted to do was sleep. Everything surrounding him seemed so beautiful. He knew inside his head he lay in a shit pit but somehow the drugs brought out the beauty in even the worse situations. His eyes rolled as Ged could be heard mumbling as he got off.

"Orr I can't be arsed waiting for ya." Ged left Shaun in silence. Pulling the covers over his body Shaun found some calm away from all his problems. He was off his head.

★

Julie headed down Rochdale Road. Her head was dipped as the wind started to pick up. Her small leather jacket had more than seen its day as she pulled it together to try and keep warm. The zip was broken so she held it together with a strong grip. Standing in her usual place she twisted her body from side to side trying to keep warm. The area seemed quiet as she leant against an old wall. From where she stood she could see Strangeways. Each brick looked ancient and she wondered what it looked like when it was first built. Julie had always escaped any prison sentence in the past and knew if they locked her away she would definitely struggle to cope. In the distance she could see a white van approaching. She lifted her body from the wall and prepared herself to meet the punter.

"You looking for some fun?" The man cast his eyes on her scrawny body. He was an Asian man and looked quite fat. As she placed her head inside the car window she could smell the stale aroma of curry and spices. The man touched his crotch as he spoke in a foreign accent.

"Get inside."

Julie loosened her coat. The punter licked his lips as he could now see the top of her breasts. His eyes looked excited as he started the engine and drove off to a nearby alleyway. Once the car came to a halt he slid his seat back. Julie knew to always get the money first and asked him what she could do for him. Stroking his chin he held his head back.

"I want you to give me a wank and let me come in your mouth," his words were nauseating as he spoke further. "I want to press my cock around your mouth when I shoot my load as well." Julie was used to this kind of talk from her punters and told him it was twenty quid. Lifting his fat arse up from the seat he dug into his jeans searching for some cash. She watched him as he pulled one ten-pound note from his pocket. He sat counting the change and held what he had out towards her. "I've got sixteen pounds twenty-two pence."

Julie screwed her face up. She was sick to death of people talking the piss out of her and let him know it. "I said twenty quid not sixteen pound something." The man knew she was desperate and started to put the money back into his pocket. He was cocky as he spoke.

"I can get what I want for a tenner. That blonde girl back there usually sorts me out." He looked at the money again and held it one last time. "So, take it or leave it. It's up to you. It won't take you long; believe me I'm feeling very horny." Julie knew she had no choice. Punters came a lot worse than him and she knew if she sucked him off she wouldn't have to stay out all night selling her body. Grabbing the money she slid it into her coat pocket.

The man started to pull his strides down and position himself. Julie hated where her life had taken her and some days she thought she was cursed. She fell forward onto his lap and gripped his brown penis in her hands. Julie closed her eyes and tried to think of happier times in her life. The man's cock smelt like onion bhajis. She could also see nob cheese all around the rim of it. Her eyes squeezed together as she felt his warm pole slide into her mouth. She could feel his hands placed heavily on her head as he pushed himself deep inside her throat. You could now hear moans and groans and Julie knew it wouldn't be long before he shot his load. Her hand strummed his cock faster and faster. She could feel his body tensing. As he requested she pulled his penis from her mouth and let him squirt his muck all around her mouth. The man was ranting some foreign words as he ejaculated. Once he'd finished he pulled her head up and tried to kiss her. Her mouth was covered in spunk. She pulled away from him quickly wiping her mouth as quick as she could.

The man looked happy and after he had straightened his clothes he started the van. When he pulled up at the area where he'd picked her up he turned his head the other way as she left the car. Julie jerked her body forward and slid from the van with the shame she always felt when she'd just been with a punter.

A few other prostitutes stood on the street. Julie went straight towards them and tried to bum a cig. Some of the women had been on the game for years. They'd told her in the past that things didn't get any better on the streets, they just got worse. A lot of them were junkies. You could tell by their thin bodies that the drug had stolen all their self-respect.

Standing next to a middle aged woman Julie bummed a cig from her. The woman was dressed in a short black skirt with fishnet stockings and a figure hugging red blouse. Her make-up was over the top and you could see her wrinkled face seeping through it. The prostitute handed her a light for her cig. Standing back from the kerb they both took deep drags from their cigarettes. Within a few minutes a punter came along and took the woman away. Julie sat on the floor with her knees up to her chest still smoking.

The night went on and Julie had more nob ends than weekends. She felt like a sperm bank. As she walked home her knickers were overflowing with spunk from her punters. She didn't even make them wear condoms. Counting her money she held sixty pounds in her hands. The money would just about cover her drugs for the next day.

Julie lived for heroin and nothing else in the world seemed to matter as long as the brown powder was in her veins. The walk back to the flat took about twenty minutes. As she stood in the lift she looked in a dirty mirror. She wiped her coat over a small part of it and could see the face of a heroin addict. Tears filled her eyes and she placed her finger in her mouth to wet it. Her index finger now wiped the mascara that stained her eyes underneath. Feeling guilty she knew she would have to come up with a story to tell Shaun about her whereabouts that night. Quickly she dug her hand into her knickers and shoved them all around her fanny. Bringing her hand out she smelt her fingers. Her face looked sick and she knew she would have to have a wash before she went anywhere near him. Julie stepped from the lift and knocked on the door.

"Fucking hell where the fuck have you been?" Shaun asked angrily when she got back. "I thought you said you wouldn't be long?."

Julie walked into the flat and muttered under her breath. She couldn't look him in the eye and spoke with a low voice. "Oh I got sidetracked. I saw my old mate and we sat gabbing for a bit. I didn't know it was that late." Shaun threw himself on the chair and calmed down. He was starving and hoped she had some cash to get something to eat. Watching her sit down he asked her if she'd seen Ged.

"Nar, isn't he back yet?" she rolled her eyes. "Oh don't worry about him; he's probably with his little tart somewhere." Shaun asked about the girlfriend and smiled at the thought of Ged never mentioning her to him. He quickly changed the subject

"You got any money or what? I'm fucking starving. There's nowt in the fridge except a mouldy tomato?" Julie threw her money on the table and Shaun sat up amazed. He knew she didn't have any money earlier and interrogated her about it. "Where have you got that from? I thought you were skint. You snidey bitch!" Julie kicked her black ankle boots off and came up with another story.

"I was skint. My mate owed me some cash from the other week and she gave it me back tonight. That one of the reasons I stayed talking to her." Shaun stood from his chair and made his way back into the bedroom for his clothes. Once he returned he held the arm of the chair while he slid his jeans on.

"Do you want owt or what? I'm gonna go to the chippy on Rochdale Road?" Julie's appetite had long gone. She told him she'd already eaten and told him to take some money from the table. Shaun scraped up the cash and told her he wouldn't be long. Once the front door closed she pulled herself from the chair and headed to the bathroom for a quick wash before he returned.

Ged could be heard in the hallway and Julie held her ear to the door as she heard someone talking to him. Once she knew it was Lizzy, his fucked-up girlfriend, she screwed her face up. Lizzy was a head-case and a butty short of a picnic. She was a raving baghead and would do anything for a quick fix. Julie finished washing herself in the bathroom and headed back to the front room.

Ged and Lizzy were getting ready to inject the smack

and Julie noticed a ten pound missing from her money. She quickly re-counted it and looked at Lizzy with hate in her eyes.

"Where's my fucking tenner. It was there a minute ago?" Lizzy stopped what she was doing and stared into her face.

"Ay ya little slag. I hope you're not saying I've had it away?" Julie was shaking inside and tried to be fearless but her shaking hands showed she was scared.

"Well there's only you two in here. It was there when I went to the bathroom," her hands were waving about in Lizzy's face. "Don't tell me it's just fucking disappeared!"

Lizzy moved closer to her as Ged carried on preparing the drugs. "I've got money. So why the fuck would I nick yours?"

Julie knew she was fighting a losing battle and backed away. She'd had dealings with her in the past and knew she wouldn't think twice about twatting her. Throwing herself onto a chair she gazed around the flat. She could see Lizzy looking menacingly at the side of her and hoped Shaun would hurry back. Lizzy was an out and out bitch. She made no secret that she didn't like Julie. Slowly she made her way back to Ged's side. The drugs were ready and Ged handed her the syringe full of smack. Julie watched TV and didn't bother talking to either of them. Lizzy was clenching her fist together. She was struggling to find a vein. Years of drug use had left her with collapsed veins. She finally gave up trying to find one in her arm and decided to inject in between her toes instead.

There was a knock at the door and Julie stood up quickly to answer it. Shaun entered eating chips, curry and rice. "Fucking hell starver!" Julie gasped, "Watch ya fingers, greedy balls." Shaun made his way into the front room. He placed his food on the side as he peeled his coat off. Julie looked upset. Shaun sat on the corner of her chair with one arm drooped over her as he carried on eating. His eyes focused on Ged and Lizzy. He hadn't met her before and he spoke to Ged who was now laid on the sofa. Shaun giggled.

"You're a dark horse aren't you?" He stretched his hand out towards Lizzy. "I'm Shaun by the way." He looked at her and she smiled back. Ged lifted his head from the couch.

"Why am I a dark horse then?" Shaun fell onto the chair with Julie and smiled.

"You didn't say you had a woman."

Ged sat up and interrupted before Lizzy could speak, "Lizzy's just my fuck buddy aren't you love?" She threw a nearby pillow at him and laughed.

"You cheeky twat. I'm your fucking girlfriend and I have been for the last few years. Why haven't you told him about me ay?" Lizzy was on one now and looked angry. Ged could tell he'd hurt her feelings and jumped up to make amends.

"Orr come here, my little precious. I've not told him about you because he's been in nick and it never came into the conversation." Lizzy pulled away as he laughed and tried to kiss her. She was trying not to laugh but Ged knew she was only kidding. Shaun walked over to her and gave her a hug.

"I'm Shaun." Lizzy introduced herself as Ged watched them both with worried eyes. Lizzy was a good grafter and often provided Ged with drugs. He didn't want to lose her and hugged her as she sat back down. He watched the connection between them and knew in he would have to watch Shaun like a hawk.

Julie sat oblivious to it all. She still felt angry about

her missing tenner. She dug Shaun in the waist and asked him if he was ready for bed. Shaun stood up and stretched. Lizzy had stirred something inside him and he felt horny. He said goodnight to them both and pulled Julie from the chair.

"Come on then baggy fanny. Let's see what tonight holds." Julie shook her head and smirked. She knew he was showing off and put him back in his place.

"Ay my fanny might be baggy, but let's see if ya nob can grow to fill it. You couldn't get a hard on before, remember screw dick." Shaun looked shocked. She grabbed his arm pulling him into the bedroom before he could reply. Ged could be heard laughing. He was shouting to him as he left the room.

"I can get hold of some Viagra if you need some our kid. Nothing worse than a floppy cock, is there mate?" Ged rolled about laughing.

Shaun felt angry at Julie's comment and slouched onto the bed. "What the fuck are you telling them about that for? My dick is perfectly fine. I'll have you know." He shook it from his pants. "Look it's like a baby's arm now." He pulled his strides fully down now and revealed his proud cock. Julie smiled.

"Ay don't give what you can't fucking take. You said I had a baggy fanny remember. What do you expect?" Shaun pulled his t-shirt over his head and lay naked on the bed waiting for her to reveal herself to him. He watched her take her clothes off. Her body was pale and he could see her ribs through her skin. The knickers she wore had seen better days and he wished he had a decent bird instead of her. Once she peeled her underwear off he smirked at her bushy fanny.

"Fuck me Julie, that's some pubic mound innit. When

was the last time you trimmed it?" she smiled and jumped on the bed beside him. As she lay down he sat up. The palm of his hand now hovered over her fanny as he slowly pressed down on her pubic hair.

"Have you got a plank of wood or summat?" he joked. She looked confused as she replied to him.

"Nar. What do ya need a fucking plank of wood for?" He giggled as he grabbed her bony arm.

"To tie across my arse, so I don't fall in ya growler. Fucking hell I would never be seen again if I got lost in that lot."

She punched him playfully on his arm. He made her smile so much. They both lay giggling. Julie made the first move and started to kiss him softly. She teased her tongue around his lips and eventually he kissed her back. Sex was quite straightforward. He didn't dare give her oral because once he'd stuck his fingers inside her he could smell the aroma of stale fish and knew licking her muffin would make him feel sick. Julie did, however, suck a mean cock. She was more than willing to show him her moves in the bedroom. Sex was good and it wasn't long before his toes were curling and he was shooting his load.

Julie felt like her mission was complete and fell back onto the bed. She hadn't really had any enjoyment from Shaun but she didn't mind. She hoped in time sex would get better between them and she too would feel the excitement of an orgasm. Lay in each other's arms they fell asleep. Shaun struggled at first to stop his mind from working overtime but eventually he found sleep with the help from his pebble.

Next morning birds could be heard outside the window. Shaun opened his eyes and felt a pain deep in his guts. He thought he might have had food poisoning but as he sat up he realised it was his body calling out for heroin. He sat against the cold bedroom wall and shivered.

Shaun remembered days gone by and how his mother was the one who used to wake him up with a cup of tea and some toast. All he had now was his addiction for smack shaking his body every morning to wake him. He looked at Julie as he searched for his t-shirt. Her hair was all over the place and he could see spit dribbling from the side of her mouth as she slept. Sneaking from the bedroom he made his way to the kitchen. He needed a brew as his mouth felt raw.

Entering the kitchen he could see Lizzy stood there with her back to him. She was wearing one of Ged's t-shirts that barely covered her arse cheeks. Shaun gazed at every inch of her legs and knew he wouldn't mind getting in between them in the near future. As she turned around she caught him scanning her body.

"Do ya want a brew Shaun?" she said pretending to ignore his prying eyes. Shaun nodded and rested one of his arms on the kitchen door-frame. The kitchen was only small. The sides were covered in grease and the stove looked like it hadn't been cleaned in years. He watched as she pulled a white cup from the sink. He could see the brown circles inside it and asked her to wash it again before she used it. She smiled as she rinsed it.

"The cups are all like that. They're fucking minging aren't they?" Lizzy moaned. Shaun agreed and took the cup from her hand to examine it further.

"I'm fucking scrubbing this again. How long has it been in the sink for?" She handed him the cups and watched as he squeezed the shabby cloth inside it.

"When I'm out today I'll pick us some decent cups up," he moaned. "Ged and Julie can use the dirty ones. They don't seem arsed anyway do they?" They both giggled and he handed the clean cups back to her while she placed a t-bag and some sugar into them. After she'd made the brews they headed to the front room. Lizzy looked at Shaun and weighed him up. You could tell she thought he was cute as she licked her lips. She knew in time she would be more than just his friend.

Shaun sipped his cup of tea. He was shaking and you could see small sweat balls gathering around his forehead. He looked rough. Lizzy knew he was rattling and passed him a small bag of brown powder from her coat pocket.

"Here, sort ya self out. I'm going to score in a bit anyway. So I don't need it for now. You can pay me back when ya get yourself sorted out." Shaun grabbed it from her hands gratefully. She passed him a dirty needle from the table and told him it was the one she'd used previously. His eyes looked at the needle and he knew the dangers of sharing but that didn't deter him because his body needed a hit as soon as possible.

At first he struggled to tie the shoe lace around his arm, but with Lizzy's help he soon found a vein. As the drugs hit him she smiled at him. Lizzy was at his side. She looked as if she was leaning in for a kiss but the voice of Ged behind her made her jump. As she turned to face him he looked angry as he scratched his head.

"Why didn't you wake me up?"

"You were asleep so I just thought I would grab a brew," she said panicking. This seemed enough for Ged but as he looked at Shaun he knew she'd shared their drugs with him. He grabbed Shaun's cup from the table and took a drink. Bringing his knees to his chest he let her know he wasn't happy.

"Have you given him our gear?" Lizzy nodded and

spoke casually.

"Yeah he was roasting his nuts off. I've told him to sort us out later. Don't worry." Ged shook his head and she could see he was livid.

"He better fucking had do. I'm not grafting my balls off all day to supply him with shit."

"For fuck's sake man," Lizzy huffed, "He's ya mate isn't he. He's just got out of nick. He's bound to be on his arse for a bit until he gets himself sorted." Ged knew she was right but he didn't like to admit that he was jealous of the attention she was giving Shaun. He backed off still moaning.

"Well as long as he does. He can come out with me today anyway. I've got a few things to look at that should earn us a few quid."

By now Shaun was in a world of his own. He didn't hear a word they were saying. He'd planned to go and see his mother today and a few other friends he hadn't seen for a while. Julie had heard all the commotion and stood at the door shouting.

"What's all the fucking noise about? People are trying to sleep ya know?"

Lizzy had just about had enough of her moaning and pounced on her. "Listen Sleeping Beauty. If you don't like it here fuck off and stay somewhere else. I'm sure one of ya punters will put you up." Julie's widened as she looked at Shaun. She prayed he hadn't heard her and tried to defend herself.

"I'm just saying that's all. Ged, can I make a drink?" He nodded. As Julie left to go into the kitchen he moaned at Lizzy.

"What's ya problem with her? Every time she tries to speak to you, you're a nasty bitch."

Lizzy screwed her face up and hated that he was trying to protect Julie. "She's a dirty fucking scrubber. Shaun deserves better than her. She'll probably give him AIDs or summat like that. You know she's a dirty slag. I can't fucking stand her." Ged placed a finger over his mouth to quieten her. He then told her Shaun didn't know Julie was on the game. Lizzy smiled cunningly and knew in the future she could have her at her beck and call with that information. She smirked as Julie came back into the room.

They sat smoking. Shaun was like a corpse at the side of them and Julie dug her fingers into his ribs to try and get him to move. She had to leave soon and didn't want him dossing all day. After all she was going out to get money for drugs so why wasn't he?

When he'd recovered, Shaun and Ged left the flat together. They walked at speed down the main road. A few kids were gathered outside some shops. The youths could be heard shouting abuse at them both as they walked passed.

"Dirty bagheads! You got owt to sell?" Ged gave them a look that could kill as he turned his head but that didn't deter them. They shouted even louder now.

"Smackheads. Probably going to sell ya arses aren't you?" Shaun wanted to run back to them but Ged pulled at his arm.

"Mate just leave 'em. They're always like that. If you show the nobs it bothers you, they just do it all the more." Shaun shoved his two fingers in the air and rammed them towards the kids. He laughed at Ged as they both carried on walking towards the local shopping centre.

Shaun looked as if he was dragging his legs along as he walked. Ged had seen some televisions in the local supermarket earlier. He was sure they could have a couple away if they played their cards right. Heading towards the Asda in Harpurhey they planned their next move.

Harpurhey looked like a ghost town. Shaun remembered how it used to be back in the day. He dipped his head as he watched fellow smackheads planning their next graft at the shopping centre. This was just another normal day in the life of a smackhead.

Chapter Seventeen

Gladys sat beside her son's hospital bed. Mike, Shaun's father, sat with her. Over the last few weeks they had somehow learnt how to speak to each other without shouting. Gladys looked tired. She was trying to wash her son's face. She lived in hope every day that he would pull through. Over the time that had passed she just sat staring at her son's face every hour of every day. She watched every time his body twitched and prayed he would wake up soon.

Mike had been there too. Gladys had told him to "fuck off" on many occasions but he just ignored her. Drinking tea and smoking cigs at the hospital was how they spent their days now. They had sat around Shaun's bedside and laughed and cried at some of the things he had done in the past to both of them. Gladys always blamed her break-up with Mike for the way Shaun had turned out, but she knew deep down inside Shaun was always set for disaster even from being a small child.

Mike couldn't get his head round why anyone would take drugs in the first place and he questioned Gladys everyday to try and get into the mind of his son. As they sat round the hospital bed Gladys began to tell Mike the life her son had led. She took him back to the first time she knew her son was a heroin addict. As she spoke every wrinkle in her face seemed to go deeper. Her facial expressions showed him just how much hurt she felt in her heart. Her words were slow at first and she fidgeted with her hands constantly as Mike listened eagerly.

"I didn't know what a drug addict looked like Mike. I

mean there isn't any book that explains what to look out for is there?" Gladys shook her head as she continued. "I saw he was changing when he got out of prison but I just put it down to him being in nick for so long." Mike slowly reached for her hand and stroked it slowly as she carried on talking.

"I've been to hell and back with him ya know. Each time he hit rock bottom, it was me who he came to you know. I've seen him on his knees screaming for money for drugs." Gladys pulled her coat around her and looked cold. "He's not only broke my heart ya know. He's shattered it into a million pieces. In fact I don't think I have a heartbeat anymore," she smiled sarcastically. "It's a wonder I'm still alive." Mike pulled his chair closer to hers. His own torment now set in and he told her how much he regretted ever leaving her. Gladys held her head up and fought back the tears. Mike told her she didn't have to continue if she didn't want to but she insisted and told him she wanted him to know exactly why their son had tried to end his own life.

Gladys played with the cuff of her sleeve as she continued. Her eyes shut slightly as if she was reliving every second of the torment. "The first time I saw him after he got out of nick was only for a few hours. He came to the house about half-ten at night. He looked tired and his eyes looked glazed over. I just thought he'd been smoking that wacky backy or summat." Mike smiled and told her it was called marijuana. She chuckled "Well whatever it is, he looked fucked," she continued. "He knew I was on my own and he just sat staring looking around the living room." Her head turned to the side and she looked to the corner of the room as she spoke. "When I think back he was just probably seeing what he could nick from me to sell for drugs. I feel a right daft cunt now. Why didn't I see it Mike? Am I that vulnerable?" Mike told her to calm down and went to the other side of the room to get her a drink of water.

When he returned he watched as she sipped the cold liquid. Gladys now sat up straight and looked angry. "He asked me for some of my Temazepam tablets," she nodded her head at him. "You know the ones I get from the doctors to help me sleep." He remembered and waited for her to continue.

"He told me he wasn't sleeping. I just thought I would be helping him and give him about four of them. I told him not to take them all at once but I watched him neck the fucking lot of them right in front of me. I went mad at him ya know but he didn't seem to care." Gladys looked so sad. "To me he just looked like he'd given up on life and wanted to sleep his life away." She chewed on her lips. "I know how he felt and I probably made excuses for him in my own mind."

Mike looked gobsmacked. "What he took four? Fucking hell I bet he slept for days didn't he?" Gladys sighed.

"Oh I wish. He stayed at mine for a while longer and then fucked off. When he'd gone I noticed my purse was missing. I searched all over for it. I thought I had lost it at first." Mike commented on her forgetful mind and laughed as he remembered her face in the past when she'd lost something. She sat straight in the chair and looked at Shaun lay in the bed as she continued.

"I searched fucking everywhere for my purse and finally gave up and collapsed on the chair where Shaun had sat earlier. I felt something sticking in my arse and that's when I saw my purse. It was open slightly. I knew exactly how much I had in it because I had just got paid." The nurse entered the room and quickly made a few adjustments to Shaun's pillows. She smiled at the couple and left the room telling them she was just outside if they needed her. The hospital had been very supportive to Shaun's family. Gladys promised that if her son ever pulled through she would buy them a box of chocolates. Mike urged her to keep talking.

"I opened my purse and twenty quid was missing. I didn't have to think about whether I had spent it because I was one hundred percent sure it was there earlier." Mike looked angry and called Shaun a "thieving bastard" under his breath. He told Gladys that she should have barred him from the house from that day on but as he looked at her he knew that the unconditional love a mother had for her son would never let her do that.

Gladys rubbed at her legs. "It's fucking freezing" she moaned. Licking her dry lips she carried on. "I was gonna go and chase him but it was too late. I knew he would deny it anyway so what was the point? I just made sure that whenever the thieving cunt came to the house again my purse was always by my side."

Mike swept his hair from his forehead. Looking down at his feet he tapped his toes. His head lifted up and he looked at the mound in the bed that was his son. Sighing he turned to Gladys. "Why didn't you tell Paul about him robbing from you? Surely he would have sorted him out." Gladys screwed her face up.

"Paul wasn't in that night. Anyway all he would have done was knocked ten tons of shit out of him and what would that have solved? I still wouldn't have got my money back." Gladys told him she needed a cig and he helped her put her put her coat on as they both went outside.

Gladys carried on talking when they sat on the bench

outside. It was cold and they huddled together. She told him of all the other things he'd stolen from her. This included gold necklaces, rings and even her clothing. Mike couldn't believe his ears. Her eyes welled up as she rocked. Her face looked in pain as the words struggled to come out. "He tried hanging himself once you know. I come in the house one night after bingo and caught him in the act. He'd fell asleep on the chair before I was due to go out, so I thought I would just leave him asleep until I got back .I mean he's my son and anything of value had been nicked by him a long time ago." Mike held his hands close to his neck and looked frightened. She took a long drag of her cig.

"I just walked in the house and needed a piss. As I opened the door there he was lying on the floor crying. He had a rope hanging from his neck. I didn't click at first what was happening but when I did I fell to pieces. He told me the rope had snapped because of his weight. I know it's not funny but when he told me I laughed. I think it was nerves." Mike looked at her and shook his head, he couldn't see the funny side of it and called her mad. She continued and tried to make him see what had happened.

"Our Shaun was the one who was laughing Mike. He sat holding the rope in his hands and rubbing his head. He told me he'd hit the large handrail when the rope snapped. So instead of hanging himself he had a big massive bruise on the side of his face." Mike raised a smile but still couldn't see the funny side of it. He now asked what she did after she found him and asked if he got medical help. She looked calm and looked him straight in the eyes. She realised what she should have done back then but at the time she wasn't thinking straight.

"Did I 'eck phone an ambulance. I made him a brew and sat talking to him for a bit. He just told me it was a daft thing to do and he just felt down in himself. I gave him two Temazepams and told him to go to bed." Mike shrugged his shoulders. Gladys went on the defensive. "It's alright you saying you should have done this and should have done that. I was on my fucking own and had to deal with it the only way I knew how. Imagine if I would have phoned you and told you your son had tried hanging himself. I know what you would have said the same as you always said when I phoned you for help." She mimicked his voice now and took the piss out of the way he used to speak to her. Her face changed and she sat forward and blew her cheeks out a little. "'Hung himself! Is he okay?'"

"Mind you I don't blame him living with you," Mike interrupted, "He was probably looking for the easy way out!" Gladys' face filled with a smile and Mike couldn't help but smile at her. His face looked endearing and he remembered when he loved her with all his heart. She continued taking the piss out of him and they both chuckled loudly. Gladys was on a roll and to look at them you wouldn't think their son lay in a coma in a critical condition.

Gladys confessed that over the years she just turned a blind eye to lots of Shaun's crimes. Katie had bought her a large lamp for her birthday a few years before and she'd placed it under the stairs in a box for when she'd re-decorated. She looked sad as she told Mike the story about it. "I was just walking home from our John's one night when I looked through my neighbour's window. You know Jack don't you?" Mike nodded. "I think everyone has a look through windows as they walking passed don't they? It just kills the time. And you know me I'm a bit of a nosey fucker."

"Yeah you've always been a nosey bastard."

Gladys smiled and nudged him in the waist. "Cheeky fucker!" she giggled. Mike urged her to go on. "The neighbour had his curtains fully opened. You could see them all sat in the living room as clear as anything. As I walked a little further to go inside my gate. I saw it." Mike was sat upright in his chair and urged her to keep speaking.

"What did you see love?"

Gladys bit her lip and a tear fell onto her cheek. As she wiped it away she stared at her ex-husband. "My lamp. The one our Katie bought me. The neighbours had it on a table in the window. I wasn't sure at first and ran inside the house. As I looked under the stairs I knew it was pointless. I had a gut feeling and already knew it wasn't there." Mike was holding her hand and he began to speak.

"What he nicked your lamp from the house?" Gladys nodded and he grabbed her in his arms hugging her.

"Orrr Gladys. I'm so, so sorry. I just didn't know how bad things really were with him. You never told me. So how could I have helped?" Gladys was angry and she kept remembering the past.

"You didn't give a fuck about anything but yourself. I was left to cope with everything. You wonder why I'm a nervous wreck? It wasn't just Shaun who had troubles ya know. Our Katie was getting knocked about by her fella as well. I felt helpless. I had no one to turn to." She gritted her teeth at him, she was on one now. "So don't preach to me about the choices I made." Gladys dragged herself away from him and sat with her nose up in the air. Mike looked as if he was thinking and he started to confess to some of the things his son had nicked from him in the past. His voice was low.

"There were times when he had me over as well. I

sent him to the bookie's one day with twenty quid for a bet. My mate had given me a tip and it was a dead cert to win. When he come to my house I wasn't ready and asked him to nip round to the bookies with it. The race was twenty minutes away and I would never have made it." Mike rubbed his hands in front of him and huffed. "The fucker took my money and the bet and I didn't see him for months after that." Gladys was still upset and struggled to get her breath. They got up and headed back to the ward.

"He was a thieving fucker. There's no doubt about it Mike. He owes me his life. If I had a pound for every time he'd borrowed money from me and swore on every cunt's life that he would bring it back when he got his giro I would be a rich woman." Gladys reached for her brown leather bag . The bag looked old. She searched inside it and pulled out her purse. Opening it up, she searched the little compartment in the back of it. She pulled out a small photograph and passed it to Mike.

"Look at him there. He looks so well doesn't he?" Mike held the picture and tears came to his eyes. Gladys quickly took the photo back from him and gazed at it as she spoke.

"He's been through so much. He has tried to get clean you know. He just couldn't do it." A silence filled the room and they both sat looking at their son. Gladys squeezed her arms around her body and broke. It was all getting too much for her.

"Did you know he was selling his body, Mike?"

Standing up from his chair as if boiling water had been poured over him Mike screamed at her. "What the fuck do you mean, selling his body?" Mike marched about the room. He held his hands up into the air. "No, stop right there. I can't take much more of this." Gladys continued and watched as he trudged around in total shock.

"Our Katie saw him in town. We'd all heard rumours, but you just ignore them don't you?" her head sunk low as she played with her fingernails. "Katie followed him one night and she came home heartbroken after she had seen him stood there looking for punters. She told me she watched him get in a car with a man and how she waited for him to return. Shaun didn't know we knew. Our Katie wanted to keep it like that, but I couldn't hold my tongue."

Mike sat back down and looked white in the face. The tears he'd kept bottled now poured from his eyes. Gladys reached over and held his hand. She didn't look at him she just kept on talking. "I told Shaun what I knew and called him all the bent bastards under the sun. He just sat there Mike and cried. He never denied it. Later that day he was found in the park half-dead. He'd taken tablets again and tried to end his life." She sipped a mouthful of water. "Fucking hell when I look back it was every week he was trying to kill himself. We got him medical help and even a counsellor from the hospital but nothing seemed to get through to him. It was like he'd just given up and wanted to die."

Mike went to his son's side and stroked his face. Gladys came to join him. They watched as Shaun's eyes flickered. He looked sad. The days were passing fast and Shaun s hope of ever waking up were slim. His parents hugged each other and prayed he would come through the other side.

Chapter Eighteen

Shaun's life had gone downhill pretty fast. His face now showed the signs of a long term junkie. His skin was grey and his cheek bones stuck out from his face. His once toned body was just a sack of bones. Shaun's collarbone stuck out from his anorexic body. His waist no longer existed and all his clothes hung from him.

In times of distress he would go to Moston cemetery where his friend Colby was laid to rest. Pinching flowers from other graves on his way in, Shaun would always place some on his mate's resting place. He didn't care that the flowers were from someone else's grave for their loved one, he just saw it as borrowing.

Colby's grave always looked well maintained. The words on his black headstone always made Shaun fill up. As his tears fell he placed his hand on the headstone and stroked the letters of his friend's name.

"Fucking hell mate. I'm in such a mess. I'd be better off with you." He sank to the ground and his head rested on the head stone. He looked like he was whispering to the grave. Shaun sat reading some cards that were at the side of him and held one to his heart.

"I miss you so much. You would have got my arse in gear wouldn't you? I'm a bad smackhead now Colby. Like the people we used to laugh at, I've become one of them. Even my family have disowned me mate." His head dipped as he pulled his hood up over his head. His knees were up to his chest and his arms cradled around them. Small droplets of rain started to fall and Shaun looked up towards the heavens.

"Please Lord, help me. I don't want to live like this anymore. Please, please." Shaun sobbed and but only a few birds heard his plea. The brown sparrows hopped near him and seemed to stare at him. As he snivelled, he wiped his nose on his sleeve.

"Right mate. I've got to go. If you can hear me Colby, please help me." Shaun walked from the graveside and dug his hands into his pocket rubbing his pebble frantically. A few people looked at him as he came to the exit and could see he was upset. His pace quickened as he got to the main road. Shaun was roasting for drugs again.

Julie was out selling her body again and Shaun had told her he would come and meet her down Cheetham Hill as soon as he made some money. Lizzy had told him months before that she was on the game. He didn't seem to mind. She was supplying him with drugs and that was all that mattered to him these days. Julie was the one who got Shaun selling his arse. One night, as he waited for her, she had stood for over an hour without a punter and he could see her holding her stomach. They were both desperate. Shaun's pain felt like boiling hot coals were being dropped onto his skin. Sinking his head he prayed his roast would soon would be over.

Shaun heard a car engine approaching and lifted his head from his knees. As he saw it drive past Julie he mumbled under his breath and looked gutted. The red car now started to pull up slowly near him. At first he thought it was someone asking for directions and stood up ready to help. He could see an older man of about fifty in the driving seat. Twisting his pebble in his pocket he walked towards the car. The man looked well dressed and the window was wound half way down. He could hear him talking and stuck his head inside the window. The man looked him up and down before he spoke.

"Are you looking for business?" Shaun wanted to jump in the car and kick fuck out of the old pervert but his words were locked into his mouth. He watched the man counting his money on his lap and froze as he held two twenties in front of him. The punter spoke in a Manchester accent. "So, are you getting in or what?"

Shaun felt like he was in a dream and nothing seemed real. Before he knew it he was sat in the car being driven away. Julie had seen him disappear but just thought it was someone he knew. The car came to a standstill and the old fart started unzipping his pants. He sat covering his nob with one wrinkled hand. Shaun tried to think of his next move. The money was on the dashboard and his mind was racing. He wasn't gay. He knew that so why was he even in the car with this man? The punter passed him the money. Shaun shoved it in his back pocket. The gobble was over quite quickly and he made him come over his own legs. He told him there was no way he was swallowing it. It was over in a flash. The man just zipped up his strides and drove away with a contented smirk on his face.

Shaun sat in an alleyway twiddling his pebble in his pocket. He pulled it up towards his face and stroked it along his cheek. His body was shaking more than ever now and his tears were flowing like a river of self-despair. He stood up and made his way to score. He didn't think of telling Julie where he was and wanted to have all the drugs to himself. This was his little secret and he would never tell anyone what he'd done to feed his habit.

Later, back in Tavistock Square, his heart sank as he entered the phone box. He quickly dialled the number for the dealer and told him what he wanted. The square was well known for dealing and another druggie stood a bit away from him waiting to score too.

Shaun sat on a small concrete wall. His arse felt cold. Looking at the row of shops he remembered happier times when he and his mates use to knock about there. Things had changed so much since then. Women now held their purses close to their chest and anything valuable would be hidden away from the preying smackheads that waited there. Police often patrolled the square but at this late hour it looked like a ghost town.

A silver Mondeo pulled up and Shaun walked towards it with speed. The deal was done in seconds and the car sped off. Holding the small bag of brown powder he made his way to his mother's house. She would be in bed by now and he could inject there without sharing it with Julie. He now walked as if he'd shit himself and the sweat was more than visible on his forehead.

His mother's house looked in darkness as he approached. He could see a small light on in her bedroom window and knew she could still be up reading. Gladys would often read until late and he hoped she might still be awake to let him in.

Looking for a small stone in the garden he threw it up towards her bedroom window. Within seconds he saw Gladys's worried face at the window. Her face stuck to the glass and he could see her struggling to see who it was. Shaun stood back and waved his hands in the air.

"Mam it's me. Open the door will ya?"

He knew by her face he was gonna get an earful and prepared for a tongue-lashing. The sound of the key in the back door let him know she was there. As she opened the door she was wearing her pink fluffy housecoat. Her hair looked a mess and you could tell she had just woken up.

"What fucking time do you call this? I'm sick to death of you coming here at all hours waking me up. I don't sleep at the best of times and you're not helping." Shaun pushed past her and smiled.

"For fuck's sake mam. I've had shit with Julie and I had nowhere else to stay. You wouldn't want me sleeping on the street would you?" His mother pulled a sour face and headed back to bed in a huff. He could hear her still moaning as she went up the stairs. "Fuck off ya moaning twat!" he mumbled.

Looking round the living room he went to his secret hiding place that contained his syringes and all the stuff he needed to inject the heroin. Gathering all he needed his hands shook as he tied his mother's old scarf tightly onto his upper arm. Shaun had turned on the small light and he was struggling to find a vein. Finally the silver pin entered his skin. He felt the rush and sunk onto a chair. The hit was never as good as the first time but he still chased the feeling. The needle remained inserted into his vein as he loosened the scarf around it. He looked spaced out and just sat staring with his eyes half-opened.

Gladys lay in bed and started reading again. Sleep was a million miles away now and she couldn't relax knowing her son was downstairs. Holding her book in her hands she listened carefully. She thought Shaun would have followed her up to bed but there was no sign of him. Quickly she searched for her purse. Her face went white as she realised she'd left it downstairs. She mumbled under her breath as she made her way to the living room. "If he's been in my purse I'll fucking kill him! I haven't got a penny to my name and if he thinks he can steal from me I'll show him." Gladys crept inside the living room and could just about see hers son's arm hanging from the chair. As she

turned the main light on her body froze as she saw his arm
with the syringe still sticking in it. She stopped breathing
and held her hand over her mouth. She was frozen. As she
made her way nearer to him she thought he was dead. She
frantically shook his body.

"Shaun, Shaun wake up!" she could see his eyes
flickering and sighed. Gladys pulled the needle from his
vein and quickly threw it onto the table as if it was poison.
Dark red blood trickled down his arm. She felt as though
her head was going to burst and she held her hands to her
head screaming.

"You dirty, dirty bastard. Fucking injecting drugs in
your own mother's house. Have you got no respect?"
Shaun rolled over and covered his face as Gladys took off
her white slipper and set about him. Her face was red with
anger as each word she spoke she meant.

"I brought you into this world and I'll take you out
of it. You fucking disgust me." Her hand was swinging the
slipper onto Shaun's body. Her words were fierce as she
whacked him. "You dirty, dirty cunt." Gripping his t-shirt
she yanked him from the chair onto the floor. Shaun just
covered his face and hid away the shame he felt.

Gladys eventually got Shaun to bed. She wanted to
get him out of her house but the fear of him leaving sent
shivers down her spine. She didn't want to have his death
on her conscience. Watching him climb into bed, her
heart broke in two. Slamming the bedroom door Gladys
collapsed. Her life was all about her son and the worse
thing was, she knew it. Everyday all she worried about was
his safety, whether he'd eaten and even if he was still alive.
She'd imagined in her head so many times the day the
police would come knocking on her door to tell her he
was dead. Her other children were sick of her and the way

she worried about him. So many times in the past Katie and Paul had told her that they needed her as well but she just ignored them telling them Shaun had problems.

For years now her son had ruled her life and she couldn't see things ever changing. Dragging herself up from her knees she entered her bedroom. Lighting a cig she stared at the walls. They'd seen so many tears over the years and she expected them to see a lot more before her time was up. Sitting back on her bed she pulled the small fur blanket around her shoulders. She was still shaking. Every noise she heard throughout the night she would get up out of bed and go and check on Shaun. It annoyed her how he was sleeping and she couldn't sleep a wink.

The following morning Gladys entered Shaun's bedroom. Their eyes met and he tried to smile at her. She looked livid but he knew he could win her round. He'd done it all his life and today was no different.

"Do us a brew mam. My mouth tastes hanging." Gladys shook her head and left the room heading downstairs. Shaun heard the sound of her stirring his brew downstairs and smiled. Dragging himself out of bed he quickly went for a piss in the toilet.

Shaun entered the bathroom and was faced with the mirror on the wall. He didn't want to look at himself but it felt like the mirror was a magnet and he was drawn toward it. He knew how much he'd changed and stared blankly. Filling the sink with cold water he threw it over his face. The water could never clean away his sins but he swilled it around his face as if it would. Grabbing a small hand-towel from the radiator he patted it on his face. Taking a deep breath he headed down stairs to meet his mother.

Shaun sat in the chair watching the TV. The Jeremy Kyle show was on and he watched it with interest. Gladys came in holding his brew and two pieces of toast. There was no way she would let him leave the house without eating, she just couldn't do it. Shaun thanked her as he took the cup from her grip. She sat near him and lit a cig. Gladys knew she would have to mention the night before and spoke in a calming tone.

"Shaun I'm not having that in my house. You're lucky I didn't phone the police on you." He carried on watching the TV as he spoke casually.

"I'm sorry mam. It's just my head was up my arse and all that last night. I won't do it again," Gladys felt a wave of love flow through her body. She sat looking at him eat his toast and spoke.

"Why can't you try and get clean Shaun. You can go to the doctors and get that stuff they give you to get off heroin." Shaun turned and faced her.

"You mean Methadone mam." She nodded.

"Yeah that's it. Why don't you let me book you in at the doctors? I'll come with you if you want?" Shaun looked at her cunningly.

"It's not as easy as that mam. I'll need help to get off the shit. It doesn't happen overnight."

His mother came to his side and cradled him with tears in her eyes. "I'll help you all I can son. We can get through this together you know." Shaun dipped his head onto her lap and pretended to cry. His mother stroked his head. He knew the moment was right and seized the opportunity to get some money off her.

"Okay mam. I just need to go and score one last time. I'm roasting already and the time we get in to see the doctor I'll be on the floor. Can you lend me twenty quid?" Gladys was quiet. She seemed to be deep in thought as she stroked her son's head on her lap. She knew it was wrong to give him money, but it was going to be his last time wasn't it, she thought. Shaun raised his head and the crocodile tears he'd forced from his eyes were visible. His mother wiped them away with her finger and spoke.

"Alright. I'll give you the money. I don't want it back either. I just want you to get clean and off drugs." He bounced up from her knees and urged her to give him the money. He wasn't listening to a word she said and just concentrated on the money she was getting from her purse. As she passed it to him she gave him some orders.

"I'm going to phone the doctors now. I'll make sure you get an appointment for about four o'clock is that okay?" Shaun grabbed the money from her hand and quickly grabbed his coat.

"Yeah I'll be back later mam. Don't worry I won't let you down." He left the house slamming the door behind him. Gladys felt like she was winning for once in her life and sat on the chair beside the phone. Once she'd got through to the doctors she made the appointment for quarter past four. A smile filled her face and she thought of a life without her son on drugs.

Katie entered the back door. Gladys couldn't wait to tell her the news and lit a cig as she spoke proudly. Her voice was giddy.

"Shaun's going to the doctors later. He's already booked in you know. He wants to get clean and off the smack."

Katie raised her eyes and sighed. She had her own problems and needed her mother's advice. As she listened to her mam going on she knew she would have to take her problems elsewhere. Katie had a black eye and Gladys hadn't even noticed it as she was too engrossed in Shaun's life.

Katie made a brew and watched as Gladys cleaned up.

She seemed alive again and full of life. As her mother spoke it was Shaun this and Shaun that. Katie held in her anger. For as long as she could remember her brother had always been the apple of her mother's eye. She resented that he'd taken all her mother's love and left none for her and Paul. Gladys came back into the front room and she was dressed. She hung her black fur coat over the chair and dusted it down with her flat palm as it hung there. The black fur coat was her mother's pride and joy and she only wore it when she was going somewhere special. The anger inside Katie was boiling and she couldn't take it anymore. As she watched Gladys buzzing like a bumble bee she let rip.

"What's the fur coat all about? You're only going to the fucking doctors, not to meet the Queen." Gladys screwed her face up and walked to her side.

"Listen you. I'm making the effort for our Shaun. He's trying you know. You want to try and give him some support as well. He's your brother." Katie stood up and grabbed her bag. She couldn't stand a moment more listening to her bull shit. She walked to the door, but as she held the handle down to leave she turned her head towards Gladys.

"Mam, he's a fucking baghead. Once a smackhead, always a smackhead. You're fucking stupid if you think he's coming back here later. Trust me he'll be shooting up somewhere with his scumbag mates. The sooner you stop treating him like your blue eyed boy the better. You do have other kids who need you too, you know." Gladys scowled and opened fire. She knew her daughter's words were true but she couldn't help defending Shaun.

"You have always been the same Katie. What's the matter, aren't you getting all my attention for a change or something?" Katie nearly choked. She was fuming as she let her have it back.

"Attention from you. You must be fucking joking. It was my birthday last week. Where's my fucking card," she said sarcastically, "Oh I forgot. You're so caught up in that junkie's life that you don't care about your other kids. Anyway, you do what you're doing. Let's see whose laughing later when you're sat there twiddling your thumbs waiting for that tosser." Katie slammed the back door and left. Gladys carried on getting ready and all that was on her mind was that her son was going to get clean from drugs. She imagined him without drugs in his life and a smiled filled her face as she sat watching the clock for the rest of the day.

The clock ticked loudly as Gladys lit another cig. It was half past four and there was still no sign of him. Gladys stood at the back-door and scanned the area. She lived in hope he was running late and sat waiting with her black fur coat on.

Shaun sat in Ged's flat listening to his CD. "Heaven Knows I'm Miserable Now" was being played at full volume. The CD was the only thing he owned now. It held so many memories for him and no matter how low he got he would never sell it. Sitting with a roll up hanging from his mouth he heard Julie coming into the flat. When she entered she slapped him around the head.

"Where the fuck did you get off to last night. I sat waiting for you, for ages. Where did you go?" Shaun fidgeted about and made some poor excuse up. She didn't believe him for one minute. Julie sat down and stared at him.

"If I find out that you're banging someone else Shaun it's over, trust me." Shaun sniggered and loved that she got jealous. He reached over to her and grabbed her hand.

"Why would I be shagging someone else when I've got you? I've told you it was my mate who wanted a quick job doing. It took longer than I thought so I just got my head down at my mam's that's all. Come here and give me a kiss." Julie was onto him and she knew in the future she would have to keep a closer eye on him. He was up to something. She gave into him and kissed him passionately. Once he had her back into his grip he asked her if she'd seen anything of Ged or Lizzy. Julie shrugged her shoulders and told him she stayed at her mates last night and this was the first time she'd stepped in the flat all day. Shaun didn't seem too bothered about Ged and Lizzy's whereabouts. He flicked through the tunes on his CD . He held the cover to his chest and sang the words loudly. Julie smiled and tried to join in even though she didn't know the song.

Suddenly there was a knock at the door. Shaun shit himself as it sounded like the dibble. He quickly picked the drugs up from the table and shoved it into Julie's hand. "Get that shit shifted. That's all we need, getting done for possession." Julie quickly shoved the drugs down the front of her knickers. They were both running about the living room like headless chickens. Shaun stood still and told her to open the door.

"Right, fuck it. Go and see who it is. They've got fuck all on us anyway." Julie was hesitant but he grabbed her shoulder and pushed her towards the front door. She could be heard moaning as she trudged up the hallway.

Julie opened the door. It was Lizzy. She looked distraught as she pushed past her without saying a word. As she entered the front room Shaun was by her side and could see something was wrong.

"What's up Lizzy. Where's Ged?" Julie stood watching

her and Lizzy began to tell them what had happened.

"I knew it was on top. It's Ged, he's a raving fucking lunatic. We saw a handbag on a car seat near Asda. It looked as if it had something worth having away in it." Shaun passed her a roll-up and waited until she lit it before he urged her to continue. "He had his iron bar in his pants. You know the one, don't you Shaun?" He nodded and she carried on. "It was on top straight away. As soon as he smashed the window the dibble were more or less at our side. I fucking ran off. They weren't arsed over me. They just wanted Ged."

Shaun blew a long breath from his mouth. Julie couldn't help but feel happy. She wanted Lizzy to go under and now Ged was gone from the house it made her feel like the alpha female. Lizzy was angry as she ranted. "We'd just fucking scored as well. The fucker has still got the drugs on him. What the fuck am I gonna do now. I need a fix and I'm skint?" Shaun looked over to his girlfriend. He could tell by her face she wasn't willing to share any drugs with her. Julie wanted to see her roast her tits off and spoke in a cocky voice as she screwed her face up at Shaun.

"Well we've got nowt. You'll have to sell ya motty with me tonight down Cheetham Hill."

Julie loved watching Lizzy's face sink. The times in the past when she'd called her for being on the game and now it was payback time. She smirked as she watched her face crumble. Julie was on her high horse and took great pleasure in watching the bitch struggle.

"The first time is the worst love. Just get off ya head and you don't care after that. That's what I do innit Shaun?" He nodded as he sat watching Julie getting the better of Lizzy for the first time ever. Julie was triumphant and Lizzy knew what she was doing. The two women carried on discussing the new job opportunity for Lizzy as Shaun put his coat on.

"I'm just nipping down to Collyhurst police station. I'll see what they are charging him with and that." Lizzy asked if he wanted her to go with him but he declined. Julie walked to his side and quickly kissed him. She watched Lizzy from the corner of her eye. She wanted to show her how in love they were and to warn her off from ever trying to get it on with her man.

Shaun broke free from her grip and looked at her strangely. It was quite out of character for her and he wondered what she was up to. Quickly he checked himself in the mirror and said goodbye to the girls. Shaun's feet were on fire .He had no intentions of going to the police station and headed to his mother's house. He knew he had some decent clothes there to get changed into. The weather was quite warm. He slung his coat over his shoulder as he walked through the Shiredale Estate in Harpurhey. All day he'd thought about a money-making idea and tonight was the night to put his plans into action. Opening his mother's back gate he kicked an old mattress from behind it. The back door was open and he walked straight inside. Quickly glancing round the living room he shouted.

"Mam, where are you?" Gladys appeared at the top of the stairs with her toothbrush still hanging from her mouth. She had an angry look on her face and he remembered the twenty pound she'd given him earlier. Thinking quickly on his feet he started to walk up towards her with both his arms held out in front of him. He pleaded with her and tried to wrap his arms around her. She wriggled and pulled the toothbrush from her mouth.

"You can fuck right off. I trusted you. You lying no-good bastard. Don't think I'll ever listen to your bullshit again." Shaun still tried to grip her and knew he would have to work harder to get her back on side.

"Mam, I know I've let you down. For fuck's sake. I just shit myself. It's hard ya know. I'm going for a job tonight in Yates's bar in town so hopefully that will start me off on my road to recovery." Gladys looked at him. She wanted to believe him so much but she couldn't tell if he was lying or not. He walked into his old bedroom and searched the old pine wardrobe. As he sat on his knees he looked at his old clothes. Pulling a light blue pair of jeans out he searched inside until he found a white shirt. Standing back to his feet he kicked the other clothes back inside. Shaun listened to his mother pulling the ironing-board out and gathered his clothes.

Gladys was stood with her back to him on the landing. He sneaked behind her and slowly reached his head round her face to kiss her on the cheek. His mother wasn't angry anymore and smiled at him.

"You're still a letdown Shaun. And you owe me twenty quid now, because you can think again if you think I'm paying for your drugs." Shaun agreed and told her when he was back on his feet he would pay her back in full all the money he owed her. He even told her he would pay for a holiday for her in the future. Gladys believed every word the lying toe-rag was telling her. He handed her his clothes and smirked as he asked her to run the iron over them. Gladys loved the change in her son and took the clothes from his grip with a smile on her face. She watched him go into the bathroom and once she heard the bath being run she shouted to him.

"Shaun are you getting a bath?" He stuck his head from behind the door and nodded. Her face lit up and she joked with him. "It's not Christmas you know son. I'll have to stop hiding my money under the soap now." Shaun looked puzzled at her words. His head came back to the door.

"What do you mean hiding your money under the soap?" As she chuckled she gripped between her legs as she nearly pissed herself laughing.

"Well you never touch the soap. So it's a safe place to hide anything isn't it?" Shaun rolled his eyes and closed the bathroom door behind him as Gladys was left laughing out loud on the landing. She was singing now.

Dipping his toe into the bath he hopped back onto the floor. As he added more cold water he looked at his toe nails. They looked black and overgrown. In fact they looked like hooves more than toe nails. Grabbing his mother's nail clippers from the window sill he placed his foot on the side of the bath and leant down to cut them. His feet looked weird after he'd cut them. Shaun smiled as he thought he'd now gone from a size nine feet to a size seven once he'd lost the long toe-nails. His skeletal body dipped into the warm water. As he submerged himself beneath the water you could see all the bruises where he'd injected heroin. Rubbing at his black and blue skin he knew the marks would never disappear from his arms. Heroin would always be trapped inside his body and he didn't need to look at the track-marks to know how much of a low-life he'd become.

Shaun lay soaking in the bath. He even started singing as he washed his hair. Gladys could hear him from outside and thought the dark days of dealing with her drug addict son were almost over. She placed his neatly pressed clothing over the banister at the top of the stairs and entered his bedroom to get him some clean boxer shorts. Gladys knocked on the bathroom door holding his clean underwear and a fluffy white bath towel. The door briefly opened and he took the items from her.

Shaun paraded on the landing wearing the bath towel hung round his waist. Walking into his mother's room he looked at her deodorants on her set of drawers. Quickly spraying his armpits he inhaled the fumes. Lifting the towel up he sprayed the floral scent between his legs with a smile on his face. From the corner of his eye he saw his mother's brown tablet bottle at the side of him. His fingers trembled as he tried to get the lid off it before he was detected. Shaking the white pills onto his hand he checked what they were. His face lit up when he saw the words "Diazepam" written on the small white tablet. Leaving the room he kept the pills clenched tightly in his fist.

The feel of fresh clothes on his skin felt good. It had been a long time since his clothes had had that clean smell about them. He held the shirt up to his nose and inhaled the freshness, before he stood in the mirror and put it on. His old trainers looked shabby. The once white laces hung from the shoes in a desperate way. Pulling the wardrobe door open he searched for some shoes his brother Paul had given him years before. The shoes were a family joke. All the family referred to them as Shaun's dancing shoes. The shoes were dusty and needed a good wipe down. As he placed them on his feet he turned his heel up and looked at the black shoe in the mirror. A smile came to his face and Shaun did a little dance in the mirror with his sparkling clean shoes on.

As he walked into the front room his mother smiled. She hadn't seen him look this good in a long time. He looked like the son she once knew. Her face looked proud as she stood up behind him straightening his collar. Shaun looked presentable and Gladys reached inside her purse as he was set to leave.

"Here, get some cigs or something." He didn't hesitate and took the money straight from her hand. Shaun kissed her on the side of the cheek.

"Wish me luck ay mam. This could be the start of the new me." Her eyes filled with tears and she hugged him.

"Let's hope so son. All I've ever wanted is for you to be okay." He nodded and smirked.

"Right mam. I've got to go. I'll come and see you later if I have any time." Gladys went on to tell him not to bother as she would be asleep by the time he'd finished work. Shaun agreed and left the house with a spring in his step. The old aftershave he'd found that must have belonged to his dad smelt clean and fresh. The Old Spice had done its trick and he inhaled its fragrance as he walked into the night air.

Chapter Nineteen

Shaun sat in Cheetham Hill for ages but still there was no sign of a punter so headed to Manchester city centre. He'd heard in the past that a lot of rent boys use to hang about near Sackville Street.

As he walked through the dimly lit streets he looked at a few of the men who stood there. Some just looked liked everyday guys but some of them looked like death on legs. Standing near a wall one of the lads came to his side and asked him for a light. He dug in his pocket and flicked the flame for him. The young male passed him a cig and Shaun didn't have to be asked twice. The lad introduced himself as Ralph. He had red hair but it was cut very close to his head. His body looked toned and a nipple ring stood out from under his tightly fitted white t-shirt. He quickly interrogated Shaun and within a few minutes he knew Shaun was fresh meat to the streets.

Ralph smiled as a car pulled up. He winked at Shaun and told him if he was still there when he got back he would come and see him. Shaun flicked his cig onto the pavement. As he twisted his pebble in his pocket he felt the tablets he'd stolen earlier. Popping them one by one he swigged at a bottle of White Ace he'd bought from the shop earlier. He necked all the tablets in one go.

A white transit van now pulled up and the passenger-side door flung open. Two white males sat looking at him. They looked quite manly and both of them had goatee beards. The one nearest to Shaun spoke.

"You getting in son? You can earn some good money

tonight if you're up for it?" The man patted the seat and waited on Shaun's reply. Shaun's eyes rolled as he tried to focus. Before he knew it, he was sat in the van being driven away from the city centre. The journey wasn't long and few words were spoken. As they pulled up at a block of flats Shaun realised he was in Ancoats. Shaun followed the men as they left the van. They were laughing and joking between themselves. The punters looked toned and very strong. One of them had a scar above his left eye that made him look rough and ready. Standing in the lift one of the men spoke to Shaun.

"You don't speak much do you?" Shaun couldn't have spoken if he'd wanted to. He tried to answer him as the lift door opened but nothing came out. Shaun's legs manoeuvred forward. He was so spaced out he felt as if he was walking on air. The red door opened in front of him and he followed the lead of the men into the house.

The flat was well presented. A red leather sofa sat on one side of the room with a glass table in front of it. Cream curtains hung neatly from the window. They looked like silk. Every pleat in them was perfect and you could tell someone took pride in them. One of the men went into the kitchen and came back with a large bottle of Brandy. He poured three glasses and handed one to Shaun. Before long cocaine was being cut into neat lines on the table and all three of them were snorting it like pigs.

Time passed and the man with a scar over his eye grabbed at Shaun. He pulled him in front of him and began to undress him. Shaun was off his head and oblivious to what was about to happen. The two men were now both naked and dragged at Shaun's body like a piece of meat. They ripped the shirt from him and began to pull his lifeless body between them. He was like a rag doll. His face was now pressed down into the floor and he could feel his arse being penetrated. Wriggling around he tried to fight them off but they were too strong. His head was pulled up from the floor and the other punter tried shoving his cock into his mouth. They were sick bastards.

With a cock stuck in his mouth and one up his arse Shaun knew he was being raped. He only ever wanted to give a wank out or a gobble but this was horrific. The two men subjected Shaun to at least two hours of sick perverted sex. When they'd finished with him they threw the money at his trembling body. Shaun's legs felt like jelly as he got his clothes together. Once he was dressed he couldn't wait to get away from the two arse bandits. Shaun picked up the crumpled money from the floor and staggered from the flat. He was mumbling under his breath as the tears fell. "Fucking sausage jockeys. Don't think you're gonna get away with this."

Fastening his jeans in the lift he vomited. His arsehole was on fire and he had difficulty walking. The buttons from his shirt were gone and he held it together with one hand as he left the lift. All that was on his mind was to get more drugs inside him. He wanted heroin and anything else that was going. He retched as he hit the cold night air. Shaun spewed his ring up again as he carried on walking. Tears were stored in the corner of his eyes now but not a single tear fell. His eyes glazed over as he struggled for breath. Finding a nearby bench, Shaun keeled over onto it. He lay across it and hugged his arms around his body rocking. He'd been through some shit in his life but this was by far the worst. He'd been raped. How could he ever tell anyone? He searched his mind for the answers but all he came up with was that he deserved it. After all he was now a rent-boy what did he expect?

His eyes rolled as he stared into the night. His vision was blurred as he tried to focus at the stars but he was fighting a losing battle. Losing his balance from the bench he rolled onto the ground. His body felt like lead as he tried to pull himself up. Scanning the area he knew he needed to get home somehow. But which way was home? He tried to think as he leant against an overfilled litter bin at the side of him.

On autopilot Shaun somehow found himself heading towards the flats in Harpurhey. The lifts were broken again as he stood with one hand on the wall waiting for it to come. As he read the notice saying "Out of Order" he kicked at the lift doors and headed towards the staircase. His legs felt tired and at one point he sat on the cold concrete stairs unable to go on. His emotions were ready to burst and his trauma was still there at the front of his mind. Holding his shirt together he held onto the wall to stand up. His face twisted up as his anger now boiled inside him. His clenched fist holding his shirt together looked white. You could see his bones through the paper thin skin. As he knocked on the door he kicked the bottom of it hoping someone would hear him.

Julie answered wearing one of his old t-shirts. As she turned to walk back inside he could see her baggy knickers hanging down. Julie went straight to bed. She was angry as she quickly glanced at him before she left his sight. Shaun quickly ran a bath. When it was ready he ripped his clothes from his body as if they were on fire. The soap didn't clean him the way he wanted it to. Nothing would ever wash away the man he'd become. Rubbing at his skin vigorously his skin looked red. As he washed his arse hole he wanted to be sick. It felt different. He quickly jumped from the bath and grabbed an old white towel at the side of him.

Julie sat up in the bed as she watched him wobble into the bedroom. She grabbed the quilt up towards her neck. Flinging the bath towel to the floor he fell onto the bed. Gripping the covers hard she yanked them over her shoulders as she lay down facing the away from him. Julie fidgeted about in the bed. You could see her eyes were still open and she was ready for war. Turning to face him she poked her stump-like finger in his face.

"Don't take me for a prick. If you have got some other slapper just fucking tell me and I'm out of here." She watched his face but he was out of it and mumbling. Putting her face to his she smelt the overpowering smell of the soap he'd just used. Gripping his shoulder and lifting him slightly from the bed she screamed into his face.

"That's why you've have had a bath innit. You dirty bastard. Did you think I would smell the sex all over you?" She dropped him back onto the bed and grabbed the blankets. With the quilt under her arm she left the room to sleep on the sofa. As she left she let him have a piece of her mind. "What goes around, comes around arsehole. Just fucking watch me now dickhead," before she slammed the bedroom behind her. Shaun was half-conscious and dug his head into the stale mattress. He knew he would have to come up with some believable story by the morning. Julie was all he had. His eyelids closed and he tried to keep warm without blankets.

The next morning Shaun was awoken from a deep sleep by a sharp pain. His face looked white as he felt his arse and realised that's where the pain was coming from. Looking at his hand he could see blood on his fingers and dived from the bed fearing he was going to die. Grabbing a pair of shorts he hurried to the bathroom. Once the door was locked he sat on the toilet as the spasms of pain shot through his arse. Shaun seemed full of wind and each fart made a loud blasting noise as it left his arse. He was now shitting like a new born baby. Ged was soon banging on the door.

"Come on hurry the fuck up. I need a piss." Shaun was glad to hear Ged's voice and even happier that he'd got out of the police station. When he finished he opened the door.

"You alright mate. Did they let you out last night or what?" Ged pushed past him and stood pissing as he answered him.

"Yeah I got out about half eleven. Lizzy said you went down to see what was happening to me but you never come back." Scratching his balls Shaun began to lie.

"Yeah I was on my way down to the police station when I got talking to my old mate Mark. You remember him don't ya?" Ged nodded as he carried on lying. "Before I knew it we were off our heads. We drank about eight bottles of White Ace." Shaun raised his eyebrows and whispered. "Julie's seen her arse because I didn't get in until late."

Ged shook his nob over the toilet bowl and smiled. He followed him to the front room. Julie was on the sofa with the quilt pulled over her head. Ged pointed at her as he made a funny face to Shaun. The room stank of sweaty socks and stale cigarette smoke. Shaun cautiously sat on the end of the couch and could see Julie's feet sticking out from under the blanket. With a smile on his face he placed his index finger to his mouth and whispered to Ged to be quiet. At first he tickled underneath her foot but she remained still. Seeing long hairs on her big toe he carefully grabbed hold of one of them and yanked at it. Julie revealed herself from under the blanket with a face that would kill.

Her hair was stuck up all over the place and the make-up she'd worn the night before was still visible on her face.

"You daft cunt. What the fuck are you doing that for?" Shaun jumped on her and began to kiss her arms. The sound of his lips puckering together could be heard as he kissed all the way up her arm. Within a few seconds she saw the funny side of things and welcomed Shaun back into her arms. As he sat next to her like a devoted puppy she made it known she still wanted answers of where he was the night before. As she started speaking Ged left the room. He didn't want to be involved in any of the dispute and headed back to the bedroom to wake Lizzy. Julie started her interrogation.

"Right no bullshit. Where was you last night?" Shaun started to answer but she jumped in. "Listen you came in and got straight in the bath. What does that tell me? Why else would you have got in the bath if you wasn't washing fanny from ya nob?" Shaun looked at her and paused. He knew she was on to something and dug deep for a story that would win her over. Shaun had his hands spread out in front of him.

"Julie on my life I wasn't with anyone else. I feel a twat telling you this but you won't believe what happened." Julie sat up and pulled her legs in front of her. She urged him to continue.

"Shaun, just fucking get on with it. If you're telling me where you was, stop fucking hanging about." Losing eye contact with her he stared at the front wall. The wallpaper was still hanging down from the ceiling and he promised one day he would paste it back up. Julie dug her clenched fist into his ribs.

"Right, right", he shouted, "for fuck's sake." He licked his bottom lip and held her hand as he spoke. "I was at

Mark's. You know Mark?" She nodded quickly. "Well we had a smoke and that and we were drinking all night. I told him I was going a few times, but you know what he's like he just kept on passing me beers." Julie held her head to the side as she lit a cig. He asked her to light him one before he continued. Taking a deep drag from his cig he blew the smoke into her eyes.

"I was fine till I hit the fresh air you know. I don't know what came over me. I just farted. At first I thought it was just the cold on my legs, but as I carried on walking I realised I had followed through." Julie pissed laughing. He knew she loved the story and continued. "Fuck me Julie, the shit was all over my legs. I must have had a bad hit or summit. As I walked I could smell it. It was fucking hanging, I can tell you." Julie was made up with the story and she believed every word the lying fucker told her. She could hear the others coming into the room and pissed herself as she repeated his story to them.

The four junkies now sat in the front room. As if someone had twitched a button on the back of their necks they all looked agitated. Ged was rubbing his sweaty palms together and Lizzy was wiping sweat from her face. Ged grabbed his jeans from the side and started to put his trainers on. Any money they had between them was put onto table. Ged quickly counted it, there was £15. Shaun kept quiet about the £20 he had and looked away as Ged spoke.

"Fucking hell. Is that all we've got? That's not enough to score for four of us." Lizzy fidgeted about and looked at Julie. She knew she was out on the game last night and she'd only put a tenner on the table. She looked at her with devious eyes as she probed her.

"Is that all ya earned last night? A fucking tenner?"

Julie was up in arms and was frothing at the mouth.

"Yeah it is. It was dead last night. Anyway a tenner is more than you have put on the table, so get off my fucking back. If I had any more money I would put it on the table." Lizzy backed down. She still gave her an evil look though. Shaun broke the atmosphere. He stood tall and stretched his rattling body.

"Let's hit Asda. They have some garden furniture near the exit. I clocked it the other day." Ged didn't need telling twice and urged his fellow druggies to get ready. The girls both sat there like gun-slingers at dawn. They stared at each other and Julie was at breaking point. She couldn't stand another minute in the same room as the raving smackhead and told Shaun she would come with them. Lizzy now followed her lead. She knew if she didn't go with them she wouldn't get any drugs until later. Both girls left the front room to get ready and the lads urged them to be as quick as they could.

Asda was buzzing. The nearby market was on that day and it seemed everyone in Harpurhey and Moston was out shopping. Ged walked into the superstore. His eyes clocked the boxed garden sets straight away. Shaun told the girls to have a wander around the market to see what they could have away. They both hesitated at first but once Shaun screwed his face up at them both they left his side and trudged towards the market. The sound of people chatting filled the air. People were sat eating in the cafe and Lizzy told Julie how hungry she was. Julie couldn't have given a flying shit about her appetite and carried on walking towards the bedding stalls.

Ged and Shaun walked up and down a few aisles in Asda. They were casing up the job before they put their plan into action. They'd learnt from past experience that

if they hung around any longer than necessary it would
be on top and the security would be on them like a rash.
By now Shaun was sweating buckets. He wiped the palm
of his hand across his face. His head was dipped low and
he struggled for breath. Every time he was gonna do a job,
he felt like he was going to have a heart attack and today
was no different. Ged grabbed a large box containing the
garden set and Shaun took the back end of it. They quickly
left the store. The box was heavy and Shaun found it hard
to keep a good grip. A few people who knew them both,
smiled as they watched them leave the store. Harpurhey
was full of shoplifters and grafters and it was an everyday
occurrence to see somebody up to no good.

They headed down Rochdale Road carrying the
large box. As soon as they could, they hit the side-streets.
Ged led them to an alleyway at the side of Conran Street.
He dropped the box onto the floor. Ged shook his hands
vigorously as he paced the floor.

"My fucking fingers are on fire. I couldn't have carried
it another second. It's fucking heavy innit?" Shaun agreed.
Both of them stood panting for breath. They knew they
needed a buyer. Ged asked who they should approach
first.

"What about err... that guy who lives on the Two
Hundred Estate he's always got cash. Peter Kenyon I
think he's called." Shaun knew exactly who he meant and
agreed.

"Yeah he buys anything. You wait here and I'll run over
and see if he wants it. How much are we asking for it?"
Ged pulled the box from the wall and looked at the picture
of the garden set. It had four chairs a table and an umbrella.
The retail price was on a sticker at the top of the box and
Ged read it out.

"It says here seventy-nine ninety-nine. Let's say thirty-five quid. What do you think?" Shaun nodded and set off to the buyer's house.

Peter Kenyon had lived on the Two Hundred estate for years. He was always into this, that and the other. He was well known for having a few bob and all the grafters went to him first with any knock-off stuff. The back gates of Peter's house were opened. Shaun popped his head inside and whistled hoping to get someone's attention. A large man now appeared. He pulled his face as he looked at Shaun. Peter came walking towards him looking fierce. Shaun panicked and stuttered.

"Hiya mate. I've got a brand new garden set still in the box if ya interested?" Peter walked right near him and caused him to step back out of the garden. Shaun hadn't dealt with Peter before and the buyer wanted to know the ins and outs of a cat's arse hole. Peter could be seen checking all the cars outside as they drove past his house. He'd had run-ins with the dibble so many times in the past and didn't want them on his case again. Once he was sure Shaun wasn't undercover police he let him stand in the garden. Peter asked him about all the other criminals in the area and once he was confident he was part of them he asked about what he was selling. Shaun explained what he had and how much he wanted for it. Peter shook his head. He told him he wasn't really interested in the garden set as he already had one. This was the trick of most buyers in the area and Shaun knew it only too well. They made out they weren't keen on the item and often waited for the smackheads to drop the price to an absolute bargain before they showed any interest. Peter thought for a while and told him he would come and have a look at it in his white Transit van. Shaun jumped in the passenger seat and they headed to meet Ged.

Ged was pleased to see them and spoke directly to Peter telling him the price and how the goods were still in the box and brand new. Peter could see Ged was roasting his nuts off and he knew the garden set would be his for next to nothing. He asked them where it was from and tried picking the box up on his own. Ged told him how heavy it was and watched him drop it back on the floor. This was another bargaining point for Peter as he knew the lads would have to carry it about with them if he didn't buy it. Kicking at the wall Pete made them an offer.

"I don't really want it lads but I'll take it off your hands. I'll give you twenty quid for it." Ged gasped.

"Fuck off mate. It's boxed up and everything. We can easily get thirty-five for it." Peter played the part well and started to walk away. Ged was desperate and gritted his teeth as he shouted him back.

"Right give us twenty. You know you've got a bargain, don't you?" Peter smirked but insisted he didn't really want it. The lads helped him load it into his van and watched as he drove away.

Ged was fuming. "Conning cunt!" he snarled as he watched him drive away. He looked at Shaun.

"Tell ya what. It fucking bugs me how these cheeky bastards take the piss out of us. We're smackheads not fucking mental patients. He knew we were rattling. I had no choice but to sell it to him did I?" Shaun wasn't arsed, he just wanted to score and told Ged to shut up fucking moaning. They both walked to Tavistock Square and used the pay-phone to place their order.

The process was much the same as every other time they scored. They would ring a number and someone would deliver the drugs. Very few words were ever spoken between the courier and the addict. It was just a case of exchanging the cash for brown. Once they had the heroin they hurried back to the flat. They both looked as if they'd shit themselves as they marched across the road with speed.

The front door was opened when they got back to the flat and you could hear Julie talking to Lizzy. The day had been good for them both, too. They seemed to be friends for now. Once Julie saw Shaun she told him of the stuff they'd had away. Lizzy now joined in the conversation and told them both they'd earned thirty quid from the stuff they'd nicked. Julie spoke of legs of lamb, packets of bacon and razor blades she'd had away. They were always top sellers and wouldn't remain in a junkie's possession long, once they were for sale.

The four of them shot the heroin deep into their veins. The day had only just begun and they all knew they had to go back out to earn some more money. Each of them was spending at least sixty quid a day on drugs. It just seemed that every day that went by, their habits got bigger. They would take anything that was going. Pills, beer and every now and then Ged would buy a stone, otherwise known as crack. Shaun had seen him in the past smoking crack through a pipe and wondered what the rush felt like. Crack was a treat for Ged and he only bought a stone when he'd had a good day's grafting.

Wasting their lives, they sat gazing into thin air. They all had a similar look about them; dark circles around their eyes and grey looking complexions. The girls' hair looked dull and their once white teeth looked like brown mouldy stumps. The clothing they wore was old and tattered and not fit for the bin. The small television on a wooden side cabinet was the only real possession Ged had in the flat.

Many a day when he'd been desperate for drugs he would take his TV to the local cash generator store. Some drug dealers let the junkies pay for drugs with knocked-off stuff. They were always placing orders with the junkies for stuff they needed.

Shaun sat on the chair and needed to get out. He felt suffocated and weak. His legs trembled as he tried to stand. The heroin had made him feel strange. He feared he was going to die. Julie was out of it and never said a word to him as he left. Once into the open air Shaun tried to walk to his mother's house. As he crossed the main road his body slumped to the ground onto the pavement. Within minutes the traffic was at a standstill and onlookers were trying to help him. An ambulance had been phoned. A middle-aged woman sat stoking the side of Shaun's face unaware he was a drug addict. Thick white froth hung from his mouth. His body was shaking slightly and his eyes were rolling to the back of his head. Everybody looked scared and prayed the medical help to hurry up.

Someone who knew Shaun ran to inform his sister Katie. She didn't live far from where he lay. As she ran to his side in her pyjamas she gripped her coat tighter around her body. Her hair was screwed up on top of her head in a bun. She could feel everyone's eyes on her as she bent down. The woman who was holding Shaun in her arms passed him over to Katie. As she stood up her body was shaking and she found it hard to hold back her emotions. Looking into her brother's face Katie whispered.

"Our kid, come on. Don't be dying on me. My mam will go mad if you leave her." Her tears fell onto his face as the sound of help arriving filtered the air. Within seconds the medics had Shaun in the back of the ambulance and on his way to hospital. Katie told one of the lads at the side of her who knew her to run and tell her mam what had happened.

Stepping in the back of the ambulance Katie sat on a small seat at the side of her brother. She hadn't really seen him for months and the life he led had broken the bond they used to share. He'd stolen from Katie months before and she swore she would never forgive him but her heart couldn't stop caring for him.

The medic was monitoring Shaun's body functions. He looked like he was a breath away from death. Everyone worried he wouldn't make it. As they pulled up outside the hospital he was rushed to a small room where the doctors inserted a drip into his arm. Katie cringed as she watched the doctor placing the drip in his arm. He must have forgotten Katie was there and commented on how bad the drug-addicts veins were.

Katie was now asked to leave the room. She looked at Shaun's face and hoped this wasn't the last time she saw him alive. Chewing on her bottom lip she walked outside. Katie had her own problems at the moment and the years of torment from her own boyfriend had taken its toll on her. Her body looked thin and her clothes hung from her. She looked like a bag of rags. Looking at her face you could see the remains of yet another black eye. If you wouldn't have known her, you would have said she was a baghead as well. Sitting in the waiting room she watched all the people coming and going into the hospital. Looking at her dirty feet through her flip-flops she tried to hide them from view. Katie turned her head as she heard the screaming voice of a woman from outside. As she looked closer she could see it was her mother. Gladys was hysterical.

"Where is he Katie?" she screamed. Katie stood to her feet and helped her mother sit down. Gladys was making a scene. "I want to see my fucking son. Tell me where he is." She was waving her arms in the air and wasn't listening to a word her daughter said. Gladys made her way to the main doors that led to where Shaun was and shouted the doctors. "My son is in here. I need to see him. Please."

The doctor walked past her and didn't give her a second look. He was more than used to people causing a scene in the casualty department and ignored her. She now entered the other side of the doors. The nurse on duty quickly took her arm and pulled her to the side out of the way. Gladys fell to her knees and pleaded with her to help. The young nurse left her side and quickly checked her notes. She could see her talking to one of the doctors and Gladys watched her every movement. When the nurse came back to her she told her she'd located Shaun. Gladys didn't even think about Katie in the waiting room and headed into Shaun's room like a charging bull.

Gladys froze for a few seconds and looked at all the wires that were attached to her son. Looking at the nurse she trembled.

"What's wrong with him? Please tell me he's going to be okay." The nurse felt her pain as she walked to her side.

"We are doing all we can. He's a lucky man I can tell you. A few hours more and we would have lost him. Whatever he's taken has nearly killed him." Gladys stood at the side of his hospital bed. She knew without asking her that she meant drugs. Her face was filled with shame and somehow she felt she was to blame. Gladys tried to explain to the nurse that her son was really a good lad and it was just the crowd he'd gotten in with that made him this way. The nurse left the room. Gladys was heartbroken. Her tears dropped onto the bed-sheets as she fell onto the bed at the side of him. Her shoulders could be seen shaking as the pain of a son addicted to drugs broke her heart. Katie now entered the room.

Shaun's sister stood at the bottom of the bed and watched the familiar sight of her mother crying again. Holding her body close she cried too. Gladys heard sobbing and lifted her head. Katie stared at her and awaited the arms of her mother to try and console her but they never came. All Gladys could see was her son and nothing or no one else seemed to matter.

The days passed and for the first time in Shaun's life he'd admitted he needed help. The hospital had put him in touch with a drugs worker and a mental health team. The day he left hospital he left as a man trying to get free from drugs. Gladys also made him an appointment for the doctors trying to get him as much help as possible. Methadone was his only ticket away from heroin.

Shaun felt weak and Gladys was at his side like a crutch all through the following weeks. She waited on him hand and foot. She was never far from his side. As you looked at Shaun now he looked like a person who'd been recovering from a serious illness and was now coming to the end of it. His skin still looked grey, but every day that passed small droplets of red happiness filled his skin. Gladys fed Shaun like a newborn baby. She watched every mouthful of food he swallowed and smiled at the thought of her son being normal again.

When the day of the mental health appointment came round, Shaun felt scared about going. Gladys wasn't taking any chances and told him she would go with him. She told him she would wait outside. The waiting room looked nice and clean. The walls were painted white and navy blue chairs filled the waiting area. A few other people sat waiting and Gladys looked at them wondering what their problems were. She looked at Shaun differently than the other patients. No way in the world did she class him as having mental health issues. Once Shaun informed the receptionist he was there he sat down in the chair next to his mother. Gladys came closer to his side and whispered from the side of her mouth.

"That one doesn't look right in the fucking head. Watch her," Shaun gazed over to the woman and watched her curling her hair roughly. She did look strange he thought. Shaun felt sick inside. Was he a crank now? He gasped and thought about getting off.

Shaun's name was called and he was led to a small office not far from the waiting room. Gladys hugged him before he left and told him everything was going to be alright. His face looked angry as he tried to push her away from him. He gritted his teeth as he murmured to her.

"Mam, will you fuck off. I'm not a kid ya know." Her face sunk as she backed off. Watching him leave her side she sat back down and picked up a magazine to read. The consultant told Shaun to take a seat. He picked up his notes and began to read them. Once he'd quickly read through them he introduced himself as Doctor Edwards. Shaun nodded and felt uneasy. Doctor Edwards had a friendly face. He was about fifty and had a handsome look about him. Pulling his chair closer to Shaun he began to ask about his life and his drugs intake. Once he'd finished he sat looking at Shaun and asked him why he took drugs. Shaun felt uneasy and pulled at his sleeve as he fidgeted. In his palm gripped tightly the doctor could see his pebble and asked what it was. Shaun opened his hand fully and revealed for the first time his soulmate. He rolled his thumb over it as he explained.

"I've had it for years doctor. It just helps me keep calm."
Stroking the small pebble in his fingers he continued. "It's
kind of my friend if you know what I mean?" Shaun looked
deep in thought before he spoke again. "It doesn't judge
me. It's always there with me no matter what happens."
Doctor Edward looked surprised and asked to hold the
pebble. Shaun slowly passed it to him and watched eagerly
as he examined it further. Once he passed it back to him
the conversation continued.

"Why do you take drugs Shaun?" Shaun raised his
eyebrows and looked from side to side. No one had ever
asked him this question before. He searched for the answer.
His head dipped and you could see his eyes welling up. As
his lip trembled the doctor passed him a tissue from the
side. Shaun tried to answer as tears fell on his cheek

"I don't know really. At first it was for a buzz. But
now I can't live without them. It takes all my pain away I
suppose." He urged him to continue.

"What pain is that Shaun?" Shaun held his head in his
hands. He pulled at his clothing and punched himself in
the chest.

"The pain of what I've become. I've done some bad
things for drugs. You don't know the half of it doctor."
Sitting watching Shaun's face he crossed his legs and
waited for the answer to his question. Shaun looked hot as
he wiped his forehead. He asked for a drink. Once he was
refreshed Shaun raised his eyes to the roof. His emotions
were calm now and he sniffed hard through his nostrils.

"I think my dad leaving was the start of it. I just went
wild and didn't give a fuck anymore." His body bent over
now as he lifted his foot onto his lap. Playing with his
shoelaces he continued. "Nobody seemed to care about

me. My mam was a nervous wreck, and my brother and sister were just craving love like me," he paused and tapped his fingers on his teeth. "I suppose I started abusing my body because I felt nobody cared. I think it was a cry for help." He now looked deep in thought before he finished speaking, "but no one ever helped."

The doctor had heard so many times in the past the reasons why people didn't feel normal. He knew getting Shaun talking about his pain was a good start and carried on probing into his life.

"Did you not tell anyone in your family the way you felt? What about your dad?" Shaun sighed. His face was filled with a painful smile.

"My dad was a bastard. He wasted my mother all the time. It's a wonder she isn't on drugs as well as me the life she's had."

The consultant nodded. "So how old were you when you first started taking drugs?" Shaun's face turned to the side and his eyes looked puzzled.

"I think I was about thirteen. I can't really remember. It wasn't heroin to start with it was just the glue." Shaun's face showed signs of embarrassment as he continued. "It all went downhill when I got put into care. Some serious shit happened when I went in that place." His words were slow now and each word was a struggle to get out. When he finally spoke of his mate Colby and the ordeal of the abuse he sobbed into his hands. The hour passed and Shaun's session was coming to an end. The doctor gave him another appointment and told him he would see him soon. Shaun now stood up and told him that he needed something to help him sleep at night. He spoke quickly as he knew it was now or never to get some more medication.

"My nerves are bad as well Doctor. I feel shaky all

the time. Can't you give me something to help sort that out too?" The doctor wrote him a prescription for some sleeping tablets and some Diazepam. As he took the green prescription from his hand he thanked him from the bottom of his heart. Gladys saw Shaun at the side of her and noticed the prescription. Quickly she pulled it from his grip as he tried to grab it back. She quickly read the names of the tablets and sighed.

"Why has he given you more tablets? You're on Methadone now. That's all you need isn't it?" Shaun started to walk from the waiting room and held his temper until they got outside. He let rip at her.

"I need summat to help me sleep don't I, ya muppet. And the Diazapam is to help chill me out. Just fucking keep out of my business, fucking nurse Nightingale."

Gladys shrugged her shoulders. "Well don't be taking them all at once. What did he say anyway?" Shaun carried on walking and lit a cig as Gladys wanted to know the ins and outs of everything. Shaun just gave her a look and she knew to back down as she could see he was agitated. "I'm only trying to help!" she mumbled.

Heading home on the bus, all Shaun could think about was popping his pills once he'd got them from the chemist. All he wanted to do was sleep. Looking at his mother's face he knew he couldn't stand much more of her chatting shit. She was suffocating him and he needed to get away from her as soon as possible. Shaun got his tablets and watched his mother's face sink when he told her he was going to stay at Ged's flat. She ranted and raved in the front room and told him if he left now he would never be allowed to come back. Shaun had heard it all before and ignored her. Before he left he tried to hug her but she broke free and give him a piece of her mind.

"Selfish, selfish bastard. We all run about after you and make sure you're alright. Them smackheads don't give a flying fuck about you. Go on. Run back to the shower of shit. See if I care." Gladys did care and as soon as he left she phoned Katie crying. She snivelled

"He's fucked off again Katie." Her hands gripped the phone and you could see her knuckles sticking out from her hand. Katie could be heard telling her just to give up on him but Gladys screamed down the phone line at her. "It's always the same with you Katie! It's always left to me to sort him out. I can't do it no more. I may as well be fucking dead. You can fuck off as well." She slammed the phone down. "Selfish bastards the lot of you!" she screamed into the empty room.

Gladys reached for her cigs. Her hands were shaking uncontrollably. Searching her handbag she clicked the lid from her tablet bottle. She knew she was only required to take one tablet a day but she poured two out and necked them both. Sitting staring into space she looked suicidal.

Shaun walked into the flat and Ged welcomed him back with open arms. A double bed was now situated in the living room and some new faces lay sprawled across it. Ged briefly explained the reasons why he hadn't been to see Shaun in the hospital and that seemed enough to bring their friendship back together. Julie sat looking at him and opened her arms out wide showing him she'd missed him.

Emptying his supply of tablets out onto the table, he showed the group his medication. He told them about his appointment with the consultant and how easy it was to get the pills. Ged seemed jealous when he showed him the small bottle of Methadone. He knew in the future Shaun didn't have to roast like him anymore. Sharing his tablets with Julie and Ged they all sat back and enjoyed the mellow feeling they all felt.

Chapter Twenty

Shaun's life didn't get much better. He still went to see the mental health doctor regularly and always got a monthly supply of tablets. His drug-intake was now bigger than ever. He still scored even though he had his Methadone script. Crack was his new-found love and Ged and himself often smoked a pipe together. His appearance was ten times worse than it had ever been. His self-respect had totally disappeared.

Selling his arse was an everyday occurrence to Shaun now. Even Ged was doing it. Shaun had told him one night when he was off his head what he was doing and told him it was easy money. Julie and Lizzy didn't care what they did as long as there was cash on the table at the end of the day. The two men had become ruthless. They had no morals anymore and stole from anyone.

The two of them were well known all over the shopping centres and life as a criminal was hard. Drug dealers sold them shit now and knew there was fuck all they could do about it. One day they got home with a bag of drugs and realised it was some spices that they had bought and not smack.

Lizzy was the worst smackhead out of them all and her habit was never ending. She stole from the group and even sold clothes she'd nicked from people's washing lines. Ged still loved her though and always defended her when the shit hit the fan. Shaun couldn't stand the little slag a moment more. She'd stolen his leather coat. Ok, it was a coat he had stolen from a car months before but that wasn't the point. He didn't mean it to go all pear-shaped but when she came in one day searching for drugs he made sure she could see a bag of spices and shit on the table. He didn't tell her it was snide shit and smirked as he left the room knowing she would inject it.

His joke backfired and Lizzy was pronounced dead at nine forty-five that same night. Ged was devastated and told everyone he was going to do himself in too. Shaun felt bad but something inside him loved watching Ged suffer just the way he had when Lauren had died years before. It was payback Shaun thought. His debt was now settled.

Lizzy's funeral was a quiet affair. Not a lot of people came. Blackley crematorium was almost empty. Her mother and father came. They both seemed like empty shells as they sat listening to the service. Lizzy's mother hugged her husband as the small part of Lizzy's youth was read out aloud to the church. The priest told of a girl who had everything going for her. A girl who enjoyed dancing and loved life as a child. As he continued the priest looked at Ged, Shaun and Julie. It was as if he was speaking only to them. He spoke about self-respect and how people could be led down the wrong path. Not one of them moved an inch as he spoke. When he finished speaking they all sat down and listened to the rest of the service.

Walking to her resting place, Shaun held Julie close. She was shaking and her teeth were chattering together. A few cars were parked up at the side of them and Shaun saw a black leather coat hung over the front seat. He made sure no one was looking and quickly tried the door. Once he knew it was opened he casually climbed into it and grabbed the coat as if it belonged to him. Placing it round Julie's shoulders he followed the mourners to the graveside.

Gathering around Lizzy's resting place the priest said

his final words. The brown coffin was now lowered to the ground. Her parents threw a red rose down onto the coffin and the rest of the people followed throwing a small piece of dirt into it from a small mound at the side of them.

Ged stood alone as everyone left the graveside. Shaun had stood with him but he asked him to leave to give him a moment on his own. The wind was howling past his ears as he stood looking down onto the coffin. His legs didn't look safe and he nearly fell into the grave a few times. Bending down he sat on the small piece of grass at the side of him. His hands pulled at the grass and each handful he pulled he threw down onto the coffin. He looked drugged out of his mind as he spoke.

"Fucking hell Lizzy. What the fuck am I gonna do without you?" His head fell into his hands and he sobbed. Shaun watched him from nearby and felt his pain. He stood hovering for a few minutes and told Julie to go and wait at the bus stop whilst he got Ged. His feet trudged through the muddy grass. The thick mud seemed to hold his feet for longer than necessary. Each step he took seemed to take forever. As he got near him he could hear his heartfelt words.

"I'll be with you soon Lizzy. I died a long time ago, just like you I suppose. Drugs have turned us into zombies. I hate who I have become." Shaun coughed and Ged raised his head. Wiping the tears from his face he came to Shaun's side.

"I'm done in mate. I loved her so much. She was a crank I know, but she was my crank." Shaun raised his arm and placed it around Ged's neck. Shaun tried to console him as they walked.

"You'll be fine Ged. It just takes time that's all." Ged mumbled something back but Shaun was showing his new coat off and didn't hear him.

"Ay check this out. I had it away before from one of the cars." Ged quickly glanced at it but wasn't in the mood. Shaun could see his timing was wrong and headed to Julie who was stood shivering at the bus stop.

The family had organised a bit of a wake at the local pub. Lizzy's parents made it known that none of them were welcome and they all steered clear. They could have done with an invite as they were starving and desperate for food. Standing at the bus stop Julie asked for Shaun's coat. The wind was picking up and black clouds were visible in the sky. The black leggings she wore were wafer thin and full of holes. Gripping Shaun she told him she was gutted inside. Placing her head onto his shoulders they all waited for the bus. Ged searched the floor area for cig dimps and pocketed the ones he found.

Back at the flat wasn't much better. The house was so depressing. Everyone's face had a story to tell. Each person looked like they had the worries of the world on their shoulders. They didn't have a penny between them and the fridge hadn't seen food for months. Any money they had these days was purely for drugs. Food was a distant memory.

Shaun headed to the bedroom and hid his new coat out of sight. If he thought for one minute he could have sold it he would have but it wasn't that clever and no one would have given a penny for it. Finding a space under the bed he rolled the coat up. Lying on the floor he pushed it to the back. Shaun sat thinking how depressed he was feeling. Looking at a pen and paper from the side he thought about ending his life. Slowly he reached for the black pen and within minutes he'd composed a suicide letter. He wasn't ready to say goodbye yet so he folded the paper and reached under the bed and placed the letter in the inside pocket of the leather jacket he'd just stolen.

Back in the front room he told Ged and Julie he was going out. He hadn't seen his mother for weeks and he felt the urge to go and see her. Nobody said goodbye to him and no cared if he was there or not. Ged was smoking dimps and Julie was sat picking her toe-nails.

Today was the worst day in Shaun's life. He'd felt low before but never like this. Every crime he'd ever committed was on his mind and all the people he'd let down in the past were there in his mind's eye. If he closed his eyes he could see them all pointing the finger at him. His mother's face was there at the front of all these people. He could see the sadness in her eyes. Shaking his head quickly he tried to rid his thoughts of her vision but the sound of his mother's voice still rang loud in his ears.

★

Gladys sat smoking in front of the TV as he entered. She didn't move to look at him she just grabbed her purse nearer to her side. Her words were harsh as she spoke to him.

"I've got no money, so don't bother asking."

Shaun felt like he'd been stabbed in the heart. His mother held no love in her eyes for him anymore. All he could see was hate. He moved closer and tried to make conversation.

"I've just come to see you that's all. I don't want any money," he huffed, "for fuck's sake mam." He watched her closely. Her eyes rolled and she seemed empty inside. In the past when he'd been low she'd always given him hope and pulled him back out of the darkness, but today she seemed lower than he'd ever seen her. In the past he'd even asked her to commit suicide with him as he was scared to die alone. He now realised how much of a shite life he'd led her. Digging deep inside his heart the words came to his mouth and he felt he needed to thank her for all she'd ever done for him.

"Mam," he whispered. He slowly came to sit on the back of her chair and stoked her neck. She never moved she just continued watching the TV as if he wasn't there. "Mam I feel strange. I need you to know just how sorry I am for all that I've put you through. I'm sorry you know." Gladys slowly closed her eyes and you could just see her slowly shaking her head as if to block his words out. He continued. "I am trying mam. I just can't do it."

Shaun sat at her feet and hugged her ankles. Gladys bit on her bottom lip as she tried to hold back the tears. He'd lied to her so much in the past and she didn't want to fall for anymore more of his bullshit. Shaun lay sobbing at her feet for a few minutes. He needed her to love him, but he could see she was empty. Picking himself up from the floor he dried his tears. He knew deep down inside he'd sucked every bit of life from his mother and left without speaking another word. As he left a single tear fell onto Gladys's cheek but she never moved an inch from where she was sat.

His next port of call was his sister's house. He hadn't seen Katie in a long time. As he crossed the main road to her house his tears were flowing. Walking down her path he prayed she opened the door and not her nobhead boyfriend. It seemed to take forever but his prayers were answered and Katie stood in her pink pyjamas staring at him with a cocky look on her face. His words choked him and he gasped for breath. Katie had seen so many of his crocodile tears over the years and was numb to any emotion she felt for him. She looked him up and down and looked behind her before she spoke to him.

"What do you want?"

He wanted to shout out that he wanted his family back and to be free from drugs but he just hunched his shoulders and remained silent. She looked agitated as she kept looking behind her again and spoke quickly. "Listen he's in, so don't come here starting trouble. I can't be doing with it all." Shaun looked at her face and could see she had troubles of her own. He paused for a minute and just told her he loved her. He walked out from the garden. Katie looked shocked and had expected him to ask for money. Her eyes followed him and she would have run after him only for her boyfriend shouting her from inside. As she closed the front door she couldn't help but feel sorry for her brother.

Night time was falling and all he had to keep him company was his pebble. He made his way to the town centre and sold his arse throughout the night. Shaun had sex with at least four men that night but couldn't remember the following day. He had pressed his self-destruct button now and he prayed every night that he wouldn't see the morning.

Every day was more or less the same and after a few months he couldn't stand himself any longer. Julie had moved on to another smackhead and Ged was like him, waiting to die. Shaun would stick anything into his veins these days and on a few occasions he'd injected Temazepams. The flat was home to more than five addicts now. He never took the time to get to know them and just went back to the flat to sleep.

Heroin was no longer the mental block he needed. All his crimes were still there even after a hit. His drug habit grew to £80 a day and not even selling his arse could pay for the drugs his body demanded. He often sold his Methadone and pills to fellow druggies to buy crack, but even the rush from that wasn't enough these days.

Lying in bed that night he just stared around the bedroom. Sleep was a million miles away as his years of betrayal floated through his mind. He was shaking from the inside as he pulled the paper-thin sheet around his body to stop his body feeling cold. The light from outside the window was shining onto him and as he turned he could see a moth fighting with the light. He looked amazed as he watched the moth attacking the light. Shaun raised his head as he heard the door opening. It was Ged, he stood still for a minute then whispered.

"Are you awake Shaun?"

"Yeah. I can't fucking sleep. My head's up my arse. I feel strange."

"Me too mate. I just feel as if I'm here on borrowed time. If ya know what I mean." Shaun did know what he meant and sat up.

"Have you got any cigs?" Ged shook his head.

"Nar, but if you want we can go on a dimp picking trail."

Shaun threw his legs from the bed and searched for the clothes he'd worn constantly for over two weeks. Once he was dressed they both hit the streets looking for cig ends.

The men looked depressed as their eyes searched on the floor for dimps. Ged took him to a local spot outside one of the pubs where he was almost certain of finding some big cigarette dimps. Trying to unfold a stumped out cig Ged smiled as he sat on a small wooden- bench.

"Tell ya what mate. This is the lowest I've been in a long time. I know I'm a baghead but I just can't shake this feeling from me. I think of Lizzy every day and sometimes wish I was the one who died and not her. I just feel so lonely."

Shaun agreed with him. He would have given an arm and a leg just to be held and for someone just to tell him they loved him. Shaun's hair was thinning now. All the shit he'd injected into his body over the years was having a dramatic effect on him. He had two white teeth at the front of his mouth and the rest were brown pegs. His fingers looked swelled and he told Ged that he thought he had septicaemia. Ged laughed. They sat smoking dimps for at least an hour before they headed home. Neither of them felt any better and it was quite obvious one of them would take their life pretty soon. Just before they neared the flats Shaun froze. Ged asked him what was the matter.

"I'm just gonna nip and see an old friend. I won't be long."

Shaun made his way to Moston cemetery. Once there he climbed the small iron-gates at the main entrance. As he walked through the graveyard he could hear an owl hooting in the distance. He froze and tried to locate it but it was hid in the darkness guarded by the trees. The walk didn't take very long to Colby's grave. As he reached it he sat close to the headstone. One hand held it and the other was on the floor. It was pitch black and the only light came from a nearby street light. Bringing his knees up to his chest he tried to stop himself trembling with fear. His mouth felt dry as he licked his lips. Taking a minute to get his words together he began to speak to Colby.

"I'm coming to see you soon mate. I hope you're ready for me? I can't do it anymore Colby." Running his fingers through his hair he continued, "No one cares whether I live or die. Even my mam has given up all hope on me mate."

He gripped his ankles and squeezed at them. "Never ever thought my mam would give up on me, but, ay, it's my own fault isn't it?" His head fell forward onto the headstone.

He reached inside his pocket for his pebble. Bringing it up closer to his face he kissed it slowly. "This is all I've got Colby. A fucking pebble. I suppose it's a lot like me really. Cold and lifeless." Rubbing the pebble on his cheeks he closed his eyes and wished the touch was that of someone who loved him. Shaun sat for a while in silence. He could hear something in the distance and knew that rats weren't that far away from him. Tying his shoelaces he spoke his final words to his best friend.

"Right then Colby. I will be there soon. So get the beer in ay?" Pulling his coat closer to his body he left the cemetery.

★

The following morning Shaun's mind was made up. His life was no longer worth living and he couldn't go on anymore. He planned every step to end his life. Running the bath he made sure he had clean underwear to put on. His mother had always warned him about not changing his underwear. He could hear her in his mind saying "Make sure you have changed your underpants Shaun, you could get knocked over today." His smile stayed on his face for a few minutes as he thought about his mother and her funny sayings.

Sat in the bath he rubbed the small piece of soap about his body. It was strange because no matter how much he rubbed at his skin he never felt clean. Shaun used a bit of washing up liquid that was on the side to wash his hair with. The small growth he had round his mouth was now shaved away with a rusty razor blade that was in a cup at the end of the bath. It was Ged's razor and Shaun knew even if it was full of germs it wouldn't matter anyway, as today was the last day of his life.

Wrapping the dirty bath towel round his body he walked back to his bedroom with his clean underwear in his hands. Shaun had enough drugs for one last good hit. Once he was ready he started to inject the drugs deep into his veins. He also popped the last few Diazapam he had left.

Walking into the front room he looked at the sad lives in front of him. Ged was sat talking to the group. He was trying to come up with some plan to earn them some much needed money. Shaun went to the small CD player and placed his disc inside. The Smiths song "Every Day is like Sunday" now played at full blast. Ged told him to turn it down but he smiled at him and winked as he disappeared back into the bedroom. Shaun found his coat and zipped it up. The hood swung around the back of it and he tried to grab it to straighten it out. Stood in his room he started to sing the words of the song. He took a deep breath and headed to the balcony. No one asked him what he was doing and no one cared that he was outside. All that the people inside cared about was their next fix and how much money they could earn. Shaun had had enough and today he was going to end his life.

"Goodbye cruel world," he whispered as he passed Ged for the last time.

Chapter Twenty-one

Shaun's family were stood around his bed. The doctors had told them that he'd taken a turn for the worse and didn't have a lot of time left. A lot of his organs were shutting down. It was only a matter of time before Shaun was gone.

Gladys stood with her two children and her ex-husband the night Shaun left this world. He never regained consciousness. Gladys was surprisingly brave and held Paul and Katie at her side as the heart-monitor stopped bleeping. Katie fell to the bed like a lead weight and sobbed her heart out. Paul had never been one for words. He held his tears back until he was away from them all.

Gladys walked slowly to Shaun's bedside as his heartbeat disappeared from the screen. The doctors in the room left and gave them time alone once they'd done all the essential medical work. Mike came to her side and cupped her waist as she lifted Shaun's head from the bed. Her words were heart wrenching and all the family cried as she spoke.

"You're not in any more pain now son. We never stopped loving you. My heart has also stopped beating." She jerked back the rush of tears. Taking a deep breath she carried on saying her goodbyes. "The hole you have left in my life will never be filled. I'm sorry son. I wish I could have helped you more, but I just didn't know how." Katie grabbed her as her body was falling. "You sucked every bit of life from me Shaun and I didn't have any strength left." Shaun's dad held her as she sobbed onto her son's head. Her hands were gripped firmly round him. It looked like she was never letting go. Katie was now at the other side of the bed. She held the cold hand of her brother. The veins were still blue. She shook her head as she tried to say goodbye.

"Our kid. I didn't ever think in a million years you would be gone. All the things I wanted to say to you will now be held in my heart forever. I lost you a long time ago to drugs. I know we have both said things in the past that we didn't mean, but I have always loved you, bruv." Katie sank her head on the bed and she could feel her mother's hand stroking her head from the other side of the bed.

That day another family from Harpurhey lost a man they loved to drugs. Many more drug addicts would follow and lots of families would mourn the death of people they loved. After time Shaun's family left his bedside. Each of them had regrets, of words unspoken and love they never shared. They all headed back to Glady's house.

Family and friends were already round at the house offering their condolences to the family. Harpurhey was a large community and they stuck together in times of sorrow. Mothers and fathers of other drug addicts stood watching the family and prayed they wouldn't have to suffer the same torment of losing a child to drugs.

Gladys sat in her chair and looked inconsolable. The only time she moved was to light a cigarette. Katie was brewing up for everyone and trying to keep her emotions stable for the sake of the household. Each person who came to Shaun's mother's side cried as they offered their sympathy. Gladys was like a ticking bomb and when one of the neighbours mentioned Shaun was a drug addict she sprung from her chair like a scalded cat.

"Don't you ever call my Shaun a drug addict! He was my son. Don't speak about him as if you knew him. None

of you fuckers gave a shit about him when he was alive!"
Gladys raised her hand and pointed her finger around the
room. Her eyes were filled with madness as she spit the
words out of her mouth as if they were on fire.

"It's alright for all of you! You still have your sons and
daughters. I have fuck all now without him." Katie dipped
her head. Her father was at the side of her and cradled her
in his arms as Gladys let rip. "And don't think I don't know
what you lot are all saying behind my back." Her head was
held high as she chewed on her lips. She paced the living
room floor looking at each of them with a look to kill in
her eyes. She lifted her hand to the ceiling. "And yeah I did
live for my son! So fucking what! No matter what he did
I always stuck by him. Just like we all do for our children."
Paul came to her side. His words were soft.

"Mam, come on, you're upset. You need to calm down."
Shaking his hand from her body she screamed at him.

"You! You were just the same as all the fucking others.
You didn't give Shaun the time of day. All you ever did was
hit him. Bullying bastard, that's all you were." Paul huffed
and looked at his father for help but he was consoling
Katie. Gladys walked away from him and continued in her
abusive language.

"When he had knocked off stuff you were all round
him like flies round shit. Yeah you all loved the bargains
didn't you? Did you ever think for one minute that with
the money he was buying fucking drugs?"

Katie was breaking free from her father's grip she
couldn't stand back anymore. She ran at her mother and
years of frustration broke free. "He robbed you blind and
everyone else. Don't pretend he was this big loving son
because he didn't give a shit about you or anyone else."
Gladys was trying to grab her now but Paul restrained her

as she opened fire.

"Stop kidding yourself mother. He was a dirty drug addict. He didn't give a shit about anyone but himself and getting wrecked." Katie knew her words were harsh and backed off as Gladys flopped to the floor. The neighbours started to disappear one by one. Within minutes all that was left was Shaun's immediate family.

The sound of sobbing could be heard. The moment was heart wrenching as Mike came to Gladys's side. Reaching down to where she lay he lifted her to her feet. Her legs were like jelly and she couldn't stand up unaided. Her hands hung round his neck as he placed her back on the sofa. Katie felt guilty and stood staring at the walls.

A family was destroyed. None of them had any words left to say. Nothing could ever take away the pain they all felt inside. Paul went inside his mother's bag and searched for her tablets. Grabbing a glass of water from the kitchen he spoke quietly to his mother.

"Mam, take a couple of these. You need to relax. You're gonna have a heart attack otherwise." His mother lifted her head. Her hair was stuck to her cheeks through the tears she'd wept. Wiping her eyes she took the two tablets from his palm and washed them down with a swig of water. Katie looked at the bottle of pills. She'd taken them in the past when she couldn't cope. Looking at Paul she asked him for a couple too. Within minutes all the family had popped a pill.

Later that night and Katie had made some sandwiches but they just stood on the small plate at the centre of the table curling at the edges.

Gladys's eyes were heavy. In her hand she held Shaun's pebble. Every now and then she would hold it tightly in her fist and place it next to her heart. She looked as if she was speaking to it as she held it to her chest. You could see her mouth moving slowly but no words were coming out.

Katie searched the old mahogany cabinet in the front room. She found the old family photo album. At first she held it inside the cabinet and didn't know whether to bring it out or not. Her fingers gripped the corner of the silver album. Slowly she placed it under her arm and brought it to show them. Paul could see her from the corner of his eyes and smiled. Paul called out to her.

"Come and sit here Katie and let's have a look at it." She walked to the sofa and nudged him over with her arse as she sat down. He pulled the album closer so he could get a good look. Opening the first page they both laughed as they saw a picture of the three of them when they were on holiday in Blackpool years before. Paul was pissing himself as he shouted over to his dad.

"Is that the hair cut you gave me dad?"

Mike walked over and bent down to look at the picture closer. His eyes screwed up as he struggled to see without his glasses. Lifting his head back up, he laughed out loud.

"Ay that was the dog's bollocks, that hair cut. You looked like George Best." Paul sighed and nudged Katie.

"Fucking George Best! More like Fred West." Katie shouted out now as she pointed at her hair in the picture.

"Fucking hell, mine's no better. I look like ya wife Rose." The three of them sat laughing. Gladys was watching them all and wanted to see what they were laughing about. She knew her son's face would be there in the photo album and stood up to join them. Sitting on the arm of the chair she leant across Paul's shoulder to get a closer look.

As the pages turned they all laughed and cried. Towards the back of the album Shaun stood from the page in his communion clothes. He looked like an angel, as if butter wouldn't melt in his mouth. Gladys examined the picture closer and spoke of the clothes he wore.

"We got his communion suit made for him didn't we Mike?" Shaun's dad nodded. He didn't remember but just agreed to keep her happy. "Mrs Sullivan made it for us. It was all made from white silk." Her face looked happy as if she could see him still wearing it. "Shaun hated it. He said the material made him itch. Fucking hell I remember it as if it was yesterday." All in the room now sat forward and listened to her every word. "I watched him in the church and he was pulling at the shirt. He was gonna rip it and I had to give him the eyes when he looked at me and mouthed to leave it alone." Gladys pulled the photo from the album and looked at it in more detail. "Poor fucker!" she chuckled, "when he come home after the church his legs were red raw." Katie smiled and remembered her brother's first communion. She took the photo from her and laughed.

"He had first degree burns mam, not just red raw." They all laughed as the photos were passed about. Lots more snaps were looked at. One of Shaun as a drug addict stared at them all from the page. Katie looked at Paul and they were going to ignore it and turn the page but Gladys stopped them.

"Look at the state of him there." Gladys shook her head and sighed. "He swore blind that he was wasn't on drugs. Do you remember it was our Susan's engagement party?" They all knew the time she was talking about and looking at the photo in more detail. You could tell he was off his head. His eyes looked like piss holes in the snow and his skin was grey even on the snap-shot. Even his sweat was visible on the photo. Mike held the picture and shook his head. He could see the skeletal frame of his son. Tears fell onto his cheek and he broke down for the first time.

Katie jumped to hold him but Gladys was already there at his side. Her lips were trembling as she spoke.

"He's at peace now Mike. Our son is finally at Peace." Paul and Katie joined them both and the family cried together. The days that lay ahead were going to be hard and they knew the funeral was just around the corner.

Chapter Twenty-two

Gladys sat in the house and smoked like a chimney. She'd been to the chapel of rest every night Shaun had been there and spent hours talking to her dead son. Walking into the chapel of rest for the first time Gladys felt strange. As she sat down beside the coffin she felt her heart pounding in her chest. The coffin was brown. White silk filled the inside of it. The gold handles on the side of the coffin looked highly polished and Gladys stroked her hands over them as she spoke to Shaun.

"I can't say goodbye son. I wish it was me who was lay there and not you. How am I supposed to go on when I know you're not here anymore?" Her hand touched Shaun's. Gladys's face changed as she felt his fingers for the last time. He felt cold. Digging in her pocket Gladys pulled something out and held it in her grip. As she started to speak she stood up and leant into the coffin. Opening Shaun's hands she struggled to place the pebble inside. Tears fell onto his black suit as she spoke.

"I know this kept you calm son. You always had it in times of trouble didn't you?" Still stood up she dusted the white fluff from his pants. The suit he wore was Paul's. It looked massive on Shaun's thin body but it was all they had to make him look respectable. Gladys looked down at his shoes and cried as she laughed.

"Them fucking dancing shoes. You hated them didn't you?" She looked closely at his feet and realised how much of a twat her son looked in them. Pulling at the hem of his trousers she tried to cover the shoes up.

The clock ticked loudly on the wall in the chapel of rest. This was the last night she would ever sit with her son. All the other family members had been to see him but she never left his side. Time was ticking away. She rocked her body as the time neared for her to leave him. Holding his hand to her face she said her last goodbyes.

"I've got to go soon son. One day we'll be together again. I'll never forget you son. Good night, God bless. Sleep tight." Gladys's eyes streamed with tears. If she would have sat there long enough she would have flooded the room with her grief. For the last time she kissed her son and made sure the pebble was still in his grip.

"Goodbye Shaun," she whispered as she left the room.

★

On the morning of the funeral the heavens opened. The clouds in the sky were black and looked angry. The residents of Harpurhey were all out in force and ready to attend the service. There had been a collection amongst the neighbours on the estate. With the money they had bought Shaun a big wreath saying his name in red and white flowers. Shaun had been a united fan and lots of the flowers were of that theme.

The funeral cars pulled up and Shaun's coffin was on show in the back of it. People started to take flowers over to the funeral director. He was placing them neatly next to the coffin. The cul-de-sac was filled with people and they all respected Shaun's funeral by wearing black.

Katie came from the house first. Her dad was holding her up. It was obvious she was devastated. Her boyfriend stood with the crowd and shook his head as he watched her sob. Gladys now came into sight and Paul was at her side. Her face looked ravaged and the effort she'd made to try and look her best couldn't hide the tears she'd cried. Her body was shaking and it was visible to everyone just how bad she was. Once inside the car she lit a cig and stared out of the window. The funeral cars slowly left the street. Young lads took off their baseball caps as the black cars passed them. Katie had organised most of the funeral and had told the driver to take Shaun's funeral to places he'd knocked about in when he was a kid.

The cars drove past Conran Street market and lots of people stood on the street watching the funeral pass. Katie noticed Ged and Julie stood at the roadside. They nodded at her as they passed. She'd seen Ged days before and he'd told her he would be at the church for the service. She smiled at him as they passed. She knew he must be nipping on the market first to have some stuff away before he came.

The next place they stopped at was The Two Hundred pub. Shaun had spent a lot of time inside the pub selling his knock off stuff. The staff and a few regulars stood outside. As the cars passed they lifted their glasses into the air as a sign of respect. Peter Kenyon, one of Shaun's friends and buyers was also there. He'd put money behind the bar in the pub for the wake after the funeral. He told Gladys that Shaun had been a good lad and he wanted to pay his respects, after all he'd earned a right few quid because of him and didn't have to worry about money anymore. He was loaded.

The cars finally headed up Rochdale Road, although not everybody paid their respects. Shaun had robbed a lot of people in the past. Katie saw one middle-aged woman mouthing "Dirty smackhead" as the cars passed. She wanted to jump out of the car and punch her right in the face but realised it wasn't the time or the place.

The church grounds were packed with people as the

cars pulled up. All Shaun's old friends were there. Most of them were also drug addicts and dipped their heads as the family drove passed.

Katie been to the flat with Ged earlier in the week and found Shaun's Smiths CD. The nights before his funeral she'd played the disc time and time again to try and find the right song for him. In the end she found a song called "Asleep." The words just said it all. It was Shaun's life in a song, she thought. She cried as she listened to the words. Katie also picked another song but made sure it wasn't as morbid as the first because she wanted Shaun to be remembered as the happy person he once was before the drugs took over his life.

The coffin was pulled from the back of the hearse. Ged had been asked to carry the coffin along with Shaun's dad and brother but declined saying he was too weak. Family members now held the coffin on their shoulders as they slowly walked into the church. The song played softly in the background as the coffin was placed at the altar.

St Patrick's was packed out. As the song played you could hear sobbing from the congregation. Gladys sat at the front of the church with Katie by her side. When the coffin was placed firmly on the stand, Mike and Paul joined them.

The wooden benches felt cold and hard as they sat on them. The priest now placed a photograph of Shaun onto the coffin and walked to the side of the church. Gladys had decided to use the photograph of Shaun when he was in his prime.

The priest had a bald head and wore a robe with deep purple stripes down the side of it. His black pants were visible underneath it and Katie wondered why he hadn't taken them off. As the priest cleared his throat he began to tell them the life of Shaun Cook. Gladys smiled as he spoke about Shaun's early years. He told the congregation that he'd had been very artistic man and could have been a very good artist if he would have ever taken that road. Paul had prepared a few words for the funeral and it was his job to speak to the mourners and set the record straight about his brother.

There was silence in the church as Ged and Julie opened the door at the back of the church. Everybody turned their heads towards them and tutted. Ged looked off his head. His eyes were dancing all over the place as were Julie's at the side of him. They both sat down as Paul was led to the lectern to speak about his brother. Paul looked white as he unfolded the large piece of paper in front of him. All the family had had a say in the words and it was his job to deliver them. Twisting his fingers together Paul began.

"Thanks everyone for coming, Shaun would have been buzzing to know so many people cared about him." He pulled at his shirt and he looked as if he was suffocating. Katie sat forward on the bench and folded her hands together as she listened. "Shaun was a drug addict. We all knew that about him, didn't we?" The heads in the church nodded. Paul looked towards Ged and Julie and spoke directly to them hoping they would learn from his brother's death. "Anyone who has had someone they love on drugs will know what kind of a life our family has had. We all found it hard to cope. His habit was our habit because we all suffered because of it." A lump formed in Paul's throat as he swallowed hard. "I can only ask that people will try to change and think of their own families before it's too late. I've lost a brother and a friend because of drugs. Our family will never forget Shaun and I hope people can see beyond his drug addiction. He was kind-hearted and just

got lost in a world of drugs." Paul dropped his head and
could hear the sound of people crying. His own tears now
fell and Mike stood up to bring him back to the bench.

Gladys sat in shock. Her body quivered. Her mouth
looked dry as she licked her lips constantly. Her black fur
coat was held with one hand tightly holding it together.

The Requiem mass went on for an hour. The priest
now led the mourners to lay Shaun to rest. The funeral
procession now drove to Moston cemetery. Katie held
the silver CD player by the graveside and played "This
Charming Man" as his body was lowered into the ground.

Gladys picked the soil up from beside her feet and
dropped it onto the coffin. The rest of the people followed
her lead as the music played in the background. Ged
watched Gladys's face and thought about his own mother.
He hadn't seen her in years and wondered if she would be
the same if he lost his life. Julie was rocking and the tablets
she'd taken numbed any emotion she felt.

The family left the graveside as the rain started. Each
droplet hit Gladys' face felt like a lump of lead. All she
wanted to do was to go home and sleep. The days that had
passed had caught up with her and her eyes were closing.
Katie told her that she needed to go back to the pub just
for one drink to pay her respects. Gladys agreed, even
though she couldn't stand the thought of people sat there
getting pissed.

The pub was packed out within minutes and the noise
of people talking was deafening. The buffet was opened
and everyone made their way to the free food. Mike came
to sit at the side of Gladys.

"He's had a good send off hasn't he?" Gladys nodded.
"I didn't realise that he had that many friends."

"Fucking friends my arse," she growled, "They're just

people who he shared drugs with and filled their pockets. He had no real friends; otherwise he wouldn't be lying dead would he?" Mike reached for her hand but she pulled it away as she swigged her glass of Brandy. Gladys was on the turn now and Mike made a quick exit before she started on him.

Paul stood with Ged and Julie. He preached at them both about taking drugs. Ged could understand his hurt and promised Paul he would try and get help. Julie was a lost cause and just stared away from him not listening to a word he said. Paul grabbed Ged's hand.

"Promise me mate. For our Shaun's sake. Please get clean and make your family proud." Ged's eyes filled up. No one had ever spoken to him like that before and he seemed to take in every word.

The night in the pub went on into the early hours of the morning and the Cook family had given Shaun a send off to be proud of. Gladys had gone home with her sister earlier on and left Katie, Paul and Mike in the pub drowning their sorrows.

For the first time in days Gladys was on her own. Her sister had put her in bed and left hours before. Looking at the ceiling she spoke to herself.

"Shaun, are you there son? If you are speak to me please. I just need to know you're okay." The silence was chilling and Gladys sat up in the bed repeating her words but this time she was shouting them. "Just like you isn't it Shaun? Leaving me, when I need you the most. Well fuck off. See if I care." Gladys grabbed the cover and buried her head under the sheets hoping she wouldn't see daylight again. The room felt cold and for minutes you could hear the sound of crying from under the sheets.

Mike, Katie and Paul all came back into the family

home around five o'clock in the morning. All of them were
pissed as farts. Katie looked a wreck. She'd been arguing
with her boyfriend and finally ended up telling him to
fuck off. He'd gone for her big time but Paul stepped in
with some of his mates and saw him off. Paul flung himself
onto a chair and kicked his shoes off. Mike was in the
fridge looking for something to eat. He was starving. Katie
sat on a dining-room chair and rubbed her feet as she
pulled her shoes off. Admiring her feet in front of her she
shouted to her dad to make her a butty. The sound of Mike
cutting some salad on the side was loud and Paul giggled.
He shouted in a sarcastic tone.

"Fucking hell can't you make any more noise? You'll
have me mam up if you don't quieten things down." Mike
shoved his head from the kitchen and smiled as he rammed
two fingers up towards Gladys lying in bed. They all
chuckled. Katie stood and told them she would just go and
check on her as they hadn't seen her for hours. Holding the
wall Katie made her way upstairs. Her head was spinning
and she felt sick. Each stair seemed to take forever to get
up. Katie giggled as she farted on the last stair. Holding her
fingers over her mouth she swayed towards the bedroom
door.

The bedroom was in darkness. Her mother's body could
be seen under the blankets. Katie crept into the room and
looked at the body in the bed. She wanted to make sure
Gladys was still breathing and stood over the covers until
they moved. With a sigh she left the room. She could see
her mother's body wriggling about in the bed.

Katie was going to go downstairs but Shaun's bedroom
door stared at her. She felt like it had magical powers over
her. She couldn't help entering the room. Pressing the
silver door handle down she rubbed at her arms. You could

see her hairs standing up on her skin. Katie sat on the bed. Her flat palm stroked the place where her brother used to sleep. Lifting the pillow she held it up to her nose and inhaled deeply. Her eyes closed as tears fell. Whispering under her breath she lay down slowly still hugging the pillow close to her.

"I can still smell you, our kid. Your sweaty head is still here on the pillow." She folded the pillow and slid it under her head still inhaling. Pulling the quilt she yanked it from both sides of the bed and enveloped herself inside it. Her eyes just looked around the room. Katie's fingers felt the wall paper. Using her finger nail she wrote Shaun's name on the wall followed by I love you. Katie cried herself to sleep. All through the night she held her brother's pillow close to her as she slept.

Chapter Twenty-three

Ged sat in the flat and glanced at his fellow users. Shaun's death had been a wake-up call for him. He wanted so much to try and turn his life round. Seeing Gladys at the funeral made him think more about his own mother and he wanted to go and see her.

Washing his face in the bathroom mirror he pulled at his skin. His skin was baggy and full of spots. His complexion was weird. It was neither white nor grey. It just had a colour of its own that didn't look healthy. As he opened his mouth to brush his teeth he could see stumps of black and brown pegs where his teeth used to be. He shook his head.

Ged looked for some decent clothes to wear. He'd not seen his mother in years and he wanted to look his best. Heading to Shaun's old bedroom he searched the wardrobe. As he pulled Shaun's old track-suit bottoms out he smiled.

"You don't mind do you Shaun?" he said tilting his head and speaking to the ceiling. Slipping the pants on over his boxer shorts he looked ten times bigger than he really was. The bottoms were a size too large. Shaun had nicked the wrong size months before by mistake. He claimed they were his big grafting pants as he could fit loads of knock-off inside them. Ged walked up and down the bedroom. He laughed as he pulled at the leg. Dipping his head he looked under the bed for any trainers that might be lurking there. Stretching his arm out he swept all the items out towards him.

Ged sat looking at the group of odd trainers. There wasn't one matching pair. Sighing he kicked at them. As he moaned under his breath his eyes focused on a black leather coat. Wiping the dust from it he held it up into the air. His face changed. Ged looked puzzled. He sat holding the coat for a few minutes, then he remembered Lizzy's funeral the day Shaun had it away. Standing to his feet he tried the coat on. It was a bit big but it was much better than anything else he owned. He quickly threw a t-shirt on from the wardrobe and placed the coat over it. He was ready to go once he'd found some trainers.

Ged walked down the street where his mother lived. He walked slowly and was in two minds whether or not to turn back home. The weather was turning. His hand dug into the jacket pocket. The lining was ripped and he could feel things moving around inside it. Digging his hand in deeper he could feel a large piece of paper. Ged stood still and took the coat off. Stretching his hand inside the black lining his fingers gripped a piece of paper. Sitting on a nearby wall he unfolded it. On the front of it in capital letters it read 'Mam' with one kiss at the side of it.

His hands were shaking as he began to read the letter. Unfolding the paper fully he sat reading it. Ged could be heard sniffling. After a few minutes he folded the letter carefully and placed it gently back inside his pocket. Whatever was written in the letter made Ged run to his mother's house.

★

Marjorie came to the door as she heard someone knocking. She thought it was another salesman and she could be heard moaning as she came to open the door.

"I don't want any new windows, or anything else

you're selling. You're wasting your time," she said as she opened the door. Her eyes focused on Ged. His mother could be seen gasping for breath as she held one hand up against the wall. Marjorie was in her mid-sixties and looked after herself. Ged's dad Eric was at work and she hesitated speaking when she first saw her son. Ged stood with a look in his eyes that told her he needed help. Her first response would have usually been to tell him to fuck off, but this time he looked different. Ged held his tears back as he spoke to his mother.

"Mam, can I come in and talk to you. I promise I won't stay long. Honest." Sweeping her hair from her face she glanced up and down the street to see if any of the neighbours were watching. Eric wasn't due home for a while yet and she hadn't seen her son for a long time. She opened the door wide and invited him inside. As he came into the front room she spoke. Reluctantly she asked him in.

"Just sit there and don't move. You know you're not allowed anywhere in this house." Her face looked frantic as she found her purse. Walking towards it she placed it at the side of her where she could see it. She sat down. Ged watched her and knew he deserved the way she was treating him. He'd stolen loads of stuff from the family in the past and didn't blame his mother for her actions. Her eyes burned into him. She looked like she could see right into his soul. Ged sat forward.

"How are ya mam?" Marjorie wriggled about in the chair and gulped.

"I'm as fine as can be expected. How are you?" he smiled softly.

"I'm not good mam. So much has happened. I'm so down and can't seem to pull myself back up." His mother looked at him and wondered if he was trying to have her over for some cash. She quickly spoke.

"I've got no money, so don't be asking me for owt." He dipped his head as a river of tears ran from his eyes.

"I don't need money mam. I need help. I need you." He was shaking. "I wanna get clean and get off the shit." Marjorie choked. Never in all the years of his drug use had Ged asked her for help. She was still apprehensive about him and questioned her son. Marjorie sat forward in her seat. She looked as if she was fighting with her hands to stop them comforting her son.

"How can I help you? You can only help yourself. You've never wanted help before, so why now?" Her words seemed cold and callous but he knew how much hurt and pain he'd caused her in the past. He pleaded.

"Mam... please! I can't go on. I just need you to help me. Please." His words dug into her heart like a twelve inch knife. She sat shaking her head slowly and knew he was desperate.

Ged cried. His mother sat glued to her chair and she found it hard to help him. Eventually she was at his side. Her eyes closed as she rested her head on his.

"Son... son." she sighed, "I want to believe you, but think of all the shit you have told us in the past. I just don't know you anymore." Ged yelled his emotions from the bottom of his heart.

"Mam. I'll change. I promise you. Can I come back here? Please. I swear I won't let you down ever again." Marjorie sobbed as she held the bag of bones that was her son. Her eyes were closed as tears fell. She knew her husband would have kittens if he knew Ged was even in the house never mind moving back in with them again. Biting down on her lip she made a decision.

"I'll have to speak to your dad. You know it won't be easy, but if you're being honest with me then I'll help you." He fell to the ground between his mother's knees. His eyes looked at hers as he begged her from the bottom of his heart.

"Please mam. I swear to you. Never again will I touch drugs." Ged gripped her two hands in front of him and squeezed them together. She nodded her head and she accepted his plea for help.

"You better get upstairs and get in that bath if you want to stay here. You stink." A smile filled her face and she led him upstairs.

"Right get in the bath. And use some soap." Ged didn't argue and followed her instructions. She placed a white fluffy towel on the toilet seat and told him to throw his clothes down once he'd got out of the bath so she could wash them. She left the bathroom and closed the door. Ged began to run the water into the bath. His body was weak and he didn't think he could lift his legs into it. His mother knocked on the door and shouted.

"There's some clothes outside the door and clean underwear." His lips trembled as he sat in the bath.

"Thanks mam", he whispered. The sound of his mother heading downstairs could be heard. Sliding into the bath his body lay flat. The warmth from the water made him feel safe. It felt like a warm blanket of love had been wrapped around his skin.

Ged disappeared under the water. When he re-appeared all his hair was stuck to his face. His mother's mirror was sparkling clean and he sat up to look into it. His face had already changed from earlier. It seemed full of hope. Scrubbing his body he inhaled the fragrance from the soap. He'd never felt so clean in years. Even the water he lay in smelt clean. Finding a razor on the side he scraped at his face removing the stubble.

Once he was dried, he grabbed the clean clothes from outside the door. He halted as he could smell the familiar aroma of bacon being cooked. Heading downstairs his mother handed him a bacon butty and a mug of piping-hot tea. She smiled as she led him into the front room. As he sat down she spoke in a firm voice.

"I've just spoken to your dad on the phone and told him what's happened." She paused as Ged's face dropped.

"He wasn't over the moon... but he said you can stay." He smiled and shook his head as she continued.

"There's rules though. We're not taking any shit. The first time you fuck up, you're out. No chances, no nothing. You'll be straight out of here on your arse, trust me." He sucked up hard through his nose as he replied.

"Thanks mam. I won't let you down. I know it's going to be hard but I'm going to do it. I owe it to Shaun to get clean." Marjorie knew all about Shaun's death and agreed. She started to speak about it and watched her son deflate as he spoke about him.

Ged quickly moved towards his jacket. Marjorie thought he was leaving. She stood up and clenched her fists. As she saw him search through his coat she relaxed and sat back down. He passed her the letter.

His mother reached for her reading-glasses and hung them over her nose as she sat back in the chair reading. Her hand gripped around her throat as she read the words. Once she'd finished she looked up over her glasses and shrugged her shoulders.

"Is this letter meant for Shaun's mother?" Ged nodded. "Has she read it yet?" Ged shook his head.

"No I've just found it in Shaun's old coat. I didn't know

it was there. He must have written it before he died."

"Oh, the poor woman," she sobbed reaching for a box of tissues at the side of her. Gripping the letter to her heart she took a deep breath.

"You need to go and give it to his mother. It's something she will need to read. Perhaps she might understand why he didn't want to go on anymore." Ged reached over and took the letter from her hands. He folded it and placed it into his tracksuit bottoms.

"I know mam. I'm going to take it round later. I think it's something he wanted her to read." Ged bit into his butty. He found it hard to eat and his mother watched him struggle to eat every mouthful. She spoke about the days ahead and told him his family would help him as much as possible. Marjorie knew it wouldn't be plain sailing but lived in hope he would come through the other side.

They both sat talking for hours and before they knew it the sound of his father opening the front- door could be heard. Ged sat up straight in the chair and his body tensed. The last time he'd seen Eric he'd punched Ged right in the face. He'd dragged him from the house after he found out he'd stolen from them again. Ged faced the door as his dad came into sight.

Eric was sixty-seven. He still worked out and had a good body for his age. As soon as his eyes hit Ged's he screwed his face up remembering all the hurt he'd caused his family. Marjorie could see this and jumped up from her chair.

"Do you want a brew love? The kettle's just boiled." Eric took his coat off and pulled a rolled-up newspaper from his pocket. He nodded to his wife. Ged felt uneasy and fidgeted. When his mother disappeared Ged spoke to his father while he was reading the newspaper.

"Dad... I'm gonna get clean you know. I know I've let you down in the past, but trust me this time please." Ged sat back in the chair but no words were spoken.

Marjorie came back from the kitchen holding two cups. Quickly she placed them on the table and returned back to bring a plate of biscuits. Eric peered slowly over the paper. His face scrunched up in anger.

"What the fuck are they for!" he ranted sarcastically, "he's not returning from the fucking war or something. Have you forgotten what he's done?" Marjorie felt wounded. She sunk her body into the armchair. She knew he was right but she just wanted a peaceful life. As she crossed her legs she retaliated.

"For Christ's sake Eric. Just give him a chance. Let's see if he can change." Ged stood up and went towards his coat. His face was filled with regret as he spoke.

"Mam, I'm gonna get off. I don't want to cause any trouble." As if she shit her knickers she jumped to her feet.

"You sit right back down." Her eyes burnt into Eric with a look that could kill. She grabbed Ged's arm to sit him back down.

"You park your arse back down there son. You're going nowhere." Eric threw his newspaper to the floor. As he stood up he pointed into his son's face.

"You might be able to have her over, but I'm gonna be watching you like a hawk." He left the room and you could hear him stamping up the stairs. Marjorie sat twiddling her thumbs. Her eyes focused on Ged. Shaking her head she reached her hand over to him.

"You better not let me down. He'll come round without water. Just give him time." Ged gritted his teeth and looked up towards the ceiling. He knew his dad was still angry with him and hoped in time he could prove him wrong. Looking at the clock he searched his pockets for the letter.

"Mam I'm just gonna whizz over to Gladys's and give her this." He waved the letter in front of her. Marjorie agreed and told him not to be long as she was making the tea. Watching him leave she prayed he would stick to his word. Ged grabbed his coat and came to his mother's side. He quickly pecked her on the cheek and told her he wouldn't be long.

Glady's house was much the same as he remembered it. He hadn't been to Shaun's mother's house in ages. Knocking at the front door he stood waiting patiently. Stepping back he looked up at the windows for any sign of someone being in. Katie's face appeared at the window. She knocked on the window and waved her hand. Ged stood kicking the floor as she opened the door.

"Alright Ged. To what do we owe the honour?" Katie smiled. Ged had always secretly fancied her in the past. He blushed.

"Ermm..." he struggled for words. "Is ya mam in?" Katie looked at him and looked shocked and held her head to the side. She opened the door slowly and told him to come in.

Katie stood with her arm over the living-room door as Ged stood looking at Gladys. Her eyes watched his every move and she thought he was up to something. Telling her mam he was there she told Ged to sit down. Katie sat at the dining table and lit a cigarette.

"Hiya Gladys. Are you okay?" Her eyes turned to him and she looked in a world of her own. Taking a few minutes Gladys answered him.

"Yeah son. I'm getting by." Gladys searched his face and realised he'd never come to her house unless Shaun was in trouble. Sitting up in her chair she gave a weak stretch.

"Katie put the kettle on will ya? Do you want one Ged? I've got some nice cakes to go with it." He refused. Katie stormed into the kitchen. You could hear her filling the kettle with water. She stood by the door not wanting to miss the reason why he was there.

Gladys spoke briefly about the weather. Ged sat forward in his chair as he searched his pocket for the letter. Katie was on her tip-toes trying to see what it was he pulled from his pocket. Reaching over to Gladys he passed her the letter and sat back cupping his hands between his legs.

Slowly Gladys looked at Ged. His eyes filled with tears and he was unable to tell her what was inside the letter. Slowly she unfolded the crumpled piece of paper. The words looked blurred to her. She held the paper away from her eyes. Her eyesight had deteriorated over the years and she shouted to Katie to pass her some reading glasses she'd recently bought from the chemist.

Katie passed her mother the spectacles. She was sat on the arm of the chair trying to read over her shoulder. Gladys told her to finish the cup of tea and told her not to be so fucking nosey. Placing the plastic grey frames on her face the words looked clearer. Within seconds she realised the letter was from Shaun and raised her head to Ged.

"What... Where is this from?" Ged was still a mess and bit down onto his lip. Katie was back by her side holding a brew. She wasn't moving for love nor money now. Gladys held a single hand round her neck stroking it slowly. She started reading. Her eyes screwed up as she tried to read the small handwriting.

'Dear Mam.
Where do I start? Where do I begin? I don't think I'm

gonna be around much longer and needed to set the record straight with you. I know in the past I've been a twat with you, but none of it was your fault. I'm a nob-head and just got caught up in a world of drugs and other shit. Mam... I hate what I've done and the person I've become. I know your probably crying now reading this letter and shaking your head telling yourself I'm wrong, but deep down mam, you know I'm right.

I've been mixed up in some sick shit lately. I've even been selling my body mam. It kills me to even to say that to you. It was the drugs mam. They just got a grip of me and made me into a monster. Every night I feel like ending it all, but I shit myself and can't go through with it. I might one day, ay? I wish I would have been everything you wanted me to be. I look around at other people and I wish I could have had a normal life. Nobody cares about me anymore mam. My family, my friends. No one. I know you do but I've hurt you so much. I don't know how you do it. I've just let you down time after time.

Perhaps you'll never read this letter; perhaps I'll never take my own life. Mam I'm shitting myself. The thought of dying on my own terrifies me. Still a big baby aren't I? Anyway mam I just wanted to tell you thanks. Thanks is all I can say. There isn't a word that will ever explain what you mean to me and I don't know how else to say it. I love you mam and I'm sorry.

Tell our Katie I love her too. Make sure she gets rid of that nob-head boyfriend. He's a cunt and always will be. She deserves better. I've got nowt to say to Paul or my dad except I love em. I love you all. Please try and remember me the way I was and not the way I ended up.

My mind's all over the place at the moment mam. I can't think of what else to say. I might finish this letter later or some

other time. I love you mam. Sorry.
    Always Shaun xxxx'

Tears fell down Gladys's face as she dropped the letter on her lap. Katie reached over and read it. The room felt cold and Katie sat reading the letter twiddling her hair in her fingers. Ged stood up as she finished reading.

"I found it in his coat Gladys. I only found it today. It was under his bed." Holding her head back into the chair she shook her head slowly. Katie placed her hand on her shoulder but she shrugged her away. Ged bent down and kissed Gladys on the cheek. He felt uneasy and knew she was going to blow any minute. He said goodbye to Katie and left.

"Mam, it's so sad. He must have known exactly what he was going to do." Her mother stood from her chair.

"I need a wee," she muttered. Gladys headed to the toilet. Her shoulders were hunched and her body felt weak. Katie read the letter over and over as she sobbed. She spoke to herself.

"Ya fucking dickhead Shaun. Why the fuck did you have to go and kill ya self. We could have got through it ya know." Gladys walked back into the room. Katie watched as she popped three Diazapam in her mouth. She swilled them down with a swig of her brew. Watching her sit down Katie shook her head.

"Mam you better stop necking them tablets like they're Smarties. You've been taking loads over the last few weeks." Her mother's face turned red. She confronted her and screamed.

"Since when have you become a fucking doctor? I'll take how many I want." Katie huffed.

"Well you'll just make yourself ill won't you?" Gladys

ran at her with fists of fury pummelling them into her body. She'd snapped.

"Get out. Fuck off. Who do you think you are dictating to me?" Katie scuffled with her. She finally gripped her hands from her body. She spoke no words as she walked away from her and grabbed her coat. Gladys flung herself back onto the chair.

Katie walked towards the front door and paused. She looked as if she was thinking whether or not to go back into the living room. After a few seconds she opened the front door and left, slamming the door behind her.

The house was in silence.

Weeks passed and Gladys still popped her pills. Katie still come to see her and tried her best to pull her through the heartbreak.

Gladys died on the 3rd of May that year. The doctors thought it was suicide at first, but they discovered she'd had a massive heart attack. Everyone said she died of a broken heart and I for one believe them.

Gladys had lived and died for her son and somehow I think she is happy now. The Cook family carried on living with the loss of their brother and mother and Katie still tells stories to her children about the good times they shared. She doesn't tell them the details of her brother's death but she warns them about drugs and how they can ruin your life.

Katie left her boyfriend not long after her mother's death and found happiness with someone who did deserve her. She still kept in contact with her brother and father and they spoke regularly.

Ged kept to his promise to his parents and stayed off

the drugs. Don't get me wrong he did slip off the wagon a few times but over the years he turned his life round. He often went to Shaun's graveside and spoke with him about his new life without drugs.

To this day Tavistock Square in Harpurhey Manchester still looks like a ghost town. If you close your eyes and listen carefully I'm sure you can still hear the laughter of all those youngsters who used to play there when they were kids.

The people who lost their lives to heroin will always be a part of Harpurhey's history and I for one will always remember them as the people they were and not who they became. Next time you see a drug addict begging on some street corner or looking like they need help, remember they weren't always like that and probably have their own story why they sold their soul to drugs.

Nobody is born bad, it's life that makes them that way.

THE END

ONE MORE TIME...

A NOVEL BY MICHAEL DILWORTH

Falling in love was never easy for Liam Kirk, until he met valerie Walters. Their relationship — if you could call it that — was strained, least of all because she was still the girlfriend of an old mate. This, however, didn't stop them embarking on an affair which ended rather abruptly.

Fast forward 13 years and Liam has just completed his first novel based on his relationship with val — without changing her name. This wouldn't be such a problem if she hadn't just gate-crashed liam's life for a second time and was now reading his account of their relationship.

Will they have the happy ending liam wished for all those years ago? or will val get the better of him one More Time? Set in various Lancastrian pubs and Californian coffee bars, this wry novel marks the writing debut of Michael Dilworth.

ABOUT THE AUTHOR

Born and raised in Silverdale, Lancaster, Michael Dilworth always loved telling stories. Having spent a fair few years writing for football fanzines, Mick decided to take his writing to the next level by writing a novel. Listing his biggest influences as Nick Hornby and Bill Bryson, he started to write a book loosely based on his own youthful antics. Mick currently resides in heysham with his wife and two children.